MISSISSIPPI ROLL

The Wild Cards Universe

The Original Triad

Wild Cards

Aces High

Jokers Wild

The Card Sharks Triad

Card Sharks

Marked Cards

Black Trump

The Puppetman Quartet

Aces Abroad

Down and Dirty

Ace in the Hole

Dead Man's Hand

Stand-Alones

Deuces Down

Death Draws Five

The Committee Triad

Inside Straight

Busted Flush

Suicide Kings

The Rox Triad

One-Eyed Jacks

Jokertown Shuffle

Dealer's Choice

The Fort Freak Triad

Fort Freak

Lowball

High Stakes

The Novels

Double Solitaire

Turn of the Cards

Mississippi Roll

MISSISSIPPI ROLL

Edited by
George R. R. Martin

Written by

Stephen Leigh | David D. Levine
John Jos. Miller | Kevin Andrew Murphy
Cherie Priest | Carrie Vaughn

TOR

A TOM DOHERTY ASSOCIATES BOOK

New York

MISSISSIPPI ROLL

Copyright © 2017 by George R. R. Martin and the Wild Cards Trust

A Tor Book
Published by Tom Doherty Associates
175 Fifth Avenue
New York, NY 10010

www.tor-forge.com

Tor® is a registered trademark of Macmillan Publishing Group, LLC.

The Library of Congress Cataloging-in-Publication Data is available upon request.

ISBN 978-0-7653-9052-3 (hardcover)
ISBN 978-0-7653-9054-7 (ebook)

Our books may be purchased in bulk for promotional, educational, or business use. Please contact your local bookseller or the Macmillan Corporate and Premium Sales Department at 1-800-221-7945, extension 5442, or by email at MacmillanSpecialMarkets@macmillan.com.

First Edition: December 2017

Printed in the United States of America

0 9 8 7 6 5 4 3 2 1

For Edward Bryant
brother-in-arms
father to gators
our ace on roller skates

Copyright
Acknowledgments

♣ ♦ ♠ ♥

Mississippi Roll Rules

Mississippi Roll is a seven-card stud poker game.
The rules are as follows:

1. Seven cards are dealt to each player, facedown.
2. Each player passes one card to the player on his left.
3. Each player passes two cards to the player on his left.
4. Each player passes three cards to the player on his left.
5. Each player discards two cards from his hand, arranges the five remaining cards in the order he wishes to reveal them, and places his hand facedown in a pack before him on the table.
6. The players roll their top card. A round of betting follows, starting with the player with the high card showing.
7. The remaining cards are revealed one by one, with each roll followed by a round of betting.
8. The high hand and low hand split the pot.

MISSISSIPPI ROLL

In the Shadow of
Tall Stacks

by Stephen Leigh

Part 1

February 27, 1951

MARDI GRAS WAS LONG past—a full three weeks ago, which unfortunately meant that the bulk of the tourists had vanished back to wherever they'd come from, which in turn meant that it had been a few weeks since the steamboat *Natchez* had last seen anything resembling a full house for its daily local cruises. At nine in the morning, it was sixty-seven degrees and ninety-seven percent humidity; not raining, though a thick, wet fog still cloaked the Mississippi and the wharf where the *Natchez* was docked near Jackson Square and the French Quarter. There was barely any breeze, and the fog seemed to squat on New Orleans like some gigantic and foul specter, muffling what little noise the not-quite-awake city mustered.

Wilbur Leathers, captain and owner of the *Natchez*, wasn't entirely awake himself, admittedly. The steamboat's engineer, Patrick O'Flaherty, had roused him an hour ago; he'd wanted to fire up the boilers and check questionable pressure readings in several of the lines before they left the dock to head upriver. The engineer's knock had also awakened Eleanor, Wilbur's wife. Wilbur had told O'Flaherty to go ahead, then dressed, kissed the sleepy Eleanor, and gone down intending to supervise the work. He'd also—at Eleanor's request—started a pot of coffee in the tiny crew mess on the main deck. He held two steaming mugs in his hands as he emerged onto the foredeck. Wilbur heard the boilers to the rear of the main deck already producing a good head of steam and hissing through the 'scape pipes up on the hurricane deck. He sniffed the curling steam from the coffee mugs: his own simply black, Eleanor's au lait and flavored with chicory.

Eleanor had told him only two days ago that she was certain she was pregnant, having missed her second time of the month a few weeks ago, and now experiencing nausea in the mornings. He'd hugged her tight, both of them ecstatic about the news. He was going to be a father. They were going to start their family. He already loved Eleanor more than ever, four years into their marriage, and he was certain that his son or daughter would only increase the bliss.

The only storm clouds on the horizon of their future were financial ones, though those were tall and plentiful.

Wilbur glanced eastward to where a dim glow heralded the sun that would eventually dissipate the fog. Wilbur judged that it would be an hour or more before the fog cleared enough for easy navigation: a shame. For several reasons, he wanted to be out on the river and heading north to Baton Rouge as soon as possible. Only four of the staterooms were currently booked, but it wasn't likely that any more were going to fill on a Tuesday morning three weeks after Mardi Gras. They wouldn't be *entirely* deadheading; there were crates of good china stacked on the deck due in Memphis by Tuesday next, as well as boxes of felt hats, shoes, and boots destined for the St. Louis markets, but those were barely enough to pay the bills.

Wilbur heaved a sigh, shaking his head.

"Is that my coffee, darling?" He heard Eleanor's voice from above, and looked up to see her leaning over the railing of the hurricane deck, smiling at him and already dressed for the day. He raised one of the mugs toward her.

"Right here, love."

"Then bring it up." She scowled theatrically at him, with a grin lurking on her lips. "Unless you want to deal with a very grumpy wife all morning."

He laughed. "Coming right up. But I still have to check on O'Flaherty." Wilbur turned toward the stairs, then stopped. A figure was stalking through the fog and up the gangway of the boat. "Oh no," Wilbur muttered. "Just what I need this morning. . . ." Then, loudly enough that the man stepping onto the *Natchez*'s main deck could hear him: "Mr. Carpenter, what brings you out so early in the morning?"

Marcus Carpenter was a burly, solid, and florid man in a suit that already looked rumpled and slept-in despite the early-morning hour—or maybe the man had been up all night. He looked sour and angry to Wilbur, but then Wilbur had rarely seen the man show any other emotions. "You know what I want, Leathers." Carpenter glanced up to where Eleanor stood watching, then at the two mugs of coffee steaming in Wilbur's hands. "Perhaps you and I should discuss this privately."

"Perhaps we should," Wilbur told him. He lifted the mug in his left hand toward Eleanor, watching from above, and placed her mug on the railing of the foredeck as Eleanor nodded to him. He took a long swallow from his mug and placed it alongside Eleanor's. "Let's go back to the boiler room," he told Carpenter. "I have to check on my engineer anyway."

Carpenter gave a shrug. Wilbur led the man back through the door of the main deck, down between the crates stacked there, and into the passage that led back to the boiler and engine rooms. Carpenter followed, and as they entered the short corridor that held the sleeping barracks for deckhands and roustabouts, his voice growled at Wilbur's back. "Look, I ain't here to beat around the goddamn bush. I want the money you owe to me and my associates, and I want it today, Leathers. You said you'd have it after Mardi Gras, but somehow none of us have seen a fucking penny so far."

Such vile language . . . Carpenter's habitual spewing of profanity wasn't the only reason that Wilbur despised the man, but it certainly fit the image.

The heat of the boilers and the hissing of steam surged around them as Wilbur opened the wooden door at the end of the corridor. He couldn't see O'Flaherty; the man must have gone farther astern to the engine room. Wilbur turned back to Carpenter, who filled the doorway of the boiler room as if blocking Wilbur from retreating that way. "Look, Mr. Carpenter," Wilbur said, "Mardi Gras just wasn't as profitable as we'd hoped, and I had some unexpected expenses for repairs on top of that—"

"Yeah, yeah," Carpenter interrupted. "That's the same old crap you handed me last time, and your excuses ain't gonna pay back the loan we gave you or the interest you're racking up. We're not happy. When we're not happy, my job is to ensure that you're not going to be fucking happy either."

"Give me just another week, Mr. Carpenter. I'll get you at least the interest on the loan."

"A week? And let you take off upriver and maybe never come back?" Carpenter was already shaking his head. He waved a hand at the boilers. "Not a fucking chance. You already got steam up, so there's no 'week' for you or even another day. I need to see the goddamn green in my hand, and I need to see it now." Carpenter took a surprisingly quick step toward Wilbur, a hand the size of a holiday ham reaching for him before he could retreat, grabbing Wilbur by the collar of his brocaded captain's jacket and twisting. "I see that green or you're going to be seeing red," Carpenter told him. His breath reeked of cigarettes and coffee.

Wilbur glanced down at the hand holding him. His eyes narrowed as he felt heat rising up his neck: "that infamous Leathers temper," as his mother and Eleanor both called it. "You'll let go of me, Carpenter. Now."

"Or you'll do *what*?" Carpenter scoffed, the retort sending a spray of saliva into Wilbur's face. With that, Wilbur sent a punch over the larger man's arm, slamming his fist hard into Carpenter's cheek; the man let go of Wilbur, staggering back a step. Then, with a shout, Carpenter charged back in, his huge hands fisted now. Wilbur tried to block the blows, but one connected hard with the side of his face, sending him down to the deck. Carpenter's foot came back, the toe of his shoe driving hard into Wilbur's stomach, doubling him over as all the air left him.

Through a growing haze of blood and anger, Wilbur saw a large pipe wrench on the decking under one of the boilers. He snatched at the tool, warm from the heat of the boilers, and brought it down hard on Carpenter's shoe. He heard bones crack in Carpenter's foot as the man howled. "Shit! You fucking *asshole!*"

Wilbur managed to get his feet under him, hunched over as he waved the wrench in his hand toward Carpenter. He took a step toward the man, raising the pipe again. "This is *my* boat, not yours!" he shouted as he advanced. "I built her and she's *mine*. You'll get your money in due time, all of it—I keep my promises and I pay my debts. Now get the *hell* off my boat or I'll throw you off." The curse word was an indication of just how furious Wilbur had become: he'd always been taught that gentlemen never cursed, and despite the fact that he heard profanity regularly from crewmembers, dockworkers, and the likes of Carpenter, he only rarely used such language himself. He took another step toward Carpenter, still waving the wrench.

What happened then would remain indelibly in his memory. As if in slow motion, he saw Carpenter reach under his suit jacket and pull out a snub-nosed revolver. The first shot went wild, hitting one of the steam pipes and sending a cloud of searing, scalding heat over Wilbur.

In that moment, even amidst the adrenaline surge and before Carpenter could pull the trigger again, Wilbur felt something shift and change and *break* inside him, the sensation taking his breath away and making him drop the wrench from the shock and pain. His body no longer seemed completely his. Wilbur was still trying to make sense of what was happening to him when the next two shots hit him directly in the chest.

He expected to feel pain. He didn't—not from the steam, not from the bullet wounds. Enveloped in the surging, deadly cloud, he felt himself fall, sprawling and bleeding on the deck. Inside, though—that change was still happening, still tearing at him, even as he felt his body dying around him.

"You fucking *asshole!*" Carpenter shouted, standing one-footed and looking down at him as Wilbur tried to shape words, tried to shout or scream or wail, though nothing emerged from his mouth. "Maybe I'll just take out the interest from that pretty wife of yours, you goddamn bastard."

Carpenter spat on the body, turned, and started to limp away toward the foredeck and gangway. Toward where, Wilbur was very afraid, Eleanor would be. His rage engulfed him, as hissing and furious as the steam venting from the pipes. Within the steam, he felt power surge within him. He rose, screaming wordlessly as he rushed toward Carpenter.

The man's mouth opened, his eyes widened almost comically, as if Wilbur were the vision of some monstrous creature leaping toward him as he lifted his hands to ward off the attack. Wilbur expected to feel the shock of their collision, but there was none. Instead—strangely, impossibly—he was *inside* Carpenter. "No! Fuck! You're *burning* me!" the man shouted, and Wilbur heard that scream as if it were his own voice, and he heard Carpenter's thoughts as well. *Shit! Shit! It hurts. It's burning me, and I can't breathe! Can't breathe . . .* Carpenter's hands flailed at his own body as if trying to put out an invisible fire, and Wilbur felt the motion of Carpenter's hands as his own. Wilbur could see through the man's eyes as well, and he saw his own body bleeding on the floor of the boiler room, eyes open and unseeing as steam continued to flow outward over it.

"Is that *me?* How?" he gasped, and he heard his words emerge from Carpenter's throat. But he could also feel the searing agony in the man's body, and Wilbur took a step away from the man as Carpenter collapsed on the floor, twitching and vomiting dark blood and bile before going still.

Stream wreathed Wilbur as he stared now at two bodies in the room: Carpenter's and his own. "Wilbur!" he heard Eleanor shout distantly, and from the engine room farther to the rear of the *Natchez*, O'Flaherty also called out: "Cap'n? M'God, what's happened here?"

The hissing steam around Wilbur died as O'Flaherty cut off the flow to the pipes. O'Flaherty hurried forward, glancing at Carpenter before crouching down alongside Wilbur's impossibly disconnected and bleeding body, ignoring the Wilbur standing behind him dripping cooling steam.

"O'Flaherty," Wilbur said, "I don't know what's going on, but I'm right here. Behind you. Look at me, man." He reached out to touch the engineer on the shoulder; his hand, pressing hard, went straight into the man, leaving behind a spreading wet stain on his coveralls. O'Flaherty, for his part, jumped up and slapped at his shoulder with a curse.

"Feck, I'm burned. I t'ought I shut off—" He stopped. He stared at Wilbur. His face went pale. "Sweet bleedin' Jaysus, 'tis the cap'n's haint," he whispered, his Irish-accented brogue heavy as he scrambled backwards away from Wilbur like a scuttling crab, pushing with his feet and hands.

They both heard growing cries of alarm from the foredeck: Eleanor's voice, as well as the deeper shouts of sleepy deckhands roused by the gunshots. O'Flaherty found his footing and went running toward the sound. With a glance back at the bodies (*That can't be me. That can't be me lying there dead.*) Wilbur followed. O'Flaherty had let the door to the boiler room shut behind him. Wilbur reached out to push it open; the door didn't move but his hand went through it as it had into Carpenter and O'Flaherty. Wilbur drew back and tried again with the same result. This time, he continued to push—his entire body passing reluctantly through the door, like pushing through a sheet of gelatin.

He didn't pause to wonder at that; he went through the corridor, among the stacks of crates, and out onto the foredeck. A couple of deckhands had gathered there, trying to find the source of the disturbance. O'Flaherty was holding Eleanor, who struggled in his grasp, trying to go toward the boiler room. "Yah should'nah see the cap'n that way," O'Flaherty was telling Eleanor, "nor his haint."

"I need to . . . I need . . ." Eleanor gasped, then broke into a deep sobbing as she sagged in O'Flaherty's arms.

"He's gone, Missus Leathers. Gone. I'm so sorry," O'Flaherty whispered, clutching her. Wilbur could see the two mugs of coffee, still sitting on the foredeck rail. "At least he took that bastard Carpenter with him."

"Eleanor, he's wrong. I'm not dead." Wilbur moved behind O'Flaherty so he could look into Eleanor's face. "I'm right here." Her gaze stared through him, a wisp contained within the fog-draped sunlight, as Eleanor continued to sob in O'Flaherty's arms. He could feel his body cooling, water puddling where he stood. "Eleanor, O'Flaherty—talk to me!" Neither of them responded.

Wilbur reached out—careful not to press too hard—to touch Eleanor's shoulder. He saw the fabric of her robe darken as his fingertips touched her, drops of water spreading out and steaming in the cooler air as Eleanor drew back in alarm. He pulled his hand back, startled. His world and New Orleans reeled around him suddenly in a drunken, wild dance.

"I'm not dead," he whispered to Eleanor, to the fog, to the boat, to the river. "I'm here. I'm not dead. I'm right here."

No one answered.

♣ ♦ ♠ ♥

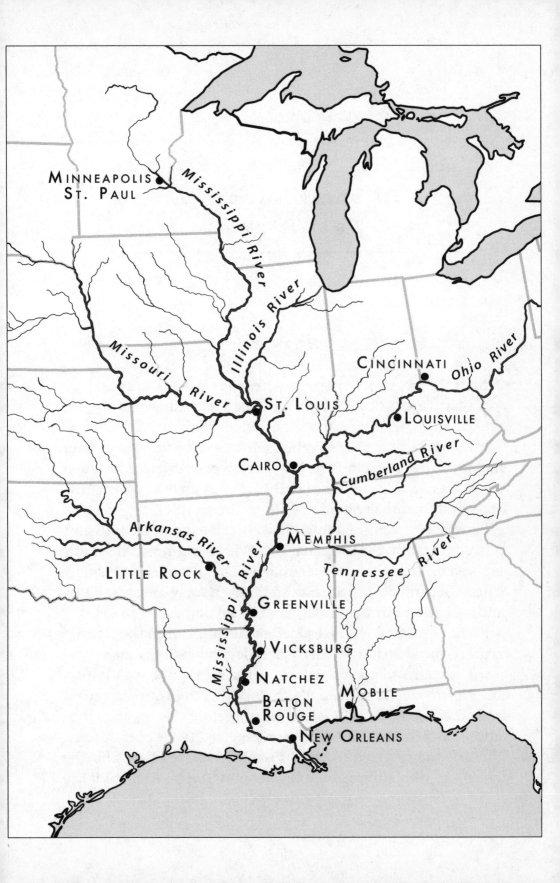

In the Shadow of
Tall Stacks

Part 2

October 2016

RIGHT HERE" WILBUR LEATHERS stayed. For sixty-five years.

He had no choice. When Eleanor left the *Natchez* later that day in 1951, Wilbur tried to follow her and found he could not. It was as if an invisible wall had been erected around the steamboat, one that would not allow him to pass.

Eleanor had vanished into New Orleans and never returned to the boat again; the body that was Wilbur-but-not-Wilbur was removed by the police coroner, followed by that of the internally boiled Carpenter. Both corpses were taken away, presumably to autopsies and eventual burial. Wilbur would never know.

He remained on the *Natchez*, never aging: not as the *Natchez* changed owners over the slow decades; not as new men (and now a woman) stepped aboard to captain her; not as innumerable crewmembers came and went; not as the *Natchez* herself aged and became steadily more shabby before undergoing renovations, a cycle that had now been repeated twice over. "Steam Wilbur," they started to call him: the crewmembers and the passengers who glimpsed him as he found he could materialize himself at will when the steam was up on the boat. "Steam Wilbur": the most famous haint on what was known now as the most haunted steamboat on the Mississippi.

Only he was the *only* haint. All the other supposed ghosts existed only in the pamphlets the current owners of the boat distributed, with sometimes lurid details of the "haints" aboard. Wilbur had seen the pamphlets and read the stories of the ghosts who reputedly were aboard: for instance, eleven-year-old Lizbeth Hamilton, touted as a "wispy, translucent figure seen on the darkest nights on the main deck, where she died in a tragic fall." Wilbur had actually witnessed Lizbeth's death in 1978 as the *Natchez* was steaming downriver from St. Louis and passing Cape Girardeau. Lizbeth had been dressed in a Billy Joel T-shirt and jeans, her brown hair in pigtails with strands escaping from baby blue ribbons. It had been windy and rather cold that October night, with a light drizzle spraying the decks. Lizbeth's parents had booked passage for Vicksburg to meet relatives. The *Natchez*, under new ownership and new captainship again, was—in Wilbur's view—growing increasingly shabby and sloppily run. Lizbeth had left her parents' cabin on the boiler deck; Wilbur heard her running footsteps from where he was prowling on the texas deck, and he glanced over the railing in time to see her slip on a thin layer of ice that had formed on the deck. Her momentum took her to the railing; she clutched at it, screaming in panic, but the railing was loose and Wilbur heard the crack of rotten wood. Lizbeth went over still holding the broken railing, falling hard onto the main deck and breaking her neck.

But no ghost had risen from her poor corpse. No ghost haunted the main deck, or any other. Not the passenger named Robert who messily committed suicide in 1958 in his stateroom; not the wife found by her husband in flagrante delicto with another man in 1963—her lover fled naked for his life before jumping overboard to safety, but the husband had strangled his unfaithful wife to death before the then-captain and crew, alerted by the uproar, overpowered him; not the drunken and clumsy idiot who managed to fall backward over the railing into the thrashing paddle wheel in 1988.

Those who died on the *Natchez*—and there had been a few more over the years—never stayed on the *Natchez*. Wilbur had no other haints as companions, despite the owners' advertisements, intended to entice and titillate potential passengers.

Of which there were currently quite a few. The *Natchez* was readying to leave her home port of New Orleans and head upriver, first to St. Louis, then back down the Mississippi a bit to the confluence of the Ohio and on up the Ohio to Cincinnati, where the steamboat would be part of Cincinnati's periodic Tall Stacks festival. Many of the passengers had booked passage specifically to attend the festival, though there were also those who were traveling to one or another of the towns and cities along the way.

For Wilbur, the Tall Stacks festivals were a somewhat bittersweet reminder of old times: a dozen or so steamboats lined up along Riverboat Row, even if the majority of them weren't *real* steamboats anymore but pale imitations—diesel-powered excursion boats whose paddles were there purely for decoration, or overgrown abominations like the *American Queen*. The festival reminded him of tales that his father had long ago told him, woven from his own childhood growing up with Wilbur's grandfather Thomas Leathers, who had built and captained the first eight steamboats named *Natchez*.

Still, Wilbur would normally have been looking forward to Tall Stacks, especially since his *Natchez* was scheduled to race against the *Belle of Louisville* and the *Delta Queen* once they arrived. A previous *Natchez* had famously raced (and lost to) the *Robert E. Lee*, a scene celebrated in the huge painting that dominated the main salon on the boiler deck.

But the rumors Wilbur was hearing rather dampened any enthusiasm he might have mustered. Wilbur "talked" often enough with Jeremiah Smalls, his one confidant on the *Natchez* and the boat's chief pilot for the last dozen years. According to Jeremiah, it appeared that the current owners of the *Natchez* were considering "options" for making the boat more profitable—and some of those options terrified Wilbur, seeing as this boat was also his prison.

Over the years, then the decades, Wilbur told himself that his was a just sentence; he'd killed Carpenter in a rage, and so he deserved this exile on the boat he'd built for committing the sin of murder. He deserved losing Eleanor, who must now be ninety years old or already dead. He deserved the punishment of never knowing his son or daughter, if Eleanor had perhaps remarried and had other children, if perhaps there were grandchildren of his out in the world.

Justice. Karma. Payment for his sins. Wilbur had been brought up Methodist, but he'd lost his faith somewhere along the way. He didn't know if there was a God or not, but whether it was God's hand or simple fate that had marooned him on his own vessel, it was his sentence to bear.

It was a bright day in New Orleans, and Wilbur hadn't taken in steam in hours. Even filled with steam and willing himself to be visible, in sunlight he'd be little more than a passing wisp of cloud, perhaps a stray, soggy refugee from the stacks or the 'scape pipes or a leaking radiator. But Wilbur was content to be invisible at the moment. He walked the main deck—at least, that was his perception of what he was doing, though he'd seen his reflection in a window or mirror many times over the decades, and to an outsider, he was a specter gliding soundlessly just above the boards. There were far more people on board than usual for the *Natchez*; it was looking like this would be a profitable trip, and he entertained the thought that this might change the minds of the consortium that owned the boat.

As he turned the corner of the promenade and moved toward the gangway leading to the dock, three young men, laden with odd pieces of equipment, were coming toward him, talking excitedly among themselves. They'd come aboard the night before: two brothers, Ryan and Kevin Forge, and Sean Venters, a cousin. According to Jeremiah, they had a cable television TV show (both cable and television being technologies that simply made Wilbur shake his steamy head in mingled wonder and disgust) called *The Dead Report*, where they investigated the paranormal. They were aboard looking for the *Natchez*'s nonexistent ghosts . . . and especially Steam Wilbur.

"The EMF fields are fluctuating like crazy," Sean was saying to Ryan as Kevin filmed their interaction, walking backward. "We're close to something." Wilbur had to step/glide aside quickly to avoid having Kevin pass directly through him—he didn't intend to give the ghost hunters anything to talk about on their show.

"Supposedly there's a ghost around here—a little girl named Lizbeth," Ryan said. He was dark-haired and muscular, with tattoos crawling his arms (another new societal change that made Wilbur shake his head—even the sailors Wilbur had known in the war hadn't defaced their bodies *this* much). "If we can find a cold spot, maybe we can make contact with her. . . ."

Wilbur let the trio pass him, then continued around to the dock side of the ship.

♣

The *Natchez* was bustling with activity everywhere. The dock side of the main deck was swarming with visitors and passengers, the air was alive with chatter as deckhands and roustabouts doubled as bellboys, carrying luggage from the dock onto the steamboat and up to the staterooms and cabins on the boiler deck.

Wilbur could see Captain Marjorie Montaigne looking like she'd just stepped out from the late 1800s in her captain's uniform with its ostentatious piping and embroidery. Montaigne had taken over as captain of the *Natchez* almost a decade ago; as far as Wilbur was concerned, if none of the captains since his death had been as competent as *he'd* been, he had to grudgingly admit Montaigne had managed to turn around or at least stop the decline of the *Natchez* during her tenure.

She was also a lesbian, and admitted that openly—another new societal twitch that Wilbur didn't quite understand or agree with. In *his* day, one kept such things tightly closeted and one *never* talked about them. Still, he had to allow that Montaigne did her job as captain well enough, and though it was still a rarity to see a female captain on the river, she was more than a match for the sometimes crude and misogynistic crewmembers. Wilbur's own aunt, Blanche Leathers, had become captain of the *Natchez* way back in 1894, long before women were at all common in the workplace, let alone running a steamboat on the Mississippi. At least Montaigne was following a Leathers tradition, even if she wasn't family.

Captain Montaigne was greeting arrivals at the gangway leading down to the wharf as Wilbur drifted past her, unseen. He'd overheard earlier talk from the captain that there might be several wild card aces among the entertainers as well as the passengers at various points along the cruise; in fact, the Jokertown Boys, a joker boy band that had been famous a decade and a half ago, had been aboard for some time now, having most recently played the night before. Their supposed music failed to impress Wilbur, who still preferred the big band sound of the '40s and early '50s, or classic New Orleans jazz. The band's keyboardist, "Gimcrack"—a stupid name, in Wilbur's opinion—had also been hired to play the boat's calliope during the cruises, though at the moment it was silent, the boilers still waiting to be fully fired up tomorrow evening when the *Natchez* would be under way.

He saw Kitty Strobe, the junior pilot for the *Natchez*, walking toward the stairs, probably heading up to the pilothouse to help Jeremiah with preparations for getting under way. As usual, despite the New Orleans heat, she was wearing a large baggy sweater and long pants, as well as large dark sunglasses. Wilbur smiled to himself: he knew why she dressed that way, even if no one else on the boat was aware of it.

Captain Montaigne was speaking with a man who looked distressingly like a cartoon fox, accompanied by a woman who sported cat's ears, nose, and whiskers in an otherwise normal face. *Jokers*, Wilbur thought. *Or aces* . . . "Mr. Yamauchi, Ms. Otto, welcome aboard," the captain said with her Cajun accent. "I'm glad to see both of you. Your equipment and luggage arrived yesterday. I have your stateroom ready; your luggage is there waiting for you. I assume you'll want to take a look at the Bayou Lounge, as that's where you'll be performing your act; I'll have one of the deckhands escort you up there. The Jokertown Boys will be sharing the bill with you. . . ."

Her voice trailed off as Wilbur drifted on past her and up the staircase, causing a descending deckhand to shudder as Wilbur passed partially through the man. Since the boilers were still cool, Wilbur was invisible, barely warm, and relatively dry at the moment.

Wilbur continued up past the boiler deck and texas deck until he was standing on the open hurricane deck atop the boat. Wilbur stood near the calliope, a classic Thomas J. Nichol–built steam calliope salvaged from the sunken remains of the side-wheeler *Island Queen*, destroyed by fire. Wilbur had paid to lovingly (and expensively) have the calliope restored. The acquisition of the calliope had been one of Wilbur's proudest accomplishments when he'd built this iteration of his family's *Natchez* boats, that and the fact that he'd also been able to salvage murals and paintings from the eighth *Natchez*, built by his grandfather.

He'd built the *Natchez* to be as much a part of him as he was now part of it.

Neither Jeremiah nor Kitty Strobe was in the pilothouse, so Wilbur continued up the short flight of stairs and into the enclosure. There was the bell made of 250 melted silver dollars that Wilbur had salvaged from the SS *J. D. Ayres;* the steam whistle from a steamboat that sank in 1908 on the Monongahela River;

the massive white oak and steel wheel from the *Hamiltonian*, and the ornate control and communications panels, refurbished and modernized over long decades by the boat's subsequent owners, far different from the time when Wilbur had stood here. Alive. With Eleanor at his side.

Eleanor . . . The pilothouse's expansive windows allowed Wilbur to see the river and New Orleans in all directions. From his vantage point, he could view the wharf, the French Quarter, and nearby Jackson Square. He looked out over New Orleans, wondering if she was still there somewhere, wondering if their child was out there as well. *Eleanor, what kind of life did Carpenter steal from us? Where would we have gone, what would we have become?*

Of course, he'd also stolen Carpenter's life. He'd sometimes wondered if Carpenter had had a family, if his wife and maybe his kids had expected him to come home for dinner that February night so many decades ago. *I'm still paying for that. I wonder if Carpenter's doing the same somewhere, or maybe everything just ended for him then, even if it didn't for me. . . .*

Wilbur turned his gaze eastward past the huge stern wheelhouse and down the wide Mississippi. That was where the MS *Gustav Schröder*, a rusting, decrepit cargo ship flying the Liberian flag, was moored near the river's intersection with the Intracoastal Waterway, guarded by the Coast Guard cutter *Triton* and boats from the New Orleans Port Police—all of them five miles downriver. With the river's curves and all the other river traffic, Wilbur couldn't make out the ship from this distance, but *Schröder* had been the subject of lots of talk and gossip and arguments aboard the *Natchez* in recent days. The vessel was reputedly stuffed with more than nine hundred refugees from Kazakhstan, wherever the hell that was, and the *Schröder* was out of fuel and food. According to the news reports from Jeremiah's radio, a very few passengers with the proper papers had been permitted to disembark; the rest were still aboard, forbidden to come ashore.

That seemed to please the majority of the crew, from what Wilbur had overheard.

"We don't need those fuckin' foreign jokers," Mickey Lee Payne, the assistant "mud" clerk, had declared only two nights ago, down on the main deck where the crew had gathered in one of the bunk rooms. Mickey Lee, in Wilbur's opinion, was mostly a scrawny, loudmouthed bigot; if Wilbur were captain, he'd have the man tossed off the boat. . . . Though he had to admit that his own grandfather had probably been a bigot of the same stripe. "We got enough of our own freaks. Who the hell knows how many of 'em might be infectious? Did you fucking *see* the pictures from over there? Christ! Thousands and thousands of people died, and the rest went bugfuck. They were eating fucking *babies*. You ask me, that new guy that took control over there has the right idea getting rid of the jokers. I say we need to do the same kinda strong leadership: close the damn borders, send 'em back, and good riddance." There'd been a rumble of general agreement with Mickey Lee's statement from many of the crew.

For Wilbur, Kazakhstan and its problems seemed as distant as the moon. His world was the *Natchez*. No, it was good enough for the moment to simply stand in the pilothouse as he had back when he'd still been alive and look out over the Quarter, watching the bustle on the dock and on the river around him and anticipating another voyage upriver, even if he was no longer the boat's captain. He thought about the steamboat race that would be the showpiece of the Tall Stacks festival in Cincinnati, imagining the *Natchez* steaming past her competitors. In that moment, he would feel some satisfaction. In that moment, he might see the *Natchez* less as a prison and more as the boat he'd been so proud to create. His legacy, born of imagination and memories and the dreams of his ancestors. The only child it would seem he'd ever know.

He could imagine that sweet moment already: his *Natchez* demonstrating what a magnificent boat she was, even in her seventieth decade. He caressed the wheel in front of him, stroking it like a lover, laying his hand there and letting it sink gently into the wood, merging his being with the boat. *Part of me. Always part of me . . .*

It was a beautiful day. There would be beautiful nights to come, as well, with a nearly full boat, the steam up in the boilers, and the paddle wheel lashing the brown water of the river as they moved upriver. *Soon. Very soon. Eleanor, I'm afraid I'm leaving you again, if you're still out there. And this time I don't know if I'll be back.*

Wilbur shook his head at the thought and scowled. His exile on the *Natchez* was only bearable when they were on the river with the paddle wheel thrashing the water. *Soon . . .*

The rest of the time . . . well, that was hardly worth thinking about.

Wingless Angel

By John Jos. Miller

B Y THE TIME BILLY Ray had arrived on site the MS *Gustav Schröder* had been anchored downriver from the New Orleans passenger ship terminals for almost two days. He and his SCARE team—part of it, anyway; the rest hadn't yet arrived—stood on the north bank of the Mississippi River. The *Schröder* was anchored downstream, with the *Triton*, a Coast Guard cutter, anchored nearby to make sure none of the refugees slipped away. There was no doubt that the Van Rennsaeler administration was determined to keep the Kazakh refugees off American soil, though possible sanctuary in the French Quarter was only a moderate swim away.

Ray eyed the *Schröder* dubiously from his vantage point on the riverbank, which was adjacent to a small dock near the cruise ship terminal where a Port Police launch was moored. The freighter was too distant to discern details, but Ray was pretty sure that she was no titan of the seas.

"How many refugees did AG Cruz say were crammed on that tub?" he asked, frowning.

"Nine hundred and thirty-seven," the Midnight Angel said quietly at his side. Her voice was empty of inflection. She could have been talking about sacks of potatoes, not people.

"She doesn't look big enough to lug nine hundred and

thirty-seven toasters across the Atlantic, let alone that many people," Ray mused.

He glanced at her as she stood next to him, SCARE Agent Moon by her side. In human form Moon was a small, deformed joker who could barely crawl, but the wild card had given her the power to transform into any canid species she could envision, living or extinct, from the Chihuahua to the dire wolf. She was currently a big, fluffy sable collie whose resemblance to TV's beloved Lassie was uncanny. Ray knew she'd chosen her most friendly form intentionally for the Angel's benefit as it was the most comforting avatar in her repertoire. Ray caught Moon's eye and nodded. Her tail thumped the ground sympathetically.

The Angel was staring into the distance, at nothing, really. She was gaunt, her eyes sunken and blank. That was better, Ray reflected, than the haunted look they usually had, an expression she'd rarely been able to shake since their return from Kazakhstan. A month ago, deep in a fit of despondency even greater than usual, she'd shaved off the mane of thick, dark hair that had hung down to her waist. The new growth was streaked with white. She no longer wore her leathers, even on a mission, for they reminded her too much of the nightmare of Talas. Instead she had on khaki slacks and a thick, long-sleeved, shapeless pullover. Despite the heat and humidity of the New Orleans summer day, her face was pale and sweatless.

Moon pressed against her side and whined softly, but the Angel didn't respond. She only stared unseeingly as a tall black woman, a bit beyond statuesque, approached the three SCARE agents. The newcomer was middle-aged, with straightened hair worn in a stiff updo with descending ringlets. Her mannish tailored suit was much too heavy for the New Orleans climate and she was paying for her dubious fashion choice with droplets of perspiration running down her face. Ray's own suit was faultlessly tailored linen, superbly suited for the local climate. Ray recognized her from the attorney general's description.

"Agent Jones?"

She reached into a pocket of her suit and produced a badge, holding it up for all to see. "Ms. Evangelique Jones," she said, with the emphasis on the *Ms.* "Immigration and Customs Enforcement."

"Right, ICE," Ray said in an unimpressed tone. "Attorney General Cruz informed me that you were in charge of this. . . ." Ray's voice ran down and he gestured vaguely out to the *Schröder.*

"That's right," she said. "My job is to ensure that these so-called refugees don't set foot on American soil without proper authorization. That those without papers take their dirty genes back to wherever they came from or to whatever hellhole will accept them. But not here."

"Hellhole?" For the first time the Angel seemed engaged. She turned and looked at Jones. "What do you know about hell?"

She caught Jones's gaze with her own bleak stare and the ICE agent paused in whatever she'd intended to say. "Well—I—"

Ray cleared his throat and Jones's attention shifted back to him. "All right. And exactly where are we in this . . . situation?"

Her lips tightened in a grimace. "Apparently this little scheme to subvert American immigration law is being perpetrated by a known prostitute, a Ukrainian national with connections to the Russian mafia named Olena Davydenko, and—"

"Olena?" Ray said.

"Are you *deaf*, Mr. Ray?" Jones asked. "Or am I speaking in some foreign—"

Ray and the Angel stared at each other, ignoring the ICE agent as Moon looked on with her narrow gaze fixed on the newcomer.

"We knew that these refugees were Kazakhs," Ray said thoughtfully, "but no one told us that Davydenko was involved in this."

"And if she is, he must be, too," the Angel said harshly.

Jones, her eyes shifting between them, frowned. "If by he, you mean her partner in miscegenation—"

"Infamous Black Tongue," the Angel said as Ray said simultaneously, "Miscegenation?"

"You two are the *rudest* people I have ever met," Jones said, "always interrupting—"

"Sorry," Ray interrupted. "It's just that the Angel and I have a history with those two—we were all at Talas, though I got there at the end. The Angel did a lot of the heavy lifting. That included a mano-a-mano battle with the Black Tongue himself." His gaze narrowed. "I wish I'd been there for that."

"Yes." Jones looked at them as if their actions were part of some kind of dubious activity. "I read all about it."

"I just mention it so you know that we're not unaware of the refugees' background."

"That's all yesterday's news," Jones said. "We have more important matters to deal with now." She looked at them thoughtfully. "I suppose you'd better come along. I have some news to deliver to the miscreants on the *Schröder*." Jones walked past them toward the police launch moored at the nearby dock meant for small river craft.

"Good news, I hope," Ray said.

"Oh yes."

Jones strode over the gangway and an officer from the New Orleans Port Police helped her down into the bow of the launch that would ferry them to the *Schröder*. Ray and the Angel followed, with Moon bringing up the rear. The officer looked at Moon skeptically as she jumped down into the bow next to the Angel. It seemed as if he wanted to say something, but bit back his words as the Angel just looked at him. They cast off and started toward the freighter moored in the middle of the river.

As they glided along with the current, they passed demonstrators who had gathered on the riverbank in two distinct groups separated by a police barrier and a squadron of New Orleans city cops. The larger bunch were maybe a hundred strong. Most carried signs that were either anti–wild carder or pro–Liberty Party, which had unexpectedly swept Pauline van Rennsaeler to the presidency the previous November. Others waved random historical battle or political flags that had no connection to the current refugee crisis.

The smaller group numbered no more than twenty. Their banners showed sympathy for the trapped refugees, some proclaiming their allegiance to the JADL, the Joker Anti-Defamation League.

"What a freak show," Ray muttered.

"I hope you're not referring to these fine Americans exercising their constitutional right to free speech," Jones said.

Ray was saved from answering her question as they reached the *Schröder*. She looked even more dubious from up close. The freighter was a battered, rusty, near-dilapidated wreck that had probably spent her maiden voyage dodging German submarines during World War II. Of course she flew the Liberian flag, which meant that she operated under the laxest licensing and inspection regime in the entire nautical world.

The only way to board her was a rickety ladder extending down from the main deck. The police launch sidled close and Jones led the way up the ladder. Ray followed, with the Angel carrying Moon in one arm as her paws couldn't handle the narrow steps. Jones was puffing as she reached the end of the climb and accepted an extended hand to help her over the top and onto the *Schröder*'s deck.

"Thank you—" she began to say as she looked up, then fell silent.

The man standing before her smiled and released her hand. He was old but distinguished looking, in a gray charcoal-colored suit that Ray's practiced eye told him cost more than twice his own. His long and still abundant silver hair was pulled back in a ponytail and he leaned on a heavy wooden cane. His shoes, like his suit, were handmade and expensive. The right one encased an obvious prosthesis, which extended upward into an artificial leg, the extent of which was hidden by an expertly tailored pants leg. He smiled at Jones as she gained the deck.

Three companions stood grouped behind him. One was a man of similar age, smaller, with a lined, pale face that showed no expression at all as he looked over the newcomers. The second was a striking woman in a formfitting blue silk shirt tucked into tight blue jeans that showcased her splendid figure. It was, Ray realized, a theme of a sort. Her skin was a deep rich blue, her thick, long hair a shade darker, and her eyes the clear cerulean of a cloudless summer sky. The third person was a young man in a black suit with a priest's collar. He was serious-looking in an intense way, with regular features, dark eyes, and short dark hair.

"Agents Ray and Angel," the silver-haired man said. "Pleased to see you. Splendid work, saving the world and all that. Splendid." He looked at Moon, whom the Angel had set down on the deck. "And this is?"

"SCARE Agent Moon," the Angel said.

"A were-canid," Ray explained as Moon thumped her tail against the deck.

"Of course," the man said. He turned toward Jones. "I am Dr. Pretorius. You must be Ms. Jones, the ICE agent in charge. I've been retained to represent the *Schröder* refugees in their attempt to secure political asylum."

"By whom?" Jones asked in a somewhat less pleasant tone.

Pretorius smiled. "The Joker Anti-Defamation League." He gestured toward the three who stood by him. "This is Mr. Robicheaux and Ms. Blue, their representatives." He indicated the young man. "And Father Joachim Aguilera of the Church of Jesus Christ, Joker."

If Robicheaux was a joker, Ray thought, his deformities were hidden. Unlike Pretorius, his clothing was that of a working man. He wore a short-sleeved shirt tucked into worn jeans and work boots that had seen hard use. His eyes were dark and, like his expression, opaque as his gaze swept them all. He nodded. Ray nodded back.

"We have much to discuss. The others are waiting. If you will follow me." Pretorius leaned heavily on his cane as he limped away.

They fell in line behind the lawyer. As he led them across the main deck, Ray's nostrils flared. The *Schröder*'s interior matched its exterior in terms of grime, rust, and general decrepitude. The deck needed a new paint job, not to mention a thorough washing. Usually, Ray thought—though his experience with boats of any kind was rather limited—you see crewmen bustling about on errands and chores, taking care of vital upkeep and minor repairs. But they saw no one, crew or passengers, as they made their way to a hatch leading down into the ship's hold. It was so quiet that it was more than a little eerie. The *Schröder* might as well have been manned by a crew of ghosts.

Ray and the Angel exchanged glances. *She can feel it, too,* he thought. He glanced at Moon and saw her sniff the air. An expression of disgust washed over her lean-jawed face. Ray lacked the acute senses that Moon had, but he could smell the stench, too. Had smelled it since they'd reached the deck. It was getting worse, and it hit them like a slap on the face when Pretorius led them down the ladder into the ship's hold.

The vessel's only cargo was inside. People. They were everywhere in the gloom of the poorly lit, practically unvented hold. Men, women, and children looked at them wearily as they descended the ladder, hunger, hope, and fear in their eyes. Ray guessed that this trip had been as hellish as the demon-haunted last days of their home city of Talas. Most were gaunt. Many just lay on the dirty bedding that was their only protection against the harshness of the hold's metal floor. Ray had been in better-smelling swamps. He didn't want to even try to imagine the privations these people had undergone during their voyage.

Ray and the Angel kept stoic expressions on their faces, but Jones recoiled and audibly gagged.

"My God," she said, "don't you people bathe?"

"In what?" asked the woman approaching them. Her voice was bitter and bore an east European accent. Ray recognized her as Olena Davydenko, the daughter of a deceased Ukrainian mobster. She'd used her dead father's fortune to finance this desperate quest for safety and freedom. Olena looked at them cooly. She was blond and pretty, Ray thought, in a brittle, high-fashion sort of way. She was accompanied by a young woman who was a bare inch or two over five feet. She had clear pale skin that had a golden sheen to it. And she was staring at the Angel, who seemed uncomfortably aware of her gaze. At least the Black Tongue was nowhere in sight. If IBT and the Angel came face-to-face again— Ray pushed the thought away and forced himself to concentrate on the here and now.

"We have barely enough water to drink," Olena continued bitterly. "We have no food, no fuel, no medical supplies—"

"Not my concern!" Jones snapped. "You people should have been better prepared for your little cruise."

Pretorius held up his hands. "This is all beside the point."

"The point being," Jones said implacably, "that of all the people who decided to take this trip, very few have the proper documentation or even family members already living in the United States willing to sponsor them. No one lacking a sponsor or the proper documents will be allowed off this ship."

Dr. Pretorius gestured to an angry Olena, who handed him an expensive-looking briefcase. Ray figured that while most of the onlooking refugees probably couldn't follow the conversation in English, they had no problems understanding the gist of it. Pretorius extracted an impressively thick document from the briefcase and handed it to Jones.

She glanced at it. "What's this?"

"A brief requesting political asylum for all my clients," Pretorius said. "The government in Kazakhstan has collapsed. The warlords are fighting over the scraps of their country, but they all agree on one thing. They fear, wrongly and unjustly, that somehow the plague that struck Talas was brought on by the wild card virus and that the madness that destroyed the city was somehow spread by the jokers living there. Nonsense, of course, but that's not stopping them from waging genocide against all wild carders. These people couldn't stay in Talas and be killed. They can't go back. They're claiming asylum."

"You know that this must be adjudicated at higher levels of government—"

"I ask for an expedited hearing. In the meantime, we need food, water, medical—"

"I'm sure they do." Jones started back up the ladder, taking Pretorius's brief with her.

The joker lawyer looked at Ray. "That was pleasant."

"Yeah," Ray said. He was starting to have a very bad feeling about this mission. It wasn't as cut-and-dried as it had first seemed. He hadn't signed up to bully helpless jokers, women and children among them.

The young woman standing with Olena looked at Angel and spoke in accented but clear English. "I am called Tulpar. I was in Talas, too. I saw you fighting monsters. They called you the Angel of the Alleyways, the Madonna of the Blade—"

The Angel looked down. "I lost it."

A look of sympathy crossed the girl's face. "I see that your pain is great. But you helped us once. The people, the children, are starving—"

The Angel turned her face, stood silent for a moment, then followed Jones up the ladder.

Moon whined and went after her, taking the ladder carefully. Ray looked at Pretorius, who was watching with pursed lips, and then at the Kazakh girl. "She's been hurt deeper than you know by what happened in Talas."

"I could see it on her face," she said.

Ray nodded and hurried after them. Jones had crossed the deck and was going down to the waiting Port Police launch. The Angel, again holding Moon with the agent's front paws over her shoulder, was following.

Ray, feeling helpless, watched her. It had been a very difficult time, with the Angel growing more withdrawn and despondent despite the counseling she'd had. Ray had thought that maybe getting her out into the field might start her back on the road to who she'd once been, but, if anything, it seemed she was getting worse. He didn't know where to turn himself, or what to do, and that helplessness was churning deep inside and turning to an anger that he couldn't focus on any one person or thing. It was just grinding at him.

He started down after the Angel as sudden shouting from the riverbank caught his attention. A group of the anti-refugee protesters from the Liberty Party had surged against the flimsy barrier separating them from the pro-refugee JADL contingent and were breaking through the thin blue line that was all that kept the two groups apart.

"Crap," Ray said.

He glanced down. The Angel, too, had paused on her way down and was watching the drama unfold on the riverbank.

"Hurry up," Ray called. "We've got to stop this before someone gets hurt!"

The Angel nodded and dropped the remaining dozen feet or so to the launch's deck, landed lightly, and set Moon down. Ray swarmed down the ladder like a monkey in a major hurry and in a moment was at the Angel's side.

"Cast off," he shouted. "Head for the landing across the river!"

"I give the orders here, Ray," Jones said coldly. "Just what are your intentions?"

"My intentions," he said in a dangerously level voice, "are to keep people from getting hurt." He locked eyes with the officer in charge of the launch.

"Yes, sir," she said crisply.

Jones sighed. "Very well. Though I don't know what you can do."

"You'd be surprised," the Angel said.

The launch cast away from the *Schröder* and swept out in an arc, taking them to the northern bank, as everyone onboard watched what was happening on shore with concern.

The small JADL contingent was holding their ground as the anti-refugee protesters broke through the police barrier. Ray and the others on the launch could hear their angry shouts as they ran, screaming and waving their signs. The one in the lead was a heavyset man whose sign read *Go Home Genetic Waist!* The ones following him shoved aside the few cops who were bobbing helplessly in the mob's wake like corks in an unleashed torrent.

"Oh crap," Ray repeated.

And as the protesters approached the JADL demonstrators—slowly, because their signs weighed them down and most weren't in the best shape and it was a very hot and humid day—the zombies began to appear.

They didn't pop up out of thin air, but instead hauled themselves out of the river, climbing the steps at the landing toward which the launch was heading, like corpses rising from a watery grave. And make no mistake, they all were dead as shit. Not one was complete. Some were missing only fingers or an ear or an eye, others were less whole. Their sodden clothes oozed stinking seawater, which nicely complemented their body odors—a combination of rotting flesh and astringent embalming chemicals. The protesters outnumbered them ten to one, but Ray figured that the zombies were probably more intent on their purpose.

"Goddammit!" Ray swore aloud. He felt a sudden twinge of despair when the Angel didn't respond to his blasphemy. She never did, anymore. "Goddammit!" he repeated.

"Sweet Jesus," Jones said.

"You've never seen a zombie attack before?" the Angel asked, conversationally.

"Swing it around parallel to the shore," Ray shouted as the launch neared the riverbank. He climbed out on the bow.

"What is he doing *now?*" Jones wondered.

"He's going to make someone pay," the Angel said softly, but she didn't say for what.

Moon whined by her side.

"Go ahead and help him, if you want." Moon put a paw on

her knee, beseechingly. "It doesn't matter," the Angel said in a faraway voice. "They're only zombies."

By now the protesters were all quite aware of the creatures shambling toward them. The mob's first reaction was to stumble to an uncertain halt, stand, and stare. Ray wanted to scream aloud to Hoodoo Mama—only she could be orchestrating this—but that would sound silly. "Josephine" was too formal, and "Joey"—he'd never called her that. The anger continued to build in him—the months and months of watching the Angel grow ever more inward, ever more detached, ever more untouchable and desolate—and he found his voice in a wordless cry of his own rage and despair.

He leaped as the launch swung around as he'd directed, setting a new unofficial world record for the standing long jump, and hit halfway up the stairway going up the riverbank. He stuck his landing and was moving a moment after his feet touched ground.

Moon followed him. She leaped from the bow, her fur flowing in the air as she dove into the water and came up swimming, reaching the foot of the staircase as Ray clambered up to the top.

By now, the shambling newcomers had inserted themselves between the two groups of demonstrators, a half score undead facing the larger contingent of the living. As the reeking zombies continued their slow approach, the demonstrators turned en masse and, bumbling and battering against one another, retreated. Many added to the chaos by screaming incoherently. Some threw away their signs, some used them to bludgeon a way to safety.

Many suddenly also realized that Ray was coming toward them with the speed of a runaway train and a look on his face that was not entirely rational. Moon followed behind him, barking ferociously. He heard Moon, but his heart sank when he realized that the Angel had remained on the launch, looking on. It all just made him even more angry.

Some protesters fled; some froze in fear, creating a major traffic jam as those behind them either blundered to a halt or tried to fight through the paralyzed clumps of humanity.

Ray hit the scrum of uncertain protesters like the running back he'd been in college. It all came back to him, like a riding a bicycle that'd been parked for forty years. He smiled crazily as he headed for an imaginary goal line, jinking and darting through the defenders, none laying a hand on him, his eyes on the prize ahead.

The biggest of the zombies, a huge man who'd once been black but was now a washed-out, grayish color, was in the lead. He had a nasty bullet hole in his forehead, but that didn't seem to be bothering him any as he reached for the unlucky protester at the rear of the pack. She'd fallen down and the zombie was looming over her, opening wide jaws, which showed gaps where, Ray guessed, gold teeth had once gleamed.

A last moment of cognition, of recognition of danger, must have flickered through the dim recesses of the zombie's brain, for a whisper of what looked to Ray like surprise passed over his face, and then Ray leaped over his intended victim and hit him at full speed, shoulder first, arms wrapped around him.

The zombie came apart.

Fuck, Ray thought, *I'm wearing a new suit.*

He clutched the top half of the zombie's body, various organs dangling from it like really ugly candy hanging from a shattered piñata. The zombie's bottom half, from the ass down, hit the asphalt walkway and skidded. Ray's forward momentum shot them into another zombie and the two and a half of them hit the ground in a tangle of limbs.

Ray had rarely—no, never—been so disgusted in his life. He was covered by water-soaked zombie goo, his new suit was ruined, and he was still, in general, pissed off. The zombie on the bottom of the dog-pile tried to bite him, and Ray put his fist through its face, smashing it like a two-week-old Halloween pumpkin. Then he was on his feet, stamping, until the zombie's chest was a flattened mass of fetid flesh and shattered bones.

If the remaining zombies in Ray's vicinity had any humanity left about them, or even some low degree of animal cunning, they would've fled. But no. They were zombies. They converged on their new, nearest target.

Ray realized that all the protesters had gotten to safety—out of the corner of his eye he saw the cops helping some of them and Moon was harassing and gnawing off bits of other zombies—but he wasn't done yet. He had to hit something to work the anger out of his system, and zombies made good targets.

He grabbed the right wrist of the nearest and flipped it to the ground. He put his foot—his shoes, too, were finished, Ray realized—in its armpit and twisted. The arm came off like a well-roasted chicken wing and Ray was just in time to duck and whirl and smack another attacking zombie right in the face with his unconventional yet effective flail.

The zombie's head sailed off its rather scrawny neck and it twirled in a little uncertain dance and immediately fell over the edge of the riverbank, bounced a few times, and was swallowed by the waiting river. Ray whirled about, but the other zombies had stopped in their tracks.

"Come on, you sons of bitches," Ray shouted, though two of the zombies were clearly women. He didn't really care.

But they, or more properly, Hoodoo Mama, had had enough. She wasn't exactly frugal with her undead soldiers, but neither did she waste them for no reason. Those left standing all turned in unison and marched toward the riverbank.

"Come on!" Ray shouted in frustration. "Come on!"

But no one heeded his challenge.

"Shit!" Ray yelled. Still enraged, he hurled the zombie arm at the last zombie before it could jump off the bank, hitting it in the back and knocking it into the river below. Ray took a deep breath. "Shit," he repeated, more quietly this time.

He stalked back to the clump of protesters. Moon trotted next to him, her beautiful coat soaked in zombie goo, sneezing and hacking up bits from her narrow-jawed mouth.

"Thanks," Ray said.

She wagged her tail.

The launch had landed during the fight and Jones had disembarked, followed by Ray and the Port Police crew.

Jones planted herself in front of him. "Agent Ray—" she began, but stopped when Ray raised his right hand and she saw the look in his eyes.

He was covered in gore, soaked in embalming chemicals and bodily fluids, smeared with rotting flesh and squashed organs.

"I'm going back to the motel now," he said. He was surprised to hear the calmness in his voice. "I have to take a shower." He looked at his wife. The look in her eyes—was it sorrow? Loss? Nothing at all?—bit deeper than any wound he'd ever received in his forty years in government service.

The Angel and Moon followed him as he walked away.

♠

"Who told you where I live?" Joey Hebert asked sullenly as Ray stood before the door of her shotgun shack. The picket fence around the front yard was more gray than white and had more gaps in it than a meth head's dental work. The front porch sagged and the entire building listed uncertainly like a drunken sailor. "It was Bubbles, wasn't it?"

Ray suppressed a sigh. He'd decided to take this one on alone, leaving the Angel and Moon at the Motel 6 where they were staying. He feared that Hoodoo Mama might remind her even more of Talas. Months of therapy had done little to help the Angel. Sitting around D.C. hadn't helped either. He'd hoped that what he thought would be a relatively innocuous assignment might start to shake her out of her depression, but the Angel wasn't responding at all to being in the field. The shields she'd erected around herself after Talas were still impenetrable. And now Ray had to worry about the twists the mission was taking. *Well, one thing at a time.*

"Let me in, Joey." He decided on the informal approach. "We have to talk."

Hoodoo Mama glared at him. She was a scrawny, young black woman with an expression that was mostly always angry. Ray knew the feeling.

"We have to talk," he repeated flatly.

After a moment she said, "I guess I can't make you shut your mouth." She opened the screen door and stepped aside.

The front room was a mess. Ray's sense of neatness was offended. The room was poorly lit by a single forty-watt bulb in a floor lamp that stood next to a dirty, beat-up sofa. The coffee table in front of it was littered with old Chinese food and pizza boxes, the worn carpet was splotched with dried mud and less identifiable stains. The room smelled of dust and decay and death. "Jesus," Ray said, "would it hurt to have one of your zombies run a broom through this place occasionally?"

Joey shrugged defensively. "I just got back into town—right before I heard about the ship of refugees being held up in the harbor. They're mostly wild carders, you know."

"Yes, I know," Ray said patiently. "And you're not helping—"

"*Someone's* got to help them, Mr. High-and-Mighty Government Man," Joey said, bitterly. "*Someone's* got to keep them safe from those creepy-ass Liberty Party motherfuckers."

"That's my job," Ray said.

"Are you going to do it?"

Ray's crooked features suddenly froze in a clenched-tooth grin. "You ever heard of me shirking my duty?"

"What is your duty, Mr. High-and-Mighty Government Man?" Joey replied.

"Trust me," he said, and repeated after her unamused bark of laughter, "trust me. If you want, keep an eye on the situation—I know you have a legion of dead pigeons and rats you use as spies. Have an entire division of zombies on hand just in case things go wrong. But for Christ's sake, keep them out of sight. You're not

helping by having the walking dead show up at every little prov-
ocation."

Joey eyed him, Ray thought, with more speculation than
distrust. "You got a plan to save those poor people?"

"I'm working on one," Ray said. It almost surprised him to
realize that he was. But in her own unsubtle way, he realized that
Joey was right.

She nodded. "All right. If you said you had one I wouldn't believe you, because no one can save them. They're fucked. But I'll be
damned if I'm just going to let them quietly sail off to their doom."

"I'll take your word on that." Ray turned to leave, stopped,
and looked back. "And Bubbles said to call her. Your cell phone
isn't working and she's worried about you."

"Damn it!" Hoodoo Mama said as Ray let the screen door
bang shut after him.

He went down the sagging wooden stairs carefully, fully aware
that there could be an army of small dead things with sharp
pointy teeth under them that Joey could send after him. But he
felt that they had found at least a tiny bit of common ground,
and zombies were one less thing he had to worry about, for now.
There were plenty of others.

Like the man sitting in the locked black Escalade he'd left
parked up the street from Joey's shack. There were no working
streetlights in Hoodoo Mama's neighborhood, so Ray could barely
discern the silhouette in the front passenger seat. He thought
that it was a man, a small man, perhaps a boy. He seemed utterly
unconcerned as Ray approached the vehicle, so Ray simply opened
the driver's side door and bent down to look in.

From close up Ray could see that he was indeed a small, slight
white man, probably in his early seventies. He had a pleasant face
that had been roughly treated by the passage of time. What hair
wasn't covered by his porkpie hat was white and cut short. Ray
suddenly recognized him. "You're the JADL guy from the boat.
Robicheaux, right?"

He smiled. His teeth were even and white. "Right, Mr. Ray."

"Can I help you?"

"No, but I want to help you." He had a Cajun accent.

Why not? Ray thought. A small old dude was just who he needed on his side. "How?" Ray slid into the car and closed the door.

"Information, Mr. Ray. I know what's going on among the refugees—and it's not good."

Ray sighed as he pulled into the deserted street. "What's happening?"

"They're scared, Mr. Ray. Tired and hungry. They were hoping for sanctuary and have been turned away—"

"Pretorius says they have a shot—"

"No. Asylum will be granted to a token few—the Handsmith and his son, the ace Tulpar, maybe two dozen passengers in all. Aces and nats, every one."

"And the jokers?"

"Van Rennsaeler made a deal with the British PM—they're sending them to Rathlin Island."

Ray frowned. "That rock off the coast of Northern Ireland?"

"It was once a joker colony. Pretty much abandoned these days."

"So they're sending them to some gulag—out of sight and out of mind."

"That's the plan."

"I can hear the *but* you left unsaid."

The old man smiled wryly. "Very perceptive, Mr. Ray. There are several *buts*. The Handsmith has refused the deal, as has Tulpar. There's talk of mutiny aboard the ship—of taking it over and trying for Brazil, Africa, maybe."

Ray snorted. "Yeah, Jesus, great idea."

"There's more. A few of the refugees belong to a joker terrorist gang—the Twisted Fists. Others are starting to listen to them."

"To do what?" Ray asked. "Go up against the U.S. Coast Guard?"

"They are desperate."

"It would be a bloodbath."

"Which is something your job is to prevent."

Ray pulled the Escalade over to the side of the street and slammed it into park.

"How'd this come down to *me*?" he asked. "I don't speak for the government. I *work* for the government."

The old man looked at him, his lined face composed. "If not you, who then?"

"Shit," Ray said.

"But for the fortunate turn of the card, you and I could be one of those jokers." If he was a joker, Ray thought, it didn't show. An ace, maybe? Ray had never heard of him, but that meant little. Your card could turn when you were seven or seventy, or maybe he had some crappy little power that attracted no attention in the wild card world. "If as a nation we turn our back on a handful of brothers and sisters whose only crime was to be born in a savage land, how long will it be before other ships are sent to Rathlin, packed with those of our own nation who some people still despise? What then, Mr. Ray?"

"Shit," Ray said again.

"But," the old man said thoughtfully, "all is not entirely lost. The JADL has been in contact with a man who calls himself Witness. For a million dollars he's offered to provide haven for the refugees in Cuba. That island isn't exactly, uh, strict when it comes to immigration, and, uh, other laws. It could easily absorb a few hundred refugees, or act as a transit point once they acquire proper identification."

But Ray's mind had turned back a decade. "This guy calls himself Witness," he asked, "what's he look like?"

◆

The Angel was still awake when Ray returned to their hotel room. She slept very little, ate very little, and never smiled. She was sitting on the bed, watching some Mexican talk show. Ray knew that she didn't speak Spanish. It was all noise to her, like the rest of the world washing through her head but failing to distract her from the horrors she'd faced in Talas.

"I'm back," he said, eliciting only a flicker of interest. "You'll never guess who I ran into."

Her eyes slid over to him, which was encouraging.

"The JADL guy we met on the ship," he said, undressing down to his underwear and carefully hanging up his suit in the hotel room's closet. The room was small, but neat, one of the lesser chains as SCARE didn't have the budget to put its agents up at the really nice places with gyms and saunas and free breakfasts. But Ray didn't much care as long as it was clean.

The night was hot and humid, but the Angel had cranked up the air conditioner until it was bordering on wintry in the room. Ray got into the bed next to her.

"The small man? He seemed nice," the Angel said. There was a faraway look in her eyes.

"Yeah." Ray looked at her thoughtfully. "But he's in the fight, in his own way."

"What do you mean?" the Angel asked.

Ray kept the smile off his face. At least he'd engaged her, aroused her curiosity. That was something.

"He's working with the JADL, trying to help the refugees." Ray relayed the information that'd been given to him, but when he was partway through the Angel turned her attention back to the television screen. "Only thing is, along with the nutjobs trying to keep the refugees off American soil, apparently there's another problem festering behind the scenes. The Twisted Fists may get involved." That evoked no interest. "And a group headed by some guy who calls himself Witness."

This captured the Angel's attention. She turned her gaze back upon Ray. "The Witness?" she asked.

Ray nodded. "He fits the description."

Angel, looking thoughtful, relaxed, shifted against Ray's chest, laying her head on his shoulder.

"The Witness," she repeated.

He held her a long time as her breathing relaxed and her eyes slowly closed and at last she fell asleep. Moving slowly and carefully, he reached out for the remote and turned off the television. Now, finally, he could sleep, too.

♥

The rest of the team arrived the next morning when Ray, the Angel, and Moon were eating breakfast in the motel's coffee shop. The Angel was listlessly picking at her pancakes. Ray himself had almost as little appetite lately as his wife, but he managed to finish his omelet between feeding Moon cut-up bits of her breakfast steak. She was still a collie. She preferred a canid form for public appearances, and Ray was long used to dealing with recalcitrant waitresses and busybody onlookers. He handled their questions, usually, with patient explanations, but today he wasn't in the mood and resorted to his best glare, sometimes reinforced by a flash of his official badge. It worked.

Two tall, thin, pale, well-dressed men approached their table, accompanied by another agent wearing fatigues, a camo T-shirt, and combat boots.

Ray nodded as they stopped before the table. "Harry, Max." He paused. "Colonel," he added dryly.

The "Colonel" was directed at the newcomer in fatigues. He was young, as were the other two, but much more nondescript, with fair hair, a fair complexion, and light blond hair. His eyebrows were almost invisible against his pale complexion. He was a former army corporal from Fairbanks, Alaska, named Alan Spencer. He'd competed on the second season of *American Hero*, jumping several ranks by calling himself "Colonel Centigrade." After failing to win the game show he'd transferred out of the army into SCARE.

"I hab a cold," he announced in a nasal, sniffling voice.

Ray exchanged glances with the Angel, but decided not to

comment on the irony of Centigrade's statement. Colonel Centigrade was a bit of a fuckup and his freezing powers weren't the most reliable. He wasn't exactly vital to the plan that Ray was evolving in his mind, whereas Harrison and Maximillian Klingensmith were. They were identical twins, down to the black eye patch each wore over his left eye and the sweep of inky black feathers that covered their scalps in lieu of hair. Their nicknames, derived from their joker aspect and from parents who had academic backgrounds in, respectively, ornithology and Nordic studies, were Huginn and Munnin.

"You boys have breakfast yet?" Ray asked.

"No, sir," they all said in unison.

"Take a seat," he said, moving closer to the Angel. He liked the Klingensmith twins. They were respectful, resourceful, and quite useful. They piled into the booth, Spencer's ass half hanging over the bench's edge. "Here's what we're going to do. . . ."

♣

The zombie intervention between the JADL demonstrators and the anti–wild card protesters had the unfortunate effect of intensifying the conflict. The ensuing publicity brought out not only more protesters on both sides—many more on the anti–wild card side—but literally hundreds of curious bystanders who were determined to view the next scene in the drama unreeling before their eager eyes. The number of police officers manning the barrier keeping the opposing groups apart had also increased dramatically, but Ray could easily read the concern on their faces. Something had to be done to defuse the situation before real violence erupted.

Ray was hopeful that his talk with Hoodoo Mama had dissuaded her from further use of her undead hordes—at least for now—but the swelling numbers of participants on both sides of the controversy had him worried.

The pro-refugee faction had maybe doubled in size, but the numbers of those protesting against the Kazakh newcomers had swelled almost exponentially, both in numbers and in passion.

It was hard to say what looked angrier, the crowd waving their signs and screaming imprecations at the moored freighter, or the morning sky, which was black with thunderheads that threatened a cloudburst at any moment. It was not a happy morning, and Ray saw that the only thing that could possibly make it worse was about to occur.

Evangelique Jones arrived on the scene. She looked glad to see Ray, which immediately made him suspicious. "Well, Director Ray," she said with a smile that was smug and gloating at the same time, "word has come down from Washington. Their final decision, so to say."

Ray flashed back to what he'd learned the night before.

"They've decided on asylum? That was fast."

Evangelique nodded. "Twenty-nine of them will be afforded political refugee status. The rest will be accorded sanctuary on an island off the coast of Northern Ireland—"

"Rathlin," Ray interrupted.

She looked at him suspiciously. "How did you know?"

Ray shrugged. He didn't want to give away his source of inside information. He should have kept his mouth shut, but it was too late. "Where else could it be? I mean—it's been used as a joker sanctuary in the past."

"Yessss," the ICE agent said. Before she could add anything, a huge clap of thunder sounded and lightning streaked across the sky and it opened up to a steady fall of rain.

Ray looked up as the droplets pattered upon his face, soaking him almost instantly. "Maybe this'll disperse the crowd," he said hopefully.

But the sudden downpour did nothing to break up the mob that was now surging back and forth in a wavelike manner. It served instead to seem to rile them up, make them even more convinced of their anger.

"Hey," Ray suddenly said, "I know those guys!"

Jones frowned. "Who?"

"Him," Ray said, and then corrected himself, "I mean them."

He pointed to a large figure at the head of the JADL contingent. He—they—were a large joker bifurcated from the waist up with two torsos, two sets of shoulders and arms, and, of course, two heads. Each held a sign in a brawny arm. One read *Welcome refugees!*, the other, *Foreigners go home!* They seemed to be arguing with each other. Their argument quickly evolved into a shoving match that a couple of cops moved in quickly to break up, then stopped, stumped.

"I used them as an informant back in the day—Rick and Mick." Ray sighed. "They could never get along."

The onlookers and both batches of protesters were enjoying the show, shouting encouragement at them and egging them on. They started swatting at each other with their signs. The pair overtipped and crashed into one of the segments of waist-high fencing that separated the two groups. Their weight crushed it to the ground, bringing down a section of fence maybe ten feet long.

For a moment there was silence, then an angry surge forward by the larger anti–wild card faction, who saw a clear path to the JADL demonstrators.

"Crap," Ray muttered. He realized that he was saying that a lot lately. He looked almost desperately at his team. They were too few to do much against the hundreds surging forward to take out their frustrations on the smaller number of joker counterprotesters. If only Washington had supplied him with some heavy hitters they could at least—

"Centigrade!" Ray suddenly barked. He couldn't make himself add the man's self-appointed rank.

Spencer stepped forward, a little uncertainly. "Sir?" he asked in a more hesitant than military manner.

"Do your stuff."

"Sir?"

Ray gestured at the scene before them. "Make it snow. Make it snow like it was fucking Christmas."

It finally dawned on the colonel. "Yes, sir!" He stepped away from the others.

"What in the world?" Jones asked as Spencer's face froze in a mask of fierce concentration. A minute passed, then she angrily turned to Ray. "If you don't tell me what that man—"

Ray pointed his right hand at her to shush her and pointed to the sky with his left.

You could just barely see it against the dark thunderheads and the streams of rain as the first snowflakes formed. A cool breeze swept down over them as in an area maybe a hundred yards across and directly above the heads of the demonstrators, sleet started to fall among the raindrops.

When the first bits of ice hit the protesters an uncertain note rumbled through the crowd. Some looked up unbelievingly at the sky. Some pointed, some cried out loud. As the rain fell it was turning to snow about fifty or sixty feet above their heads. Snow. In New Orleans. In the summer. It was . . . unnatural . . .

Within moments the surging crowd had stopped. Everyone, the bystanders, the demonstrators on both sides, the cops standing gallantly between them, looked up at the sky, mixed wonder and fear on their faces.

Ray and the others, still getting soaked by the warm rain, could nonetheless feel the chilling breeze blowing from the pocket of extraordinary weather that was now pelting down on the demonstrators as a mix of big, fluffy snowflakes and freezing sleet.

Ray looked from the sky to Colonel Centigrade. His teeth were clenched now, his face was white. Cords stood out on his neck and he was shaking. He looked about ready to collapse.

"Hold on!" Ray barked. "Concentrate! Another minute—"

The demonstrators had withstood the muggy heat, the harsh sun, even zombies, all of which were to be expected in New

Orleans. But a snowstorm? No. That was freakishly grotesque. Voodoo of the worst sort. And goddamned cold.

The mass of demonstrators broke and ran, streaming away through various cross streets, along with the crowd that had gathered to watch the show, leaving only the puzzled and shivering police still manning the barricades.

"All right, Centigrade," Ray snapped, "at ease!"

Spencer swayed on his feet and would have collapsed if Maximillian Klingensmith hadn't grabbed him. Or maybe it was Harrison. Ray wasn't sure.

"He did that?" Jones asked unbelievingly.

Ray nodded, smiling at Spencer, who was grinning weakly as he leaned on his fellow agent.

"Yes, he did," Ray said proudly.

She barely, Ray noted, suppressed a shiver as a flicker of— what?—disgust, perhaps, flashed across her face. "All right." Jones looked up at the sky. It was still raining. "I suppose he can't stop that?"

Ray shook his head. "Not part of his powers."

"No. Of course not." Jones ran her hand through her hair, which had collapsed in soggy ringlets around her face, pushing it back. "Well, rain or shine, it's my duty to serve these papers."

Ray hazarded a guess. "Max?"

The agent keeping Colonel Centigrade from collapsing with weariness nodded.

"Take the colonel back to the motel." He'd earned that with his heroic efforts, Ray thought. "Get him whatever he needs— food, drink, dry clothes."

"Yes, sir," Max said, and Spencer managed a tiny sneeze.

"And for God's sake," Ray added, "get him something for that cold." He looked at Jones. "The rest of us will accompany Agent Jones to the *Schröder*."

"I don't think that's necessary," Jones said.

"I'm in charge of your security," Ray replied, "and I think it is. After all, you're going to be delivering news to a large number of people who might take it very badly."

Jones frowned. "Perhaps you're right."

"Perhaps I am," Ray said.

♠

The conditions aboard the *Schröder* hadn't changed. It would be hard, Ray reflected, for it to get much worse, and there was no way it was going to get any better.

Jones had ordered the ship's entire complement to gather on deck, probably, Ray thought, because she'd learned somehow that the news had already reached the refugees, who were regarding her with what could only be silent anger on their faces. Or maybe, he thought, she was just being cautious and figured that she'd be safer there than down in the hold. And also because it just smelled so bad down there.

Backed by Ray, Moon, the Angel, and the Klingensmith brother known as Huginn, she stood on a small raised platform on the bow in front of a set of hatches that led down into the hold, waiting impatiently as all crew and passengers gathered around on the main deck. Fortunately the rain had ceased just before they'd boarded the ship and the blazing sun was doing its best to dry up all the excess moisture that had leaked down from the sky. Ray could feel steam rising from his suit.

It took more than a few minutes for them all to assemble. Olena stood before Jones, who looked down impassively from the height of the raised platform from which she could survey the deck. Dr. Pretorius stood with Olena, as did the young woman ace, Tulpar, and the Handsmith, a broad, chunky man with his hands wrapped in strips of burlap. His son, Nurassyl, was next to him, looking like a ghost draped in a sheet, his exposed flesh glistening with the moisture that he exuded, supported by a platform of tiny wriggling tentacles in lieu of feet. Ray recognized some others from the initial meeting, though the JADL representatives were both missing, as was the young priest.

Ray heard the Angel suddenly hiss angrily and he turned and saw Marcus Morgan, the Infamous Black Tongue, coiled behind and partly concealed by a freight derrick midway down the deck. From the waist up he was naked, exposing the body of a fit, young African-American man. He was naked from the waist down, too, but the rest of him was that of an outsized coral snake, glistening in alternating bands of black, yellow, and scarlet scales. He made the largest anaconda look like a garter snake.

The Angel clenched her teeth, took a step forward. Ray laid a warning hand on her shoulder and she angrily shrugged it off. She and IBT, as he called himself, had fought a personal duel at the conclusion of the Talas episode that had left her badly wounded. It had taken her months to recover from her injuries and that had coincided with her long slide into post-traumatic stress.

Ray was unsure what effect seeing him again would have on her. Basically, it seemed to be making her angry, which was something at least. He didn't know if it was good or bad, but at least his presence was eliciting some sort of reaction.

Jones cleared her throat and began to speak.

"I am Evangelique Jones, of Immigration and Customs Enforcement. I have passed on to Washington your lawyer's"—and here she fixed Dr. Pretorius with a hard stare that he calmly returned—"brief, which has been considered at the highest levels of government. The request for asylum has been granted—"

At this seemingly miraculous reversal of their fortunes an eruption of cheers exploded from the refugees, which built higher and higher as those who understood English translated for those who didn't. Jones fell silent and looked on with a small smile on her face until the cheering and hugging and cries of joy slowly died down.

Ray could hardly believe the evident glee she was taking in

delivering her message in this provocative manner. Even the Angel seemed to forget about IBT and stared at her incredulously.

"—to the following individuals," Jones continued in a loud, satisfied voice. "Olena Davydenko. The individual known as the Handsmith. His son, Nurassyl. Inkar Omarov, also known as the Tulpar—"

She continued to read off the names, slowly, sonorously, enjoying the looks on the faces below her as the hope began to drain out of them as they realized that all of those who'd been granted asylum were the few nats among them, the even fewer aces, and those rare jokers with useful abilities or money. After reading off the twenty-ninth name Jones folded the document and looked up impassively.

"The rest of you," she intoned, "will remain aboard the *Schröder* until such time she can be refueled, whence she shall leave the territorial water of the United States and set course to Rathlin Island off the coast of Northern Ireland, where you shall be granted permanent refuge."

"This is outrageous!" Pretorius shouted. "I shall appeal!"

Jones looked at him calmly. "As I told you, this has been considered at the highest levels of the American government. There is no appeal."

"I will not leave my people," the Handsmith shouted.

His cry was echoed by others whom Jones had named, anger in every voice.

"Moon," Ray said quietly. "Get ready to change."

The collie standing by the Angel's side nodded.

The crowd of refugees made an almost instinctive surge forward. Jones, nonplussed, blinked at the anger and hatred she saw on the hundreds of faces before them.

"Now," Ray said, and instead of a friendly collie, a dire wolf stood on the platform with them, six hundred pounds of sin with fangs like a saber-toothed tiger.

The crowd stopped as one, though IBT slithered forward, shouldering aside refugees as he pushed his way to the front.

Inkar Omarov transformed as quickly and smoothly as Moon had, becoming the Tulpar of Kazakh legend, the golden-coated, eagle-winged horse with razor-sharp hooves.

"*Stop!*" Dr. Pretorius limped forward, pushing himself to stand between Jones and the SCARE agents and the seething crowd of refugees. "Nothing will be solved by violence! There is another way. There *must be* another way."

The aging lawyer dominated the scene by the sheer force of his personality, stemming the tide of rage before it overwhelmed the situation.

"You expect us to turn away and slink off into the darkness," Olena said heatedly, "when we have no fuel, no food? How can we even hope to recross the Atlantic—"

"As I told you," Jones said with surprising calmness, "the United States will be more than pleased to fill your fuel tanks. It's a cheap enough price to pay to be rid of you."

"But the food," Olena added, "we're almost out—"

Jones shrugged. "Can't help you there," she said. "There's been no official requisition for supplies—"

Ray had suddenly had enough. "Screw that," he said. He reached into his back pants pocket, took out his wallet. "Harry," he said to the agent by his side, "take this." He handed him a credit card. "Go clean out a 7-Eleven or something. Get a boat-load of food—"

"Director Ray," Jones said in a hard voice.

"We're talking about children, here," Ray said stiffly. "Children, women, old people—hell, no one deserves to starve."

"Wait," Pretorius said. He took his own wallet out of a pocket in his jacket and extracted a card. "I appreciate the generous of-fer, Agent Ray." He held out a card. "But take mine. It probably has a higher limit."

It was black.

Ray and Pretorius locked gazes, and Ray nodded. "Do it," he said to the young agent. He quirked an eyebrow, and Huginn nodded. He stepped away from the others and took the card

Pretorius offered. He turned, headed for the police launch that was awaiting them.

"Well," Jones said. "Is anyone accompanying us to shore?"

There was a ripple in the crowd, as if a wind were blowing, but not one of the named refugees stepped forward.

Jones swept them with her gaze. "Fools," she said. She followed Huginn to the launch.

"Let's go." Ray took the Angel's arm, and she started at the touch, like a nervous horse. She looked at him with something of the old fire in her eyes, then nodded.

"Moon," Ray said, "you'd better power down. I don't think there's enough room in the launch for you in this form."

The agent was a collie before Ray could blink. She smiled and wagged her tail.

Ray turned to Pretorius. "Harry will be back with the food as soon as he can."

"Thank you," Pretorius said simply.

Ray shrugged. "Like I said. None of these people deserve to starve." Then he added in a low voice that only the lawyer could hear, "One of the boys is going to stick around for a while. Kind of keep an eye on things."

"I understand," Pretorius said. "He'll be safe."

"Maybe," Ray said, "there is a way where we can work this out."

◆

Evangelique Jones was as good as her word. By that afternoon a tanker had moseyed up to the *Schröder* and was pumping enough fuel into her tanks to get them back across the Atlantic.

Ray and the rest of the SCARE team waited on the riverbank. Some protestors from both sides had reassembled, but the earlier storm had taken the starch out of their attitude. Rick and Mick were not to be seen. *Probably,* Ray thought, *off arguing about what to have for dinner.*

Ray realized that it would all eventually build up until it started to chafe and something set it off again. More violence was inevitable as long as the *Schröder* was moored in sight of everyone. He hoped that she wouldn't be there much longer. He was sympathetic to the plight of the refugees, but there wasn't much he could do for them, other than ensure their safety when they were still under his watch. And that he was going to do.

They waited patiently until Harry Klingensmith returned with a rental truck full of food and supplies.

They helped the crew of the police launch, moored as usual at the small dock near their vantage point, load the supplies. It took several trips for the launch to ferry it all across to the *Schröder*. Obviously, there wasn't enough to provide provisions for the refugees for a voyage across the ocean, but for now it would furnish them with a decent meal after days of rationing.

It took a couple of hours to get all the groceries unloaded. When the task was finished Ray thanked the launch's crew for their help and then he and the others headed back to the motel. No one noticed that Max Klingensmith had remained on the *Schröder*.

♥

They all crowded into the room shared by Ray and the Angel. Colonel Centigrade was lying on the bed, still exhausted and fighting his bad head cold. Moon, still in her collie form, curled up next to him on the bed, but watched alertly as Harrison Klingensmith took the room's only comfortable chair, settled into it. The Angel looked on with some interest while Ray paced restlessly back and forth across the small room.

"What can you see?" he asked the pale, scarecrow-thin SCARE agent.

Huginn screwed both eyes shut tightly, frowning with concentration. When he opened them he stared at the plain, dull green drapes drawn across the hotel room window.

"I see," he intoned in a soft, faraway voice, "people eating."

Ray made an impatient sound.

"Munnin," he added, "is panning the room. It looks mostly calm. Most seem resigned, some are angry."

He went on, narrating the scene as if it were a movie, relaying what his twin brother could see with his own left eye. His right eye saw just the blank cloth of the drapery he was staring at. This mixed vision shared by two minds could be disorienting as hell, which was why he concentrated his own sight on a neutral view. His brother also saw what he saw from his left eye. Their ace had no distance limit and could never be turned off. Unfortunately— or, for them, perhaps fortunately—vision was the only sense they shared, and it had taken long and hard practice to get used to the disorientation this collective sight caused. It was, of course, an ideal means of instantaneously transferring information.

"Hold on—something's happening. Max is leaving the hold where most of the refugees are encamped."

"Why?" Ray stopped pacing.

"Hard to say. He's being stealthy, though. Sneaking. He's good at that. Sticking to shadows, ducking. He's on deck. It's dark now, nighttime. He's watching a small launch approach. Men are coming aboard."

"How many?"

"I count eight. Max is going to the bridge. Olena's there with the captain and some of his officers and the man you described as the JADL liaison, who's talking to them. He looks worried, like he's trying to tell them something they're not believing. Max is concealed outside the bridge, but he can hear them. Hold on. He's writing something—we carry pads to communicate complicated messages. I can read it as he writes. Robicheaux says that you can't trust the man called Witness. He's gotten in touch with his contacts in Cuba—someone from the Gambione family. No one in Havana knows anything about the *Schröder* getting asylum there. But they know this guy Witness—he's heavily into human trafficking."

"I knew it," the Angel said between clenched teeth. "I knew they couldn't trust the bastard."

"Wait—the men are coming to the bridge. Max is retreating into deeper cover. The one leading them is big, blond, muscles like a weightlifter. Handsome, except for a smashed nose. The men with him are armed. They're dragging the old guy from the bridge, Olena is trying to stop them but they're pushing her down. She's screaming. They're—they're throwing the old guy off the side of the ship. That guy, that snake guy is coming fast, to the bridge. They're shooting at him—"

"Damn!" Ray said. "We've got to get there, fast! We should have staked out someplace closer, dammit!"

"The *Schröder*'s engines are starting. There's commotion on the Coast Guard cutter. Lights are going on all over her!"

"Angel—" Ray said.

"I can't help you," she said numbly. "You know I can't." She couldn't look him in the eyes.

Ray stood before her, took her arms, and lifted her from her chair. Supporting her weight, he held her upright before him.

"You have to," he said. "But not me. You have to help those people on that goddamned boat. There's no telling what will happen to them."

"I'm sorry—"

"I know you are," Ray said earnestly. "And I know you're hurt. I understand if you can't do this anymore. But if you have anything left, now's the time to dig down deep and find it. Just get me there—that's all you have to do. I promise."

Ray could feel her body stiffen, her legs take her weight, and she stood upright, on her own.

"All right," she said, "but we'd better step outside."

Ray smiled. "Good point," he said. He turned to the others. "Follow as quickly as you can."

He tossed the keys to the Escalade to Huginn and hand in hand he and the Angel ran out the motel room door, down the hallway, and to a side exit off the first floor.

The night was hot and muggy, as usual for New Orleans. They stood together in the parking lot, bathed in the light of the incandescent bulbs illuminating the rows of cars.

The Angel put her arms around him. "I could drink a case of you," she murmured, and pulled him close.

He put his arms around her and they kissed. Ray felt as if he could feel the hurt and need in her and kissed her as if to draw it all out of her and into himself. After a moment he felt heat all around him and he knew it for the touch of the unburning flames that covered her wings, and suddenly they were airborne. Ray could feel the rush of the breeze from her beating wings upon his face and he laughed aloud as the Angel's strength bore him effortlessly through the sky.

The city of New Orleans was spread below them, its streets outlined by lamplights and rows of car headlights moving like tracers over the ground. After the Angel gained sufficient altitude she turned toward the river and the bend bordering the French Quarter. It took only a minute or two, traveling as the angel flies, until they could see the lighted deck of the *Schröder* moving on the river, being pursued by half a dozen launches as well as the Coast Guard cutter *Triton*, which was quickly gaining on her.

"She's under way," Ray said.

The Angel's expression was serene as a Madonna's. Ray felt a stab of happiness to see her so. All the cares and worry and anxiety were washed away from her face as she bore them both through the sky.

Ray frowned as he looked down at the ship. "She's moving pretty fast," he said. "The cutter is trying to block her way—they're going to collide!"

The ships hit with the anguished scream of shrieking metal as the Angel spiraled down to the *Schröder*'s main deck. The much larger freighter smashed the cutter aside as if she were a plastic toy. The Coast Guard vessel buckled where the freighter's prow struck her amidships. The *Schröder* continued to plow serenely upstream as the *Triton* broke into two pieces. The launches trailing the runaway freighter stopped to pick up sailors who'd abandoned the wrecked and rapidly sinking *Triton*.

The Angel touched down on the stern of the freighter, unnoticed in the darkness.

"All right," Ray said quietly. "You stay here. I'm going to go see what the hell is going on."

The Angel shook her head. "No, I'm coming with you."

"You going to be all right?" he asked, his expression concerned.

"Maybe. I don't know. But I do know that there's someone I wouldn't mind seeing again."

"All right. If you're sure."

"I already said that I'm not." Ray didn't mind the impatience in her voice and in her expression. It was at least a sign of engagement, of a return to the world. "I'll be right behind you." She smiled and Ray liked that even better. "One sword at least thy right shall guard."

Ray remembered those same words spoken a dozen years ago and moved off into the darkness feeling whole for the first time in a long time.

The decks were deserted and quiet. His first thought was for the refugees. They found a companionway headed down into the hold and cat-footed it into the eerily lit space where they bivouacked. The lighting was provided by strung bulbs of low wattage that gleamed like will-o'-the-wisps hovering over a swamp. The air still smelled terrible. As they went silently down the ladder, they could see the mass of people sitting and standing in close ranks in the cramped hold, three men covering them with automatic rifles.

"Jesus," one of them was saying, "what a sorry-assed lot. Be lucky if one in ten of them was worth keeping."

"They are a pretty useless bunch of rag-heads. Still, I reckon some of them will bring a nice price. The rest, well, fuck 'em. They can go down with the ship when we scuttle it."

"Hey," said the third, the one in the middle, "give me a cig, will you? I need something to cover up the stench in here."

Ray reached the hold's floor, maybe twenty feet behind them.

"I need a light myself." The three men sidled together, keeping their rifles pointed at the mass of people in front of them. Many of the refugees, at least those who hadn't sunken into complete lethargy, must have seen Ray creeping as stealthily as a panther, but no one gave him away with either a look or a gesture.

One of the men cradled his rifle to his side under his arm while he bent down to light his cigarette with the match offered him by the middle man, while the third reached for a packet he kept in his shirt pocket.

Morons, Ray thought, and when he was six feet away sprung with his arms widespread.

He grabbed the collars of the man to the right and to the left and smashed both their heads into that of the man in the middle. The colliding skulls made satisfyingly loud sounds. Ray held the two up by their collars as their knees sagged while the third slipped silently to the hold's floor.

The refugees looked almost as stunned as Ray's victims as he shook the two guards like a terrier with rats in its jaws, just to make sure they were out, then swiftly checked them all for more weapons. "Well, don't just stand there," he told the refugees, "someone tie them up."

Twenty-odd prisoners leaped forward in response. It probably would have gone more efficiently if they didn't keep getting in one another's way, but Ray let them have their fun. In a few moments the three were tied and gagged and Ray had distributed their guns to refugees who professed familiarity with the weapons.

"Keep your eye on them while we take care of the rest," Ray told them.

"Let us go with you," one of the Kazakhs offered.

Ray shook his head. "This job is for professionals. You stay here and guard these bozos."

They reluctantly accepted his advice, and Ray returned to the stairway, where the Angel stood watching him.

"I didn't think you'd need my help," she said.

Ray snorted. "Not with those idiots. But there's five left. Let's check the bridge."

The Angel nodded, and they went up the walkway to the deck above, where all was still darkness. Ahead, in the bow, they could see the lit bridge and the figures who occupied it, who were unidentifiable at this distance.

They moved quietly toward the light. Halfway there, Ray put out his arm in warning and he and the Angel stopped. They could hear something slithering before them in the darkness.

"The snake," the Angel said quietly, and suddenly before them loomed IBT.

Ray thrust himself forward between him and the Angel.

"Stop right there," Ray said coldly, "or I will seriously fuck you up."

The human part of IBT's body was raised up. He was as tall as a tall man standing, while the coils of his snake body writhed behind him.

"Who are you?"

"I'm Billy Ray," Ray replied, "and I owe you big for what you did to my wife."

"Wife?" The expression on the joker-ace's face went puzzled. "I don't—" He suddenly caught sight of the Angel beside Ray. "She's your wife?"

"That's right," Ray said in a flat voice.

"I remember," the Infamous Black Tongue said. "It was in Kazakhstan, on the battlefield. Neither of us were in our right minds then."

"Whatever—" Ray said, and the Angel took his arm, stopping him before he could move.

"He's right, Billy," the Angel said. "It's what you've been telling me all this time."

"I am sorry for what happened," IBT said.

"As am I," the Angel replied. "But there's no time for apologies now. What's happening on the bridge?"

"We made a deal with the man who calls himself Witness. A million dollars to take us to refuge in Cuba. But it was all a trap—he just wanted the money and people he could sell into servitude. He plans to scuttle the ship once we're out to sea, take off the ones he thinks would be useful, and let the old and infirm drown."

"Where's the Witness?" Ray asked.

"On the bridge. He has Olena." IBT looked desperate. "We have to rescue her, but he has guns."

For the first time Ray noticed that blood was oozing out of several segments of IBT's colorful banded serpent body.

"You've been shot," Ray said.

IBT shook his head. "That's not important. He has Olena. We must rescue her."

"All right. Calm down," Ray said as he saw the desperate look return to the joker's face. "Let's see. There's five of them—"

IBT shook his head. "Three. He sent out three men to guard the refugees in the hold—"

"We took care of them," Ray said.

"—and then two sentries to patrol the deck," IBT said, then added with some satisfaction, "and I took care of them."

"Okay," Ray said. He didn't ask for details. "Uh, you didn't run into a tall, pale, skinny guy in a dark suit, did you? Probably wearing a patch over one eye."

"No," IBT said.

"Good. He's one of us."

IBT nodded.

"All right," Ray said. "Time to take the bridge."

It took only moments to arrange the ambush. IBT led them to a place of concealment where they had a decent view of the control room through the front windows shielding the bridge deck. The windows were already shot out, shattered in IBT's original hopeless assault. They could see six people in the dim light of the chamber. Two were thugs with guns, one was Olena, the other two were the captain of the *Schröder* and his mate, who was steering the ship. The last—

"It's him," the Angel said.

It was the Witness. Ray had encountered him first during the mission on which he'd met the Midnight Angel. He knew that this Witness and the Angel had a history between them, but she'd never revealed the extent of it and he'd never asked her. "Well," he said, "no sense in putting this off." He looked at IBT. "Get in place. Move when you hear the shots."

"Give me three minutes," IBT said.

"You got it," Ray said, and the Tongue slithered off into the darkness.

"You don't want to do this," the Angel said.

"Kill these guys?" Ray shrugged. "Not particularly."

"No." The Angel smiled. "You're not cold-blooded. Hot-blooded, yes. But you can't kill from ambush."

"There's always a first time," Ray said.

"Not if there's another way."

"I told you. All you had to do is get me here. I would take care of the rest."

"I love you," the Angel said.

Ray smiled. "That's good to hear."

"I know." She bowed her head. "Save me from evil, Lord," she prayed for the first time in months, "and heal this warrior's heart."

Her wings appeared and she shot up into the sky. She was above the sight line from the bridge in a second, a reverse meteor burning through the sky. In her hands, Ray saw, was her flaming sword. She flew above the bridge, cut her way through the roof, and dropped down on top of them. The sword cut two swaths through the air, left and right, and the barrels of the guns dropped, severed in two. She broke her grip on the sword's hilt and it disappeared, going wherever the hell it went when she didn't need it. Then she used her fists on them. They didn't stand a chance.

"You!" the Witness said.

"Me," the Angel agreed, and advanced on him.

He backed away, saying, "Not again, not again!"

"Hmm," Ray said, and fired two shots into the air.

IBT burst through the door and threw a couple of loops of his body around the Witness.

"The serpent!" the Witness screamed. "Oh, God, not the serpent! Save me, oh, God, save me!"

IBT started to squeeze and the Witness screamed like a little girl.

Next to Ray, Maximillian Klingensmith appeared from out of the shadows.

"Where you been?" Ray asked.

"Hiding from that snake guy," he said. "Everything under control?"

"I guess so," Ray said.

♣

But, no, Ray realized. Their troubles were far from over.

He stood in what remained of the bridge, with the Angel, Olena, IBT, and the *Schröder*'s captain and mate. The Witness, who'd fainted dead away when the IBT had grabbed him, was tied up with his surviving men in the hold. The *Schröder* was still steaming upriver, being chased by more launches and followed on the road running alongside the river by a line of screaming police cars, their sirens wailing in the night.

"Now what?" Olena said miserably. "Our last hope is gone. Cuba was our last haven. What can we do now? We can't let them be taken to Rathlin. That's a prison sentence, a virtual death sentence."

They all exchanged glances.

"Well," Ray said, "far be it from me to encourage illegal behavior, but I think your best chance is to run for it."

"What?" Olena said.

Ray shrugged. "Find someplace, run the ship aground, and leg it. Some of the refugees will probably be caught, but you can hardly have a more emotionally heart-touching revelation of their plight. The publicity will be killer. In the meantime, many will get away. It's a big country. I'm sure there's people out there willing to help, one way or another."

"But you, you say this? You represent the government."

Ray sighed. "I've represented the government for forty years, and if it's one thing I've learned, it's that the government isn't always right. The right thing for them in this case was to help your people, not turn their backs on them."

"The Lord," the Angel said quietly, "helps those who help themselves."

"There you go," Ray said.

Olena and IBT looked at each other. Then she looked at the captain.

"Can this be done safely?"

"Relatively," he said.

"But your ship?"

He sighed. "My ship is old and so am I. I think we are both ready to retire."

Olena took a deep breath. "All right," she said. "Let's do it."

♠

"Are we doing the right thing here, Angel?" Ray asked as they watched the crowd of refugees swarm the deck.

"I think you've given them their best chance," she said.

They looked at Munnin. The patch was back over his left eye. "I see nothing," he said.

"That's probably for the best," Ray said. "Better hang on."

They all grabbed onto the derrick in the center of the deck as the captain ran the ship aground. It hit the riverbank in the midst of a dark industrial area that consisted of large buildings set in a warren of narrow streets and alleys. The ship shuddered with a groaning cry of old metal tearing. Although the three kept their feet, on the deck below them many of the refugees went down. Some skidded and rolled, but most all got to their feet immediately and it was every man, woman, and child for themselves. They swarmed down gangplanks and ladders. The confident swimmers went over the side and into the water below.

The launches following them stopped dead, the police cars racing up the road skidded to a halt. The three SCARE agents watched the show unfold. It was like watching a surrealistic version of an old Keystone Kops movie with sound effects.

The refugees, vastly outnumbering their pursuers, were fleeing in all directions. Some few, of course, were caught.

Gunfire erupted from one police boat as someone started shooting at those who were swimming for it. Suddenly a vast, dark form erupted out of the river. It slammed into the launch, half lifting it out of the water. The launch rocked uncontrollably, and to Ray's astonishment he realized that the attacker was a giant alligator. It was the largest gator that Ray had ever seen, fifteen feet long if it was an inch. The gator managed to hook a leg over the edge of the boat and clambered aboard like an avenging demon. It swept the boat clean of cops using its tail and then bellowed, its cry roaring eerily into the night. Using its snout as a battering ram, it sank the boat, then slipped under the water.

"That's not something you see every day," Ray remarked.

A barge rowed by zombies cut through the water, picking up a handful of refugees. Ray could see the Handsmith and his son among them before it disappeared into the darkness.

A golden creature, the winged Tulpar, appeared on the shore and charged the lead car in the police caravan that was chasing refugees who were fleeing into the warren of warehouses and industrial plants, smashing in its hood with her razor-sharp hooves. She leaped up onto the car's roof, crumpling it, and managed to cripple half a dozen more before vanishing into the night.

The show was interrupted when Evangelique Jones appeared in one of the launches, looking up at them on the *Schröder*'s deck and shouting.

"What's going on here?" she cried. "Why aren't you helping to round up these illegal aliens?"

"Not my assignment," Ray called down.

"I'll have your badge for this!" Jones screamed at him.

"All right," Ray said. He took it out and scaled it down at her. As usual, his aim was impeccable. It hit her in her ample bosom and fell down at her feet. She stared at him, her jaw dropping.

Ray looked at the Angel. She laughed aloud for the first time in way too long. Ray smiled at her. Her aim wasn't as good. Hers plunked down into the river somewhere near the launch's bow. Ray looked at Max.

"You might want to hang on to yours."

"Yes, sir," the young agent said stoically.

"It was nice working with you," Ray said.

"Nice working with you, sir," Max replied.

Arm in arm, Ray and the Angel walked down one of the gangplanks leading to the riverbank. He felt relieved. Almost lightheaded. For the first time in years it seemed as if nothing, not a single part of his body, hurt.

"What now?" the Angel asked.

Ray pursed his lips. "I don't know," he said, and saying it felt very good.

They'd walked a couple of miles down the riverbank back toward New Orleans, when Ray suddenly stopped.

"Crap," he said. "I forgot all about the Witness and his men tied up in the *Schröder*'s hold."

The Angel looked at him. "Would you think less of me if I told you that I hadn't?"

Ray shrugged. "Oh well. Maybe someone will find them."

Laughing, they resumed their stroll, heading toward the rising sun.

In the Shadow of
Tall Stacks

Part 3

WILBUR LEATHERS FELT STEAM hissing in the boilers and surging through the lines as Travis Cottle, the current chief engineer—a coffee- and cigarette-addicted middle-aged man with graying and thinning brown hair—checked and tweaked the boilers, lines, and engines for the *Natchez*'s impending departure from New Orleans. Cottle was rather obsessive, in Wilbur's opinion, always consulting the pressure gauges within the system—which dropped briefly whenever Wilbur borrowed steam from the lines, random failures of the system that seemed to infuriate Cottle as he could find no explanation for the pressure drops. If Wilbur wanted to, he could plunge his hands into one of the lines and draw the steam into him right now, allowing it to fill his body, and sending Cottle off on yet another paroxysm of double-checking all the lines and recalibrating the gauges.

Wilbur told himself he'd do that later. Maybe he'd even allow himself to become steamily visible, and if a passenger or two glimpsed him in the dark, it would only add to the popularity of the *Natchez*—though he'd make damn certain it wasn't that obnoxious *Dead Report* crew; he didn't intend to give them the pleasure.

Still, he could almost hear the shriek of alarm and wonder that would result. *"Oh my God! Look! That's Steam Wilbur! We're actually seeing him! He's real!"* But later. Later. Maybe. He'd left Cottle to his work, finding something on the main deck that interested him far more.

He could hear the Jokertown Boys doing their late show up in the Bayou Lounge—all of the passengers seemed to be there; the main deck was largely deserted and the main gangway had been withdrawn. The Quarter lights threw their futile beams into an overcast and occasionally dripping night sky. The promenades on the deck were empty, the passengers nearly all choosing to stay inside against the threatening weather.

There was some commotion going on downriver from where they were berthed. Wilbur could see a constellation of blue and red flashing lights crowding the shore a few miles downriver, and spotlights tore at the low clouds nearby, though whatever action they were illuminating was just beyond the downriver bend. He wondered what was happening, and if it had to do with that joker freighter.

JoHanna Potts, the head clerk, waited near the head of the gangway along with a quartet of deckhands. Jack, an older Cajun man whose skin looked as crinkled and dark as alligator hide, walked anxiously along the *Natchez*'s landing at the river's edge; Jack had been hired as one of the bartenders for this cruise. Jack and JoHanna put Wilbur in mind of the old nursery rhyme about Jack Sprat and his wife: JoHanna was a wide and heavy African-American woman whose wrists and neck glittered with strands of gaudy costume jewelry; Jack, conversely, was rail-thin, normally dressed in dark pants and the white jacket he wore as bartender. But he wasn't dressed that way now; in fact, his clothes seemed to be in tatters and soaked besides, and Wilbur couldn't imagine what the old Cajun was doing out there.

As Wilbur pondered the scene, a small barge emerged from the darkness of the river. Wilbur stared at the craft in shock: it was being rowed by what appeared to be several . . . zombies. At least that's what the rotting, peeling, and discolored flesh of their bodies, the jerky movements as they paddled the barge, and the horrific smell that the breeze off the river would indicate. Jack was hurrying over to the barge and helping perhaps twenty people inside out onto the landing. When they were all on the shore, the zombie crew—if that's truly what they were—pushed away again, vanishing quickly into the night and heading back downriver.

"Go on," he heard JoHanna say to the deckhands, who swung the gangway over to the dock once more. Wilbur went to the rail of the main deck; he could see Jack herding the people from the barge toward the *Natchez*. JoHanna waved to them, and the clot of people moved quickly up the gangway and onto the boat. The first of them came up the gangway and approached JoHanna; in the deck lights, Wilbur saw the man more clearly: a face neither young nor old, lined and weathered. His clothing was ragged, soiled, and tattered; most strange was the fact that his hands were covered by burlap, the rough cloth tied around them at his wrists. It didn't look to Wilbur as if there were actual hands under those improvised mittens, nor did the man extend his hand to JoHanna. "I'm Jyrgal," he said, his voice heavily accented, his words halting. "Some call me the Handsmith. We are very grateful to you for your help." *Sounds Russian,* Wilbur thought, then he saw the others with him.

A boy stood behind Jyrgal, looking like a kid trying to play a ghost for Halloween, his head protruding from a simple sheet. The boy's skin glistened and seemed to be covered in some gelatinous goo. Wilbur couldn't see the boy's hands; they were wrapped in a fold of the sheet. *Jokers.* Another man stepped up behind the two, also a joker, with a scaled, almost fishlike face, and a beaver's tail protruding from underneath the hem of the long overcoat he wore. It struck Wilbur suddenly as the others came onto the deck of the *Natchez*, perhaps twenty of them: *These people. These jokers . . . They must be from the Schröder—some of the Kazakh refugees. What in the world are they doing here on my boat?*

The deckhands were already pulling in the gangway and

swinging it forward once more, lashing it down. Jack had somehow disappeared entirely. Wilbur could hear footsteps and calls
from the forward stairs. JoHanna gestured urgently to those jokers. "Follow me," JoHanna said. "Quietly; I can trust these men,
but we can't have anyone else seeing you. . . ."

She led them with her wide, slow walk toward the stairs at
the stern of the boat and began heavily climbing. As the last of
the refugees was halfway up the stairs, following her, additional
crewmembers began to spill out onto the main deck. "The cap'n's
putting us under way," Wilbur heard one of them say.

"She's in a fucking shitty mood, too," another replied. "Make
sure everything's ready unless you want her to bite your head off."

"Prob'ly her time of the month," one of the quartet who had
helped JoHanna called back. Rough laughter followed.

"Quit yappin' and start workin'." A tinny voice rattled the
speaker of the intercom from the pilothouse on the hurricane
deck: Jeremiah Smalls, the head pilot of the *Natchez*. "Otherwise
I'll mention that last remark to the cap'n, an' I'll help her toss
any heads she bites off over the side. I intend to pull away from
this dock in fifteen minutes. It's a lousy night, but steam's up and
time's a-wastin', people, so either do your jobs or get off the boat."

The voices faded as Wilbur followed JoHanna and the refugees: up past the boiler deck to the texas deck. Captain Montaigne was standing at the head of the stairs, watching them as
the group ascended. She nodded to JoHanna—breathing heavily
from the ascent—and to Jyrgal. If she was struck by the appearance of these people, her face showed nothing of it.

"I've made sure all the crew except Jeremiah's off this deck at
the moment—and he's up in the pilothouse, making preparations
for us to disembark," the captain said. "Some of you will be staying in adjacent staterooms up here; the rest will be moving to
one of the crew rooms down on the main deck—JoHanna will
take you down as soon as we're done here. With so many of you,
it's going to be close quarters, I'm afraid, at least at first, and
you're going to have to be quiet and careful. If you're discovered

and the authorities are called in, you'll all be deported and everyone who has helped you get here will be in great trouble. Do you understand me?"

"We do, Captain," Jyrgal answered. "JoHanna and Jack have both told us this. We'll cause you no trouble. You have my word."

"See that you keep that promise," Montaigne said. To Wilbur, she looked uncertain and more than a little worried about the prospect. Still, she nodded and allowed JoHanna to lead the little group to the stateroom toward the stern, next to JoHanna's own room. JoHanna hurried them in, then shut the door quickly behind them as Wilbur watched Captain Montaigne climb the short flight of stairs up to the hurricane deck and the pilothouse. Wilbur went to the wall of the refugees' room and pushed himself through until he stood inside, though he kept his form deliberately invisible for the moment.

"... best we could do," JoHanna was saying, with Jyrgal translating to the others. "Jyrgal will select the group to go down to the main deck with me." The captain hadn't been joking about tight quarters—even with a portion of the group leaving, this was worse than the crew bunk rooms down on the main deck. Wilbur had no idea how all of them were going to sleep, much less tolerate being in the same room for any amount of time. JoHanna pointed to an interior door to the left. "That door leads to an adjoining cabin that's also for your use. I've put mats in there for sleeping; you can roll them up for more room when you're not using them. Each room also has its own bathroom, as does the room on the main deck, so you don't need to go outside for that. I'll have a trusted crew member, maybe Jack but possibly someone else, drop off food for everyone and pick up the trays afterward. If you hear a knock like this"—JoHanna knocked on the wall: two quick raps, a pause, three more quick ones, then a last short one—"you can open the outside door. Otherwise, don't open the door for anyone else, keep it locked from the inside, and make sure the windows are always covered. Does everyone—and I mean *every* one of you—understand that?"

The group nodded, their assorted faces—most displaying obvious joker attributes—solemn. "Good," JoHanna said. "Arrangements are being made through the Joker Anti-Defamation League, the JADL, to get you to sanctuary cities along the river. We'll be dropping you off along the way, no more than two or three at a time, where you'll be given aid. In the meantime, make yourselves as comfortable as you can and stay as quiet as possible."

"You should not worry," Jyrgal told her in his slow English. "This is much better than where we were, and we are very grateful for your help."

JoHanna gave a sigh as she went to the door. "No one deserves to be treated the way you have, and I'm ashamed for my country. I'm glad we could help. I just hope . . ." She didn't finish the thought, and Wilbur watched her nod to the refugees. "All right, those who Jyrgal chose, come with me." JoHanna opened the door, peered out along the promenade, and slid out quickly, gesturing for the smaller group to follow her.

Wilbur remained behind. He stared at them—a threat to his boat and thus to his own safety—as memory swept over him. . . .

◆

It was March of 1948, and he and Eleanor, not yet a year married, were in Cincinnati, where Wilbur was supervising the finishing touches on the *Natchez*, already afloat on the Ohio and readying for its maiden voyage down the Ohio and on to the Mississippi toward its future home of New Orleans. They'd been in the Netherland Plaza Pavillion Caprice, where they'd listened to the radio broadcast of the NCAA finals game between Baylor and Kentucky. Kentucky had won, 58–42, and Alex Groza had won the Most Outstanding Player trophy for having scored fifty-four points during the tournament. There were whispers among some of the people listening that perhaps the unstoppable Groza might be one of those "aces" that people were talking about.

Now, with the ball game over and a local band playing on the stage, they were enjoying highballs at their table as the waitstaff, nearly all of them colored, circulated among the tables. Wilbur was telling Eleanor some of the history of his grandfather's sequence of *Natchez* steamboats. "He was a tough and stubborn old bird, from what I understand. Had to be, to keep building all those new boats time and time again."

"You never knew him?" Eleanor asked. She was scissoring a jeweled pendant in her fingers, the light catching on the facets of the large emerald that was its centerpiece: a gift from her parents when they'd announced their engagement.

"He died in New Orleans in 1896, twenty years before I'd be born—believe it or not, after being struck by a hit-and-run bicyclist. My dad was only three at the time." Wilbur lifted a hand at the slow beginning of his wife's smile. "Uh-uh. You're not allowed to laugh at that," he said. "It was a tragedy."

"Being killed by a hit-and-run bicycle?"

"Grandpa Thomas was eighty. Not exactly a spring chicken."

"Thought you said he was a tough and stubborn old bird. Though if he still managed to get his poor second wife pregnant in his seventies . . ." She laughed, and Wilbur had to laugh along with her.

"He saw a lot in his time," he told her. "The Civil War, for instance."

Eleanor nodded at that, sipping at her highball. One of the waiters passed the table, refilling their water glasses, his skin starkly dark against the white sleeves of his jacket. Wilbur saw her gaze follow the man. "I've been reading up on steamboats on my own, since we're going to be living on one," Eleanor said, her attention moving from the waiter back to Wilbur. "I learned that some of them used to smuggle slaves from the South. Brought them here to Cincinnati sometimes, in fact . . ." She stopped, looking embarrassed, taking another, longer sip from the glass. "Sorry," she said. "I know how your grandfather . . ."

Wilbur shrugged. "My grandfather was a man of his time and

place," he said. "Yes, he was a Confederate and unapologetic about his views. Heck, Eleanor, the sixth *Natchez* took Jefferson Davis to his home after he'd been elected president of the Confederate States of America; Granddad used his boat to transport Confederate troops to Memphis; and—according to what I've been told by family—he deliberately torched that *Natchez* in 1863 to keep her from being seized by Union forces. He never smuggled any slaves to freedom; in fact, from what I've been told, he despised the captains who did and considered them traitors. After the war, he refused to fly the Stars and Stripes flag on any of his boats—he finally, *finally* let the eighth *Natchez* raise the American flag in 1885, as she passed Vicksburg. Sometimes . . ." Wilbur managed a wan smile and lifted his own drink. "Sometimes I think I'm *glad* I never had the chance to know him. After what I saw in the war, after what we heard was done in Germany to the Jews, and the horrors the Japs inflicted on the Chinese . . . well, Grandpa Thomas's political beliefs feel like a bloody stain on my family's legacy." He grunted a short, deprecating laugh. "Families—they all have skeletons they'd prefer to keep buried."

"You're not your grandfather, Wilbur," she told him. "As you said, he was a man of his time. Any sins he might have committed aren't yours to bear." She put her hand over his on the tablecloth, her wide blue eyes searching his own. "*You* aren't *him*, Wilbur," she said with a slow emphasis. "You're a far better and wiser man. I wouldn't have fallen in love with someone who wasn't also a good and compassionate person. Which is what you are."

She leaned over and kissed him. "Now let's go upstairs to our room," she said. "And no more talking about your grandpa Thomas."

♥

He remembered how they'd made love that night, and how they'd moved aboard the Natchez two days later, which would be their home for the next three years, until that day when everything changed. . . .

Now Wilbur was looking at twenty or so ragged, tired, and frightened refugees packed into a cabin just as those smuggled slaves might have been a century and a half earlier, and the sight tore at him. Here, it seemed, was a chance for the *Natchez* to atone, at least a little, for Thomas. Here was a chance for Wilbur to do something his grandfather had refused to do.

What Eleanor, with her empathy for anyone in trouble, would have *insisted* he do. She'd called Wilbur "good and compassionate." He was afraid she'd overstated his qualities, but . . .

For Eleanor's sake, he would help Captain Montaigne, Jo-Hanna, and Jack to bring these people to freedom. He would do what he could to make sure that happened.

Wilbur went to the nearest wall, where the steam lines ran to the 'scape pipes. He could feel the warmth of the steam like a welcome embrace, and he closed his eyes, pushing his hands through the wall and into the pipe, absorbing the heat that flowed there and letting it fill him. As he took in the steam, he also allowed his form to slowly materialize in wispy clouds. With only a single light on in the otherwise dark room, he was easily visible—in the mirror installed on the far wall, he could see his semitransparent, cloud-like form: a middle-aged man in an old-fashioned captain's uniform and cap—Wilbur as he'd once been.

A young woman with a froth of lacy gills around her neck was the first of the refugees to notice him. She gasped and pointed, and a babble of voices erupted around him. The beaver-like joker glared at him threateningly. Wilbur lifted a finger to his lips, shaking his head, and they quieted, all of them moving back from the apparition. He motioned to Jyrgal to come closer; the joker did so with obvious reluctance. "I will also help you," Wilbur said slowly with an exaggerated emphasis, though he knew that none of the living could hear him. He'd hoped that the joker could manage to read his lips, but Jyrgal shook his head.

"I do not understand you," he said. Fear trembled in his voice, and a mittened hand touched his ear. "I can't hear the words . . ."

Wilbur glanced around the room for paper and a pen or pencil. Seeing none, he sighed and glided, cloud-like, over to the mirror. They moved aside as he approached, as if he were Moses parting the Red Sea. Standing in front of the mirror, he raised his hand; using his index finger as a pencil, he wrote on the mirror in steamy, blurred, and dripping letters:

YOU MUST DO AS THEY SAY. YOU MUST STAY HIDDEN.

He looked at Jyrgal. The man was staring at the writing, but Wilbur couldn't tell if he could read English or not. There was a box of tissues on a small table under the mirror; in his steam form, Wilbur was capable of handling and moving small objects. He plucked a tissue from the box and used it to wipe away the letters, then placed the now-sopping tissue back on the table. He wrote again.

I WILL ALSO HELP YOU.

Jyrgal still stared, as did the others. "Do you understand?" Wilbur asked. "Tell me."

No one answered, at least not in English. There was only the chaos of voices speaking their own language, and Jyrgal's expression didn't lend any confidence that he understood the writing.

Wilbur held out his hand to the mirror again; this time it didn't steam up as quickly, and he could see from the increasing transparency of his reflection that his steam-created body had cooled somewhat—he could never stay long in full steam form. Glancing around at the refugees around him, he chose one who looked young and in relatively good health: a rather excessively hairy young man with four arms. He slid quickly into the joker's body before the young man had time to move.

Carefully . . . After killing Carpenter by doing what he was doing now, Wilbur hadn't tried to take possession of a body for a long time, but over the decades, driven by curiosity and wanting to find a way off the *Natchez*, he had—though he'd found that even in possession of another person's body, the ship still wouldn't permit him to leave. But he knew now to allow his body to cool significantly first before entering a person, and not to stay too long.

In the moment Wilbur slid into the body of the joker from Kazakhstan, he *was* the joker. He knew the man's name: Tazhibai. He could feel Tazhibai's confusion and fear, and images of the man's memory flooded him. Wilbur ignored the glimpses of Tazhibai's life—he didn't have the luxury of time to examine them, not if he wanted Tazhibai to live.

Instead, he quickly wrenched away control of Tazhibai's body from the joker. He pointed to Jyrgal with all four arms (a decidedly strange sensation, Wilbur thought), and spoke in English. "Don't be afraid. My name is Wilbur, and I'm also here to help you," he said. "Do as JoHanna and the captain tell you, and I will also watch over all of you. Tell them, Jyrgal. Oh, and this young man isn't going to be feeling very good for the next few hours. Tell him I'm terribly sorry, but this was the easiest way for you to understand me."

With that, Wilbur slid away from the joker again. The young man's clothing was drenched, and he was suddenly and rather explosively ill from the effects of the hot steam and the water his body had taken in. "Really, really sorry," Wilbur said again, though he knew none of them could hear him now. They were all staring at him, uncertain. "Okay, then. . . . I'll check in on you later."

With that, he turned—all of them moving back quickly except for the four-armed joker, who crouched, moaning, on the floor as a young woman with incredibly long arms but only short stubs for legs put an arm around him in comfort and stared at Wilbur with decided malice. Wilbur slid across the room to the outside wall and through.

He left behind a man-shaped, dripping wet spot on the wall.

♣

As he left the refugees' cabin, Wilbur felt the boat lurch as the stern wheel suddenly engaged, followed by three short blasts from the steam whistle. The calliope wheezed and began playing "Southern Nights" as the *Natchez* nosed out from the dock, the paddles lashing the brown water into foam as it pushed the boat against the Mississippi's relentless southward current. Passengers crowded the rails down on the boiler deck, shouting loudly and holding plastic drink cups, waving to those on the shore.

They were under way.

Cool enough now that even if he wished it he was no longer easily visible, Wilbur went up the nearest starboard stairs to the hurricane deck. He could see Gimcrack, the keyboard player for the Jokertown Boys, standing at the calliope keyboard, decked out in a white dress shirt with puffy sleeves held down by sleeve garters, over which he wore a fancifully embroidered vest. The calliope's pipes vented slightly off-key bursts of white steam in response to his fingers on the keys.

Evidently Captain Montaigne had opened the stairways on the port side of the boat to the passengers, who were normally not permitted on the hurricane deck. Some of them were watching Gimcrack play or gazing out over New Orleans, glittering and alight in the night with the river a dark, winding trail in its midst. Some of the passengers appeared to be jokers themselves: a few steps away, Wilbur saw one older man with a pair of gigantic, curling ram's horns sprouting from his temples, holding hands with an extremely tall and extremely attractive older woman. *Jokers or aces?* Wilbur wondered.

The truth was that Wilbur had wondered that about himself. Every ghost he ever heard about in stories had been a cold presence; he was a hot one. And he'd seen how the wild card virus could change someone drastically: after all, he'd been there in New York to see it start.

He would never forget . . .

♠

It was September 15, 1946. . . .

Wilbur had served during the war as an ensign, then later a lieutenant (junior grade) aboard the USS *Natchez*, from 1943 until her return to Charleston for decommissioning in June of 1945. He found it amusing that he'd been assigned to a ship bearing the same name as his family's boat, even if the USS *Natchez* was a patrol frigate in the Atlantic on anti-submarine duty, and resembled a steamboat not at all. Wilbur even saw action aboard the ship as they escorted convoys, most notably when the *Natchez* sunk a German U-boat they spotted not far off Cape Henry, Virginia. For a time, Wilbur even considered making the navy a career, but then he met Eleanor at a nightclub in Charleston two weeks after leaving the USS *Natchez*. Everything about her entranced him: her dancing blue eyes, her easy smile, her laughter, the smell of her goldsilk hair, her husky, low voice that reminded him of Lauren Bacall. . . . He fell in love with her quickly and completely, and decided that serving long tours of duty at sea as he made his way up the ranks no longer seemed quite so appealing a prospect.

Wilbur was released from service a year later. He spent the next few months traveling around the Midwest and up and down the East Coast (with frequent returns to Charleston to be with Eleanor), trying to raise money from family, friends, and bankers to pursue his dream of building a new steamboat, a ninth *Natchez* like his grandfather's famous vessels. Wilbur was convinced that with the war over and the nation trying to recover, people would yearn for a return to a simpler time, and steaming along the Mississippi in a sparkling new boat with a famous name transported from a golden era would be a compelling prospect.

That was his dream, and Eleanor gladly shared the dream with him.

He'd come out of the Chrysler Building's impressive Art Deco lobby after a meeting at the Chase National Bank, the papers for a loan in his suit pocket. He walked three or four blocks up Lexington Avenue toward his room at the Hotel Lexington when he heard air raid sirens and realized everyone around him was staring up at the sky. He craned his neck, following their gazes.

From the tower-flanked Manhattan street, he watched with dozens of others to see a collection of blimps moving high over the city. As the sirens continued to blare, anti-aircraft fire boomed as fighter aircrafts buzzed like circling wasps below the growing dark clouds. Echoes of the bursting flak pounded along the street like a barrage of distant bass drums. "What's going on?" he asked a uniformed cop, standing with one foot outside his parked patrol car.

"There's someone up there with a damn A-bomb," the cop grunted with a Brooklyn Irish accent. "I'd tell you to get the hell out of here and take shelter, mister, but if it's really an A-bomb . . ." The cop shrugged, still staring up at the sky, the flak, and the red-painted jet rising above it. "Hey, Jetboy's up there . . . that's his plane heading for the blimps."

They both watched Jetboy's plane crash into the gondola of the dirigible, then shielded their eyes from the explosion that followed a few moments later as fragments of the famous ace's red airplane fell toward the city like a bloody rain.

They could see a parachute open below the gondola, and he cheered with the cop and the crowds around them, all of them thinking that it was Jetboy under that white canopy. Then, perhaps a minute later, there was a second, far larger explosion, one that sent shadows racing over Manhattan even in the daylight. "*God*damn," the cop said as the glare of the explosion faded, leaving purple afterimages chasing themselves across Wilbur's vision while more wreckage fell from the sky into the city. He saw a portion of the gondola hit the side of the Chrysler Building and rebound, tumbling down toward the crowds on Lexington Avenue. The cop grabbed his radio receiver. "Dispatch!" Wilbur heard him say. "Emergency!"

Then everything went terribly strange, wrong, and surreal.

Wilbur saw the cop's hand clench around the receiver as if he were trying to crush it, and at the same time, the man screamed, high and shrill. Wilbur could see his face: skin drawing tight against the skull, the tendons and muscles all standing out stark and tight, his eyes bulging and his tongue hanging from his mouth. The scream strangled, gagging noises emerged as the cop's entire body twisted impossibly, his torso turning 180 degrees while his lower body remained still. Wilbur heard a sickening, distinct *snap* like a dry twig being broken: the man's spine. Another snap, then another and another and another; the cop was on the ground now, the ends of broken bones erupting bloodily from his skin and clothing, his whole body writhing as if something alive had burrowed under his skin and were shrinking and drawing tight all of his muscles, tendons, and tissues.

The cop's skull cracked open with a sound like a gunshot, and brain matter splattered over Wilbur's pants and shoes. Wilbur's mouth was open in a soundless howl of horror, but now he realized that there were screams and wails rising all around him, and his gaze left the ruin of the cop's body to view the street.

It was a sight that even Hieronymus Bosch could not have imagined in his visions of hell. It was a sight that Wilbur later wished he could erase from his memory forever.

Cars were colliding madly all along Lexington; Wilbur saw a black Packard Clipper, its horn blaring and the driver slumped over the wheel, climb the curb and plow into a crowd of pedestrians before shattering a plate glass window. But that was hardly the worst of it. All around him, people were changing and dying in myriad awful ways: a woman's body melting into a human-sized gray slug oozing a trail of slime as it slithered down the sidewalk; a man screaming as purple fire engulfed his body; a young woman with a featureless face—no eyes, no nose, no mouth—clutching at her throat before collapsing; a man whose face and naked body had transformed into that of a classic red-skinned devil, laughing madly as his barbed tail slashed repeatedly across his scarlet abdomen, his laughter dying as his gray guts spilled out and the blade of the tail sliced across his throat, nearly removing his head.

Everywhere Wilbur looked, there were yet more horrors to see, more people altered into grotesque parodies of what they'd once been, more people screaming in agony and dying. He did the only thing he could think of doing.

He ran.

He didn't know then, but would learn later, that the cause of the disaster was what would be named the wild card virus. An alien virus unleashed on an unsuspecting world. The world would be forever changed as a result.

But Wilbur was one of the lucky ones. The virus hadn't affected him—at least, that was what he believed. Tens of thousands would die that day and over the next few weeks while New York City, the nation, and the entire world panicked but Wilbur managed to return to Eleanor unscathed through a landscape that was far more altered and awful than anything he'd experienced in years of war.

The moment he finally held Eleanor in his arms again—the wonderful scent of her shampoo and her perfume filling his nostrils; her body warm against his as they clutched each other; both of them weeping tears birthed in mingled joy and fear—that, at least, was a memory he would always treasure. *I will never forgot that feeling. Never . . .*

◆

Over the years, thinking back on what happened the day that Carpenter had fired his revolver at him and how he'd felt as the steam enveloped him . . . well, he had to wonder. Maybe he wasn't a haint. Perhaps he wasn't even technically dead. After all, if he was a ghost, then why hadn't he ever come across someone else like him?

Maybe, just maybe, he hadn't been spared from the wild card virus that day in New York City. Maybe instead he was one of *them.* He'd heard that the virus could manifest much later in an infected person, generally during a moment of extreme emotion. Being scalded by steam and then shot certainly qualified as such a moment. There was no way for him to know, though, nor would it make a difference in his life if he were a ghost or a joker. He was what he was.

There was another blast from the steam whistle as Gimcrack finished playing and launched into "When the Saints Go Marching In." Wilbur looked up to the large glass windows of the pilothouse, where he could see Jeremiah Smalls at the wheel. Behind him were Captain Montaigne and JoHanna, who had evidently finished dropping off the other group of refugees. Wilbur went up the stairs to the pilothouse and allowed himself to sink through the closed door. He left behind a dripping mess, but none of the three were looking that way.

". . . should be interesting between the refugees, the jokers and aces we have aboard, and those damn ghost hunters," Captain Montaigne was saying. "Everyone who needs to know about the Kazakhs already knows; we need to make sure no one else finds out. Period. And there are certain crew members who absolutely can't know."

"Mickey Lee's absolutely one," JoHanna said, her wide face set in a scowl. "He'd call the Feds in a heartbeat." Wilbur agreed with that entirely; the man was a jerk.

"And Kitty, too," Jeremiah grunted. His gaze remained on the river in front of him and the gauges and lights of the panels. "Can't say she'd do anything, but I don't think she'd like it, either. She doesn't seem to care for jokers, so it's better she don't know."

"Let's hope we can keep things settled," the captain said. "We're in for a long haul before we get to Cincinnati, and we still have the other little problem with the Natchez Consortium to worry about. But that's for later, I suppose. JoHanna, both you and I have social duties we need to get to, and we should leave Jeremiah to his work now that we're under way." She turned as if to leave but stopped. Wilbur saw her staring at the door and the water still streaking the painted wood. She glanced at Jeremiah, who nodded but said nothing. Montaigne opened the door so that JoHanna could leave ahead of her, and walked out behind her, shutting the door once again.

Wilbur knew that Captain Montaigne was aware of his presence aboard the ship, but she'd never tried to speak to him, even when she must have known or suspected he was in the room with her. Wilbur had overheard her talk to Jeremiah once about him: *"All those stories about Steam Wilbur get us decent publicity and more passengers, and that's fine with me. Beyond that, I don't want or need to know any more about him. . . ."*

Jeremiah flicked off the interior light in the pilothouse so he could more easily see outside; only the glow from the control panel in front of him illuminated the small room. "Wilbur?" Jeremiah said to the air, his attention still on the river and the wheel of the steamboat. Wilbur, in answer, went to the pipe connected to the boat's steam whistle. He curled his fingers around and into the pipe, drawing the steam from it (and hearing the calliope suddenly lower in pitch as the pressure in its supply pipes dropped in sympathy). Wilbur took in just enough steam to make himself easily visible to Jeremiah, then released the pipe. The calliope went back up to its normal pitch in a wail. At the keyboard, they saw Gimcrack shaking his head. Wilbur imagined that down in the boiler room, Cottle was cursing.

Wilbur went to the whiteboard hung from one of the window frames, with a marker tied to it with a string. He uncapped the marker. *Captain noticed I was here,* he wrote.

Jeremiah glanced quickly over to the board at the sound of the marker's squeaking. "Yeah, she did," Jeremiah said. "Didn't seem happy 'bout it, neither."

She doesn't like me.

"It ain't that. She just don't like complications, 'specially right now. So y'know 'bout our new passengers?" Jeremiah asked. Wilbur nodded. "You comfortable with what we're doin'?" Wilbur nodded again.

"That's good," Jeremiah said. The relief was obvious on the reflection of his lined face in the glass in front of him. "Y'can help us keep an eye on 'em. And maybe scare off anyone who gets too curious, huh? I'll tell the captain you're on our side. That'll ease her mind."

Good. You're busy. Talk to you later.

"You do that, hear?" Jeremiah answered.

♥

That afternoon at Baton Rouge a slow and persistent storm front was pushing dark thunderheads from west to east across the river—not that rain bothered Wilbur at all. However, that meant that most of the passengers were crowded into the saloon, the Bayou Lounge, and the dining hall areas of the boiler deck, or staying in their staterooms.

But Wilbur saw Captain Montaigne, open umbrella in hand, coming down the stairs to the main deck to stand at the head of the gangway as a black limousine pulled onto the dock. The driver got out, opened his own umbrella, and went to the rear passenger door, holding the umbrella as a man emerged from the car. Wilbur recognized him immediately. It was hard to mistake the thick white hair and neatly trimmed goatee, the wire-frame glasses, the stocky build, and the expensive cut of his three-piece suit: Kirby Jackson, the majority shareholder in the Natchez Consortium, and as such, essentially the current owner of the *Natchez*. Another suited man emerged from the front passenger door and went to the trunk, pulling out a pair of large suitcases as Jackson's driver accompanied him up the gangway in the rain, holding the umbrella over the man until he ducked under Captain Montaigne's umbrella. The man with the suitcases handed them off to a deckhand who came scurrying out to take them, then headed up the nearest stairs with them. Jackson spoke briefly to the driver and the other man, then the two made their way back to the limousine as Captain Montaigne shook hands with Jackson and escorted him up the stairs. The captain's expression was tight-lipped and sour, though Wilbur had the sense that it wasn't the weather that had put her in a bad mood.

Wilbur followed, making certain that he remained invisible. Jackson, from what Wilbur had seen and overheard, had no passion for steamboats or the *Natchez*, per se. He was strictly an "investor," pure and simple, interested only in making money from his shares in the *Natchez*. In that, he reminded Wilbur uneasily of Marcus Carpenter and his ilk. Gliding unseen behind the two, Wilbur followed them up to the texas deck, where Jo-Hanna was already standing at the open door of what was generally referred to as the "owners' stateroom"—a well-appointed chamber at the opposite end of the deck from the stateroom that contained the Kazakh refugees, and one that usually remained vacant unless one of the Natchez Consortium shareholders or their family decided to take a jaunt on the river. Wilbur slid inside the open door ahead of Jackson and the captain, going to the back wall near where the suitcases had been placed.

"You should be comfortable here, Mr. Jackson," Montaigne said. "If you need anything, please let me know personally, and I'll take care of it. I'm sure you're going to enjoy our trip to Cincinnati and the Tall Stacks festival."

"I'm sure I will, Captain," Jackson answered. His voice had a sandy growl, and his white-toothed smile was that of a man used to deploying it as a weapon. "And we should be frank here. I'm sure you've heard the rumors by now. I'm here to tell you that they're true. Cincinnati will be the last and final port of call for the *Natchez*. We've made arrangements to berth the boat permanently at the Public Landing. We'll be converting the *Natchez* into an entertainment hub, with the thought of obtaining a casino license."

"Mr. Jackson, JoHanna and I—"

Jackson cut off the captain's comment with a lifted hand. "I know. The two of you made an offer to purchase my shares from the consortium, and I and the consortium board appreciate your interest in having the *Natchez* continue on as usual. I've considered your offer, but I'm afraid I'm not interested in selling my stake—the *Natchez* is worth far more moored in Cincinnati."

Wilbur saw JoHanna and Montaigne exchange glances. "We might be able to raise our offer," she said, "if you can just give us a little time."

"Time is a commodity I don't have, unfortunately," he answered. "In fact, I already have a buyer interested in buying up the boilers for scrap." Wilbur let out a hiss at that statement. *The boilers gone. No steam . . .* "But I do have an alternate offer for the two of you. Stay with the *Natchez*, as co-managers of the new venture. Why, Marjorie, you could even remain as 'Captain' Montaigne—that would be a nice image for the patrons, I think. And you'd both be well compensated, I can guarantee you that."

Again, the two women looked to each other. "I don't know," Montaigne said. "Not being on the river . . . I'd have to think about it. JoHanna?"

JoHanna only gave a grim shrug, and Jackson smiled again. "Then do that," he said. "I don't need your answers until we get to Cincinnati. Let me talk with the other shareholders, and I'll get you more firm details on what we're offering, and we can talk again . . ."

Wilbur didn't wait to hear more. He stepped backwards into and through the wall of the stateroom, out into the weather once more. The music from the lounge a deck below was painfully cheerful.

Wilbur took the stairs up to the hurricane deck.

Jeremiah was on duty. The rain was lashing the windows of the pilothouse, the wipers squeegeeing it away, though Jeremiah's attention was more on the instruments in front of him rather than the view. Passing through the closed and locked door, Wilbur picked up the whiteboard's marker and uncapped it. He set the cap on the instrument panel in front of Jeremiah, setting it down with an audible *clack*. Jeremiah snorted at its sudden appearance.

"What's up, Wilbur?"

Kirby Jackson's aboard. Says Cincinnati is the last stop. Ever.

Jeremiah scowled and spat. "Fuck," he said. Wilbur found himself agreeing entirely with the sentiment.

"So all those lousy rumors were true, huh?" he said aloud. "I shoulda known. What do you think about all this, Wilbur?"

Sucks, he wrote on the whiteboard.

Jeremiah managed a short, unamused laugh. "Amen to that, brother. I've been piloting this old boat since before Captain Montaigne got here. Twelve years now. It just don't seem fair, I tell ya."

Life's not fair, Wilbur scribbled on the board. *Neither's death*, he added. No, none of it was fair: it wasn't fair that Carpenter stole his life and Eleanor and their child from him; wasn't fair that he was somehow bound to this boat; wasn't fair that now it appeared that the *Natchez* would never get steam up and plow the rivers again.

Jeremiah grunted as he glanced over at Wilbur's comment. "Damn straight it ain't," he said. "I get tossed out on my ass like a piece of garbage, and you . . . you're going to be stuck in goddamn Cincinnati until the *Natchez* finally rots."

The captain and JoHanna were trying to buy the boat and keep it running, Wilbur wrote. *Jackson turned down their offer.*

"Yeah, the captain mentioned that to me. And it don't surprise me none that Jackson said no if'n he thinks he can rake in more dollars with the boat parked. All the man cares about is making the most money for himself, and he don't care who gets hurt in the process. Bastard."

Maybe the captain can still come up with a better offer.

Jeremiah snorted at that. "Yeah, and we might see a flock of pigs flying over the Mississippi tomorrow, too." He shook his graying head and glanced at the clock. "Kitty's due up here for her shift in a few minutes. Me, I'm going to try to get some sleep—after I take some medicine to help me get there, if you take my drift. If you want to join me . . ."

Wilbur shook his head. He was cooling rapidly, water puddling on the pilothouse floor underneath him. *Goodnight,* he wrote on the board, then recapped the marker and erased the board with the rag Jeremiah kept there. In a flash of lightning, he could see Kitty, the second pilot, near the top of the stairs to the hurricane deck, holding an umbrella against the pounding of the rain, dressed as usual in a baggy sweater and long pants, and wearing her sunglasses even in the dark and rain. Wilbur shook his head at the sight.

Wilbur left the pilothouse the way he'd come in, moving from the pilothouse, down the stairs from the hurricane and the texas decks to the boiler deck, carefully avoiding the people on his way. He thought he might make a stop in the Bayou Lounge. The Jokertown Boys hadn't impressed him, but he'd heard some good comments about the duo called Sylvia and the Fox—the Fox being some guy that Caitlyn Beaumont, the cruise director, bragged about once having been on some TV show that Wilbur had never seen: *American Hero.* "He's gorgeous and he's actually an ace," Wilbur overheard Caitlyn telling one of the female passengers. "Not hard to look at, if you know what I mean."

He needed a diversion about now, anyway. It might stop him from thinking about the *Natchez* and Cincinnati. *Aces and jokers . . .* Curious, Wilbur passed through the wall into the lounge just as their show was starting.

♣   ♦   ♠   ♥

A Big Break in the Small Time

by Carrie Vaughn

THE BAYOU LOUNGE DIDN'T have a green room so much as a closet behind a curtain where performers could leave their things during their acts. The space had just enough room for Andrew and Sylvia to perch on folding chairs before going on for their late-night set. The late set was turning out to be not so great a slot, even with the captive audience en route between Baton Rouge and Natchez. Andrew didn't have to move to peek behind the curtain. Maybe a dozen people out there, sipping drinks and not paying attention to the stage. He sighed.

"How's it look?" Sylvia asked.

"It's great. It's looking great," he said, sounding more dispirited than he'd intended. She caught the tone and squeezed his hand.

"Aw, honey, I thought we were treating this as a vacation. Easy gig, testing out new material on a new crowd. Watching the scenery go by during the day. Maybe not worry so much."

Yeah, he definitely didn't used to worry so much. That was before he hit thirty and realized he wasn't going to be Disney cute forever.

At least he had Sylvia.

"I know. I'm just losing perspective."

"You miss Vegas."

"Yeah." His tail drooped to the floor.

This certainly wasn't the cabaret at the Flamingo, but it was a gig. Couldn't very well turn your tail on that. But for four years they'd been Sylvia and the Fox, playing two shows a night, six nights a week to a packed theater. For a while, they'd been on a dozen "don't miss" entertainment lists for their "retro cabaret act" filled with "charm and some real talent." He was the charm, she was the talent. He had no illusions about that. He still had the best reviews memorized.

But it couldn't last. Nothing ever did, not even in Vegas. They'd gotten a ton of mileage off the sheer novelty of a couple of joker lounge singers who were actually charming and attractive (once again, Andrew knew which was which)—or at least not offensive—in a kind of old-school feel-good show that was supposed to be out of fashion. Kind of thing you could bring your grandmother to.

Trouble was, grandmas died off.

At least they'd closed that gig mostly on top, not waiting until they'd been shunted off to a stage in the back of some Fremont Street casino, hoping for whatever audience trickled in for gin and tonics at the bar. At least they'd landed a couple of steps up from that. They had a couple of videos up on YouTube edging close to a million hits. By all measures, they were doing okay.

He sighed again.

Andrew used his old ace name from way back on *American Hero*, Wild Fox, because it was appropriate: he had ruddy fox ears and a luxurious thick brush of a fox tail. So rather than just being another average skinny Asian guy with floppy black hair and a manic disposition, he was almost a walking, talking cartoon. For a certain group of people who'd watched the animated *Robin Hood* at an impressionable age, he was very nearly a fetish object. He banked on it.

Sylvia Otto—she was beautiful. Smashing. Amazing, talented, kind, funny . . . the most perfect, perfect woman Andrew had ever met. At five-seven, she was an inch shorter than him. She had creamy skin, big hazel eyes, and a body that curved and dipped and was made for spandex. Sylvia the ocelot. Fuzzy, triangular ears, brindled light and dark, peeked up through her thick chestnut hair. A slender, slinky tail curled out her back. Just a hint of whiskers at her nose. Some people might call her a joker, but Andrew called her adorable. A perfect match to his fox.

He'd fallen hard for her backstage at a corporate entertainment junket and woke up every single day shocked that she chose to spend time with him. She picked him! How did that happen? He was a nerd. A dork. Lame. Weird. He got by on schtick and little else. And yet, when he walked into a room, she smiled. They'd been together for six years now and he'd just about gotten to the point where he believed she didn't stay just to be nice. Maybe, just maybe, she liked him, too.

Dogs and cats, living together. He made that joke every night and people always laughed.

She glanced at her phone, slipped it back in her bag, and gave him a peck on the cheek. "Showtime, babe. Ready?"

He couldn't go on in a funk so he smiled broadly and spread his arms. "I'm always ready, hon." He swished his tail, wiggled his ears. Yeah, he was ready.

First, before they even went out onstage, he started with an illusion. Besides Sylvia's music, this was what set them apart: Andrew could conjure illusions that looked and sounded like anything he wanted. They didn't hold up to physical contact, but he didn't need them to.

First he made a kind of wall, a secondary curtain—really useful for a stage like this. Sylvia could set up without anyone seeing her. He could make the wall or curtain look scintillating, way more interesting that just a length of fabric. A waterfall coming out of the ceiling. A curtain of flowers. A rain of diamonds. People couldn't help but pay attention.

So the audience saw a waterfall right there onstage that looked and sounded real except that nothing got wet. Then a kind of jungle-y, rhumba-y version of "Bolero" played, and the waterfall parted, revealing Andrew and Sylvia transitioning to their first real number, a Latin-beat version of the Sinatra staple "Come Fly with Me." It was meant to be retro and exotic and cheesy all at the same time, an elaborate tiki bar setting from an old movie.

Andrew wasn't a great singer—he'd had to take lessons when he went into show business. But what he lacked in skill he made up for with bravado. Expansive gestures, heartfelt crooning, winks to the audience.

The song ended, and the banter started with Andrew announcing, "Hey, welcome to the Bayou Lounge, I'm so glad to see all your smiling faces. I see we've taken on some new folks at Baton Rouge—welcome to the *Natchez*, and the romance of the Mississippi. Hey, Sylvia, you up for a little romance?"

"I *love* romance!"

Andrew turned to the crowd with a lascivious grin and wink that really shouldn't have gotten a laugh but did.

Sylvia had worked up a slew of new arrangements for songs that weren't usually part of the lounge singer routine. Instead of drawing on the Great American Songbook, she'd put together old-style swing and ragtime versions of grunge hits, crooner versions of heavy metal classics that most of their audience didn't even recognize until they sang the chorus. Old Cole Porter songs done salsa and hip-hop style. They were hoping the new material would appeal to a younger crowd. Give them something new and amazing to work with. Show off Sylvia's talent as a musician.

The Bayou Lounge wasn't really a theater, but a bar area with a stage big enough for a jazz trio and not much else. Plenty of room for him, Sylvia, and her keyboard and synthesizer setup. The bar ran along one side of the room, which occupied most of the rear of the *Natchez*'s middle boiler deck. Groups of tables and comfortable seating were clustered throughout the room. The stage lighting wasn't much brighter than the house lights—the waitstaff had to be able to see to circulate among tables throughout the show. The bar and tables were polished wood, and brass fixtures on the lights and barstools gave the place a vintage look, but the whole veneer of the place was tired rather than antique. The *Natchez* was clean but she'd seen better days.

Andrew was competent enough at this that he could look out and take stock. He noted a couple of the old biddies who'd been to every single one of their shows and made sure to smile just for them. Plenty of small groups didn't seem to be paying attention to the show at all; an undercurrent of conversation ran under the music as people bent together to talk and sip their drinks. They'd probably have a better time if they went somewhere else on the boat, but it wasn't like he could kick them out. Now, if they were being charged thirty bucks a head to get in . . .

But no, this wasn't Vegas. As much as he was tempted to drop an illusion of an exploding bomb or a giant scorpion in the middle of them, he let them be.

A group of young things was at the bar. Recent college grads, looked like, the women in tiny cocktail dresses and the men in silk shirts and slacks. No older than midtwenties, out partying on the money they got from brand-new professional jobs. Or maybe from brand-new newly vested trust funds, judging by the quality of some of the footwear.

Andrew smirked inwardly, congratulating himself on being able to make an honest living—comparatively speaking—when he spotted something he shouldn't have, and sort of wished he hadn't. One of the men, a president-of-the-frat, future-politician-looking white guy with a perfect blond haircut and a practiced smile, slipped a couple of pills in a tumbler of rum and Coke before sliding it over to a woman in a red flowered sheath dress and long black hair, stylishly tousled. The guy had very carefully blocked the view from her as he did so, deftly holding one hand just so as he dropped in the pills. But he didn't block Andrew's view of the act. Probably didn't think he needed to. Andrew was just part of the background, after all. Hired help.

In a tribute to his long experience, Andrew didn't miss a beat, but kept on with their lounge version of Britney Spears's "Toxic" even as he wanted to leap off the stage and bat the drink out of the woman's hand. Even if he'd done so, he couldn't have gotten to her in time before she lifted the glass and sipped, oblivious. The guy kept grinning. He'd wear that same grin on some future election-day press conference if he got the chance.

Andrew couldn't let it go. He just couldn't.

He finished the verse, and as Sylvia kept playing he announced, "All right, we're going to take a quick break now. I just need a minute to adjust my tail. Don't go anywhere!"

The music trailed out as Sylvia gave him a confused look. Grabbing her hand, he rushed her backstage behind the curtain.

"Hey, babe, call security."

"What? What's wrong—"

"Tell you in a sec."

He took a deep breath, concentrated, held the picture in his mind of what he wanted to do—then breathed out. Phone to her ear, Sylvia watched him. "Hi, yeah, this is Sylvia over at the Bayou Lounge, Andrew says there's something going on—" She mouthed the word *what?* at him.

"Date rape drug situation," he whispered back. Her eyes went wide and she repeated the info.

"Yeah, okay, see ya." She clicked off and glared. "Andrew—"

A wavy light flickered around him, his illusion settling into place. To an outside observer he now appeared to be someone else. He was about to ask Sylvia how he looked when she shook her head.

"I don't think so."

"What, what's wrong—"

"I don't think *Conan*-era Arnold Schwarzenegger is really what you want to go for."

"I want to be intimidating!"

"Yeah, I know. Just be big, okay? Big, not famous."

Story of their lives, that.

He breathed out again and shifted his mental image before

slipping out from behind the curtain. As far as everyone in the lounge was concerned, he was no longer manic Asian thirty-something Andrew Yamauchi. He was a big white linebacker with muscles ready to burst out of his suit. He walked straight to the bar.

The woman's rum and Coke was half gone. Her giggle was turning shrill, and the guy was looming over her, leering. Getting ready to lean in in a way that was totally skeezy even if he hadn't drugged her drink.

Andrew had to be careful. He couldn't physically confront the guy. He couldn't knock him over, punch his shoulder, or even nudge his arm, or the illusion would vanish. Not that Andrew could physically affect the guy anyway. Mostly, he had to keep the guy from doing anything to *him*. He hoped if he looked like enough of a badass the guy would back off. Sylvia was right, looking like Arnold was probably too much. So this had to be all about attitude.

He marched over, sidled up to the bar, and reached around the woman to take the tumbler of drugged cocktail out of her hand and set it out of her reach.

"Hey!" she said. Her would-be assailant clenched his hands into fists, looking like he might punch Andrew right there.

"What's wrong with you?" he exclaimed.

Andrew said to the woman, "I saw him slip pills into your drink. But, you know, maybe they were just vitamins. Maybe he's just worried about your health."

"Wait, *what?*" She got off the stool to face him down, but stumbled. Her legs seemed to go out from under her for just a second before she grabbed the bar and steadied herself. She was still with it enough to turn to the frat-boy type. *"Greg?"*

He missed a beat before managing to defend himself. "What? No, I don't know what he's talking about! I would never—"

"Still, you know. Maybe a fresh drink?" Andrew said. "Just in case."

"Molly, this guy's a creep, whatever he thinks he saw, he didn't see. Now, come on, you look tired, maybe I should walk you back—"

A guy in the audience with thick ram's horns curving out of his head, who'd been sitting in back and sipping on a tumbler of bourbon the whole show, leaned in to whisper to the woman next to him, then stood and sauntered over to the bar. He was an older guy, but he had a bearing to him. A serious gaze and an easy way of standing with his hands at his belt, like he might just be getting ready to reach for a gun. He wore a nondescript dark suit jacket, no tie, but he could just as easily have been wearing a uniform.

"There a problem here?" the joker said, in that casual way every single cop Andrew had ever encountered asked that exact question. Sylvia appeared at the guy's side, talking quickly and quietly and gesturing at the ruckus.

To the woman, Molly, Andrew said, "Do you have a friend who can maybe stay with you, make sure you're okay?"

"Molly, listen to me—"

"You can always save the drink and get it tested if you don't believe me," Andrew added, shrugging nonchalantly, trying to play it cool. Smarmy Greg hadn't tried to hit him yet, but there was still time.

Greg grabbed the drink and threw it out, right on the floor behind the bar. No possibility of testing it now.

Molly snarled at him. "It's true! You asshole! Trying to drug me? I probably would have slept with you anyway, you didn't have to *drug* me! *Fuck you!*"

She shoved him; Andrew stepped out of the way. But Greg took the moment to turn on Andrew, throwing a punch. "You cockblocking fag!"

Andrew tried to duck, he really did. But Greg clipped him—a lot harder than he was expecting, and the room turned upside down as he went spinning, and the sparkling aura of his illusion faded.

The joker with the ram's horns stepped in and deftly took the guy's wrist and shoulder, cranking him back into a lock that had douche-Greg groaning. "Get your hands off me! I'll sue you, I swear to God—"

"Not before you get brought up on a couple of charges of assault, I'm betting. Let's get you to security, hm?"

Andrew stared up at the guy—ex-cop, wanna bet?—with more than a little awe. Dreamed of a day when maybe he could afford a bodyguard. "Hey, thanks," he said, though the words sounded a little mushy.

"No problem," the guy said, and frog-marched the guy to the door, where a couple of tuxedo-wearing security guards from the casino waited.

Sylvia dropped to the floor by Andrew. "Aw, you okay?"

That probably could have gone better. He maybe should have done some more planning. Like, he should have known a big frat boy–type lunk wouldn't have any problem throwing a punch and that Andrew wouldn't have been able to maintain the illusion. That was all entirely clear in hindsight.

He sighed and leaned into Sylvia's touch. "Yeah. Just woozy."

"Honey, you know what you did? You saved the day!"

The woman, Molly, had not been completely roofied. If preventing that was the primary goal, Andrew had succeeded. He'd saved her. He perked up.

"Yeah—I guess I did!"

"I'm so proud of you!"

Light applause from the audience greeted the scene. They probably didn't know exactly what they'd seen, only that something momentous had happened. Maybe part of the show? Andrew didn't really care; clapping was usually a good sign.

Molly was getting consoled by her friends, and one of the security guys took statements from the women and from Andrew, who described seeing the guy drop pills in the drink. They got confirmation a little later that security found more pills in the guy's pocket. When they arrived at Natchez, Molly could charge the guy with attempted assault. In any case, he'd get thrown off the boat then.

In the meantime, as hoary an old cliché as it was, the show must go on. They had a couple of songs left in their set, and a bunch of guests to distract from recent unpleasantness. The whole left side of Andrew's face ached from that punch, but he didn't care. He was kind of buzzing on the good deed he'd done. He'd saved the day!

Sylvia must have seen him wincing, but never mind because she just worked it into the show. Back onstage, speaking into the mike, she said, "Hey, Wild Fox, think maybe you should get some ice on that shiner?" She glissandoed a sad trombone-sounding run on the keyboard.

He continued the banter. "Looking pretty bad, is it?" He made sure to turn that part of his face to the light. He had no idea how it looked, but maybe it'd get him some sympathy.

"I think it makes you look like a tough guy."

"It does? Well, that's not so bad then!"

"No! You know why?"

"Tell me why, Sylvia!"

Without missing a beat, as if this rambling intro—including the truncated bar fight—had all been planned, she launched into their own crazy rendition of "I Got You Babe," with Sylvia turning it into a jazz improv piece, riffing on the keyboard, paying homage to the Sonny and Cher version while adding her own flourishes that somehow made the music sound young and hip. They got to the end, and Andrew held the "I" out in the last line while gazing adoringly at Sylvia, which wasn't hard to do. Meanwhile, a giant cartoon heart appeared in the air between them, glittering with a sheen of light, sparkles popping out of it, basically looking like a greeting card made by a four-year-old with too many art supplies. A couple of *aws* drifted out from the crowd, which was gratifying.

"You've been a great crowd tonight"—a dozen people was a

crowd, right?—"really amazing. Thank you so much for being here and putting up with me—because we all know who the real talent in this outfit is, am I right?" He gestured widely to Sylvia, who blushed and smiled and twitched her feline tail, and as he knew it would the applause tripled and actually started to fill the place. "Just a couple of announcements. Tomorrow at noon there'll be karaoke right here at the Bayou Lounge, with half-off cocktails! Tomorrow, Sylvia and I will be back with a whole new show for you—because the fun never ends around here!" There, that ought to make Caitlyn happy, talking up her schedule. "Let me tell you, you're all stars in my book, every one of you, and don't let anyone tell you different."

Delivering his most charming wink and wiggling his fox ears, Andrew aimed and fired a finger gun at the audience, and the fake shots rained out a swarm of glittering gold stars, which settled on the crowd and vanished harmlessly. And people applauded. The key to pulling off grade-A showbiz cheese was to embrace it with enthusiasm. People came for the cheese, and Andrew knew how to lay it on.

He and Sylvia ended up backstage, and he was about to ask her how it went like he always did, but she put her hand on his shoulder. "Okay, honey, now you really need to get some ice on that eye."

And that was when he realized his face *really* hurt.

♣

Sylvia led him to the bar and got the bartender, Jack, to fill a Baggie with ice and wrap it in a towel. She helped him hold it in place while cooing over him, and he basked in the attention. Quietly, for a change. The place had emptied out after the show. Which meant people had stayed to see them. That was something at least.

Jack seemed ancient, his face weathered, his body thin. He had a methodical way of moving and talking in a rich Cajun accent. Probably been hired for atmosphere as much as for his bartending skills.

"You folk need anythin' else?" he asked.

Sylvia smiled. "We're fine, Jack. Thanks."

"Ma'am, if I might say, you are one lovely cat."

"Ocelot, but thank you." The distinction might have been little more than semantics, but it was important to Sylvia, so she was an ocelot. Sounded cooler that way. And she was *very* pretty.

"You seen a lot of cats, old man?" Andrew asked.

Andrew had maybe expected a laugh, but Jack leaned on the bar and gave him a significant look, like he was telling war stories. "Son, more than you will ever know." He moved off to wipe down another part of the bar.

He'd saved someone. Maybe it wasn't flashy, maybe it wasn't as big and spectacular as going off to Egypt to try to save an entire country from war. But he'd done it, stopped something bad from happening . . . and it felt *good*. His hands itched, his limbs were on fire. Spent adrenaline, he knew. But he'd never felt like this on *American Hero*. They'd done plenty of fake scenarios and fake missions, rescued actors from fake burning buildings and fake kidnapping victims. It had all felt like a high school play, inconsequential and ultimately kind of embarrassing. He literally hadn't understood it when a big chunk of the contestants quit the show to go be heroes for real, because at the time, to Andrew, there was no real. It was all publicity stunts and self-righteous nonsense.

But this, *this*—was this what the others had been feeling all along? Was this what it really felt like to be a hero?

Sylvia pulled away the ice pack and winced sympathetically. "How's that feel?"

"Fine, it's fine," he murmured.

Leaning back, she took a sip of her gin and tonic and watched him from the next barstool over. "You look poleaxed. Big day, huh?"

Words poured out. "Honey, I'm not a hero. I've known that

ever since Team Hearts on *American Hero*—" He'd been voted off the show—discarded, rather—in the seventh round, and he sort of hated that he remembered that detail. He wasn't supposed to care. It was supposed to be a joke. "But I don't know now, I just did something because I couldn't *not* do something. After what I saw, that would have made me an ass."

"A bigger ass," she said cheerfully.

"Yeah. I mean. But doing the right thing, catching that guy— that felt really good. And now I don't know what to do with my- self. Because I'm a joker but I'm also kind of an ace and a lot of people say that means I should go out and help people. And maybe I should. I don't know. I've never felt like this. What do I do?" He looked at her pleadingly. He hadn't taken a single drink of the beer sitting in front of him.

She slid off the stool and slipped her hands behind his neck. The touch comforted him, grounded him. Stopped him from feeling like he wanted to run all over the ship screaming in a fit of existential angst.

"What you did? That wasn't 'cause you're an ace. Anyone could have seen it and reported it. Anybody who's decent would have. And you're a decent guy, Andrew." She gave him a light kiss on the cheek. "You don't have to be an ace hero to be a good citizen."

She was right. She was exactly right. A good citizen, that was all. He didn't have to save the world. He just had to be a decent human being. That ought to be easy enough.

♠

Once Andrew started looking, he saw crime everywhere. Wrong- doers. Malfeasance. People being awful. People breaking the law—and he was in a position to stop them.

The next day, just after noon, Andrew was wandering along the promenade outside the Grand Saloon. The cruise director, Caitlyn Beaumont, liked for the entertainers to mingle with the guests in their downtime. Smile, wave, take a few pictures. Give the guests a little bit of a thrill, make them feel like they're part of the action, that there wasn't a space between the stage and the seats. Andrew happened to agree with her—not that he'd admit it to her face. But it was a good idea. Keeping the guests happy, enticing them to come back for more, making them feel special. All part of the show.

Hands in his trouser pockets, wearing a spiffy silk T-shirt, he strolled along. Minding his own business, but not really. A couple of his groupies spotted him and rushed over for pictures. Andrew obliged them, smiling graciously, winking conspiratorially. The cell phone snapshots took twice as long to take as they should have, but he was used to that, and the women thanked him. Not a bad gig at all. He wondered if good ol' Rusty had women rushing up to him demanding pictures.

Then he looked up the deck to see a young, unassuming woman pull a phone out of an older man's back pocket and walk away. It was so smooth, so casual, Andrew wasn't sure he'd even seen it. A group of people stood at the railing, watching barges pass by on the river. She just seemed like part of the group, wasn't even looking at her target, waiting for the right moment. The moment came—someone called and pointed out an especially interesting view—and she slipped the phone clean out and tucked it up her sleeve. Just like that.

Oh no. Andrew wasn't going to let that stand. Not on his boat.

Nonchalantly glancing out at the forest scrolling past on the shoreline, he strolled after her, as casual-like as he could manage. The woman was wearing slacks and an expensive-looking blouse that rippled as she moved, high heels that clicked on the decking. The blouse had long sleeves, which seemed odd in the sticky southern heat, but Andrew wouldn't have questioned it if he hadn't seen her hide the phone up that sleeve. The blouse was a cover.

She wasn't in a hurry. Wasn't drawing any attention to herself. That gave Andrew time to think about how to handle this.

Call security? Keep an eye on her until a security guard could arrive? Confront her himself? Maybe use a bit of sleight of hand to steal back the phone? Wasn't really time to call security, he decided. She couldn't leave the boat en route, but she could get rid of the goods and claim innocence. He thought he could handle this smoothly. He paused long enough to snap a picture of her with his phone, catching her in a moment when she leaned on the railing, turned toward him, and he could do so without being too obvious about it. There, he could pass along her picture and security could keep an eye on her.

She strolled on. He had to do something before she got to the door. Too many places for her to duck away among the staterooms and galleries of the boat's interior.

"Wild Fox!" someone called from behind him, then giggled. He knew what came next and he didn't really have time for it.

He stopped, rolled back his shoulders, and donned his broad stage smile before turning around, arms open. "Ladies!"

A couple of women, fashionable mom types in their late thirties or early forties, approached with their eyes lit up. Sometimes he never really knew if they were fans of *him*, or fans of celebrity in general and he was just the most approachable one on hand. They might never have the guts to approach, say, George Clooney—but a has-been from *American Hero*? Oh yeah. And they'd show the pictures around and someone would say, "I didn't know he was even still alive!"

The blond woman said, "We caught your show last night and just wanted to tell you how much fun it was. Just really nice, you know?"

"Thanks, that's exactly the kind of thing we like to hear," Andrew said, delivering practiced responses. Genuine—he really was grateful, and "fun" and "nice" were just what he and Sylvia were going for.

"You mind if we get a picture with you?"

He put his arms around both their shoulders and pulled them in as one of them held up her phone for the group selfie.

In the background of the shot, Andrew could see his quarry walking away. He had to go after her. Without being rude, because Caitlyn would hear about it.

They'd gotten three good pictures already but the blonde still wasn't sure about any of them and wanted to try for a fourth where she maybe wasn't blinking so much. But Andrew cut her off with a light hand on her shoulder.

"Ladies. Could you do me a big favor?" He met both their gazes earnestly.

They nodded, agreeing eagerly before he even told them what he wanted. He explained: "Can you get to the end of the deck there, past that woman in the beige shirt, and then maybe block the path? Like, just spend a good long time taking some pictures of the scenery while I corner her. Just for a few minutes. I really need to talk to her." He might have leered.

"But what about Sylvia?" one of them asked, clearly unhappy with the idea of him being unfaithful to his beautiful girlfriend. The idea appalled Andrew as well, and he reassured the woman.

"Believe me, Sylvia is my one true love in the whole world. But this chick took something that isn't hers and I'm going to get it back. Understand?" He winked and showed a little bit of pointed teeth. That fun-loving Robin Hood predator. His accomplices giggled conspiratorially. *They* didn't seem to have a problem with Wild Fox, superhero. That thought gave him some courage.

They raced ahead, making a whole big show of calling out about this or that other part of the shore, the lacy decoration along the roof over the promenade, sniping at each other about where to stand and who should hold the camera. Way over the top, but somehow that made the scenario seem more authentic, a couple of otherwise normal adults acting like little kids just because they were on a riverboat.

The pickpocket had been heading for the door but pulled up short, confronted by the low-grade idiocy before her. Hands on hips, she hesitated, seemingly taking a moment to try to figure out how to slip by the women to get to where she was going. That gave Andrew his chance.

He sidled up to her. "Hey, babe, what's a low-down chick like you doing on a nice boat like this?"

Startled, she turned, then drew herself straighter, a posture meant to be intimidating. "What? Who do you think you are—"

He was pretty sure she was about to either slap him or march away, threatening to report him. He was definitely being skeezy—a little scary how good he was at it. Before she could put on the damsel-in-distress act and let out some attention-getting scream, her grabbed her wrist, the one she'd slipped the phone up, and he really hoped she hadn't gotten rid of it or passed it off while he wasn't looking.

And she hadn't. He slid back her sleeve, revealing a pouch strapped to her forearm where she'd stashed the phone, a pair of earrings, and a wristwatch. Andrew took them all, putting them safely in his pocket.

"These"—he held up the phone—"do not belong to you."

She could argue. She could fight. Threaten him with an assault charge, whatever. But she didn't, because she had a thousand or so dollars of stolen goods on her. And she'd probably been at this awhile. She glared at him in a murderous but useless rage.

He had her arm. She didn't pull away, just waited for his next move, and he thought about maybe hauling her to the security office in the casino and seeing if he could arrest her for whatever. But the glare in her big brown eyes seemed to dare him to try it. Like, if he made a move, she would then have permission to respond. To fight.

Andrew really didn't want to fight. He was pretty sure this woman could take him. A quick stomp on his instep with those heels, he'd be crippled for life.

He let go.

He pointed at her. "Don't try this again. *Capisce?*"

She didn't say a word, just turned and marched away, hips swaying inside those silky slacks. Escaping before he could call the wrath of security down on her. Just as well, probably. He had no idea whether he'd done the right thing.

His accomplices, the women at the door, stepped aside to let her through; she hardly seemed to notice them, and they looked back at Andrew hopefully.

"Did it work?"

"Yeah!" he said brightly, even though his gut feeling was that the whole encounter had gone just a little bit wrong, and that there would be consequences. "Just great! Here, have a couple of drink vouchers. On the house."

◆

He paused a moment, took a breath. A shimmer of light, an exhalation later, and he looked like one of the casino security guys, complete with tux and name tag. Only then did he approach the man who'd been pickpocketed.

"Sir, you dropped this," Andrew said, pitching his voice right, comporting himself as somberly as he could. The way he imagined professional security guards everywhere must approach their jobs. Very seriously.

The man looked startled. "What? Oh! Oh my goodness, I didn't even notice, thank you!"

"All part of the job," he said, unable to resist a sly wink. A heroic wink, he thought of it.

Andrew-as-security nodded smartly and walked off, hands tucked behind his back, surveying his domain, regarding those under his care with an air of benevolent calm. Oh *yeah*. That was *amazing*. He was so badass he hardly knew what to do with himself.

♥

". . . and this one's pickpocketing—so old school, isn't it? Like what are we, in some Dickens novel? She seems to be mostly working the outside deck." Andrew scrolled to the next photo on his phone. He and Sylvia had a quick afternoon set in the restaurant, before the Dixieland jazz band got rolling, but after that he'd gone patrolling again and managed to secretly take a bunch of pictures, hoping to ID some of the miscreants he'd spotted over the course of the afternoon. There'd been a surprising number of them. "And this is the guy who's been palming cards in the poker room. I don't think the dealer's spotting it because he's got this slick little hidden pocket device. You probably want to check this out. And maybe the other table games. I know counting cards is technically legal, and I haven't really had a chance to watch the blackjack tables to see if there's anything skeezy going on—"

"Mr. Yamauchi. Stop."

"What?"

"This isn't your job," Captain Montaigne said. "You don't have to go patrolling the boat looking for trouble. We have crew for that."

He was in the captain's office on the *Natchez*'s third deck, the texas deck. Captain Montaigne, a no-nonsense middle-aged woman with red hair and a uniform jacket open at the collar, sat across from him at her desk, looking tired, like this was just one more thing.

"No, it's not my job, I know—that's why I'm telling you. The casino guys told me to come talk to you. It's not like I'm throwing people overboard like some kind of vigilante, I know better than that."

"Thank God," she muttered. Andrew figured he wasn't supposed to hear that.

"But I thought you'd want to know. So you can keep an eye on them. Kick them off the boat. I had no idea but there are obviously bad apples out there who see the place as their own little cash till, and I thought you'd want . . . that you'd want to know." His voice trailed off. He really did think she'd want to know. And maybe she did. But Andrew had the distinct impression that he'd done something to make the captain's life harder, not easier.

"How about I e-mail the pictures to you? Then you can compare them to some kind of database. You guys always have some kind of database—"

"I'm not the police. I don't have a database. I can't just . . . fine, okay. E-mail the pictures. I'll keep an eye out. Thank you."

Andrew grinned and strolled out of the captain's office. He didn't get far before he heard the clicking of Caitlyn Beaumont's heels coming around the walkway on the deck. She hesitated at the corner, glancing around as if searching for something. Then her gaze rested on him, and she *marched*. Straight toward him, with determination. Uh-oh . . .

She waved to catch his attention. "Andrew, can I have a word with you?"

That didn't sound good. Her tone made her sound like a school hall monitor. Like a parent. His ears flattened for just a moment before he perked them back up to listen to her like nothing was wrong.

"Hey, Caitlyn!" he called back, his smile forced.

She got up close—but not too close, and he could never figure out if it was because she didn't like Asians, jokers, or just *him*—and lowered her voice, glancing around to make sure no guests were nearby to overhear. "Andrew, *what* are you doing?"

"I'm just trying to be a good citizen," he said. "You know, helping out."

"I've had some . . ." She paused a moment, as if searching for the right word. The polite word. "*Suggestions* that whatever it is you're doing, however well meant, might be looking an awful lot like, well. Harassment." She winced, as if telling him this personally pained her.

He spread his arms. "Am I just supposed to ignore it when I see someone palming cards? Or picking pockets? Or running a con? You'd rather I let a bunch of criminals get away with it?"

"It's not your job."

Just like that. Not your job. Battle cry of the unimaginative. Caitlyn Beaumont didn't have an ounce of talent in her perfectly turned-out body, but she was the one who got to stand there and decide what he should or shouldn't do? He could rant about it, but some inner voice that was a lot smarter than he was—and that sounded a lot like Sylvia—made him stop, take a breath, and consider that this was not a fight worth fighting.

"All right," he said, his smile tight. "I'll step back. It'll be fine."

The tension left Caitlyn's face and she beamed at him. "Thank you *so much*. I knew you'd understand."

"Yeah. Sure. Of course."

She stalked off on her stilt-like high heels to take care of her next minor crisis. In the meantime, Andrew had no intention of backing off. He'd just have to figure out how to be a little more sneaky about the whole thing.

♣

Coming down the stairs and turning back around to the outside promenade, he ran into a crow. Shouldn't have been possible. The thing had wings, couldn't it get out of the way?

"Heads up! Heads up!" the thing cried, flapping its wings in Andrew's face while he threw up his arms and rocked back.

"Hey!"

"Lenore, get over here," said an amused voice.

Finally able to see again, Andrew looked to find the crow—Lenore, Roger Washburn's sidekick—coming to perch on the man's shoulder. The Amazing Ravenstone, one of the other acts on the boat. Apparently he'd been famous back in the day.

God, Andrew hoped nobody ever said that about him. "Hey there, Rodge."

"Hey."

Andrew got an idea. "Hey, I wondered—does Lenore see a lot

of stuff? Like—does she notice when things happen? Bad things. Like, you know, Lassie?"

Roger's brow furrowed. His trademark devil's horns wiggled a little when he did that. "Excuse me?"

"It's just I've been noticing things going wrong. Like, just small-time cons and things. I thought with an extra pair of eyes we could maybe cover more ground—"

"Heads up! Cawk!"

"Andrew—she's a bird. Even if she did see something wrong she wouldn't be able to tell us."

"But she talks—"

Roger smirked and tilted his head in an expression that clearly said, *Oh really?*

"Yeah, okay, just a thought. Thanks," Andrew said, quickly backpedaling. He remembered the old show business adage: Never work with children or animals. Sure thing.

Roger eased past him. "I'm on my way to my cabin. Maybe we should have lunch over the next couple days, compare notes?"

"Yeah, sure," Andrew said, and stepped aside to let Roger and Lenore by.

His cell phone dinged and he looked to find a message from Sylvia.

We're supposed to meet for dinner, babe, where are you?

Oh *no.* Yes. He glanced at the time—he was fifteen minutes late, which meant she'd been sitting there all by herself, waiting.

On my way, he texted back.

He found her in the restaurant, sitting with her chin in her hands, looking out at the churning brown water outside. Her gray brindled tail flicked back and forth out the back of her chair, which wasn't a good sign.

"Honey, I'm so sorry," Andrew said at the same time he slid into the chair across from her.

She perked up and took a long drink from her glass of wine. She'd also been nibbling from a bowl of shrimp cocktail that must have been artfully arranged before she went at it. "I went ahead and ordered."

She didn't ask if that was okay, or if he minded, which was one of the things he loved about her. She just did things. She knew her mind.

"Good, great. Can I?" He reached for one of the remaining shrimp and she nodded graciously. He didn't realize how hungry he was until just this moment. "I'm really sorry. I've been . . . distracted. I'm doing a . . . thing. I really didn't mean to stand you up. I'm *so* sorry."

"Babe, I'm not mad, I just want to know what's wrong. Something *is* wrong? I've hardly seen you all day."

He wasn't entirely sure how to explain himself. After the encounters with Captain Montaigne and Caitlyn, he was less sure of his mission.

"I'm just trying to help people, you know? After last night, I started looking around and seeing how much *crap* goes on—I thought maybe I could help." His ears drooped; his tail dragged on the floor.

"How's that going?"

"I don't know." He shrugged. "Maybe not as good as I hoped."

"What, people aren't hoisting you on their shoulders and putting your name in lights?"

He chuckled in spite of himself. "A simple thank-you would be enough."

She leaned over the table to kiss him on the nose. "Thank you, honey. Now let's get some food."

The whole meal, Andrew scanned the dining room, glancing over guests, studying the people entering and leaving, searching for anything suspicious. Someone walking a little too sneaky. Someone reaching into a bag that wasn't theirs.

Sylvia waved in front of his face to catch his attention and he flinched, startled.

"You know we've got another late set tonight, right?" she said.

Actually, he'd forgotten. He winced and tried to come up with a bunch of excuses—reasonable excuses that would get rid of that worried crease in her brow. But he couldn't think of anything.

"Yeah, I know."

She frowned. She always knew when he was giving her the show business grin. When he wasn't entirely on the same page.

"Babe, are you happy?"

"What? Of course I'm happy, what are you—"

She held out her arm. Shook her hand at him, a clear instruction for him to take hold of it. So he did, contritely, and she pulled herself to his side of the table, settling in his lap. Cuddling up, she put her arms around him and tousled his hair, rubbing his ears, and he just about started crying because no, maybe he wasn't entirely happy, and how had she figured that out just by looking at him?

"I think," he said, and sighed. "I think I may be having a midlife crisis."

"Wishing you'd maybe made a different choice at the end of *American Hero* way back when?"

"What? Oh hell no, I never wanted to go to Egypt, people *died* there. It's just . . . it's just maybe I'm not entirely sure where to go from here."

"Let's just take it a day at a time till the end of the cruise. Then maybe try for that booking in New York. That sound like a plan?"

"Sylvia, are you happy?"

"I wake up every single day grateful that I get to make music and don't have to have a real job."

"That's pretty cool, isn't it?"

"Yes, it is. And I have this pretty cute guy to hang out with."

"Oh yeah, who?"

She slapped his shoulder. "That joke's older than dirt. Like Burns and Allen old." But she giggled anyway.

"So that makes it retro and we should try to work it into the show, yeah?"

"Love you, honey." She touched her nose to his, inviting him to kiss her, which he did.

"Love you, too. I'll be at the stage at eleven. Promise. I just have to check a couple of things first."

"I know. I trust you."

And the words stabbed him in the heart, because he had such a clear picture then of the worst thing that could ever happen to him, and it wasn't dying or being maimed or tortured or anything like that. It would be Sylvia deciding she didn't trust him. His heart raced just thinking of it.

He made sure his watch was strapped on tight, and he checked it often.

♠

Andrew couldn't be chastised for just *looking*, could he? He was supposed to be circulating anyway, and nobody could fault him for keeping an eye out while he was circulating. Just a little.

In the casino, that one guy he'd spotted palming cards was at the blackjack table. Andrew knew better than to confront the cheater himself, but he did think of a whole list of disruptive scenarios that might expose what he was up to. Jump on the table and start singing show tunes, swing from the chandelier, pull a fire alarm. Actually that last one would get him in a huge amount of trouble, cause the launching of lifeboats, the end of the whole cruise maybe. So no. Instead, he talked to the pit boss. Pointed out what he'd seen before, asked the boss to keep an eye on him. Was gratified a few minutes later when, as he was just about to leave, the pit boss and his security guy politely escorted the guy away from the table and out the door.

That may not have been a huge victory, but it was a victory. One tiny blow for justice.

He took time out for a bathroom break. Public restrooms on

this deck were toward the stern, and he didn't expect to see anything out of the ordinary here—but he did. A kid coming out of the men's room, a big bag tucked under his arm, looking both ways as if to make sure the coast was clear. Lips clamped together like he was nervous.

That right there was a suspicious figure. Hunched over, looking out with a startled, anxious gaze, the kid wore boots and jeans, a sweater and a jacket over the sweater, messy hair swept under a stocking cap. The boat's air-conditioning was good but not that good. He wasn't dressed for a vacation, but like he'd just come from hiding out in a basement. Brushing against the wall, the kid furtively rounded the corner and went through a door that led to a staircase down to the main deck, clearly trying to avoid attention.

Andrew followed him because guests weren't supposed to be on the lower deck. He moved quietly—these stairs were bare, utilitarian. Not meant to be seen by the public. He'd assumed the kid was stealing something. Obviously up to something nefarious. But this was a boat on a river, en route to someplace else. He had no place to go, no place to escape. Best bet was to blend in with everyone else until he could leave, right?

Maybe he was a stowaway. Maybe he had a hiding place.

Andrew had never been down to this lowest deck, which was all engines, electrical systems, machinery. He had no reason to be here. And neither did this kid, he was betting. He moved quietly as he knew how, which was an effort. But he was able to stay just out of sight, and even though he seemed to be looking over his shoulder every five seconds, the kid didn't spot him. He fled into one of the lower deck's back corridors. The boat showed its age here, with scuffed floorboards, wood laminate doors cracked with wear. The incandescent lightbulbs made the whole place seem washed out.

Andrew had an idea. He couldn't make himself invisible, but he could pull something of a chameleon act, wrapping himself in a kind of imaginary robe, then painting the robe with whatever colors happened to be around him. It wasn't perfect, but he could blend in enough to escape a cursory search. An onlooker might spot movement, and if someone was taking pictures he'd show up clear as anything since his illusions didn't appear on camera—so long, television career. The age of ubiquitous smart-phone cameras and Instagram accounts made his power little more than a parlor trick. But you know, if no one was actually *looking* for him, he was fine.

He was pretty sure no one was looking for him.

Andrew followed his quarry into the corridor. The kid had slowed, checking ahead and behind him one more time. Andrew made himself appear blank and dark, and stood very still. The kid didn't see him. He stopped at what looked like the steam room door and quickly knocked a pattern like a code.

What was going on? Smuggling? Human trafficking? Was this some kind of underground mafioso crime ring organized under everyone's nose? Terrorist attack? This last idea gave him pause. There'd been so much in the news lately, so many disasters. It might seem ludicrous to think that some international terrorist group would decide to target some C-string tourist cruise on the Mississippi, but stranger things had happened. What better way to strike at the American heartland—

The door opened, and the kid began handing items out of the bag to the people within. And what was he smuggling? Toilet pa-per. Ragged hands grabbed a roll and pulled back. The kid smiled and slipped inside.

Toilet paper and paper towels. That was what the kid had been carrying. Smuggling. Stealing. Whatever. Items so basic they were hard to even comprehend as a target for theft.

What was going on here?

The door closed, a latch slid home, and the corridor appeared as if nothing had happened.

Andrew stared for a long time, wondering what he should do. Knock on the door, talk to the people inside to find out what was going on. Tell someone that there seemed to be stowaways on the lowest deck. But who?

This felt weird, this felt bigger than him, and he didn't know what to do.

"Mr. Yamauchi, are you supposed to be down here?"

The voice came from behind him, and he jumped, gasping. When the door shut, he'd let his camouflage illusion drop. Which meant the person standing behind him saw him.

The boat's head clerk, JoHanna Potts, stood at the end of the corridor, arms crossed, glaring with enough focus that she might spontaneously develop laser vision and make Andrew explode right there. He wouldn't mind so much—it would save him from having to get through the next few minutes. She was an older black woman, impeccable, precise, and the kind of personality you just didn't argue with. Ever. He'd met her when they'd come on board in New Orleans and filled out tax forms and direct deposit paperwork. And she was right, he was not supposed to be down here.

He put on his biggest bullshitting smile. "Hey, JoHanna! How the heck are you?" He marched to the end of the hallway, hoping maybe she would step aside and let him flee as if nothing was wrong.

She didn't budge an inch but remained a wall, blocking his way out. "Seriously. Are you supposed to be here?"

He felt like he was fourteen and playing hooky. "Well I guess, I mean. It's not like I'm *not* supposed to be down here—"

"But do you have a reason to be here?" She casually glanced at her phone. "Don't you have a performance you're supposed to be at?"

"Yeah, in half an hour maybe—"

She glared. That was all she did. Andrew took a step back. "But I thought I saw . . . is something going on down here?"

"Nothing you need to be concerned with."

So that was weird. Andrew seemed to have run up firmly

against the limits of what he could confront as the *Natchez*'s resident vigilante hero. If JoHanna was behind it, it likely wasn't bad, right? A mystery, yes, but not criminal.

"In fact, how about you just forget you saw anything at all and I won't make a complaint to Ms. Beaumont about you getting in trouble in your off hours?"

He was already one strike down with Caitlyn. This was a deal he could accept.

"Right. Okay. You have a good evening." He winked and clicked finger guns at her, because that was what he always did to make himself appear harmless. She didn't even scowl.

He fled.

◆

It was a truism that if you went looking hard enough you were bound to find something you didn't want to see. He wanted to talk to Sylvia. Ask her what he should do about what he'd seen and JoHanna's involvement. Then again, if this was something really dangerous and skeevy, he didn't want Sylvia anywhere near it. So he should just handle it on his own.

Being a hero was tough. Maybe it wasn't worth the anguished moral quandary. Besides, he was pretty sure his true mission in life was making an ass of himself onstage for other peoples' enjoyment.

Speaking of which, their next show was coming up soon and he ought to get back to the cabin to change clothes, maybe take a quick shower and freshen up. As of now, he was officially off superhero duty. Stretching his shoulders, unkinking his neck, thinking of which obnoxious dinner jacket with bedazzled lapels he ought to wear that night, he turned the corner into the hallway of cabins on the way to his and Sylvia's room.

A whole gang jumped him from behind, not ten steps away from his own door. Like they knew just where to find him and were waiting in ambush. Ninjas, a million of them. No, turned out it was just two guys and a woman. That was all it took to completely overpower Andrew Yamauchi.

Each guy grabbed an arm and wrenched back, almost lifting Andrew off his feet. He yelled and tried to twist out of their grips, but that nearly popped his shoulders out of their sockets so he settled on kicking wildly. That was when the woman moved in front of him and punched him in the junk.

That *really hurt*. He doubled over, his yell turning into a groan. She grabbed his chin and lifted, forcing him to meet her gaze. "Quiet, you," she sneered.

He knew her. Recognized her—the pickpocket from earlier in the afternoon. But he'd turned her in! He'd told security all about her! And . . . they hadn't done anything. Hadn't had enough proof, enough probable cause to lock her up until they could kick her off the boat. Well, shoot.

It suddenly occurred to him that when he confronted the pickpocket he maybe should have disguised himself. Just a little, maybe. All the rest of that afternoon he'd done such a good job of looking around, keeping a close watch, noticing everything he wasn't supposed to notice. Tracking down real, actual crime. But he hadn't seen these guys coming. But—they must have noticed him. Damn.

Andrew tried to think of how he could get out of this, and the only idea he came up with was running his mouth. "Hey, I'm pretty sure I don't owe anyone any money, but maybe I'm wrong?" His laugh sounded weak.

"We had a sweet gig going here," the woman murmured. "No one expects anything bad to happen on a boat like this. No one expects dirty tricks here in the small time. But then you had to go and be a hero."

"I've learned my lesson on that. Really. I'm not a hero, I'm not—"

"Can it," she said, and stuffed a handkerchief in his mouth, tying it in the back of his head for a gag.

Okay, this was bad. Something was going around his wrists.

Some kind of nylon cord, which would be hard to twist out of. Goon One hoisted him off his feet so Goon Two could tie those together—and yes, he now recognized both goons as the grifters from the casino. They hefted him over their shoulders and carried him bodily away, while the woman kept watch. They squished his tail in their grips.

Keeping out of sight, they hauled him to the stern. Lots of shadows on a riverboat at night. The grinding rumble of the wheel turning, water splashing off the slats, sounded monstrous back here. Even if he hadn't been gagged, no one would have heard him shout.

Andrew fought the best way he knew how. Did everything he could think of, which admittedly wasn't much. He slammed illusions at them as fast as he could think of them, conjuring whatever he thought might distract them. The ace Lohengrin, a hulking knight in full armor wielding a glowing sword, came marching along the walkway. The trio of thugs flinched, almost dropping Andrew. If he twisted just right—

But the illusion could only stand there, swinging the sword without striking anything, and the woman muttered, "It's fake. Ignore it."

Andrew tried again and again. Mafia thugs with baseball bats charged from one side and a swarm of katana-wielding ninjas from the other. Trouble was, his illusions were just that, and they couldn't make contact with the bad guys without vanishing, which they promptly did, washing against the thugs like a fog bank. He hoped the flurry of movement and light would distract them, maybe give Andrew a chance to break free.

But no. They didn't even look. He tried something a little more believable than mafiosi and ninjas. Sorority girls, a whole bunch of them, like they'd come on board for drunken revels and were now running wild all over the boat. All of them in tight little candy-colored dresses with their boobs ready to burst out, big hairsprayed hair forming an actual canopy over them when they all squeezed together. All screaming crazy high-pitched shrieks of either terror or delight, who could say which.

Surely this would get the bad guys to back off. Flee in horror. At least look up from what they were doing. But no, they didn't do a thing, stayed right on task, and the illusory crowd of sorority girls disappeared.

Andrew gave a muffled wail through the gag. He worked his jaw a little—the knot wasn't very tight, if he could just work it a little more. The fabric tasted terrible, like old socks.

His next gambit, a herd of angry velociraptors with knife-long claws and snapping mouths of angry teeth, had no effect on them. Maybe if he rained seagulls down on their heads. Maybe if he could make a giant tidal wave appear alongside the boat—

He was pretty sure he couldn't generate that much of a convincing illusion. Maybe if he'd spent the last ten years actually practicing being a hero instead of playing Vegas and corporate shindigs, he'd have a better idea of how to get out of this.

He finally spit out the gag and immediately started talking. "I'm famous, you know," he pleaded. "You can't just make me disappear and expect to get away with it."

"Watch us. Oh, sorry, you won't be around to watch!"

She said it like they'd done this kind of thing before. The two men hoisted him up on the rail. Andrew was trying to be brave but he screamed in spite of himself.

His phone rang. The notes of "The Merry-Go-Round Broke Down" from *Looney Tunes* jangled out. That made everyone stop.

"Is that a phone?" one of the guys asked.

They all looked at Andrew.

The phone was in his pocket, and that was Sylvia calling. Sylvia, wanting to know where he was because their next set started in ten minutes, and he wasn't there. He had promised she wouldn't have to track him down. And here she was, tracking him down. He had disappointed her. His shoulders slumped; he hadn't really felt defeated until that moment.

Maybe he could butt-dial and get the phone to pick up. Maybe she would hear what was happening and send help. Maybe he could tell her he loved her one last time.

The woman found his pocket, wrenched his tail out of the way—which really hurt—grabbed the phone, and stared at it a moment.

Andrew shouted, "Sylvia! I'm in trouble! Goons kidnapped me, get help! Love you, babe!"

But the woman had already tossed it over the side. Andrew was still yelling as it splashed into the waters of the Mississippi below. Andrew would no doubt follow in a moment, and Sylvia would never know what happened to him.

He was balanced on the railing; the only things keeping him in place were the two goons with painful grips on his arms. If they let go, he'd fall.

"Come on, guys. Let's talk about this." Maybe if he could hook his legs under the railing somehow. Maybe that would keep him from falling. "I mean, I couldn't have hurt you too bad, you're still here—"

One of the goons said, "Funny, the more you talk the more I'm going to enjoy this."

The water below was black, foam-capped with a million whirl-pools churned up by the waterwheel. Andrew wouldn't get a chance to swim away because he'd be instantly sucked into its pull. He swallowed back bile and started to shake.

The night seemed to grow more humid, the air sticky, stifling; he couldn't breathe. So this was what impending death felt like: a broken sauna. One of the goons shivered. A warm fog settled . . . and more.

It wasn't his imagination. A mist coalesced. A ghostly figure, semiopaque, the color of dirty cotton, seemed to form right next to him. It moved closer to the three crooks.

"What—" said one of the goons.

The second one shook him. "I told you to stop that, we're not falling for your stupid illusions!"

"That's not me!" Andrew yelled. "I swear to God I am *not* doing that!"

The woman jumped back. "Jesus, did you just lick the back of my neck?"

"Did I *what*?"

The second guy jumped, too, and they both glared at each other. "Something touched me. I'm telling you, something touched me."

"Something kind of hot and wet?"

"Yeah—"

"It's the fucking joker fox—"

"No, it isn't, his illusions can't touch us. It's . . . it's . . ."

They all stared at the fog, wide-eyed. Then, the cloud of steam disappeared.

The first goon stiffened as if caught in a seizure, and grabbed Andrew's shoulder and tail, yanking them back, hard. Andrew was sure this was it, he was done for—but instead of falling forward he fell back, slamming onto the deck. Wrenched his shoulder and backside, but he didn't care, he was still on board. His shirt and tail were soaking wet.

"What're you doing!" Goon Two shouted at Goon One.

The first goon heaved a stomachful of water onto the deck. His skin was flushed red, and he was panting. "I don't know! Wasn't me, I swear, it was like something . . . something else—"

The steam returned, a sticky fog that coalesced, seeming to grow, stretching claws that reached toward the woman and her henchmen. They screamed. The woman ran, and the second goon started to. But the first, still writhing on the floor in obvious pain, grabbed his foot, almost bringing him down. The goon hauled up his buddy and the two managed to stumble off after the ringleader.

The fog, pulling back into a human shape that was somehow even more disconcerting, seemed to gaze down at Andrew for a moment. Then, it vanished. Like, there one second and gone the next, and the night was the same warm Mississippi summer as before.

Andrew lay on the deck, his tail kinked under him, gasping for breath, taking stock. Trying to figure out if he was still alive. Yeah, he was probably still alive.

Squirming, he got his tail out of the way—it immediately hurt less, which meant it probably wasn't broken, which was good. The fur on it was seriously wet and bedraggled, though. He'd have to blow-dry it before going onstage. Wriggling some more, he tried to see if he could get his hands free from the cord, maybe kick his feet loose.

He was still struggling when he heard voices coming up the walkway.

"Andrew!"

"Sylvia!"

She was at his side the next moment, along with Leo Storgman, the retired Jokertown cop. They were lifting him, cutting cords. Andrew only saw Sylvia and couldn't get the words out fast enough. "Baby, I'm so sorry, I didn't mean to miss the gig, I know you were looking for me but these guys they caught me and tied me up and I couldn't call you and I couldn't get to you and I'm so, so sorry—"

She put her hands on his cheeks. "Honey, I know, it's okay! Calm down!"

"But, but—"

"It's okay," she explained. She was smiling, and things couldn't be so bad if she was smiling. "When I called you, the answer button on your phone must have gotten pushed because I heard the whole thing. Leo was right there, so I grabbed him and came to find you. And here we are!"

"Hey, Leo." Andrew tried to wave, but his hands were still half tied so it came out as a shrug.

"Andrew," Storgman answered wryly.

"And what about the bad guys?" Andrew said.

"Casino security caught them running down the deck,

screaming like lunatics. They're locked up in the captain's office now. We'll dock by morning and the Natchez cops are on their way."

And then Andrew's hands were free, and the first thing he did was hug Sylvia. "I'm so happy to see you."

"What happened?" she asked. He wanted to cling to her forever, but she pulled back enough so she could look him over and check for wounds. "You're soaking wet!"

His memories of the last few minutes sorted themselves out, clarified. He still wasn't sure he could explain it. He looked for fog, but there was nothing. Not so much as a low-hanging cloud. The sky was clear. A few stars twinkled.

"I don't know," he said, shrugging because he knew the explanation was unsatisfactory. "They had me hanging over the railing. I should have fallen, except . . . it was like the fog grabbed me. Saved me."

"You know the boat's supposed to be haunted," Leo said.

"That's just stories," Andrew said, but weakly. Unconvinced. "I don't know what happened. I'm just glad it did."

"Come on, you," Sylvia said, taking his arm and helping him to his feet. "I'll give Caitlyn a call and let her know we'll have to skip our set tonight. She'll probably make us host sing-along bingo to make up for it—"

"No," Andrew said. "No canceling. I can do it. I want to do it."

"But baby, you still look like . . . well, you look like you saw a ghost."

He nodded firmly. "Doesn't matter. The show must go on."

♥

They spent a hurried fifteen minutes back in their cabin cleaning up and getting ready. The set might start late, but they'd be there. Andrew jumped out of the shower and buttoned up his shirt while Sylvia ran the blow-dryer over his tail to get the fur nice and fluffy.

"I feel like an idiot," he said, part of a running monologue that had been going on for a while. "I could have been killed. What the hell did I think I was doing? Never again. Never, never again."

He finished with the shirt and started on the bow tie. Sylvia put away the dryer and helped him with his jacket. She looked great, of course: she wore a black sequined dress and a big red hibiscus in her hair. She looked like a '40s pinup. With cat ears.

She straightened his tie. "Well then. Did you learn your lesson?"

He nodded. "Heroing is for chumps."

"No, silly," she said. Smiling, her whiskers twitching, she held his face in her hands and sang softly, " 'I love you just the way you are.' "

As always she was right. The lesson: he was exactly where he was supposed to be, and there was a lot to be said for that.

Just a few minutes later they were onstage at the Bayou Lounge, warming up the crowd, basking in the lights. The place was full tonight, and Andrew soaked it in.

"Hey, Sylvia!"

"Hey, Andrew!"

"Can I ask you a question?" He started the sequence of illusions for this number. First, a cartoony yellow canary perched at the end of the keyboard, ruffling its wings.

"Ask away, babe!" She started playing a vague little tune on the keys.

A couple more birds, red and blue, one short and fat and one slender, appeared. One perched on the lights, the other fluttered from one side of the stage to the other.

"Sylvia, can you tell me . . ." Even more birds, some of them flapping over the audience so that people looked up to follow their flight, but most of them clustered around the keyboard, hopping on the cables, dancing under the stage lights. "Can you tell me . . . please tell me . . . why . . . do . . . birds—"

And on the words "suddenly appear," the half dozen birds

exploded into a flock, a swarm. Dozens of birds tweeting and chirping all over the lounge, but most especially around Sylvia, and the whole audience gasped and oohed with delight. It was like they'd all landed inside a cartoon, which was just how Andrew planned it.

The next morning, the picturesque town of Natchez spread out from the docks; behind them, the lacework of steel struts on the Natchez-Vidalia Bridge gleamed gold in the sun. The riverboat looked like a palace, and Andrew got to stand at the railing and watch the police lead a would-be rapist and the three members of what turned out to be a gang of grifters who'd thought working the boat would be easy pickings down the gangplank in handcuffs. *Sayonara, losers,* Andrew thought at them.

Sylvia was with him, looking gorgeous in the morning light, wearing a billowy sundress, her hair flickering in a slight breeze. They were drinking mimosas in tall glasses. Made Andrew feel like a rock star.

She raised hers in a toast. "It's been a pretty good trip so far, don't you think?"

Andrew grinned, clinking his glass to hers. "The best, babe. The best."

In the Shadow of
Tall Stacks

Part 4

WILBUR WAS FEELING RATHER smug about having saved the illusionist from being tossed overboard. Helping rid his boat of thieves left a glow on his attitude, and watching the police escort the criminals down the gangway to the waiting police cars was a delight. If he'd solid hands with which to do so, he would have applauded their departure.

The pleasure that Wilbur felt, looking out over the town of Natchez—the city after which Thomas Leathers had named all his steamboats—wasn't destined to last long. The *Natchez* had berthed at Natchez Under-the-Hill along Silver Street, the historic district, with the steep green river bluff (and the ruins of Fort Rosalie in the city park there) rising behind the buildings. Just upriver the Magnolia Bluffs Casino extended out over the river's shore—a stark reminder to Wilbur of the *Natchez*'s own possible fate.

Natchez was also a sanctuary city, and the first stop where a few of the Kazakhs were to depart the boat, as Wilbur knew from Jeremiah and from listening to conversations between JoHanna, Jack, and Captain Montaigne. That would be another pleasure, seeing at least a few of them leaving the boat toward a more hopeful future.

Wilbur was watching the activity from the bow of the main deck. Now that the cops had done their work (the passengers crowding the boiler deck to gawk at the arrests), many of those aboard were making their way down to the main deck, ready to leave the boat to savor what Natchez had to offer. Captain Montaigne stood at the head of the gangway, presumably to supervise the roustabouts, while JoHanna and the bartender Jack stood nearby. On the dock, five people waited to board. One was a massive man in an expensive suit, sitting in an equally massive electric wheelchair and fanning himself against the heat and sunlight. Behind him, a large van with a wheelchair lift waited. Wilbur estimated that the man must weigh in excess of five hundred pounds and doubted that he could manage to stand on his own. Wilbur knew who he was from what he'd overheard: a Southern Baptist preacher by the name of Reverend Thaddeus Wintergreen, also known as the ace Holy Roller—and the JADL contact for the Kazakhs who would be disembarking here in Natchez.

The other quartet, three men and a woman, were dressed in dark suits, all of them with eyes concealed behind dark sunglasses. The leader of the four appeared to be a tall, thin black man, whose appearance screamed "cop" to Wilbur. The man gestured to his companions before the gangway was entirely lashed down and before the reverend could start his wheelchair rolling. Following behind, the four strode up and onto the boat, the leader's right hand fishing out an ID from his suit jacket to flash at the captain; Wilbur slid closer to the trio in time to hear the man's first words. "Martin Lowell," he said. "ICE. These other three agents are with me." He put his ID back and pulled out another sheet of paper, handing it to Captain Montaigne, who glanced at it quizzically. "That is a federal warrant giving us the right to search your boat before anyone else leaves or"—glancing back at Reverend Wintergreen—"anyone else comes aboard."

Captain Montaigne pointedly didn't look at either JoHanna or Jack. "What exactly are you looking for, Agent Lowell?"

Lowell didn't answer directly. "I've a copy of your passenger manifest, and there are a few rooms I wish to inspect. I assume you have master keys to all the staterooms?"

"My head clerk does. JoHanna, would you bring me the keys?"

JoHanna took a step forward and glowered at Lowell. Then, with a sniff, she turned and went toward her office near the boiler room. Lowell nodded to one of his men, who took up a station at the top of the gangway; Captain Montaigne went to the bottom of the stairs leading up to the boiler deck and opened a compartment in the wall there, taking out a handset. Her voice crackled over the boat's loudspeakers. "There will be a short delay before passengers can disembark. In the meantime, please enjoy a complimentary beverage in any of the bars or dining rooms on the boiler deck. We thank you for your patience and indulgence." There was some grumbling from those on the main deck, but most of the passengers were already heading toward the boiler deck. She hung up the handset and closed and locked the compartment. "I hope this won't take long, Agent Lowell," she said on her return.

Her only answer was a quick twitch of his lips. "I'd like to start with the boiler and engine rooms," he said. "Do we need keys for that?"

"You don't. Knock, and ask for Chief Engineer Cottle," Captain Montaigne answered, gesturing to the doors to the main deck saloon. "He can show you the area. I'll wait here for JoHanna."

Wilbur didn't wait to hear more; he was already following the crowd up the stairs, continuing on past the boiler deck and through the chained-off stairs to the texas deck to stateroom 3. They'd been lucky: the refugees housed on the main deck had been escorted earlier by Jack up to the texas deck so they could say their farewells to those who were supposed to leave here in Natchez—the ICE agents would find none of them there. Wilbur slid quickly into the room and willed himself to become visible at the same time, not certain what he could do but knowing he had to do something. Two were standing near the door with Jyrgal, their belongings at their feet: the two who Reverend Winter-green was to take.

"There's a problem." Wilbur mouthed the words desperately to Jyrgal, waving steamy arms. "You all need to leave this room."

Jyrgal was shaking his head. "I don't understand," he said in his ponderous English. Wilbur looked around, ready to sink into someone's body to allow him to talk, but another of the refu-gees, Nurassyl—Jyrgal's son—was already moving toward Wilbur, slithering across the floor on legs that ended not in feet but in tentacles, his flesh glistening like that of some pale, oozing jel-lyfish. The young man reached out to Wilbur with arms that, like his feet, ended in a mass of wriggling tentacles. The boy reached up to place those hands into Wilbur's steamy chest near his throat, hissing as he felt the heat. Nurassyl quickly withdrew his arms, pressing them close to his chest as he looked at Wil-bur. And Wilbur . . .

Wilbur felt a tingling spreading out from where Nurassyl had touched him, a strangely comforting sensation. "What did you—?" he started to ask, but stopped.

He *heard* his voice. Sibilant. Breathy. Steamy. Certainly not the voice he'd once had, but one that was audible and understand-able. Wilbur's hands went to his throat, marveling. He stared at Nurassyl, who had moved back near his father.

"My son has a gift," Jyrgal said. He smiled. "What were you trying to tell us?"

The question brought Wilbur back to the moment, though he continued to watch Nurassyl. "There are men aboard, from the government. They've come to search the ship. If they find you, they'll take you all away and deport you. You have to leave this room. Now."

"Where will we go?"

Good question, Wilbur thought. Where *could* they go? He had no idea which rooms the ICE agents intended to search; he was only certain that this would be one of them. He saw the door to the adjoining room. "Everyone needs to go in there," he said, pointing. "Take everything out of this room except the furniture and take it with you; it has to look like no one has been living here. Do that, then close and lock the door. As soon as it's safe, I'll come back and tell you. Hurry!"

With that, Wilbur turned to leave, but he stopped. He looked again to Nurassyl. "Thank you," he said. "I don't know how you did that, but . . . thank you." He hoped Nurassyl could see the steamy smile that spread across his face as he slipped through the wall and outside again.

He went in search of the captain and the ICE agents.

He found the captain rather quickly, waiting for the agents to emerge from the boiler room corridor. Her foot tapped the deck, betraying her anxiety. He could see the worry in her face, her jaw muscles bunched below her ears. The ring of master keys to the staterooms was clutched in her tight fingers. Making certain he wasn't visible, he put himself alongside Montaigne. He put his mouth next to her ear, speaking in a steamy whisper. "Captain, listen to me." She jerked away at the words, swiping at her ear, and Wilbur saw water on her fingers. She saw it as well, and wiped her hand on her uniform.

"What?" he heard her say in a stage whisper while staring at the door leading to the crew quarters and the boiler and engine rooms.

Wilbur leaned in again. "If they go to the stateroom on the texas deck, tell them you've closed it because of a steam leak. I'll take care of the rest."

She gave him the faintest of nods, then moved forward as the door to the crew area opened and Agent Lowell, followed by the other agents, emerged. Lowell was talking into a Bluetooth earpiece stuffed in his left ear. "We've checked the main deck, Evangelique, and we're about to check the staterooms you've marked. Don't worry; I've got this handled. I'll let you know what we find." He touched the earpiece as Captain Montaigne lifted the key ring.

"I take it you didn't find anything untoward, Agent," she told him. "I have the master keys. Which rooms did you need to see?"

Expressionless, Agent Lowell consulted his smartphone. "We'll start on the texas deck," he said. "Stateroom three."

"Stateroom three?" Montaigne told him. "I'm afraid we have a steam leak in that room, and it's closed."

Lowell gave her a thin-lipped half smile. "A steam leak? That's terribly convenient. I'll still need to see it."

Wilbur moved quickly away with Captain Montaigne's "Follow me, then," moving up to the texas deck and trusting that Montaigne would take a slower route up. Inside the stateroom, he went to the closed door of the adjoining room, allowing himself to appear to the refugees in the dark and packed interior, holding an index finger up to his lips. "You must be silent," he said. "They're coming . . ."

With that, he slipped back into the main room and thrust his hands into the wall where the lines to the 'scape pipes ran, closing his fingers around and into the delicious steam there. He let it fill him, relishing the heat that now ran through him like lifeblood. He went to the door of the stateroom and let himself remain there, the door bisecting his body, his head outside. He could see Montaigne and the trio of agents approaching. "I wouldn't go in there," Montaigne said. "The steam leak . . ."

"Strange, I don't see a warning sign on the door," Lowell answered.

"I haven't had time yet, but as you can see, the door's dripping from it," the captain answered. She held up the ring of keys. "And, after all, it's locked. A sign seems unnecessary."

"Then unlock it, please, and step aside."

Wilbur slipped back into the room. He allowed his arms, handless, to become visible as the door opened, as if they were wisps of steam. He placed himself at the open doorway as Captain Montaigne moved away and Lowell took a step inside. Wilbur pressed his body against the man, gratified when the agent nearly jumped backwards. "Christ! It's scalding in there," he gasped. The front of his suit was spattered with water drops.

"It's a steam leak," Montaigne said, as if she were speaking to a child. "Steam is hot by definition."

"Aren't you afraid of fire?" Lowell asked her.

Montaigne laughed. "It's steam. Steam is also *wet*. I'm far more worried about water damage to the stateroom. Look at your suit, and you already saw that the door's sweating with it." She said that with a glance into the room herself. "We'll have the line sealed off as soon as possible. But as you can see, there's no one there. If you still want to go in and search . . ." Montaigne let the sentence hang unfinished.

Lowell scowled. He pulled out his smartphone and looked at the screen again. "You have another stateroom on this deck—the one you reserve for shareholders. I need to see that one."

"It's currently occupied. Mr. Kirby Jackson, the primary shareholder, came aboard at Baton Rouge."

"Fine. I'll still need to see it," Lowell told her.

Captain Montaigne shrugged. "As you wish." With a final glance inside the room, as if she was looking for Wilbur, she pulled the door closed. Wilbur heard the lock engage, and the muffled footsteps of the four moving away.

He slipped back into the adjoining room. "It's safe," he told Jyrgal and the others. "You can come out now. They'll be gone soon, and after that, I'm sure JoHanna will come to get Bulat and Anara—their ride is waiting for them. Then she'll escort some of you back to the other room again." He started to leave, then stopped, looking again at Nurassyl. "Jyrgal, how do you say *thank you* in Kazakh?"

"*Paxmet,*" Jyrgal replied. Nurassyl nodded back to Wilbur with a smile.

Wilbur pointed to his mouth, still looking at Nurassyl. "*Paxmet*, Nurassyl," he said, then, turning to Jyrgal again: "Tell

Nurassyl that without his help, this wouldn't have ended well."
Wilbur inclined his head to Nurassyl as Jyrgal began to speak to
his son in their own language.

With that, Wilbur went to stand in the bathroom tub for several minutes, allowing himself to cool and for the resulting
water to drain away as the Kazakhs began to collect their belongings and move them back into the outer room.

♣

Wilbur watched from the main deck as the Reverend Wintergreen, in his wheelchair, left the *Natchez*. JoHanna and Jack
and two of the Kazakhs, accompanied him. The ICE agents had
left hours earlier, at which point Reverend Wintergreen had
come aboard, and many of the passengers had left for the local
bars, shops, and sights. A crowd of locals had also paid to come
aboard the *Natchez* to tour the boat and be entertained in the
lounge; it was eleven P.M. now, the Jokertown Boys had finished
their show, and Captain Montaigne had made the announce-
ment that all visitors must now disembark.

Wilbur watched Reverend Wintergreen's wheelchair make its
slow way down the gangway in the crowd toward his waiting
van. The Kazakhs slipped into the van as Wintergreen's driver
opened the side door and brought the side lift out to get the reverend into the vehicle. The door closed, and they drove off along
with the rest of the cars parked along Silver Street. No one seemed
to be following them.

For the second time that day, Wilbur felt a distinct sense of
satisfaction. He moved through the wall of the salon on the main
deck and into the crew corridors.

Even in his bodily days, Wilbur had enjoyed spending time
in the heat and noise of the boiler and engine rooms: to him, they
were the beating heart chambers of the *Natchez*. It was here that
he could feel her as if she were a living entity, breathing in fire
and water and exhaling steam to drive herself forward against

the river's currents, its twists and turns and ever-changing mud-banks.

Now, it was the place where Wilbur felt most at home and returned to often, where he could most easily feed his addiction to the steam that made him come most fully alive. He almost sighed as he felt that warm, moist atmosphere surround him. He enjoyed watching Cottle (who Wilbur had privately nick-named "Coddle" for the way he treated the machinery of the boat) fiddle with the pressure in the lines. The crew had been dismissed, since the *Natchez* was berthed for the night, and no steam was needed beyond what was already in the system. Wilbur expected to find himself alone. He was surprised to hear voices coming from near the entrance to the boiler room. He slid between the boilers toward the voices.

". . . know what to do when the time comes." The voice was familiar, and as Wilbur passed the boilers, he saw Kirby Jackson in his expensive suit, talking to Chief Engineer Cottle.

"I don't know, sir," Cottle answered. He took a sip from his ever-present coffee mug—Wilbur wondered how the man ever managed to sleep, since he went through several pots a day from the cheap Mr. Coffee machine in the crew mess.

"I know *you*, Travis." Jackson's voice was warm honey and gravel. "Look, my friend, either way things go, you're out of a job once we get to Cincinnati. How easy was it for you to find this one, eh? I'm offering you your chance to retire in style. Why not take it?"

"But this—"

"Now, Travis," Jackson interrupted. "I've told you what needs to be done. I expect you to do it. That's best for both of us."

"But . . ."

Jackson moved close to Cottle, who looked down into his cof-fee mug. Standing over the man, Jackson shook his head. "You understand how it has to be," Jackson said, his voice darkening and going dangerously soft. "You can't back out now. I simply can't allow that. Do we understand each other?"

Cottle said nothing, only nodded once, not even looking up at Jackson.

"Good. I thought you'd see reason," Jackson said, taking a step back and raising his voice. He patted Cottle's shoulder. "Then you know what to do when the time comes. I'll make sure everything's set up on my end. You've made the right decision, Travis. You're not going to regret it, I promise you."

With another pat on the back, Jackson left the boiler room as Cottle took another long drag from his coffee mug. Wilbur went to the boilers, still holding steam, and pulled in the warmth and energy there until he had enough steam within him to make himself visible if he wished. Enough steam to have a voice again.

An alarm wailed as pressure dropped in the lines, then went silent. By the door, Cottle cursed.

"This is my boat, Cottle," Wilbur said, still marveling at the steamy, breathy voice that had been returned to him. A voice appropriate for a haint. "My boat."

"Who's there?" Cottle said loudly. "Who said that?" The engineer came around the boilers with a wrench raised in one hand and the coffee cup still in the other—bringing back memories of his own fight with Carpenter—but Wilbur was already moving away, passing through the walls of the boiler room and back out onto the main deck. There were a few passengers there, but Wilbur had cooled enough that he was only an errant wisp to them if they noticed him at all.

What had they been discussing? Wilbur wondered. *What was it that Cottle didn't want to do?*

♠

The next morning, the *Natchez* left Natchez, heading to Vicksburg and the cities farther upriver.

It was one of Wilbur's realizations, very quickly after his death, that he had no need of sleep. During the night, he might lean undisturbed on the railing of the hurricane deck and watch a moonlit landscape drift past the *Natchez*. That landscape had changed a lot over the decades, and especially during the day, the river was more crowded now with motorized small boats, pleasure cruisers, and barges carrying freight, but there was still a sense of being part of a long past while on the water.

His was an existence that was often solitary, but Wilbur also found that comforting. In those reflective moments, Wilbur could almost forget that he was also a prisoner here, marooned eternally on the *Natchez*. At least the Kazakh refugees stuck in their cabins would be able to leave, while Wilbur would remain here.

In the prison he'd constructed himself. He could bear that life sentence, though, as long as the *Natchez* still plied the river. As long as the steam was up. But on a *Natchez* that was no longer a boat, but just a floating bar or casino or hotel, never moving, without steam . . .

Living in Cincinnati until the Natchez rots . . . Jeremiah's words. The prospect made Wilbur feel increasingly miserable the more he thought about it. He stood at the stern on the texas deck, watching the paddle wheel's relentless churning, his thoughts running in circles in tandem with the paddles.

Selling the boilers for scrap. No steam. They'd run the calliope on compressed air like they do on the new boats. No steam, so no way for me to do much of anything. I'll just be another haint they'll talk about but never see, weak and emasculated. I'll go crazy and bored. No steam: just endless days and nights tied up on an old wrecked hulk, with people eating dinners and wedding receptions with drunken idiots dancing to lousy bands playing worn-out music. Even if the owners did eventually decide to put her back on the river for little jaunts, the boilers would be gone. They wouldn't go to the expense of putting new ones in. No. No steam. They'd just cram a diesel engine or two in the back, with the paddle wheel spinning strictly for show.

Just another replica excursion boat.

No steam. No steam. Just me stuck on a gutted boat, both of us rotting away together.

Without steam, Wilbur couldn't make himself visible or shape his cloudy form. Without steam, he couldn't handle or manipulate physical objects, no matter how light. Without steam, he couldn't enter into another person's body. Without steam, Wilbur was invisible, nothing at all. He was as addicted to steam as any heroin user to his drug.

If he thought it would work, Wilbur would have jumped over the railing and into the wheel and tried to drown himself, only he knew nothing at all would happen. He'd lost count of how many times he'd tried to leave the *Natchez,* but the boat (or whatever it was that had made Wilbur what he now was) wouldn't allow that.

From the boiler deck, someone's digital camera flashed, freezing for a moment the spray from the paddle wheel.

Eleanor and I stood here many times, just watching the paddle wheel endlessly turning and pushing us forward. "It's mesmerizing," she told him a few months after the Natchez's launch, leaning over the rail to stare down. "Meditative. I feel like I could *just* let myself fall down into the paddle wheel and the water and *just* become part of the boat."

That made Wilbur grab at her arm, as if he were afraid that she'd actually do that. "You wouldn't be part of the boat, my dear," Wilbur answered. "You'd just be dead."

As if she understood his distress, she took a step back from the rail. She smiled at him. "Are you saying that our boat could possibly hurt me? I don't think so. We built her. You built her, darling—you poured your heart and your soul into her. She's your child and she loves us too much to hurt anyone in our family. I know you, my love. You'll stay here until you die." She laced her fingers around his. "Which is going to be a long, long time from now, for both of us . . ."

Wilbur was afraid now that Eleanor had been right, that it would be far longer than he wanted or expected. Death: he'd expected that experience to be like all the cliché books and movies. He'd see the light and all his dead relatives calling him and welcoming him into heaven.

But he'd stayed with the boat. *His* boat. But the *Natchez* was not his child. No. She clasped Wilbur to her bosom like an overprotective mother, refusing to let go.

What does it mean that I'm not . . . moving on *to something else? Is that supposed to tell me that all that stuff about heaven and hell and the rest was a lie? Is this what happens to everyone who dies? Is the whole world full of ghosts stuck where they passed away, wearing what they were wearing in that moment and looking just like they did in the moment before death claimed them? Or did the wild card do this to me?*

Either way, there's no way out. At least, none that I've found.

A Chris-Craft Catalina went roaring past the *Natchez*, heading downriver, its wake throwing swells against the side of the steamer and causing the paddles to slap harder at the river, bringing Wilbur's attention back to the wheelhouse. Being stuck on the *Natchez* was one thing when his steamboat still plied the river, still running the watery trail she'd followed since he'd built her. Having her docked and maimed and crippled, and him with her . . . that wasn't a fate he could tolerate. *There* has *to be a way for me to leave or to have the* Natchez *remain as she is. There must be—one way or the other. I have to find it.*

But he had no idea even where to start.

◆

He was still brooding on the problem later that night as he prowled the decks well before dawn. With the exception of some diehards in the lounge, most of the passengers were in their cabins, sleeping or pursuing other pleasures. Wilbur was glad for the solitude as he passed along the promenade of the boiler deck. At least, he was until he saw Kitty Strobe leaning on the rail near the stairs to the texas deck and staring at the night landscape passing by. The junior pilot was attired in her usual overdressed-for-the-weather fashion, with her sunglasses firmly in place despite the fact that it must be three or four in the morning. Wilbur figured she was on her way up to the pilothouse to relieve Jeremiah.

Wilbur made certain he was invisible; no sense in startling the woman, who appeared to be brooding about her own issues. He was about to glide past Kitty when they both heard voices approaching: the ghost-hunter trio, lugging equipment and camera, and talking to one another in loud stage whispers.

"You got the key that JoHanna chick gave us?" the blond one asked. He was handling most of the equipment, with a microphone on a long pole and various devices protruding from stuffed pockets in his baggy jeans—Sean, Wilbur remembered.

The dark-haired and tattooed leader of the trio—Ryan—held up a small key on a large ring. "Stateroom thirteen," he said, not even trying for a whisper in the early-morning darkness. "Got it."

"Thirteen? You sure?" his baseball-capped brother, Kevin, interjected. He had the camera. "Dude, I thought it was eighteen."

"Thirteen, I'm pretty sure," Ryan said. "Anyway, it's supposed to be one of the haunted rooms, and it's empty right now. The captain said we could set up there until dawn. So let's get . . ."

Ryan's voice trailed off as he saw Kitty staring at them. "Hey, you're one of the pilots, aren't you," he said.

"Yeah," Kitty answered. "And you're all awfully loud for this late." Her voice was quiet enough that all three of the young men leaned in to listen. "You're those *Dead Report* guys?"

"Yep, *The Dead Report*. You've seen our show?"

Kitty shook her head.

"You should. *Great* stuff. We're getting quite a following. And we're gonna get *greater* stuff on the *Natchez*. Hey, you know where stateroom thirteen is?"

He dangled the key in front of her sunglasses as Kitty lifted a finger to her lips. "Quiet, remember? Other side of the boat. This deck. And you gotta keep it down, okay?" The three of them nodded simultaneously. "You guys really believe in this ghost stuff? You think you can talk to dead people?"

"*Hell* yes," Ryan answered excitedly, nearly shouting the words as Kitty shook her head. "Oh, yeah. Sorry," Ryan continued, dropping his voice to a husky and still very audible whisper. "You should *hear* some of the recordings we got." His hands waved like a conjurer doing a trick, exposing his tattooed arms. "Voices from *beyond the grave*," he said theatrically. "On tape."

Wilbur saw Kitty visibly shudder at that. "Whatever," she said. "Just keep it quiet."

"Sure will." The trio moved on past Wilbur and Kitty. As they did, the boom Sean was carrying whacked into the metal railing of the stairs. The sound was like a blacksmith's hammer on an anvil. Kitty glared at them as Sean grimaced. "Sorry," he said. Kitty just shook her head again.

She went back to the railing, looking at the river again, before heaving a sigh and going to the stairs. Wilbur watched her ascend toward the texas deck, then took her place at the rail.

He stood there for a long time, but the river provided no answers for him.

♣   ♦   ♠   ♥

Death on the Water

By Cherie Priest

1.

"Goddamnit, wake up and roll your ass over. Someone's trying to break in."

Leo's eyes popped open. He blinked once or twice and sat up. "What? Who? What?"

"Wake *up*," his wife commanded. The outline of her face came into focus, but the lights were off and without Leo's glasses, Wanda was just some frantic blob with a death grip on his shoulders.

Leo Storgman rarely woke up fast, and never woke up happy. "It's probably just . . . somebody's got the wrong room." He pivoted slowly on his hips and found the side of the bed, then dangled his feet—fishing around until his toes located his sandals.

She flipped on the lamp. "Here's your robe. I'll get the gun."

The thought of his wife with a 9mm lit up Leo's morning like a trash fire. He leaped to his feet and with sandals flopping he intercepted her on the path to his suitcase. "No! No, don't . . . don't do that. I'll see who it is." He took the robe and wrestled his way inside it.

Behind him, the knob rattled. A large, blunt body part slammed against the door, and somebody swore while a key scraped and jerked fruitlessly in the lock.

Leo held his eye up to the peephole, and there he saw one fishbowled face up close and personal. It belonged to a big, black-haired dude with black tattoos crawling out of his black T-shirt. A silver wallet chain dangled across the hip of his black jeans, and a black leather bracelet slipped up and down his wrist when he knocked.

Leo didn't want any trouble, but he wasn't particularly bothered by it, either. He leaned one shoulder against the door and in his best old-cop voice, he said, "Hey, asshole, this isn't your room."

Silence fell. Whispers rose.

Leo put his eye back on the peephole. Now he could see two other guys, one on either side of the man with the wrong damn key. One of them was a blond. The other had a hat. That was all he could tell from the narrow vantage of the little glass circle.

The first guy lifted up his face. His eye was as big as an apple. "Oh shit, man, I am *truly* sorry if we bothered you . . . but . . . isn't this room thirteen?"

"Yes, and it's occupied."

The guy outside pressed on. "It's occupied? Are you sure?"

"What kind of idiot question is that?"

"No, I mean, it's just . . ." The eyeball disappeared.

One of his friends pushed him aside. The newbie was leaner and less decorated. He wore a gray cap and suspenders. "Excuse me, hello?"

"Hello, and go away." Leo reflexively looked at his wrist, but he wasn't wearing a watch. "This is an ungodly hour to be running around, knocking on doors." Or so he assumed.

The dark-haired guy whined faintly from somewhere off to the right. "But our investigation doesn't end until dawn. We've got all this equipment ready and everything."

The new face at the peephole said, "I'm very sorry that we bothered you, sir, but we were told the room would be empty until the boat hits Memphis."

"Well, it's not." He teetered on the cusp of finishing off with a "fuck you and good night," but now he was curious. His hand hovered over the old-fashioned chain that did back-up duty to the dead bolt. He sighed, surrendered, and drew the chain back—then opened the door.

All three men shuffled their feet, suitably abashed. The first two looked related, but the blond one didn't match them at all. He looked like a surfer, not a Hipster of the Night. For Christ's sake, he was wearing Crocs with denim cutoffs.

The one in the hat was the most apologetic, and did the least mumbling when he began his apologies afresh. "Sir, we'll leave you alone. Again, we *do* apologize."

Leo eyed their cameras and the metal case that the blond toted—while simultaneously juggling what looked like a boom mike. "What kind of investigation are you up to?"

The dude in black wrestled his way back to the front and center and offered his hand in a firm, friendly shake. "Sir, I'm Ryan Forge from *The Dead Report,* on the Explore America channel. This is my brother Kevin, and our cousin, Sean Venters. We're here on the *Natchez* to film a special: 'Death on the Water,'" he said, jazz hands waving.

"'Death on the Water'?"

Ryan nodded earnestly and launched into his sales pitch with a sincerity to be envied by the saints. "Believe it or not, *this boat* is one of the most supernaturally active structures in the *world.* There have been over two *dozen* documented deaths on board since it launched in 1948, and at least half of those departed souls remain on board . . . riding up and down the Mississippi River for *all eternity.*"

"You . . . you're serious, aren't you?"

"*Super*-serious, sir," Ryan insisted, heroically failing to lisp. "This is our *life,* man. This is what we *do.* We communicate with spirits and enable them to find peace."

Leo asked, "How do you do that?" and immediately regretted

it, for he had unleashed a dragon. A dipshit dragon, who talked with his hands and peppered his speech with italic emphasis.

"Okay, what we do is, *first* we set up all our equipment—our cameras and recorders, and our EMF readers, and our amplifiers, and our spirit boxes, and *then* we create a base of operations—or that's what we *usually* do, but we're locked out of our base of operations right now because the bartender threw us out. So we took our light gear and thought we'd check out some of the *individual* rooms. *Wait . . .*" His eyes narrowed, and his forehead sank into a handsome, determined frown of confusion. "Does that plaque say this is the honeymoon suite?"

Wanda manifested over Leo's shoulder, all smiles and white satin. "Why, yes, it is. Hello there, boys."

Leo made room for her in the doorway.

All three faces darkened three shades of pink. All three throats required clearing at once, with the sound of three mortified lawn mowers puttering by. Ryan spoke for them all when he said, "Oh. Um. Our most *heartfelt* apologies. And congratulations, dude. To both of you, I mean. Ma'am. Dude."

Leo slipped an arm around his wife's waist. She was taller than him by an inch and a half despite his horns, but those mostly curled to the sides of his head. Even without them, she was better looking than him by a mile and a half. He knew how lucky he was. His joker card wasn't that weird, and his wife was a ten.

The guys stared studiously at everything everywhere, except for anything beneath Wanda's nightdress. Her nipples were out like stars.

Ryan successfully held his eyes above the danger line, keeping his gaze locked on Leo's frowning face. "Right. Well. Once again, sir. And madam. We apologize for the trouble. Have a . . . I hope you . . ." He floundered. "Enjoy your honeymoon some more. Without us."

On that note he turned and fled, with his cousin and brother hot on his heels. They scrambled down the deck, bumping into one another and scraping the boom mike along the wall— knocking it on every damn door they passed.

Leo shook his head. Wanda laughed. "*That* was exciting!"

Leo shut the door and kicked off his sandals. "That was annoying."

"They were very polite, though. Such gracious and *strapping* lads, weren't they? Especially the one in black. What was his name?"

"Like you don't remember it."

"Bryan something," she teased.

"Ryan something," he corrected. "And they were *ghost hunting*, I swear to God. The job market for millennials is worse than I thought."

He shrugged out of his robe and wadded it up. He chucked it at his wife, who dodged it.

Wanda shrugged out of her nightdress and wadded it up. She chucked it at Leo, who caught it with his face. "I think we've got another hour until dawn, and I'm both wide awake and conveniently naked."

"That's my favorite kind of awake."

He sat down on the bed. It didn't hide the pitched tent in his boxers, but then again, he wasn't trying to hide it. "You want to turn off the light or . . ."

"Don't you like the view?" She grinned wickedly and prowled toward him.

"I do. Very much. Yes." He leaned back. She leaned forward. She put her hands on either side of his head, and she crawled onto the bed until she straddled him—grinding gently against the warm lump in his shorts.

Until the bedside lamp's bulb popped and went out, with a sound like a wine cork.

They both froze.

"Did you do that?" he asked, thinking maybe she'd kicked it by accident. Lights on or off, he couldn't see past her breasts anyway.

"No." She sat up and rolled off him.

He protested by rolling back onto her. "Must be a bum bulb."

"No, stop it. Wait."

"What?"

Her body was tense, and not in the good way. He could feel her shoulders tighten and see the edge of her face by what little light came in around the window's shade. He didn't know where they were on the river, but there was always a little glow from the lights on the boiler deck. It was never as dark as you'd think.

"I heard something. I think I *felt* something."

"Was it—"

"Something cold," she cut him off. "On my back. Just now, like someone touched me. Right before the lightbulb blew."

He sighed and flopped down beside her. They both stared up at the ceiling, at nothing. "You're just worked up because of those boys. I didn't know you believe in ghosts."

"I don't, exactly. But I won't rule them out, either. Something touched me, Leo. A hand, right on my thigh, as cold as death."

"Death feels cold?"

"And *damp*. Like a mist, almost. Like . . ." She curled up and grabbed the edge of the blanket and drew it across her torso. "Like a humidifier."

"Death likes it moist. Got it." His pup tent deflated, and he resigned himself to a morning that would be less steamy than clammy.

"Shush. Listen. Do you hear that?"

He shushed. He listened. He heard the distant humming slap of the stern wheel churning and the creak of the old boat's boards as it trekked north through the night. He heard someone talking, but couldn't make out the words. It sounded close, and it sounded like swearing. Maybe it was coming from the Grand Saloon.

"It's just your imagination, now that you've got it running. Or maybe those idiots tried to get inside another room and woke up somebody else." But just like that, he was covered in goose bumps.

"Who do you think the ghost hunters were looking for?" Wanda asked.

"What does it matter?"

"If there's a ghost in the room, we could try talking to it. Maybe we could ask it to go away. Do you think it was a suicide? Accident? Natural causes? Or . . . something more interesting?"

Leo grabbed his pillow and crawled back into the spot where he'd been sleeping before the spook trio tried barging in. He tugged the sheet over himself, and Wanda joined him. "Leave that nonsense to those three jackasses," he told her. "We've got a *real* case to solve."

"We haven't made much progress so far."

"Tomorrow, we should . . ." He stopped himself and shook his head, rolling it back and forth on the pillow. "Or this morning, I guess—I don't know what time it is—we'll start asking around. We've just hit Vicksburg, after all. She died right around this point in the cruise, when the boat was coming down the other direction."

"I *still* say we should've gone undercover."

He laughed. "It's an insurance gig, not a RICO investigation. There's no real reason for anyone to lie to us, and we won't be in any danger."

"Unless the girl was *murdered*."

"She wasn't *murdered*. It was an accident. The only question is, was the accident her fault, or was something on the *Natchez* to blame? The boat's owners are just covering their asses, in case her family tries to sue."

"I have a really great wig, and some killer sunglasses."

He smiled at the ceiling. "*No* disguises. No undercover work—just *work*-work, as soon as the sun comes up. We've fooled around enough already."

"Are you sure?" She wormed up against him, warm and soft and reaching for his half-mast chubby of eternal optimism. It rose to the challenge like an inflatable tube man at a car dealership.

Leo mumbled an answer, something about her not being afraid of ghosts anymore. It was mostly a soup of vowels and grunts.

Wanda cackled and ducked under the blanket. She took his waistband in her teeth and dragged his underwear south, while the *Natchez* rolled softly on the river.

2.

After their predawn quickie, Leo and Wanda slept in another hour or two before heading to the Grand Saloon for breakfast. The sun was up, and the center of the boat was lit for the morning meal, so everything felt a little too bright to Leo. He pulled out his sunglasses and shoved them on, then ordered a black coffee. Wanda went for a mimosa.

The waiter buzzed off, dashed back with a pair of waters, and said he'd be right back with the menus—unless they wanted the breakfast bar? Both said "no thanks."

"*Never* pick the breakfast bar," Leo both commanded and vowed. "I'll wait for something made for me, not thrown in a trough for eighty other people."

"Well, we can survive another ten minutes. It's only what . . . seven thirty? And to think, you've already had a morning workout."

He smiled without showing any teeth and bobbed his head. "You were no slouch, yourself."

She returned the grin, added a cocked eyebrow, and adjusted her sun hat. "I know."

Before long, the uniformed server reappeared with coffee, mimosa, and menus. The Storgmans ordered and settled in to wait. Wanda sighed happily and licked bubbly orange juice off her top lip. "I've never been a morning person, but being up this early isn't all bad."

Leo shrugged. He'd been a cop for thirty years, in the city that never sleeps. Over the course of that career, he'd seen more sunrises than sunsets—as often as not, while staring down a corpse. It was never his favorite way to start the day, but he'd gotten used to it.

If anything, he would've rather seen a lifeless body than the fellow who spotted him and Wanda, waved, and invited himself over to their table. *Any lifeless body. Ideally, this guy's.* "Oh God," he muttered.

Wanda, on the other hand, lit the fuck up. "Why hello there!"

Ryan Forge grabbed a nearby empty chair. He spun it around and sat astride it in reverse, folding his arms on the narrow metal back and frowning apologetically. "Sir. Ma'am. I just want to apologize again. What happened this morning was *totally* our bad."

"No shit."

"Leo . . ." Wanda whapped him on the shoulder. "Be nice. The poor boy is trying to say he's sorry."

"We heard him the first time—and it's a good thing you had the wrong key," he said to Ryan. "Wanda was ready to come out, guns blazing."

"Guns?"

"We're private investigators." She extended a hand, limp and calling for a kiss. "I'm Wanda, and this is my husband, Leo—of Storgman and Storgman Investigations."

Ryan took her up on the smooch across the knuckles. "Always a pleasure to meet a fellow investigator, ma'am."

Leo rolled his eyes. "We're not the same *sort* of investigator."

"Yeah, I know—but it's *kind of* the same. Me and my team, we investigate old murders and deaths—we investigate the other *side*, man."

Leo wasn't having it. "Yeah, well. We investigate fresher mysteries. Real ones."

"Is that what you're doing on this boat? Investigating a fresh murder or death?"

"Stop saying that. You sound like an idiot."

Wanda shot her husband one kind of look and gave Ryan another look entirely—half benevolent mom who wanted to pat his head, and half cougar who wanted to slap his ass. "Nothing so exciting as a murder, I'm afraid. There was an accident, and a young woman died. We're here at the insurance company's request. But what about you? Who were you hoping to contact in our suite?"

Ryan hunkered down against the seat back, crossing his arms and lowering his voice. "Okay, so like, a *bunch* of people have died on board this boat. It's practically *cursed*, man. But supposably a man who committed suicide back in the eighties was staying in room thirteen."

"You just said 'supposably.'"

"Yeah, because nobody knows for sure. We can't find any hard records about it, because of maritime law, or something."

Leo pinched the bridge of his nose and rubbed it like it hurt him. "That is definitely not the reason you can't find records."

Defensively, Ryan said, "Look, man—we've got records on nine different ghosts. We've already reached two or three of them with our equipment, and there must be at *least* a dozen more on board. Just because we don't have all the details on this one suicide, that doesn't mean he isn't there."

"Your logic is flawless."

"I'm pretty good at logic."

"Oh, for fuck's sake. . . ."

"Leo, stop it. Now, Ryan, do you know the name of the man who died in our suite?"

"It's Ted. Or Fred. Or maybe Alexander."

"You're covering quite a spread there, kid." Leo looked around for the waiter and didn't see him.

"The art of investigation is a little imprecise, sometimes. As you well know, sir. Unless you're new to investigating . . ."

"Listen here, you—"

"Leo."

The waiter hovered into his peripheral vision, a tray full of food balanced on one hand and a pitcher of water in the other. Leo focused on the food. He took a deep breath and let it out slow. "I was a cop in New York for longer than you've been alive. Now I'm retired from that, and I do this, instead."

"We do this." Wanda beamed.

"We do this." He collected his roll of silverware from the napkin and dropped the cloth into his lap. "Now, if you'll excuse us, I believe our breakfast is arriving."

"Don't be ridiculous. Ryan, honey—have you eaten yet?"

"No, ma'am, I was just going to hit the breakfast bar."

"Of course you were. Enjoy your salmonella, kid."

Ryan frowned. "I don't think there's any fish on the bar. Not for breakfast."

Wanda smushed her lips together. She collected herself and said, "Go on and make yourself a plate, then pull up a seat. We'd love to have you join us."

"Thank you, ma'am—if it's all right with you, sir," he said, but did not wait for confirmation. "I'd love the opportunity to learn from your experience." Then he darted off for the bar, Wanda's eyes on his backside all the way.

The waiter delivered the food, and while he was there, he offered to refresh the coffee and mimosa. Leo added a boiler-maker to his order, because screw it. It was that kind of day already. "Why," he half asked, half accused. "Why would you do that."

"Oh, come on. Give him a break. He's sweet."

"This is our honeymoon, and he's young enough to be your . . ."

"Watch it, dear."

". . . your son. But only barely. Maybe . . . your prom baby."

"Better." She smiled.

"But he's about as dumb as a garden gnome."

"He could learn a lot from you."

"That's not why you invited him to breakfast."

"No," she agreed. "He's easy on the eyes, and so damn eager. It's adorable."

"It's shameful, you acting like this. On our *honeymoon*."

"Our *real* honeymoon was two years ago—and it was the greatest week of my life, in the greatest city in the world . . ." she said dreamily. "But I'm not dead, and I can look. *You* look, all the time."

"I do not."

"What about that cruise director? Leggy blonde, with the *Gone With the Wind* accent?"

He shoveled a mouthful of omelet into his face to buy himself time. It didn't buy him long enough. She still expected an answer. "Caitlyn somebody. Nice girl."

"You flirted with her. *Shamelessly.* Speaking of shame."

"I was trying to get us the upgrade, and it worked, didn't it . . . ?"

"That was very nice of her, to humor a dirty old man."

"It was nice of you to go along with the story. You really sold it like a champ—just two happy newlyweds . . . who'd never been able to take a proper honeymoon . . . and it would sure mean the *world* to us if we could have that suite. You had her hook, line, and sinker. You'd have made one hell of a DEA agent. Or a grifter."

"You think so?"

He nodded like his life depended on it. "You're great at everything you try, and you're the love of my life, and I will remain faithful to you until my dying breath."

"Good." She leaned over and took one of his cheeks in hand, then lovingly kissed the other. "Now, be nice. He's coming back."

Leo mumbled something unintelligible, but he accepted the smooch—and then he accepted the boilermaker, which arrived right on cue.

Ryan dropped his plate onto the table and turned the chair around so it faced the right direction. He sat down and unrolled his silverware. "Thank you so much for being so cool about all this. Man, I hate to think if we'd had the right key . . . holy shit, man. *I* could be the newest ghost on board the *Natchez*!"

"The cruise ain't over yet," Leo muttered. Upon receipt of Wanda's withering warning smirk, he added, "But . . . I'm glad no one was hurt."

"Me too, man. Me too. This boat's afterlife is getting pretty crowded."

After a round or two of chitchat and enough breakfast (and booze) to wake everyone up, Ryan asked for a few specifics about their case. Leo had already told Wanda that this wasn't a secret mission, and she was ready to share.

"There was a lounge singer named Misty Sighs," she began, as if she was setting up an episode of *Dateline*.

"Her name was Amanda Simpson," Leo corrected.

"Her *stage name* was Misty Sighs. She'd been on board for several months, singing backup for other acts—and she finally got a chance at the front microphone on the *Natchez's* last trip down the river. She was a big hit with the passengers, and she was terribly excited about the gig. She told her sister that this might be her big break."

Ryan stopped eating and leaned forward on his elbows. "And then . . . ?"

"And then, *tragically*, one morning she was found dead on the texas deck. It was wet, and she'd slipped. Hit her head. Open-and-shut case, except for the insurance company's payout to her family."

Leo explained, "They're trying to decide how little they can get away with. If the fall was caused by the boat or somebody on it, then the family can sue for a bundle. If it was Misty's own fault, it won't do them any good to try . . . if anyone bothers."

"I thought you were on your honeymoon? This sounds more like a working vacation."

Leo took a finishing gulp of his drink, then waved the glass in the direction of their waiter. *One more,* he signaled with a finger. "It's our *second* honeymoon."

"Oh . . . got it." He held his orange juice aloft. "Well, I say you should take as many honeymoons as you can get!"

Wanda held her second mimosa aloft and said, "I'll toast to that!"

3.

After breakfast, Leo and Wanda got to work. Or Leo got to work, the moment he saw the cruise director, Caitlyn Beaumont. She was reading from a clipboard and checking her phone for messages. She fretted prettily and probably swore with asterisks as she texted somebody back. (She struck Leo as the kind of girl who didn't put any vowels in her four-letter words, just in case the Good Lord was watching.)

The clipboard made a lousy texting platform, and she dropped it with a clatter.

Leo picked it up with a smile and handed it back.

She jumped, collected the clipboard, and tried not to look at his horns. He didn't take it personal. Everybody tried not to look, and if she wanted to not look, she was welcome to. "Oh! Um, thank you."

"Looks like you're having a busy morning." Wanda eyed the crates.

"Not the good kind, I'm afraid. Someone left this delivery on the deck, but I can't find anyone to move it, or anyplace else to put it." She sighed, tossed her hair prettily, and summoned her best professional Zen. "But that's not important. What can I do for you two today? I hope the honeymoon suite is up to snuff."

Leo assured her, "It's perfect, just perfect. Except for the unexpected visitors this morning, but that was nothing we couldn't handle."

"Unexpected visitors?" She frowned, and her frown said that this was definitely a problem, and it definitely needed addressing. "Sir, are you being harassed? Is it because of . . . of . . ." She used her cell phone to gesture at the sides of his head.

Wanda sighed. "No, Ms. Beaumont. Nothing like that. Everyone has been very pleasant, and no one has pointed out that my dear husband has those enormous horns above his ears."

"They're not *that* big," he insisted, not quite blushing beneath the light hue of his exposed forehead. He'd forgotten his hat. It was probably just a hint of sunburn.

"They're a good size," Wanda persisted. Then with a wicked grin, she added, "I like to grab 'em when I ride his face."

Caitlyn's face went the color of beets. "I'm sure . . . I mean . . ."

"Please forgive my wife—she thinks she's funny. Listen," he added as fast as he could. "We're pulling together a file for the Misty Sighs case, and I wanted to ask you a couple of follow-up questions."

"Oh. All right, I guess that would be . . . that's fine."

"Good, good." He pulled out a notebook and a pen. He checked the last page of notes and dove right in. "We've got the facts from the insurance statement, but there were a few things they couldn't tell us. For example, was Misty suffering from any medical conditions?"

"Not that I'm aware of."

"Did she have any recent injuries, fits, or seizures?"

"If she did, she didn't tell anybody," she said carefully.

Wanda wanted to take it a different direction. She leaned forward and asked softly, conspiratorially: "Was there any tension between her and the other girls in the show?"

Caitlyn rolled her eyes a little. "Probably. She wasn't the world's most reliable coworker. Or employee, either. She was young and pretty, and as far as she knew, that was all she needed to get by. She had a bad habit of missing shifts, and a worse habit of doing a crappy job when she *did* show up. But she was popular with the guests, and she had a friend in one of the pilots. Kitty kept asking me to cut her slack."

"Kitty?"

"Kitty Strobe. She's a junior pilot. Kind of new here. I don't know her very well . . . I don't think anybody does—she's not the outgoing type. But she got along with Misty. She's working a shift right now, but she'll be out and about this evening. However . . ." She twisted her lips like she had something distasteful to say.

"What is it?" he asked.

"Kitty's kind of funny about . . . people like you."

Leo barked a little laugh. "Don't worry, I'm used to it."

"I just hate the idea of anyone being rude."

"He's used to that, too." Wanda cocked her head. "Miss Beaumont, did Misty have a boyfriend?"

"Um . . . I'm not sure if she—"

"Girlfriend?"

"No, I don't mean it like that," Caitlyn said. "Of course she got phone numbers and love notes, but I think she had something going on with Benny Criggs."

A sturdy, middle-aged black woman was walking briskly past—but she paused and touched Leo on the arm. "I'm sorry, but are you asking about Misty?"

Caitlyn nodded and said, "These are the investigators from the insurance company. Mr. and Mrs. Storgman, this is JoHanna Potts. She's our head clerk."

She swung her head from side to side, like the whole thing was just a terrible goddamn shame. "I hope her family doesn't come after us. It's nobody's fault. Just a freak accident, is all."

Wanda nodded. "It certainly sounds like it. Did you know Misty?"

"I don't often get to know the entertainers. They come and go, and I have other business to attend. But I *did* notice her. Mostly because of that boy, Benny Criggs. She *wasn't* dating him."

Caitlyn put her phone in a pocket and tucked the clipboard under her arm. "I thought they were an item."

"Only in his dreams. He followed that girl around like a puppy." JoHanna shook her head, and shook it hard. "It was weird."

Wanda was visibly delighted by this hint of the sinister. "Where is he now?"

Caitlyn supplied, "I think he quit, the day Misty died."

Leo nodded along to his notes and looked up again. "Miss Beaumont, I don't suppose you have any contact information for this kid's family, or a fixed address other than the boat?"

"He came here from Louisville, but I don't know if he went back there. I'll look up the address for you, if you'll give me a little time. I think he had a roommate."

"Take all the time you need, sweetheart." Then to JoHanna he said, "Thank you, Ms. Potts. I'll make a few phone calls and see if I can't track him down."

"You don't think he had something to do with her death?"

"Nah, probably not. But it's our job to be thorough."

Wanda more or less agreed. "Assuming it *was* an accident . . . the more details we can fill in, the better. Thank you both so much for your time." She flashed Caitlyn a thousand-watt smile and put her arm on Leo's waist. "Come on, dear. Let's go make those phone calls."

Leo let her lead him away, but over his shoulder he said, "I'll look you up again later, about that address. Or you could look me up. We're in—"

"The honeymoon suite. Yes, sir, I remember."

Within an hour, Caitlyn had slipped contact information for Benny Criggs under the door of room thirteen, where Wanda and Leo didn't immediately notice it. They were too busy peeling off some of Wanda's second-honeymoon lingerie and giggling like high schoolers.

"Again? Really? I didn't see any blue pills in your luggage . . ."

"*You're* the one who started this round. And who needs pills when you're wearing *that*?" Something black and lacy shot across the room like a rubber band.

They found the slip of paper about thirty minutes later.

Wanda took a shower, and Leo sat around to make those phone calls at last. Before long, he learned that Benjamin

Andrew Criggs had indeed gotten off the boat when Misty died, on the boat's previous run up the river. Last the roommate heard, he'd gotten a job in a bar, somewhere conveniently close to Vicksburg—a place called Lamar's.

Leo thanked the former roommate and hung up. To Wanda he said, "It's not too far from the water, so he might be close enough to ask in person."

She emerged from the bathroom with her hair in a towel. "He's still nearby? That's interesting."

"Not really. If—for the sake of argument—he had anything to do with her death, he probably would've run farther."

"One would think. *But . . .*" She gave Leo a few seconds to shut her down. When he didn't, she kept going. "If it wasn't an accident . . . he might stick around and watch, to see if there's any suspicion."

"Eh. I doubt it."

"Can we look into him as a suspect?"

Leo closed his notebook and put his phone in his pocket. "We'll check him out for a person of interest, as a matter of due diligence. But first, we'll finish our insurance company homework. We still need to take some measurements and get some pictures."

4.

All the photos, measurements, and report-taking were eventually squared away, so Leo and Wanda retreated to a pair of lounge chairs on the boiler deck. Wanda wore an oversized hat and idly read a paperback. Leo had one beer and started snoring.

Meanwhile, the sky went orange across the river, fading to lavender from west to east. Most of the happy, lazy passengers on deck retreated to their rooms for a more formal nap than the one Leo enjoyed, or else they wandered into the Grand Saloon for some cooler air to go along with the evening meal.

Wanda wanted to join them. She nudged Leo awake with her book, then tweaked the newsboy cap he'd pulled down low across his eyes. "Wake up, sleepyhead."

He didn't raise his eyes or move the hat. "Why?"

"I'm getting hungry. Also, there's a magic show inside. I'd like to see it."

But Wanda's timing was off. Supper service didn't begin for another half hour, and the show would start another thirty minutes after that.

"Got any other ideas?" Leo asked her, thinking fondly of his Leo-shaped dent in the lounge chair.

Her eyes narrowed, and the corner of her mouth tipped up. "Well, over there—isn't that Kitty Strobe?"

He squinted in the direction where she pointed. "Yeah, that's her. Junior pilot, right?"

They'd looked her up in the staff book. She was a petite, intense-looking woman no older than Caitlyn. Her hair was light brown—almost ginger—and she wore dark sunglasses that were big enough to make her face look tiny. She strolled at a hasty pace along the boiler deck. She moved like a woman who had someplace to be, but that didn't stop Leo from getting in her way.

"Excuse me, Miss Strobe?"

She did a double take and stopped. "I'm sorry, yes?" The corner of her nose rose in an understated—but quite revolted—sneer, lifting the edge of her lip as she eyed Leo's horns. She stepped back as far away from him as she could, planting herself against the wall.

"Didn't mean to startle you," he said with a cooly apologetic bob of his head. He introduced himself and Wanda but didn't try to shake the pilot's hand. "We're working on behalf of the *Natchez*'s insurance company, looking into the death of Misty Sighs."

Her eyebrows lifted above the rim of the sunglasses. "Oh my. Yes. Misty . . . that was . . ." She hugged herself, tugging at the sweater she wore over a long-sleeved blouse. "Awful. It was just awful."

Wanda nodded agreeably, before cutting loose a sneeze that took everyone by surprise. "Excuse me!" she exclaimed. Then she took over the questions, and Leo didn't mind. She'd probably get further than he would. "I beg your pardon, Miss Strobe, but Caitlyn Beaumont said that you and Misty had become good friends."

"Well, that's true. I really adored her, and I'm just heartsick, now that she's gone."

"How long did you two know one another?" she asked.

"Not very long, in the scheme of things. I only came on board a few months ago—so I'm new here, and to be honest, I don't have many friends here. The guys are tough on me, you know? Some of them aren't too accustomed to having a woman in charge . . . or in the pilothouse, period. But Misty was sweet. We used to get drinks on the deck after our shifts, sometimes. We were both a little artsy, so we'd do this thing." She laughed awkwardly. "We called it 'Drink and Draw.' I miss it. I miss *her*."

"I'm very sorry for your loss," Wanda told her. She snuffled, then fished around in her bag for some tissues. "Sorry, I don't know what's come over me. But I was wondering, could you tell us about the night she died? Where were you? Did you see her, up on the texas deck? Was she alone?"

She faltered. "I don't . . . I don't know if I should say. After all, everyone says it was an accident. It doesn't matter now."

"If that's the case," Wanda said around a Kleenex, "then there's no harm in sharing."

Reluctantly, Kitty agreed. "I suppose not. It's just that . . . last time I saw her, she was fighting with Caitlyn in the Bayou Lounge."

"*Do tell*," she pushed.

"Caitlyn was really giving her a hard time. She'd showed up for a shift hungover or something, and she'd barely made it through her number. Benny was trying to run interference, but mostly getting in the way . . . and I remember thinking, 'That's it, I bet. Tonight's the night Caitlyn finally snaps and fires her.'"

"I hear you'd tried to cover for her, or vouch for her in the past."

"Sure, of course I did. She did love the bottomless margaritas, and maybe she wasn't always the most reliable person . . . but she was my friend."

Wanda muttered something sympathetic and wiped her nose, and Leo thanked Kitty for her time. She took off toward the stairs and ducked inside them with a fresh tissue waving.

Leo cringed as Wanda blew her nose like a foghorn. "What's gotten into you?"

"Allergies?" she guessed.

"She's not a real fucking kitty, honey."

She sighed. "I know, I know. It must be that ocelot-looking girl, or the illusionist. I think he's her boyfriend. Something about her fur, or his tail—I don't know. I saw them on the deck a few minutes ago; maybe they shed. I'll take some decongestant when we get back to the room."

"Good idea," he agreed. "Now let's find Caitlyn and see what she has to say about that night in the lounge."

Caitlyn Beaumont could be found at the other end of the boiler deck, supervising a cleanup of the shuffleboard area. She fussed about a broad spill of shrimp cocktail from a shattered bowl and pointed a cleaning crew member with a mop toward a stray splash. "Good Lord, what a mess. There's a little bit of glass over there, too—don't miss it."

Leo launched into his charm offensive. "Miss Beaumont, I hate to interrupt, but could we just ask you a couple more follow-up questions about Misty?"

Her professional friendliness darkened; but whatever shadow had passed across her face, she pushed it away in an instant. "I'm in the middle of something right now, Mr. Storgman, but—"

"I promise we'll be brief," Wanda assured her.

"But we have to do our jobs." Leo whipped out his notebook and reviewed a few lines. "Now, you didn't mention—when last we talked—that you and Misty had a loud . . . let's call it a disagreement, on the night she died."

"Oh, for heaven's sake. No, I wasn't happy with her . . . but I told you that. Who said we got in a fight?"

"Not important." He waved it away. "Is it true?"

She hugged her ever-present clipboard. "Misty was a terrible employee, and yes, I yelled at her. I told her that if she couldn't get her act together, she was fired. She did some yelling, too, and it might've looked like a fight. Benny kept getting in the way. I halfway wanted to fire him, too."

Wanda frowned. "But you said she was popular with the guests."

"Pretty girls who can sing are a dime a dozen. She wouldn't have been that hard to replace. That night, Misty showed up late and tried to use one of Roger Ravenstone's mini-shows out on the boiler deck as an excuse. Like she hadn't seen the whole thing on stage, a million times already. Then her set was just plain awful, and she tried to skip out early. I gave her the ultimatum, and she left in a huff . . . with Benny chasing after her, a minute or two later."

"Where did they go?"

"Back to the bar, I assume. Except, maybe not. That night . . . hm." She nibbled her lower lip. "She said Mickey was bothering her, and that's why she wanted to leave early: to avoid him."

Leo looked up from his notes-in-progress. "Mickey?"

"Michael Payne. He's the mud clerk, under JoHanna. Skinny white guy, about my age. Unfortunate tattoos."

Something about the way she said his name suggested that she didn't think too highly of him. "Yeah? What's he like?"

She hesitated. "I don't like to use the word *redneck* because it isn't kind . . . but that's how he strikes me. He asked Misty out awhile back, and she blew him off. From the sounds of things, he couldn't take no for an answer. I don't think he'd actually hurt her, or anybody else, but . . . I did see him in the lounge that night."

"When she left, did Mickey follow her, too?" he asked.

She thought about it. "I don't remember seeing him after she was gone, so maybe he did. Maybe he didn't. I wouldn't swear to it, either way."

"Any thoughts about where we might find Mickey now?"

"I'm sorry, but I don't know if he's working or not. Oh, that reminds me—did you catch up with Kitty?"

"Yes," he said. "We caught her earlier."

"*Please* tell me she wasn't rude," she begged. "She's entitled to her hang-ups, of course—but she doesn't usually interact with the passengers. It's not usually a problem."

"Nah, she was fine. Don't worry about it, Miss Beaumont," he said graciously. "And thanks again for your time."

Leo and Wanda left her to the last runny drips and tiny shards of the shrimp cocktail explosion and walked back toward the Grand Saloon. Wanda pulled her husband in close by the arm. "This is starting to get good."

"No it isn't. A girl either died by accident, or someone killed her. Neither of those things is good."

"You know what I mean."

"Yeah, I do." He put an arm around her waist. "You meant it was getting interesting. I'm not sure if that's true, either, but this is good practice for you."

"You think I need practice?"

"I should've said . . . good *experience* for you. I told you already, you're a natural."

She grinned. "That was a very good save. Ooh!" she declared, catching a glimpse of Leo's least favorite person on board, strolling manfully around the corner. "Let's go see what the ghost hunters are doing!"

"Let's not, and say we did."

"Don't be a grump. They're doing such *intriguing* work . . ."

"No, they aren't." But he let himself be dragged in their wake anyway, until everyone caught up together at the prow of the boat—where the sun was setting fast. There, the *Dead Report* crew was all set up and ready to do whatever the hell it was they did with all that fancy equipment.

"Wanda, *really.*"

"Shhh," she said, adding an elbow for emphasis. "They're working."

Ryan Forge struck a pose at the frontmost end of the boat, like a goth bodybuilder's version of that scene from *Titanic*. His cousin held a boom mike. His brother held a camera. He turned slowly, the spikes in his blue-black hair immobile even in the river breeze, and fixed that camera with a stare so hot it could pop a balloon.

"*Tonight*, we continue our 'Death on the Water' investigation aboard the *Natchez*—the most haunted mobile object in the history of North America or probably *anyplace*."

Kevin whispered, "What about that train we did in season two . . . ?"

But Ryan shrugged it off. "Okay, that train was pretty haunted. But this is *definitely* the most haunted mobile object that moves on the *water*."

Leo opened his mouth. Wanda's glare shut it again.

"Last night, we successfully communicated with Debbie Canfield, a greeting card saleswoman from Raleigh who was found dead in her room, back in 1994. We honor her, and we thank her for taking the time to whisper her message into the audio recorder. *Sympathies*, that's what she said." He looked aside at Sean, and said in a less bombastic voice, "We'll play the clip of that, once we get the sound file cleaned up." Sean nodded. Ryan nodded back, and returned his manly gaze of earnest intensity to the camera. "*Sympathies*, and *best wishes*. We send sympathies and best wishes to you, too, Debbie. Rest in peace, ma'am."

Leo sucked in his breath.

"Calm your tits," Wanda commanded through her teeth.

"They're calm as a coma."

"Keep it that way."

Ryan stalked slowly to the right, and the camera followed him. "But tonight we're on the lookout for a man named Harvey

Schneider, who threw himself overboard from this very spot, so as to kill himself, one tragic night in 1966. His wife had left him, his boss had fired him, and his dog had died. He had nothing left to live for. So he took a bottle from the bar, finished most of it, and climbed the rail." Here, he patted the rail for emphasis. "He closed his eyes. He stood here, with his feet on the bars and the wind on his face . . ." With his back to the river, he tried to do likewise. He got as far as one foot up, and the other foot slipping around on the deck, before he changed his mind and merely struck a resigned, pensive pose with his eyes shut and his nose in the air. "And he gave up on life." Ryan exhaled heavily and put his hands on his hips.

"That's a good spot for a break, isn't it?" asked his brother, dipping the camera to the side.

"Sure, sure. We'll cut there and run the forty-five-second ShockSnack promo, then we'll pick back up in his room."

"Which room was that?"

Sean answered for him. "Number eighteen. We've got the right room this time, and the cruise director swore to God there's nobody inside. Number thirteen was just a mix-up. Something about somebody's shit handwriting."

Wanda giggled loud enough for Ryan to finally notice her. "Mrs. Storgman!"

"Hello again, boys—and I do hope we're not interrupting your *fascinating* work," she said, laying on the bullshit a little thicker than was strictly necessary, in Leo's opinion.

Sean lowered the boom mike, and Kevin set down his camera.

Ryan came over and shook his head. "Nah, we were just cutting away for a commercial break."

"For . . . ShockSnack?" Leo asked, unsure if he'd heard correctly.

"ShockSnack! The thousand-volt energy bar!" he explained in his best advertising voice. "They're our primary sponsor. What can we do for you?" he asked, reaching in to give Wanda's hand its now-customary smooch of greeting.

"I've been thinking . . ." She accepted the kiss and batted her eyelashes so hard they could put out a brush fire. "You hunt ghosts, and we are looking into a girl's death. Do you think there's any chance you could use your equipment to help us reach her?"

Ryan crossed his bulky, tattooed arms and then fondled his chin with one hand. "Maybe," he said thoughtfully. "It depends on if she stayed, or if she crossed over."

"Crossed over to where?" Leo asked with great pessimism.

"To the other side," Sean replied in a similar tone. He might've been a surfer king who smelled faintly of Corona Light, but the look in his eye said that never mind the razzle-dazzle—he was just along for the ride. Maybe the whole gang wasn't as dumb as their front man made them look.

Ryan didn't notice. "But if she's still here . . . we might be able to get her talking. What can you tell us about her?"

Wanda reminded him of the basics and told him about how Misty had been found on the texas deck.

"That is just fucking tragic," Ryan declared with a sad, slow swing of his head. "Sure, I'm game. Let's go see if we can reach her."

Since the texas deck was off-limits to everyone but the crew, the ghost hunters texted Caitlyn Beaumont for permission to proceed. She pinged them back immediately with a yellow thumbs-up, so they all trekked up there to stare at the patch of bare flooring. It had been scrubbed a number of times since the unfortunate death of Misty Sighs.

"I think I can see a stain, right there," Ryan said.

"There's no stain," Leo argued. "Even if there was, you couldn't see it. She died weeks ago." The light was still out. The deck was heavily shadowed with what Ryan no doubt considered excellent mood lighting.

Kevin agreed with his brother. "Naw, man. It's right there. It's like, in the shape of her body. There's a darker bit over here, where her head must've been. Was there a lot of blood?"

"You're both insane."

But Wanda played along. "Ooh, I think you're right. It is a little darker over here. I bet there *was* a lot of blood. You can't just get that out with . . . with plain old bleach, or cold water." She winked to let Leo see the little twinkle in her eye. "That poor girl. On the one hand, I hope she rests in peace. On the other . . . dear boys, I would *deeply* appreciate it if you could help."

"Sean, get the mike up and the mixing software loaded. Kevin, cue up the camera and give us some light."

Sean got down on one knee and opened up the case that held their laptop. "Are you sure about this?"

"Yeah, I'm sure. If we get anything, we'll work it into the show."

"All right, Ryan. It's your call."

"And I already *made* it," he said firmly, like this resolved everything—including any and all gambling debts, breaches of contract, or conflicts in the Middle East.

Ten minutes later, Leo was trying not to punch Sean Venters, who was worming a microphone line up his shirt and attaching it to his collar. "Here, man. Just like this. Sorry. Don't mean to get personal."

"I don't know why you won't put Wanda on camera, instead of me."

"She refused. She said you'd do it."

"I bet she did." He squirmed when Sean's hands fiddled with the small foam nubbie at his neck.

"Almost done. Here, it clips on like this. Don't worry. You're going to look awesome on camera. Your horns are totally badass."

"Thanks. I grew them myself."

Sean grinned, patted the mike, and tested it quickly. "Don't let Ryan and Kev rattle you. They're true believers, that's all. And don't forget, all our shows are backed up to the TV website. So if you're an asshole on camera for five seconds, you're an asshole on the internet until the end of time. Or until the grid goes down in the zombie apocalypse."

"Cheery outlook you've got there, kid."

"Hey, you spend enough time looking up murders and sanitariums and wars and shit, and you'll get pretty cheery, too."

"I was a homicide cop."

Sean paused, and then bobbed his head full of sun-kissed curls. "So that's why *you're* such a cheery fucker."

"Damn right."

Ryan arrived, and Sean stepped back to retrieve the mike. He hitched it to his rig and let it ride high above the scene. Kevin took a step back, adjusted the light from the camera, and signaled that he was ready.

"Three . . . two . . ." He bobbed his chin at Kevin to stand in for the count of "one." "I'm standing here with investigator Leo Storgman. Mr. Storgman, what can you tell us about the Misty Sighs case?"

Leo cleared his throat, wiped a smear of sweat from his forehead with the back of his hand, and squinted into the lens. "She died on the last run of the *Natchez*, on the deck right here."

"On this very spot?"

"Almost exactly—she died at the Vicksburg stop. She was a singer, part of the entertainment crew. One night the deck was wet; somebody'd been mopping, it wasn't the weather. She slipped in the mop water, fell and hit her head, and that was it. She was twenty-two years old, unmarried, born in Indianapolis. Left behind a pair of grieving parents and an older sister."

Ryan chuckled. To the camera he said, "Our friend here is a retired cop, and it shows." Back to Leo, he asked, "Is there any question, then, that she might have been murdered, or otherwise killed?"

"We have . . ." Leo looked over at his wife, who shot him the thumbs-up with both barrels. He looked at Ryan Forge, the true believer and ShockSnack spokesbro, and he sighed. "We have questions. That's why we're trying to reach her . . . her spirit . . . I guess."

"That's why you need our *help*," Ryan said with that same level of intense seriousness he used for everything from movie reviews to mass casualties.

Leo gave up entirely. "Yeah. That's why we need your help."

Ryan tossed his head at Kevin and said, "Cut—that's a wrap for now."

"For now?" Wanda asked. "I thought we were going ghost hunting."

"Oh, we are," Ryan promised. "This was just the pulmonary footage, to set up the investigation."

"Pulmonary . . ."

"You know, the stuff we shoot first."

"Preliminary?" Leo guessed.

Ryan was already walking away. "Business can wait for another hour, right?"

"I suppose . . . ?" Wanda offered, though she sounded confused.

"Cool, because they're about to serve dinner in the Grand Saloon, and after that, I hear there's a magic show. Come on, and sit with us. It'll be a blast!" Then he declared as he wandered off, "I fucking *love* magic shows."

5.

Things were hopping in the Bayou Lounge, and the Amazing Ravenstone and the Jokertown Boys were killing it.

Wanda liked the talking bird, though Leo was a little suspicious of it. (As a general rule, he was suspicious of anything that could talk without moving its lips. Much less anything that could talk without any lips at all.) But Ravenstone had a set of horns, albeit smaller than his own, and Leo felt a tug of solidarity with the jokers onstage. That friendly tug was replaced with a pang of primal concern when the raven flapped over to his table, fixed him with a beady-eyed stare, and said—plain as day—"*Who sees in the dark?*"

Leo gave the Ravenstone a puzzled frown, and the magician gave it back. "Lenore?" he called the bird.

She replied, *"In the dark!"*

"Lenore, my dear . . ." He held out his arm.

The bird cocked its head back and forth, then hopped up and flew back to her handler's extended wrist. People clapped a little uncertainly. The magician played it off with a flourish and returned to the setup for his next trick.

Leo wasn't much interested in whatever the next one might be. The old detective was distracted, and getting fussy.

This whole ghost-hunting business was utter nonsense, and he was annoyed that Wanda had glommed on to the handsome hunters. They couldn't possibly be any help, because there was no such thing as ghosts. There shouldn't be any such thing as talking birds, either, and he didn't *fucking love magic shows* like the bulky moron seated to his left.

"Excuse me a minute," he finally said. He rose to his feet and pushed his chair under the table.

"Leo?"

"I just want some air."

He pretended to walk toward the public restrooms, but passed them and headed back out to the boiler deck instead. He sighed in a deep breath of overly warm air that smelled like river water and seagull shit, and sighed out a gust that smelled like the two drinks he'd downed during the show.

He leaned forward against the rail.

The night sky was blue and very dark against the city lights of Vicksburg, sparkling along the shore and beyond it. The mighty Mississippi slapped softly against the boat's hull. Laughter and cheers rose up from the Bayou Lounge, where his wife was probably enjoying some filthy thoughts about a man young enough to be her grandson.

Something about that damn bird stuck in his head.

Who sees in the dark? A nonsensical message from an avian

brain the size of a caper, that's all. Not a clue. Not a sign. Just a glitch in a magic show.

He thought about it anyway. He wondered what the answer was, if there even was one.

A rousing cheer and a cheerful thunder of applause rose up from the Bayou Lounge, so the magic show was probably over. The audience was probably finishing up drinks and wandering up and out to the decks to watch the city lights and get crapped on by the occasional bird.

Wanda and the *Dead Report*'s crew spied him and collectively flagged him down. "Honey, where did you go? You missed the big finish."

"I'll pick up the pieces of my shattered life and move on."

"Great! Because we've got our equipment ready to rock!" Ryan Forge declared. "Let's go back up to the texas deck and talk to a ghost."

Caitlyn Beaumont joined them there, making sure the deck remained "employees and other authorized personnel only." Gently, firmly, she helped clear the scene. Then she approached Ryan Forge, her eyes all big and gooey.

"If there's anything else I can do for you, just holler!" she said, and he couldn't tell if she was offering coffee and crowd control, or a quickie in the nearest broom closet.

The camera came on, and with it, the vividly diffused spotlight. Everybody blinked until all eyes had adjusted, and then Ryan launched into his showman's patter. "Here I have my spirit box, a device that uses radio-wave static and a word bank to allow spirits to communicate with us. We'll start with this, and see if we can reach the spirit of this poor lounge singer, this sad, unfortunate girl . . . who met her end one fateful night upon *this very spot*."

He held up the little box, which had the size and complexity of an old Walkman. When he pressed a button, a loud white noise fizzed forth, filling the air with the sound of a million bees. "So let's see if Misty is with us, and if she's willing to talk."

Caitlyn withdrew to the nearest rail and leaned against it, just out of the camera's sight line. She exhaled dreamily in Ryan's direction and clutched her clipboard to her chest.

"Misty Sighs!" he called out to the deck, like he was issuing a warrant for her arrest. "You died on this spot, from what looked like an accident . . . but what might have been a crime that was much, much more sinister in nature. Can you tell us . . . were you murdered, or did you just die?"

Together they listened to the static, for three seconds, four seconds, six seconds. The hum hiccupped and a word coughed through between the stations.

Rutabaga.

Everyone jumped, even Leo. "Did . . . did that thing just say . . . ?"

"Rutabaga!" Ryan announced triumphantly.

Cattle drive.

"Cattle drive!" everyone repeated, like a pep rally cheer.

"These words don't mean anything," Leo complained. "They're fucking nonsense!"

"Shut up, sweetheart."

"Oh come *on*, Wanda. . . ."

Thursday.

"Fuck a bunch of this," he muttered, and turned away from the scene. Whether or not he'd heard a ghost talking before, this was definitely not a ghost talking *now*. That stupid spirit box was probably picking up ambient chatter in the Grand Saloon.

Labradoodle.

Hovering under one of the still-working lights, he spied a skinny white guy in a trucker cap, holding a can of Coke and watching the proceedings. Something about his posture, or maybe the hat, or maybe the way he spit into the soda can . . . it added up to *redneck*, whether Caitlyn Beaumont liked that word or not. And she hadn't chased him away, so that meant he was an employee.

He approached. "Hey, are you Mickey? Mickey Payne?"

The guy looked confused. "Huh?"

"You. Mickey Payne. Yes or no?"

"That's me. Who wants to know?"

Diphthong.

Leo held out his hand, and Mickey shook it uncertainly. "Leo Storgman, of Storgman and Storgman Investigations. I'm here working for the boat's insurance company, looking into the death of Misty Sighs. I understand you knew her?"

He blanched, then said, "Sure. Hang on." Then he took a moment to spit a big gob of tobacco and juice into the can, apparently emptying the contents of his lip. "Sorry. They don't like it when we smoke on board."

"Right. Because chewing tobacco is . . . less disgusting."

"What do you want, man?"

Festoon.

"I hear that Misty was avoiding you."

"So what if she was?"

"So, she's dead."

"Accidentally dead," Mickey said pointedly. "That's what everybody says."

"Sometimes everybody's wrong. Did you creep her out, or what?"

"I *asked* her out, and she said no. I tried again. She said no again. But the third time's the charm, right?"

"More like you can't take a hint. The night she died, she left the Grand Saloon and you followed her." Leo played his guess. "Where did she go?"

Mickey blushed to the brim of his hat. "It wasn't like that. I didn't chase her down or anything, I just wanted to explain myself. I wanted to make sure she knew that I wasn't a jerk, and she didn't have to be afraid of me."

"Yeah, women love that—when you follow them around, after they've told you to get lost. So you went after her, wanting to talk. Then what happened?"

He tossed his sloshing soda can into a trash can a couple of feet away. "I lost her up here on the texas deck. There are always a couple of lights out, okay? But she wasn't alone—I know that for damn sure."

Leo wasn't sure he believed him, but he played along. "Who else was here?"

Squelch.

"She was arguing with somebody—I heard her yelling, and someone else was whispering back. Angry whispering, you know?"

"Who do you think it was?"

Mickey glanced over Leo's shoulder, and apparently didn't see anyone who might give a damn about anything he had to say. Still, he kept his voice down. "I think it might've been my boss."

"Ms. Potts? What was she doing up there?"

"She said she was just picking up after one of the new cleaning crew guys, but when she came back down the stairs, she was acting pretty shifty. She was annoyed when she realized I'd seen her, and she acted like *I* was the one sneaking around. I was just looking for Misty, but by the time anybody found Misty . . ." He made a show of looking sad, hanging his head. "It was too late. Never gonna get that third chance."

"That *does* sound suspicious. Did you say anything about seeing Ms. Potts to anybody, at the time?"

"No way, man. She's my *boss*. But she's been hanging out up there a whole lot after Misty's death, and it's starting to look weird. Besides, everybody said . . ." He looked up at the ghost-hunting crew and watched them wrestle with the spirit box. "Everybody said it was an accident. It had to be an accident."

"What makes you so sure?"

Mickey didn't answer the question. He only said, as he stared off past Leo at the ghost hunters on the boiler deck: "It was *totally* an accident."

6.

Leo spotted Caitlyn at breakfast and waved her over. The bags under her eyes said she hadn't slept terribly well, but she stood up straighter and smiled. "Good morning, Storgmans."

"Good morning, Miss Beaumont, and I have just one last question: Did Misty leave anything on board the boat, or have you returned her personal effects back to her family?"

"I think we've still got a box. I meant to ship it weeks ago, but I've been so busy . . . I just haven't gotten around to it yet."

"Could we take a look at the contents?"

She scrunched up her mouth, like she was looking for an excuse to say no but couldn't come up with one. "I guess that would be all right. Let me finish up here, and I'll have it sent to your room."

Caitlyn was as good as her word. By the time the Storgmans had finished their morning meal and returned to their cabin, a file box was sitting on the bed with a note that wished them a nice day. It also had a smiley face at the end.

"She's cute," Leo mused.

"Fucking adorable," Wanda agreed somewhat less enthusiastically. "So what's inside?"

He lifted the lid and set it beside the box on the bed. "Some clothes . . ." He pulled out several sequined dresses that were each small enough to fit in somebody's purse, three pairs of strappy high heels, and some tiny, lacy pajamas with bunnies on them. There were also some tank tops: one from PETA advertising that she'd rather go naked than wear fur, one from the Talladega Speedway, and one from a vegetarian restaurant called Sluggo's.

Two pairs of cutoff denim shorts that would've barely covered a Barbie's behind.

"What else?"

"Some underwear and the like. A couple of sketchbooks, yeah—look at this. What was it Kitty said? Drink and draw? Check it out." He held up a loosely drawn image of the Amazing Ravenstone. He was out on the boiler deck, entertaining a child with a simple trick involving scarves.

"It really looks like him!"

"Yeah, she had some talent."

Down at the bottom of the box were a few artist's pencils and erasers. There was also a pouch that held tampons, a bottle of mixed pills, and a fistful of receipts. "Anything useful in here . . . ?" Leo refused to wear bifocals and he didn't have his cheaters handy, so he passed some of the receipts to Wanda.

"Mostly supper from the Grand Saloon, and a lot of bottomless margaritas. I mean, a *lot* of them. Looks like she ate at the buffet, but not always. In the evenings, she preferred bar food. Barbecue nachos, buffalo wings, and loaded fries."

"Buffalo wings?" He pointed at the tank tops. "From the PETA princess?"

Wanda looked over at the shirts. "Maybe those were a gift, or a thrift-store find."

"Maybe the food was for somebody else." He spread the receipts out across the bed and put them in chronological order. "This was the last one: several strawberry margaritas, and a couple of bacon Bloody Marys."

"This one's from the night she died. She couldn't have drunk all that by herself."

"Benny might've helped. We know he was around." He pulled another receipt out of the pile. "Check it out: this one's from Lamar's Party Hole. The roommate said he got a job at a place called Lamar's. This must be it."

"'Karaoke and the strongest drinks in town,'" Wanda read

aloud from the bottom of the scrap of paper. "When's that one dated?"

"A week before she died."

"Huh." She reached into the box and pulled out a single flip-flop. She turned it over in her hand and spied something on the bottom, stuck in a glob. When she brought it closer to take a better look, her nose twitched. She rubbed it, then scratched it and set the shoe aside.

"What's that?"

"There's some hair stuck to the bottom. It's making my eyes water."

"Hair, or fur?" He picked it up and inspected it for himself. There was a small clump of fur wedged in a black wad of something that might've once been chewing gum, or possibly tar. It was reddish, and it made him think immediately of Wild Fox's tail. "Maybe you're allergic to foxes."

"Foxes?"

"Isn't that his name? Wild Fox? The other magician."

"I don't think I'm allergic to foxes," she said drolly. "I was fine during the show—"

"From all the way out in the audience," he pointed out.

"Still. That hair could've come from anyplace. Where's the other shoe?"

"Don't see it in here, and that's pretty much everything. What do you say we hit the shore and see if your phone can get us to Lamar's."

Thirty minutes later Leo and Wanda had an Uber driver with green hair, an assortment of eyes that made her face look rather spiderlike, and an encyclopedic knowledge of the greater Vicksburg area. "Been here all my life!" she informed them. "Ask me anything! Civil War? I'll give you casualties, stats, and locales of local battlefield parks. Civic government? I've been on the city council, the education committee, and in parks and rec. Hit me!"

"How far away is Lamar's?" Leo asked.

The driver lifted a finger and said, "Ah! Lamar's Party Hole.

Established 1997 as a karaoke bar, and since evolved into a full-service restaurant and bar, specializing in cuisine that could best be described as soul-food-meets-bar-food. Be sure to try the fried green tomatoes with a special house-made buffalo sauce!"

"How long will it take us to get there?"

"More than five minutes, fewer than ten! It's a popular stop for folks riding the river cruises, close enough to get off the water and back to the boat in no time flat."

The driver was right, and Leo was glad to be out of the vehicle when they pulled up to a tall, narrow building with a big neon sign that featured an anthropomorphic shrimp that was holding a fishing pole. "Have a great time!" the driver called as she drove away, tires squealing in the gravel.

Wanda waved her off, and Leo climbed the short front steps to the door. It opened with the chime of a small gold bell.

Inside, the place was too nice to call a dive bar, and too ratty to mistake for a chain. Fishing nets were strung from corner to corner, and the occasional ship's wheel hung on the bits of wall that weren't occupied by signed photos of minor celebrities and karaoke stars alike. It smelled like fried corn bread, grease, and beer.

They were a little early for lunch, but the hostess offered to seat them.

"No thanks," Leo told her. "We're actually looking for someone: a guy named Benny Criggs. Heard he works here."

She summoned him from the kitchen, from whence he brought a plastic tub. The hostess pointed out Leo and Wanda and ushered him toward them.

Benny put down the tub. "Hi. Um, I'm Benny?"

Leo was about to ask if he was sure, when Wanda held out her hand and quickly said, "Hello, darling. It's a pleasure to meet you. I'm Wanda Storgman and this is my husband, Leo. We're doing a bit of investigation for the insurance company that holds a riverboat called the *Natchez*."

He took her hand and shook it, then scratched at the back

of his neck. "Um . . . I don't work on the *Natchez* anymore. I work here, as a barback. And I bus tables. That kind of thing."

Leo nodded and pulled out his Moleskine. He clicked his pen into the ready position. "But you used to work there. You left when Misty Sighs died, last time the boat passed through here."

"I didn't have anything to do with that," he said fast. "That was an accident, everybody said so."

"Yeah, everybody says so. But we're covering our bases. The night Misty died, you were with her in the Bayou Lounge, while Caitlyn gave her the third degree about being a shitty employee."

He swallowed. "That sounds right."

"Did you follow her, when she left?"

"Yes," he said cautiously. "But only because that guy Mickey Lee was watching her all weird-like. I was trying to look out for her."

"Where did she go?"

"Up to the texas deck. It was dark, though. I lost her. I think Mickey lost her, too. I ran into him, coming back down the other way. He bumped into me, really hard, and told me to fuck off."

Wanda nodded sympathetically. "Leo already talked to him. He didn't mention seeing you, but he mentioned JoHanna Potts. He also heard Misty yelling at someone."

His mouth twisted in confusion. "I saw Ms. Potts, that's true. And I *did* hear Misty talking. I wouldn't say she was yelling, but she sounded drunk and annoyed. Ms. Potts, though . . . she came out of one of the cargo doors, right before the spot where the light was out. I could barely see her, and I don't think she saw me."

"What was she doing up there?"

"Batting clean-up for her nephew. She'd gotten him hired, and he wasn't doing the world's best job, or that's how I heard it. It's not the kind of place she usually had any business, but . . ." He shrugged weakly. "Mickey didn't have any business up there, either. Neither did I." Benny opened his mouth like he wanted to say something else, then stopped himself.

Wanda saw him pause, and gently urged him to continue. "What is it, darling? Is there something you'd like to tell us?"

He looked nervously at Leo, then back to Wanda. "I'm . . . I'm not in any trouble, am I? You're not police?"

"Did you do something wrong?" Leo asked him.

Wanda overrode him. "No, nothing like that. We aren't cops, and you're not in trouble."

"What if I did something that was . . . a *little* wrong? I didn't hurt anybody," he said before anyone could ask. "I just . . ." His voice fell to a whisper. "I found Misty's body, okay? I tripped over her, in the dark. I slipped in her blood, and I . . ." He gulped dryly. "I freaked out! I hollered for help, but I knew she was dead. There was so much blood. I couldn't see it all, but it was all over me, and I had this *moment*, you know? I was on my hands and knees on the deck and I found her sweater. She was holding it in her left hand, so I picked it up, and I . . . I kept it."

"You *kept* it?" Leo stopped writing.

"She must have been carrying it. I panicked, see? I wanted something that belonged to her. God, you must think I'm pathetic."

"It's not pathetic, it's sweet," Wanda cooed. "Oh my, that's why you came to work here, isn't it? You used to come here together."

Miserably, he nodded. "We came here on our first date."

"First date?" Leo asked dubiously.

"Only date," he said, even more sadly. "I miss her so much, that's all. I swear, I'm not some kind of weirdo."

"Keep telling yourself that. Let me see this sweater."

Benny recoiled. "I don't have it here! It's at home, at my new apartment."

"Have you washed it?" Leo demanded.

"I washed it twice, and then I had it dry-cleaned, too. I wasn't trying to cover my tracks, or get rid of any evidence, I swear! But it had this weird orange fur on it, and it made my hands itchy."

Leo's eyes narrowed. He snapped the notebook shut. "Okay. I've heard enough."

Wanda gave him the side-eye. "What? You have?"

"Yup. Get out your phone, and get us a car. Let's go back to the boat."

7.

Wanda walked back up the ramp, onto the *Natchez*. "We could've gotten some lunch first. Lamar's looked like a fun place to eat."

"The food on board is fine." Leo joined her on the deck, and looked toward the Grand Saloon. Lunchtime stragglers were still wandering toward the buffet or picking out tables. "Let's get something here. I bet we can find everybody we need around the buffet, anyway."

"Everyone we need?"

"Yeah, I've got a theory. Let's round up the usual suspects." When she gave him a puzzled frown, he added, "It's just an expression."

"I know, but we left creeper Benny in Vicksburg. Isn't he at the top of the list?"

"No, he's not a suspect anymore. Come on, let's see who we else we can find."

His wife shook her head. "But he stole her sweater and kept it. That's *awfully* suspicious, if you ask me."

"No, he didn't. Take her sweater, I mean." He strolled toward the seating area and stared around, pinpointing persons of interest.

Caitlyn Beaumont came up behind him and tapped him on the shoulder. "Mr. Storgman?"

"Oh! Hi there, Miss Beaumont. Hey, would you do me a favor?"

"Anything you need, just ask."

"Is anyone using the backstage area of the Bayou Lounge?"

"Not right now."

"Good. I want to call a meeting there. Could you scare up the following people, and have them meet us there in fifteen minutes?" He took a napkin and wrote a couple of names. "And don't let any of them leave the boat."

"Sir . . . is there something I should know?" She looked down at the napkin. "I think these people are on shift right now . . ."

"That's why I'm giving you some time to bring them around. Besides, I need to make a phone call before we have this chat. Please, see if you can round them up—and bring your own sweet self, too."

"I'll see what I can do." She walked away, pausing to give Leo a worried look over her shoulder, and kept going.

"Phone call?"

"Vicksburg PD."

Wanda gave every appearance of trying very, very hard not to jump up and down and squeal. "Misty *was* murdered!"

"Quieter, dear. Let's just say she was killed. Maybe manslaughtered, I don't know yet." He pulled out his phone, and as he made for the backstage area, he pulled up a number for the local police.

By the time Leo ducked around the curtain and stage, he had received assurances that a unit was on the way. And by the time he realized they weren't alone backstage, it was too late for him to chase down Caitlyn and suggest a different spot for a meetup.

"Storgmans!" announced Ryan Forge. The other two members of *Dead Report* took up the cheer. "Good to see you again, dude. Seriously."

"Nobody's supposed to be back here right now," Leo grumped.

"Oh, we didn't reserve the space or anything. We just heard rumor of a magician's assistant who drowned on *that very stage,* back in the 1970s. He was doing the Houdini trick with the water tank. *Super* dangerous. He died and *everything.*"

"Have you got any good EVPs?" Wanda asked, suddenly all hip to the lingo.

"Usually we wait until nightfall to shoot for voice recordings," said Sean, who was snacking on a small plate of deli meat and cheese he'd swiped from the buffet. "But our fearless leader thought he saw a spirit back here."

"I *did* see a spirit. I've seen him *several* times. I think he's fucking with me," Ryan complained conspiratorially. "He's an old-fashioned-looking guy, like from the forties or something." Then he added, to the room at large: "And I want him to know that he doesn't scare me!"

"*Who* doesn't scare you?" JoHanna Potts put her head around the curtain.

Leo welcomed her inside the somewhat darkened space, where the buzz of the lunchtime crowd was muffled by the curtains, the boxes, and the equipment. "Come on in, Ms. Potts. You too, Mickey. I see you."

Mickey Lee Payne came in behind her, and then Kitty Strobe, wearing her big round sunglasses. "What are we doing here?" she asked, as if she wasn't sure whether or not to expect a response.

"Good question." Caitlyn brought up the rear. She pulled the curtain back into place behind herself, offering the group a small measure of privacy. "Mr. Storgman? What's going on?"

"We're talking about Misty Sighs," he declared.

"The ghost?" asked Kevin.

"She's not a . . ." Leo didn't swear, but he grumbled with a lot of asterisks. "Never mind. She's dead, that's the thing."

"From an accident!" Caitlyn exclaimed.

"Maybe it was an accident and maybe it wasn't. That's what we're here to talk about. I want you all to help me piece together what happened the night she died."

All three of the *Natchez* employees began to protest, but

Wanda held up her hands. "Everybody, please. Hear him out. We're just trying to finish our report for the insurance company."

Leo nodded approvingly. She'd made a good call, to frame it that way. It'd keep the perp from bolting. He wished he'd thought of it, but slipping back into cop mode had been too easy. He'd forgotten the absence of his trusty badge.

He tried not to watch as Wanda went over to Sean and whispered something in his ear. He nodded and winked at Leo. Leo didn't return the wink. He pulled out his notebook, flipped through a couple of pages, and flipped back again.

He took a deep breath and began. "On the last cruise of the *Natchez*, Amanda Simpson—better known as Misty Sighs—died on the texas deck, right here outside of Vicksburg. We can all agree on that, can't we?"

Everyone nodded, even Ryan Forge—who couldn't have confirmed anything more complex than his birthday.

"On the night she died, Misty left work in the Grand Saloon, and went up to the texas deck, where there was at least one light out. But she didn't go alone. Ms. Potts, you were also on the texas deck that night. Do you want to tell me why?"

Her face went not just blank—but stony. "Not particularly."

"I'll settle for that," Leo said. "What I really want to know is whether or not you heard an argument."

She shifted her weight back and forth, very slightly.

"You've already admitted you were there."

The clerk caved. "Fine, I heard Misty. She was talking real drunk, real loud."

"To whom?" Leo asked.

"I don't know. Somebody who was hushing her, trying to calm her down. I didn't stay to listen. I had my own business to attend to."

Kitty wanted to know, "What business was that?"

She gave in and sighed heavily, and unhappily. "Well, it was Teddy's business. My nephew, on the cleaning crew. I'm not saying he left the mop bucket out there, that night—but I'm not saying he didn't either. Lord, and I went to so much trouble to bring him on board . . . for all the good it did. He got fired for sleeping on the job a couple of weeks later."

Satisfied, Leo let it go. "So here's the big question: Who was Misty arguing with? Anyone could've said it was anybody else. It could've been lovesick Benny, who believed they were truly meant to be—and was totally wrong. It could've been Mickey—who was halfway stalking her. But I don't think it was either one of you."

"No?" Ryan Forge hung on Leo's every word.

When Leo glanced back, he saw Sean sitting beside him—his hand discreetly holding the record button on one of their audio devices. "No," he said, returning his attention to the assembled crewmembers.

"Why not?" asked Sean.

Leo grunted impatiently. "You guys stay out of this." Then he answered the question, regardless. "Because the texas deck was a busy place that night. Ms. Strobe, you were also there."

"What?" she said, too fast for it to sound casual. "No I wasn't."

"Yeah, I think you were. Earlier that evening, you two had been down on the boiler deck, doing your drinking and drawing thing."

"So?"

"You never mentioned it, not when I asked about the night she died."

Ryan Forge made the kind of "ooooooh" noise that a roomful of third graders makes when the teacher gets a kiss from her husband.

"Shut up!" Kitty Strobe said to him, before Leo had the opportunity. "That doesn't mean anything."

"Not by itself, no. But I have a theory."

"You're crazy if you think I had anything to do with Misty's death. I told you, she was my only friend on board this boat. Why would I hurt her?"

Leo sat down on the edge of the stage and faced the dim-lit room. "I don't think you did it on purpose, necessarily. Here's partly what I *know* happened, and partly what I *bet* happened: You and Misty sat on the deck and drew pictures while you drank. Ravenstone was putting on a little show for some kids out there. That's why she was late getting to work," he said to Caitlyn. "Not because she was watching the show, but because she was drawing it." Back to Kitty, he continued, "At some point, while you two were talking . . . your secret came out. Maybe you confessed after a few bacon Bloody Marys. Maybe Misty guessed."

"Secret?" Her voice was tight and high.

"You wanted her to keep quiet about it, and you knew she was a drinker and a blabber. You begged her. Pleaded with her. But she had to get to work while she still had a job so she left you there. After the show, she went up to the texas deck—probably trying to get away from the two dumbass boys who wouldn't leave her alone. You were there, too. You followed her, maybe. Or maybe it was just a coincidence."

"You don't know what you're talking about."

"You'd both been drinking. It was dark and wet, and you had an unfair advantage. Do me a favor, would you? Take off those sunglasses."

"No."

He swung his feet back and forth against the stage. "I won't make you, but the police will. You're getting a mug shot."

At this, she panicked and came forward—rushing him. He almost reached for his gun, but he didn't have it on him and he wouldn't have needed it. It was just a reflex. Christ, she was fast. Way faster than she looked.

She stopped, barely a foot from his face. She whipped the glasses off, revealing a pair of vivid green eyes. "See? They're perfectly normal."

"Or very good theatrical contacts."

She didn't deny the possibility. Shrilly, she protested: "I have a sensitivity to light!"

Leo believed her, sort of. "That might be true, but that's not why you wear the long sleeves and long pants outside when it's hot enough to bake cookies on the lounge chairs. That's not the real reason you wear the sunglasses indoors and everywhere else—though it makes for a neat cover story."

Wanda snuffled. Her nose twitched. She ran her finger back and forth beneath it, trying to defuse a sneeze.

"I think you do it because of the fur. I think Kitty's *not* just a nickname."

"No," she protested, backing away. "That isn't true at all."

"I bet you're a meat eater, like any other cat. I found the receipts from the bar; Misty wasn't the one ordering the barbecue nachos or the bacon Bloody Marys. That was *you.*"

"I like nachos. I like bacon. None of this means anything."

"I bet when you take those contacts out, you can see very, *very* well in the dark. Even when you've been drinking. Even when you're only trying to convince your friend to keep her trap shut. I know you fought with her, so don't pretend you didn't."

"There's no proof. Not a bit of it."

"You sure? What about the sweater you were wearing that night?"

Her face froze. She did not ask, "What sweater?" but she looked like she wanted to.

"Benny has it. He pried it out of her hand, thinking it was hers. But I saw what that kid had in her wardrobe—tiny shorts and tiny shirts and tiny dresses, everything showing skin. Nobody on board covers up in this heat, except for you."

Kitty Strobe retreated a little farther.

Wanda sneezed. Ryan Forge ceremoniously blessed her.

"My wife, over here—" Leo gestured with one hand. "She's got allergies. Benny has them, too. He kept trying to wash the cat hair out of his souvenir."

Kitty looked at the edge of the curtain, which was now functioning as an exit. "You don't understand . . . I can't be a joker. I can't." It was hardly more than a whisper. She tugged at her collar, and the pull of her finger revealed a thin seam of light orange hair.

"But you are," Leo said calmly.

"She was going to tell everyone."

"So what?" Wanda demanded. "What's wrong with being a joker?"

"It's awkward, it's embarrassing, and I am *trying* to be taken seriously as a professional! Even when nobody knew," she said, a touch more calmly. "Even then, the stupid nickname stuck and I couldn't get out from under it—no matter how hard I tried."

He nodded slowly. "I know that feeling. Back at the precinct, before I retired, you know what they called me? Ramsey, or Ramshead. I didn't love it. Honestly, it drove me crazy at first, and then I got over myself. That's the shame here, really. I'm not saying that all the jokers whose cards turned strange have it swell—but you can live with it, and that's what you should've done. You killing Misty . . . that was a hate crime. But you didn't hate *her*. You hated yourself."

The curtain slipped aside, and two uniformed officers joined the party. "Olivia Strobe?" one of them asked.

"She's all yours." He didn't need to point her out. She was already trying to run. "You can call her Kitty."

She got about as far as the end of the stage before the cops brought her down. They picked her up and cuffed her.

"I've got her confession on tape!" Sean announced, trailing after them. "You guys! We've got it on tape! We totally helped!"

Ryan put his hands on his hips and stared into space. "We *did* totally help," he declared, with his great and ridiculous gravitas. "You guys, 'Death on the Water' is going to be our best episode *ever*."

Leo hopped down off the stage. "You know what? I bet it will be. You kids have a good time with that recording, and don't forget to share it with the nice policemen before they leave the boat." Then he put his arm around Wanda and drew her away from the ecstatic young men of *The Dead Report*. "Now come on, baby. Let's go finish this honeymoon."

In the Shadow of
Tall Stacks

Part 5

THE ARREST OF KITTY Strobe caused its own repercussions on the *Natchez*. Wilbur, still trying to understand what Kirby Jackson was insisting that Cottle had to do for him, managed to be in Jackson's stateroom when he and Captain Montaigne were discussing how to replace Kitty. "I can cover her shifts for the next few days," the captain said, "but that's only a stopgap. We have to get another licensed pilot on board ASAP. Preferably have someone brought in before our next stop."

"How cheaply can you do that?" Jackson asked.

Montaigne just glared at the man stonily. "On *my* boat," she answered, "I don't worry about *cheap*, I worry about *good*."

Jackson gave her an aggrieved sigh, then waved his hand. "Fine. Whatever. Just don't offer any kind of long-term contract. The new pilot's job is temporary. It ends once the Tall Stacks festival's over in Cincinnati. You understand?"

"Perfectly," Montaigne told him. "I'll get someone in." She turned and left the stateroom with an audible "*Cheap-ass bastard . . .*" trailing after her.

As the *Natchez* steamed upriver toward its next stop in Memphis (where more of the Kazakhs were scheduled to leave the boat), Wilbur continued to muse on his personal dilemma. He haunted the boiler room, still hoping to learn details about what Jackson expected Cottle to do, but Jackson never again approached Cottle or talked to him, at least as far as Wilbur knew. Cottle was as nervous and OCD about his precious machinery as ever.

He spent time in Jackson's stateroom to see if he could discover what the man was planning, but was ultimately disappointed. The conversations he did catch gave him no optimism. Jackson seemed to be simply enjoying the voyage, rarely talking business with anyone unless they brought up the subject.

He lurked in Captain Montaigne's quarters, hoping to overhear more details. The captain seemed to be as morose and unsettled as Wilbur, talking to JoHanna, to friends, and (especially) to the woman who Wilbur knew was her lover back in New Orleans about what she should do. Could they borrow more money and raise the offer to Jackson? Maybe they could get another mortgage on the house in New Orleans, or just sell it outright. Should she accept the management job that the owners were offering, move to Cincinnati, and remain "captain" of a boat that would never move? Should she just look for an opening on some other river craft, maybe even returning to barge work? But that was as far as things went.

Wilbur didn't talk to Montaigne or even let her know he was listening: while he might grudgingly admit that she was a decent boat's captain, and while she had played along with him with the ICE agents, he also realized that she believed being "friendly" with her crew undermined her authority, and as for Wilbur, despite the fact that Jeremiah had told her he had conversations with Wilbur, it was as if Montaigne still wanted plausible deniability concerning his existence. She was prepared to simply ignore the signs and had no interest in communicating with him normally.

That was fair enough—a certain aloofness was necessary for a captain, and Wilbur had been the same way himself with his crew when alive. She tended to privacy in personal matters; she never talked about her sexual orientation with anyone on the *Natchez*, though it was an open secret. Wilbur understood that choice as well, given the general chauvinistic attitude of most of the crews he'd known in his time.

He would be private with her about his own worries, then.

For that, he went to Jeremiah, who *was* one of the few people among the crew who the captain also confided in. He found Jeremiah writing a letter: using a fountain pen on nice, thick stationery. Jeremiah still used a fountain pen—refillable, not a cartridge. "All them little plastic things just getting thrown away," he'd told Wilbur once. "That's just a plain, sad waste." Unlike most of the crew, Jeremiah didn't own a computer or laptop; he still wrote letters when he wanted to communicate with someone outside, and wrote out checks for his few bills. He did have a cell phone, even if he rarely had it with him, but it was of the ancient, flip-phone variety. Wilbur had never seen him texting anyone with it.

That was fine with Wilbur, who also thought things had largely been better Back Then.

Jeremiah was off duty; Captain Montaigne was up in the pilot house, filling in for Kitty until the new assistant pilot came aboard. Jeremiah's quarters were like the man himself: unassuming, understated, and a little old-fashioned, but everything in it was there for a good reason. The walls were lined with pictures and drawings of riverboats, several of the *Natchez* herself. Jeremiah was drinking a rum and Coke that smelled mostly like rum, the ice tinkling in the glass as he lay down and capped the fountain pen next to the letter.

Wilbur thrust his hand into the wall to draw in steam—he knew exactly where all the steam lines were on the boat. Behind Jeremiah, he allowed himself to become fully visible. "*I* haven't heard anything new from the captain. Any new gossip you've heard?"

Jeremiah started heavily at the sound of Wilbur's voice,

spilling a bit of his drink. He craned his neck over his shoulder. "I don't know about this talkin' thing, Wilbur. It was bad enough when you'd just suddenly show up. Now you got a voice, you can scare the bejesus outta someone. Could you clear your throat or somethin' to let a body know you're there?"

"Sorry," Wilbur told him. "I'll try to remember that. But have you heard anything?"

"Well, the cap'n says she's got a new replacement pilot set to arrive by launch tomorrow. I even heard a' him: guy named Albert Mason, worked mostly on barges but for a few years was the pilot on the *Delta Queen*, so he knows steamboats. Retired a year or so ago. Cap'n must've convinced him to come back. Not like he's gonna be here long, after all."

Wilbur consoled himself with the thought that at least the *Natchez* would be in good hands until that point. "Did the captain say anything else? About the *Natchez*, I mean."

"Nope," Jeremiah said. He took a long swallow of his drink. "Not a word. Far as I know, this'll be my last trip on your old *Natchez*. Maybe my last trip pilotin' ever."

"I . . . no, *we* can't let that happen, Jeremiah."

Jeremiah set the glass down on a coaster. "There's a difference between not *wantin'* somethin' to happen and actually stoppin' it from hap'ning, Wilbur. I don't see how either of us got much chance of the latter. It's the money talkin'. It's *always* the money talkin' for people like that bastard Jackson. Always has been, always will be."

"I'm aware of the importance of money. I've had experience with that."

Jeremiah chuckled slowly. "I guess you have, seein' as you say that's what got you shot." He picked up his glass again, swirling around the ice cubes. He looked with nut-brown eyes trapped in a net of wrinkles at the wispy outline of Wilbur. "If there ain't no steam up anymore, that's gonna really mess with you, ain't it?"

"What if . . ." Wilbur hesitated, wondering if he really wanted to say the next words aloud. *Say a thing out loud, and you make it real. So be careful what you say.* That was something Eleanor sometimes used to tell him. ". . . I killed Jackson?" he finished. "I could do that easily, you know."

Jeremiah set down his whiskey glass on the desk with a sharp *crack*. He took the sheets of the letter he'd been writing and folded them in thirds. "You don't mean that," he told Wilbur as he pulled an envelope from a slot in his desk and placed the sheets inside. "You don't even want to think it."

"Why not? Wouldn't that solve the problem? No one would know how it happened, and even if they did, how are they going to arrest me?"

Jeremiah was already shaking his head. "First of all, it ain't likely to change nothin'. The man's shares would just go to his heir, and the consortium's already made up their minds. You'd just have that man's death on your conscience. You already told me you feel like you're paying for what you did to Carpenter, and that was justifiable for what he did to you. The Wilbur I know ain't got it in him to deliberately just murder someone. Face it, you ain't no killer, Wilbur."

Wilbur simply nodded his head. The truth of the statement burned within him like steam. No, he couldn't do that, couldn't stay inside the man and feel him die around him. It had been bad enough with Carpenter, and the guilt still nagged at him after decades. He couldn't imagine how he would feel—he knew Jackson had a wife, children, and grandchildren; he knew that from what he'd overheard. The loss of Eleanor had been devastating to Wilbur; he could easily imagine the desolation of Jackson's wife and children on hearing of his death, no matter what he personally thought of the man.

All the anger building up in him collapsed, cold as water.

Jeremiah grunted, as if he saw that in Wilbur's steamy posture. "I wish I could help," he said. "I really do. But that ain't the way, my friend. That ain't never the way."

"I know," Wilbur said steamily. "But I can't think of any other way out." He hesitated. Condensed steam was beginning to make the carpet wet underneath him, and he slid over a few feet. "Yet," he added finally.

"Well, when you do, let me know. Mebbe I can give you a hand. Too bad that Nurassyl couldn't fix you so you could drink again. I'd offer you a good, stiff shot in the meantime." Jeremiah lifted his glass in Wilbur's direction. "Cheers," he said.

"Cheers," Wilbur answered. There was nothing else to say.

♥

It was late in 1949, a year after the *Natchez* had started running the Mississippi. While Wilbur loved being on the river and being on the boat, it had been a difficult year financially. The monthly payments on the initial loan were due, passengers were more scarce than Wilbur had imagined, and too few companies still used riverboats to move their cargo.

Wilbur was sitting at his desk in the captain's stateroom with legal papers and bank statements arrayed in front of him. It was a dismal sight, the equivalent of overlooking a blood-soaked battlefield strewn with bodies, where there was no choice but for the general in charge to admit defeat and surrender. Wilbur was kneading his temples against the headache pounding at the inside of his skull when he heard Eleanor enter the stateroom.

"I'm afraid it's over for the boat, my love," he said aloud, without looking back at her. He didn't want to look at the disappointment or perhaps the anger he imagined would be on her face. "I don't see any way for us to go on like this. I'm not going to be able to make the next loan payments. I'm going to lose the *Natchez*. All my work, all *our* work, is just—"

He stopped. Eleanor's hand had moved in front of his face, holding a check. Wilbur blinked at the amount written there. He turned to see her face, an oddly sad smile set there. "Eleanor, how in the world . . ." He stopped, realizing he'd never seen Eleanor fully dressed without jewelry, but she was wearing none now. "What did you do? Your emerald necklace, the jewelry from your parents . . . ?"

"I sold it all," she said simply. "Our *Natchez* needed them more than I did."

"But—" Wilbur began to protest, but Eleanor put her finger to his lips, shaking her head.

"Hush," she said. "It's done. You're going to put that check in our bank account, and you're going to pay off some of our creditors."

"Eleanor, I can't do that," Wilbur protested. "Those were gifts from your family. Heirlooms."

"*You're* my family, Wilbur. The most important part of all. And this . . ." She spread her hands, gesturing around them. "This is what we've built together. Your dream. What you've always wanted."

"I have what I want. I have you."

Eleanor's smile widened at that. "That's very nice of you to say, dear. Sometimes what you have to do for family, what you have to do to achieve what you want, is to refuse to give up on them, to change whatever needs to be changed and make whatever sacrifices are necessary. That," she said, pointing at the check, "is just a small one. Those pieces of jewelry were just pretty baubles. This boat holds all of your dreams, and because of that, it's become my dream as well. So don't say anything more. This is what we need now, both of us."

Wilbur could only shake his head. He took her hands and pulled her down into an embrace. "I don't deserve you," he told her, and was rewarded with a laugh.

"Then you'd better get working to make sure you do," she told him.

He would, but in the end, the boat wouldn't make enough of a profit to save him.

♣

Wilbur left Jeremiah's cabin and went into a bright afternoon, drifting down the promenade of the texas deck toward the stairs. He figured he'd head down to the Kazakhs' cabin and talk to Jyrgal and Nurassyl, who'd begun to teach him a bit of the Kazakh language.

But he saw the familiar trio of young men in raincoats and laden with odd pieces of equipment emerge from the head of the staircase toward the bow of the boat, well away from the Kazakhs' cabin: either Captain Montaigne had given the ghost hunters permission to explore the upper decks, or they'd simply ignored the chain with the CREW ONLY sign that was usually draped across the bottom of the stairs.

"Okay! Let's get some good readings up here before someone sees us," the heavily tattooed, studded, and bejeweled Ryan was saying. "Come on . . ."

This is your own damn fault, all that worrying about your own problems. It's serendipity. Karma. You can't have these idiots prowling around up here, not with the refugees so close. Wilbur moved toward the trio, pausing once at a wall behind which he knew one of the steam pipes ran. He thrust his hand into the wall and into the pipe it hid, drawing more steam into himself and absorbing it. He knew that in the sunlight, the most the ghost hunters might see was the wispy, uncertain outline of a figure, but still made certain that the steam inside him remained unseen.

"Are you sure we should be doing this, Ryan?" Sean, the blond cousin, again carrying most of the equipment, asked. "We don't want to piss off the captain or get tossed off the boat at the next stop—the trip's just started and though we have some great footage already, there's so much more to check out."

"Christ's sakes, Sean," Ryan told him. "Quit being such a wimp. We'll just tell her the chain was down and we thought that meant we were allowed up here. C'mon, let's get to work. Sean, you scan for EMF residue; I'll get temp readings and see if there are any anemones."

Wilbur sighed at that. So did Kevin, the third young man of the group, wearing a black tee and his usual plaid newsboy cap. "Anomalies," he told Ryan. "You mean anomalies."

"Whatever." Ryan shrugged. "Just make sure you're filming everything as we go, Kevin, just in case we hit something good. Some of the crew hinted that there's weird stuff going on up here."

They started moving slowly down toward Wilbur, as Wilbur moved just as deliberately toward them. It was probably leftover irritation and frustration from his talk with Jeremiah, but Wilbur felt angry. Felt that he wanted to *do* something.

The probe Ryan was wielding was pointed directly at Wilbur, who allowed it to penetrate his body. "Shit! Look at this!" Ryan exclaimed, stopping so suddenly that Sean nearly ran into him. Kevin brought the camera close, zooming in on the instrument: the camera was a Sony, Wilbur saw. He shook his head. He'd never understood how quickly a country that they'd fought in World War II had gone from a bitter enemy to a ubiquitous consumer goods supplier. "I'm getting a reading of fifty degrees Celsius right here—that's almost hot enough to scald someone." Ryan moved the probe to his right; Wilbur stayed where he was. "Down to twenty-two degrees Celsius here: air temp. You got that, Kevin?" And back . . . "Fifty degrees again." Ryan blinked heavily. "Not a cold spot; a very hot spot."

"Steam Wilbur," the two others said nearly simultaneously.

"You guessed it," Wilbur said aloud, and was pleased to see all of them jump at the sound of his new voice. He moved then, quickly. He put his hands around the Sony being held by Kevin, allowing them to fully penetrate the device, which suddenly became very hot. Kevin dropped the camera with a curse. It was rather too heavy for Wilbur to hold; the camera bounced on the decking, and Wilbur put his feet through it. Steam condensed into water and puddled around it; they could all hear the crackle of electronics shorting out.

"You can't come up here again," Wilbur said, the words emerging in wisps of steam. "If you do, it'll be the last mistake you make. You'll end up like this . . ."

Wilbur moved quickly, entering Kevin's body. For a second, he was lost in Kevin's thoughts—*What the fuck? It's like I just stepped into a sauna . . .* —then he snatched control of the body from the young man. He forced Kevin to take a step, then another, toward the rail. He could feel Kevin fighting him, but the ghost hunter had already lost that battle; the water and heat his body was absorbing drained his energy and his will. Wilbur brought one foot over the railing, then looked back to Ryan and Sean. "Next time, I'll make him jump," he said, this time with Kevin's voice. "Then I'll force the two of you to jump right after him. Now go while you can! GO!"

With that final shout, Wilbur stepped away from Kevin, who collapsed into a soggy heap on the deck, his clothing drenched. He coughed, retched, and threw up water and whatever he'd eaten for breakfast: eggs and toast, with bits of bacon, Wilbur decided.

Sean was already lumbering toward the stairs. Ryan, to his credit and Wilbur's mild surprise, went to Kevin, helping him up. "Kevin, c'mon, little bro." With one arm around him, he slowly followed Sean, looking around him fearfully all the while, as if he expected Wilbur to jump out from the nearest cabin. They left the camera where it was.

Wilbur watched them leave. "I need to stop doing that," he muttered. "It always makes me feel so *dry*."

Wilbur crouched down next to the camera. *So small now. They used to be enormous.* He started looking for the film compartment or the button to eject the video cassette, then belatedly remembered the new cameras used neither anymore. *Everything's small now.* Flipping up the cover, he took out the memory card. Moving to the stern of the boat, he watched the paddle wheel churning below him in the wheelhouse. He held the card over the white water and the dripping paddles and let it drop. It hit one of the rising paddles, bouncing once, then vanishing into watery chaos.

He *did* feel somewhat better, having chased away the *Dead Report* kids and hopefully convinced them to stay away from the texas deck. He went back down the promenade a bit to the door of stateroom 3, and went through. *"Sälem!"* he said: *Hello.* "I thought I'd stop by for another lesson."

♠

Late the next afternoon, Captain Montaigne, JoHanna, Jeremiah, and the bartender, Jack, were ensconced in Montaigne's quarters. Wilbur had seen them gathering and was there as well, slipping in unseen while the door was open to admit JoHanna.

"I've heard from the JADL that several hundred of the captured refugees from the *Schröder* are all now on this place called Rathlin Island, not far from Belfast. That's where they'll be deporting anyone they catch. The island is quarantined and the waters around it patrolled. They've been told that any unknown boats trying to leave the island will be sunk," Jack was saying, scowling. "They're acting like these poor people are carrying a plague."

"We know better," JoHanna said. "They're just people. Nothing more. But if our group is found . . ." She let the statement hang for a moment. "Jack and I have firmed up everything with the JADL. All the drop-offs are set. But we'll still have half a dozen of the refugees with us when we reach Cincinnati—they'll be picked up there and taken to Charlotte, where their contact is a guy called Theodorus, supposedly some wealthy joker who's a big donor to the JADL."

"There ain't nothing easy or safe about any of this for anyone in this room," Jack interjected. His Cajun accent was nearly as thick as JoHanna's. "We're still days away from Cincinnati with the stops we're scheduled to make. We've already had one visit from ICE, and I'd be surprised if there ain't more. From what I've heard, there's lots of official types interested in finding Nurassyl, especially. And this Theodorus wants us to make certain he gets to Charlotte."

Jeremiah sniffed at that. "There's already been people snooping around that cabin, and I've heard some of the crew wonderin' about the meals that keep gettin' sent up there. The rumors from the crew are all over the place: that there's some big-ass star holed up there with his or her entourage who don't want to be seen, or that it's one a' them aces or jokers doing the same, or that the people in there came down with a nasty communicable disease they picked up traveling. Hard to keep it from the crew that there's people in there, and then havin' the passengers pick up on it."

"All of which is bad, if it means anyone on the boat gets curious enough to try to find out the truth. We've used the 'steam leak' excuse once already," Captain Montaigne said. She glanced around the room as she said that, as if expecting to find Wilbur, but her gaze never found him. "Okay. I'll talk to the crew personally and impress upon them that if I hear any of them gossiping about this, they'll be off the boat the next time we dock. Maybe that'll stop some of the speculation."

"Hell, make 'em swim for it, Cap'n," Jeremiah said, and everyone chuckled.

"In the meantime, let's try to make our handoffs in the sanctuary cities go smoothly. There's another one coming up."

Wilbur had heard enough. He slipped out of the room, though he was fairly sure one of those inside would notice the newly dripping wall, not that it mattered.

◆

It was dusk when Wilbur emerged from the captain's stateroom. Just looking out from the bow of the deck's promenade, he knew where he was from decades of being on the river: they were passing Woodstock Island, Mississippi, on the port side, with the town of Greenville on the starboard.

The lights of Greenville were sliding by on the eastern bank just beyond Archer Island. Greenville was already dotted with lights in the evening; little-populated Woodstock Island was a featureless green darkness with several hawks circling against a backdrop of clouds tinted red and orange by the setting sun. Several pleasure craft were still out in the main channel, though he knew many of them were heading back to their respective docks and harbors for the night.

The sight was one on which Wilbur lingered for several minutes.

He was cool enough now that he didn't need to make certain that he wasn't visible in the near-darkness. He moved down the promenade of the texas deck and slipped into stateroom 3. Now that several of the Kazakhs had left the boat, both this stateroom and the other down on the main deck were somewhat less crowded than they'd been before, but quarters were still tight. Jyrgal was in the main room, sitting in a chair in front of the coffee table, on top of which a lamp, minus the shade, had been laid. Aliya, his wife, and Nurassyl were sitting on the floor near Jyrgal along with a few other of the Kazakhs, watching. Wilbur noticed that the mittens were gone from Jyrgal's hands . . . and—like his son, Nurassyl—he didn't *have* hands. His arms ended in amorphous blobs, and set in them were steel instruments: a pair of needle-nose pliers on one, and a screwdriver and clamp on the other. He was fiddling around in the light socket of the lamp. He glanced up and Wilbur saw that he noticed the door streaked with water.

"Wilbur," Jyrgal said, and Wilbur allowed himself to become visible, though he was little more than a nearly transparent wisp, as cool as he was. Jyrgal gestured with the tools on his arms, snapping the needle-nose pliers open and shut. "The lamp, it was broken. It is fixed now." As Wilbur watched, the tools seemed to dissolve, the stubs from which they'd protruded turning a furious red that faded to pink as they shortened and settled. Aliya rose quietly from the floor and went to Jyrgal, holding his burlap mittens, which she tied gently over the stubs of his arms. Another of the jokers took the lamp, plugged it into a wall socket, and turned it on—the lamp lit immediately, and Jyrgal smiled. "Good," he said. Nurassyl clapped softly with his own shrouded hands.

"How . . ." Wilbur began, but he was interrupted by a loud roar from the adjoining room as someone shouted in Kazakh, and there were two other voices—one female, one male. Jyrgal frowned and moved quickly toward the argument. Wilbur moved with him, passing through the wall and through a steam line so that he could suck in the energy there. He emerged from the wall to see the beaver-like joker Erzhan confronting the male joker—Tazhibai—who Wilbur had briefly inhabited early in the voyage, and the long-armed but short-legged young woman who'd obviously been upset by what Wilbur had done. The two young jokers were holding hands; it was obvious that the two wished to be with each other, but that Erzhan was furious at seeing them together. Jyrgal, as well as the village elder Timur, went to Erzhan, and there was a rapid-fire and heated exchange in Kazakh, with plentiful gesticulations toward the would-be lovers. Finally, Timur led Erzhan back into the other room, while Jyrgal spoke to the two.

After a few minutes, Jyrgal came over to Wilbur. "I'm sorry. The girl is Aiman, and she is Erzhan's daughter. She and Tazhibai, well, they have fallen in love, but Erzhan disapproves of Tazhibai. He would have Aiman marry someone else, and so . . ." Jyrgal shrugged. "Is it this way here in your country?"

"Sometimes," Wilbur answered. "But here, usually, the young are allowed to find their own love, even when parents disapprove. My wife and I . . . that's how we . . . I saw her and just knew . . ." he began, then stopped. Memories burned inside him. "But I lost her when this happened." He waved his hand toward his own body. Filaments of steam moved, then fell back into place.

"I'm sorry for you, Wilbur." He looked back toward the lovers, who were holding each other and whispering. "I sometimes wish it were the same for us, but it's not. A father's wishes hold much power, and Erzhan still believes in the old traditional ways." Jyrgal looked toward the door of the other room. "I should go and speak with Erzhan. Perhaps Timur and I can convince him that he must become more . . . modern. If you'll excuse me . . ."

"Certainly," Wilbur told him, and Jyrgal bowed his head briefly and left. Wilbur watched Aiman and Tazhibai for a few moments more, then turned and left through the outer wall of the room and out into the evening.

♥

Wilbur drifted down into the Bayou Lounge just as the Jokertown Boys were starting their set. Roger Washburn, aka The Amazing Ravenstone, the leader and one of the two original members left of the once-famous pop group, was at the mike, dressed like a caricature of a riverboat gambler: top hat, fancy vest, a lace shirt, goatee, and an eye patch. His black raven sat on his shoulder. Toward the back and on one side of the small stage was an array of keyboards, with the other remaining member of the boy band behind it: Gimcrack.

Wilbur had seen hundreds of acts playing on the boat, and he thought the Jokertown Boys were one of the weaker groups ever hired: lots of cheese-laden patter from Ravenstone, magic tricks, and songs that had been played to death long before now—though Wilbur had to admit that Roger played a halfway-decent fiddle. Still. It felt as if he were entering a new circle of hell, one that Dante might have invented if he were still around: the Circle of Cheesy Musical Acts. Wilbur far preferred a good "Naw'lins" Dixieland jazz band who could also execute a driving habanera.

To make the lounge even less tolerable, Kirby Jackson was

there as well, dressed as always in an expensive suit. He seemed to be enjoying the act, which was enough to make Wilbur scowl.

"Now, we'd never advocate frequenting a house of ill repute," Roger was declaiming as he strapped on an electric guitar. "Would we, Lenore?"

The raven on his shoulder stirred, flapped its wings, and croaked out, *"Nevermore!"*

"Well, not any*more*, of course," Ravenstone answered. Wilbur sighed, though some in the audience gave a chorus of sympathetic chuckles, even while most of them seemed more interested in their drinks and their companions than in the Jokertown Boys. "But back in New Orleans, there were a few places like that, and this is the tale of one of them."

With that, Gimcrack played the opening chords of "House of the Rising Sun," Roger's guitar joining in. Wilbur sighed again and glided unseen past the patrons to the wall next to the stage. He put his hand through the wall as Roger began to sing the first verse with his surprisingly low voice; Wilbur felt for the steam pipe hidden behind it and drew in enough steam that he could feel it coursing through his arm. He kept the steam focused there and now felt for the electric cable feeding power to the stage outlets as Roger finished the first verse and started into the second. Finding the power line, he closed his steam-laden hand around it and into it, holding the grip until he felt the water condensing and beginning to drip on the copper wires, shorting them. There was an audible *snap* as the circuit breakers cut power. Wilbur felt the tingle in his arm.

The PA went abruptly and mercifully silent, Gimcrack's amp and keyboard dead, the stage lights dark.

Roger lifted a finger alight at the tip with a small flame—another of his stock magic tricks. "It appears that we must have critics among the ghosts of the *Natchez*," he said loudly—Wilbur snorted laughter at that inadvertent half-truth. Over at the bar, he saw Jack shaking his head as he prepared drinks. "We'll take a short break while the stage crew fixes the problem. Just a blown circuit, I'm sure. Don't leave; there's lots more to come. Drink up!"

Wilbur had already left, though, passing through the wall of the Bayou Lounge. He told himself that he'd only been performing a small service for the boat's passengers and thinking about Eleanor and how he'd never have had the *Natchez* at all if it weren't for her.

♣

Late the next night, Wilbur saw Captain Montaigne knock once on Kirby Jackson's stateroom door. He moved close behind her, slipping past her as Jackson opened the door and stood aside. Jackson closed the door behind Montaigne and gestured her to a chair as Wilbur stood nearby. Jackson sat at the small desk in the room, swiveling the chair to face the captain. He gestured to his laptop on the desk.

"I've reviewed your new offer to buy out my shares in the consortium, Captain. I have to admit that I'm surprised you and Ms. Potts could come up with that kind of additional funds. Stunned, in fact. You must have saved every penny we've ever paid you; either that, or the two of you have borrowed well beyond your means. It's obvious that keeping the *Natchez* on the rivers means a great deal to you. Such sentiment is very . . . admirable. I'm very impressed."

Montaigne gave the man a tight-lipped smile. "I'm glad you're impressed, Mr. Jackson. So do we have a deal, then?"

Wilbur knew the answer before the man even started to shake his head: it was in the amusement lurking behind his eyes and the way the corners of his lips curled slightly. "I'm afraid not."

Montaigne let out an exasperated huff of air. "Mr. Jackson, we've nearly doubled our previous offer, far more than you could possibly make simply selling your shares on the market. I don't understand . . ."

"That's obvious, Captain. You don't understand. I'm taking the long view and not the short-term. First, we would both have to admit that *Natchez* is already in need of serious renovations, which will be expensive, as I'm sure I don't have to tell you. Why, just last night in the lounge, the stage electricity went off and had to be repaired. So whether *Natchez* stays on the river or not, whoever owns the boat is looking at a large investment in refurbishing her—and spending that money to scrape by and barely break even on the river seems counterproductive. Having the *Natchez* docked in Cincinnati and running as a riverfront casino and attraction will, on the other hand, result in *far* more profit for me in years and decades to come—and the other consortium shareholders, of course. More than any offer you could possibly give me now." Jackson rose from his chair; Montaigne rose with him. "As I said, Captain, yours is a very generous offer, and had you made it even a year ago, I would have happily accepted. But not now. I'm sorry." Jackson opened the stateroom door. "I'm sure you can understand."

Wilbur wanted Montaigne to get angry, to shout at the man, to *do* something, anything. She didn't. She only stared at him, and the slump of her shoulders told Wilbur all he needed to know. Montaigne said nothing; she moved past Jackson and out onto the promenade of the texas deck. Jackson shut the door behind her.

Wilbur had gone to the desk. He put his hand on and through the laptop's keyboard, letting the moisture he held soak into the device. He saw the screen shudder and go dark, and he lifted his hand.

He knew what Eleanor would tell him if she could: *You're just being petty, Wilbur. It doesn't become you. You're a better person than that.*

She would be right, but it still gave him a small twinge of pleasure.

Wilbur slid through the wall of Jackson's stateroom and out

onto the deck. He didn't know how long he stood at the rail there, just staring out into the night: an hour or more. Suddenly, a black shape flapped out of the gloom and past him: a large raven.

As an omen, it couldn't bode well.

Find the Lady

By Kevin Andrew Murphy

ROGER WASHBURN DOZED FITFULLY, almost waking to the clank of his stateroom door against the battered brass corners of his antique steamer trunk. Its sides were black, vaingloriously emblazoned with *THE AMAZING RAVEN-STONE*, some turn-of-the-century conjurer who had left no other record of his passing.

Mr. Dutton, the skull-faced business mogul of Jokertown, had had it in the back of his magic shop, using it as a display stand for chapbooks and penny tricks. Roger had bought it with his first paycheck from him and taken the stage name for his own.

The open door swung idly with the roll of the boat, and to its other side, also swinging, but from the hook of a wrought-iron stand bolted to the stateroom floor, hung a vintage parrot cage, its door similarly ajar.

No parrot dwelt inside, but this was not unusual. No parrot had resided there for a long while. The cage belonged to Lenore, Roger's pet raven for more than twenty years, since he found her and her sister Annabel Lee in Central Park, knocked out of their nest by a storm.

Annabel, like her namesake, had perished. Lenore, unlike her namesake, had thrived, learning many clever tricks over the years. Sometimes too many.

The boat listed again, banging the door against the steamer trunk, louder this time, and Roger woke with a start, seeing both open doors and then the unbolted padlock on the floor, his lock-picks beside it.

Roger stared. His eyes were an intense blue and attractive in the way that only a born showman's can be, though few ever saw the left. He customarily concealed it with layers of secrecy: a flip of tawny blond hair over a black silk eye patch hiding a blackout theatrical contact that made it appear as a mysterious orb of jet to anyone allowed to see past the first two veils of deception. Roger's horns were black as well, though quite real, and firmly attached to his skull, three inches long, and devilishly becoming, burnished blacker with a bit of mustache wax.

Everyone who glimpsed his horns beneath the magician's top hat Roger usually hid them with assumed they were a gift of the wild card, a minor joker to go with his ace, that being countless parlor tricks.

Everyone was wrong.

Roger was a latent, living under the wild card's almost certain promise of death or disfigurement since childhood. His brother, Sam, an artist, had as well until his card turned in high school, giving Sam fountain pens for fingernails and a lion tail similar to the one their friend Alec sprouted when he turned into a unicorn. A few months later, after one too many times of being beaten up and called "nat boy," Roger decided he would cheat, forcing or at least forging a card from the deck himself.

A dik-dik, a small African antelope stolen from the Brooklyn Zoo, "donated" its horns, transplanted by Hodgepodge, Jokertown's back alley psychic surgeon. And once Roger had mastered all of the tricks sold by Dutton's magic shop, Cameo, a trance medium most thought to be a fraud, channeled the spirit of Blackwood the Magnificent, a legendary magician of the pre-wild card era who had taken his secrets to his grave along with a silver pocket watch.

Now Roger possessed Blackwood's secrets. And his pocket watch, too.

But Roger's most precious possession was Lenore. He gasped her name, then once again, louder, but querulous. "Lenore . . . ?"

He scrambled for his eye patch, snatching it from the nightstand and skipping the contact, grabbing his dressing gown, a long black crushed-velvet smoking jacket with *THE JOKERTOWN BOYS* appliquéd across the back in gold thread and scarlet brocade with matching reinforced epaulets to serve as raven perches.

Roger forced his pounding heart to slow, his panic to ebb, lessons he had learned from Houdini borrowing Cameo's form courtesy of a pair of handcuffs borrowed from Dutton's collection. Houdini had taught him these meditations as the way to survive the Water Torture Cell, but they were more precious to Roger as a way to survive the wild card. The alien virus often expressed itself when the mind felt the surge of extreme emotion, and as everyone knew, the deck was stacked against him, with nine jokers and ninety black queens for every ace.

Roger would not be of any use to Lenore dead.

But it was a testament to his love and devotion that he ran out onto the boiler deck of the *Natchez* exactly as he was, foregoing even his top hat.

The boards were cold and clammy under Roger's bare feet, slick with dew and the mist of the river in the predawn light. "Lenore!" he called, and again, louder, *"Lenore!"*

His voice echoed off the riverbanks—*Lenore . . . Lenore*—but there came no answering cry of *"Nevermore!"* the first word he'd taught her, the first word she'd ever said back.

He felt like he had the first time she'd gotten loose, when he'd thought he'd lost her forever. Jim had left their bedroom window open and she'd flown free. She was, after all, a wild bird. Roger had spent all day looking for her, calling till he was hoarse and croaking like a raven himself. Then he'd gone home to the orphanage, to Jim's apologies, to Alec and Paul and Sam trying to make him feel better, then crying himself to sleep, afraid that grief might kill him, almost afraid that it wouldn't, because not allowing yourself to feel was no way to live.

Then suddenly there had come a tapping, just like in the poem, but not on his chamber door, but his window. *"Never-more!"* Lenore had croaked. *"Nevermore!"*

Roger had been afraid he'd die of joy as well.

But this was the Mississippi, not New York, and the *Natchez* was not some stationary brownstone like the Jokertown orphanage but a paddle wheeler cruising up the river. If Lenore had flown to either bank, she might never find her way back.

The deck was almost deserted except for three young men fussing over some handheld gizmo with blinking LEDs. They sported tribal tats, the one holding the gizmo with a backpiece sun so large that the tips of the rays crossed under the straps of his tank top, the topmost poking beneath a mass of blond curls. The tallest wore black and enough silver jewelry to stock a goth shop, displaying his tribal marks in a band around his upper left arm, and the shortest bore no obvious ink but wore a newsboy cap and carried an overlarge video camera.

"Have—" Roger gasped. "Have you seen a raven?"

They stared. "Says 'Nevermore'?" asked the Person in Black with the inked armband.

Roger realized the camera was on as the one with the newsboy cap angled it toward him and he saw his reflection in the lens. "Yes." He winced and the reflection did as well. Roger had carefully cultivated a devilish Vandyke, but mustache wax and pillows were not a good combination. He looked like hipster Mephistopheles after a bender.

"Flew that way, Mr. Scratch." The tall PiB pointed dramatically.

"Thank you."

"All right, dudes." Roger heard the PiB's voice behind him as he turned and ran. "No ghosts this morning, but we just saw Poe's raven being chased by the Devil. . . ."

The boiler deck was deserted on the right, no ravens or persons apparent either way, and Roger was faced with a choice between the stairwell down to the main deck or the one up to the texas deck and Captain Montaigne's cabin. "Lenore!" he cried again, projecting as loudly as he could. *"Lenore!!"*

Cameo had had connections and had gotten him, Jim, Alec, and Paul into the High School of Performing Arts, where Roger had excelled at opera, a dramatic bass. *"LENORE!!!"* His voice echoed back to him, reflecting off the banks of the Mississippi, *"Lenore . . . Lenore . . . Lenore,"* and then a different word, like an old woman singing a roundelay response, *"Nevermore!"* and again *"Nevermore!"*

The voice came from the deck below. Roger unclasped the chain with the metal sign CREW ONLY with a practiced ease, reclasping it behind himself without even looking, a magician's fingers instinctively knowing the manipulation of links and chains.

The main deck was the domain of Cottle, the chief engineer, and Ms. Potts, the head clerk. The boiler room lay up ahead, along with Potts's payroll office and an endless profusion of cupboards and storage closets lining the claustrophobic hallway down the spine of the boat. The air was thick and hot with steam, and Roger's bare feet stung with the warmth, sensation returning after the chill of the perversely named boiler deck. "Lenore!" he called again, then listened.

Clanks and rattles sounded in the dimness, the only illumination being the eerie green glow of an exit sign pointing the way back out, tinting the tendrils of steam the same hue as an art nouveau absinthe poster.

Other sounds echoed in the dark, strange mutterings and unfamiliar words, but above them and intermixed, a beautiful trill of birdsong, the exact opposite of a raven's voice. Then came another voice that sounded like Lenore's croaking, but no intelligible words, or at least nothing in English, followed by other words and voices in the same language. What was it? French? Italian?

When Roger's card had turned—or at least he made everybody think it had by the Grand Guignol expedient of cutting his fingers on his new horns so that blood sprayed everywhere while he howled in agony, clutching his eyes, and slipped in the blackout contacts—he had been onstage for the school's winter gala, costumed as Mephistopheles. Roger had performed "Vous qui faites l'endormie"—"You Who Are Supposed to Be Asleep"—from Gounod's *Faust*, then segued to "Son lo spirito che nega"—"I Am the Spirit That Denies"—from Boito's *Mefistofele*.

He had placed his transformation in the second aria, right where Mephistopheles breaks singing to whistle dramatically. Roger had then staggered about the stage, covered with blood while belting out Italian in a dramatic *the show must go on* bit of scenery chewing until Mrs. Beltramo had dropped the curtain while screaming for someone to get him to the hospital.

At some point amidst his theatrics, his right contact had fallen out, lost in the blood on the stage and the babble of confusion behind the curtain. The voices Roger heard now sounded a lot like that, muffled and indistinct behind the noise of the machinery and the ship's engine.

He made his way around a column of pipes dripping with heat and condensation. The voices were louder here, and Lenore's voice as well, but he still couldn't make out what she was saying, which was strange since he knew all her phrases, including her new favorite, *"Find the Lady!"* She'd picked that one up spontaneously since Miss Beaumont, the *Natchez*'s cruise director, had asked him to stroll the boiler deck as a riverboat gambler, a role that required a lot of three-card monte.

"Find the lady, Lenore?" he called, waiting for a response. "Find the lady?"

The other voices hushed, then Roger heard Lenore's gleeful raucous cawing from behind one particular door. *"Find the Lady! Find the Lady!"*

The door was locked, covered with numerous warning signs, hazard stickers, and the words in black permanent marker:

STEAM LEAK—UNSAFE, and was secured with several padlocks besides. Roger rattled the doorknob anyway. "Lenore?"

He heard the trill of birdsong again, louder, a beautiful song like a mockingbird's only even more lovely. Roger tried the door again and again and then, with a sudden flutter, Lenore winged down the hallway and landed on his right shoulder.

"*Nevermore!*" Lenore called, followed by a raven's croaking chuckle. "*Find the Lady!*"

The birdsong called again from behind the locked door.

Lenore nodded her head enthusiastically. "*Nevermore!*"

"Have you got a boyfriend?" Roger smiled. "Does Cottle keep a canary back there? Do he and Potts have a secret poker den?"

"*Find the Lady!*" Lenore told him.

Instead, Roger found a package of Lotus biscuits in his pocket and gave her one. "Birdbrain," he admonished fondly.

"*Devil,*" Lenore said in response, as she'd been trained, then polished her beak on his right horn, making his skull vibrate and tickle.

Roger stroked her while fastening his smoking jacket's sash to her leg as an impromptu jess, considering the forbidden door. He recalled hearing some of the boiler room crew being pleased to be upgraded to actual, if tiny, cabins due to a radiator leak in their bunk room. From the sounds, the leak was not that serious, but as he knew better than anyone, everyone was entitled to their little secrets. And with his card tricks, it was not often he was invited to poker games, secret or otherwise.

"Okay, Lenore," Roger said as he held his dressing gown shut with his other hand and proceeded upstairs, "that's enough tricks for today. Now for the ones they pay us for."

"*Devil,*" Lenore repeated, then, "*The Devil made me do it!*"

It was an old punch line from an older comedian, something Lenore had learned from Mr. Dutton at the magic shop, a joke before Roger's time, but it never failed to elicit a chuckle from the older set, so Roger encouraged it.

"Not this time, birdbrain." Roger kissed his pet. "Not this time."

♠

Brunch on the *Natchez* was an elegant and elaborate affair, the best tables set up outside on the boiler deck's promenade, allowing guests to sip mimosas in the sunshine accompanied by music from the calliope high atop the hurricane deck. Usually this required someone to be physically playing the keyboard, but this was before they'd hired Jim Krakowicz, aka Gimcrack, the other remaining member of the Jokertown Boys and Roger's best friend since childhood.

Jim stuffed an overlarge bite of eggs Benedict in his mouth with a fork in one hand while with the other he pointed a battered duct-taped and rewired universal remote at the calliope and pressed play. A jolt of electricity flew out of the soldered-on antenna, arcing up two decks to the brass steam pipes like a Jacob's ladder, and the calliope immediately launched into a spirited performance of "The Entertainer."

Roger, now costumed in his top hat, brocade vest, and cutaway frock coat with Emperor Norton epaulets, knew better than to remark on this and simply took a sip of orange juice. Andrew Yamauchi, aka Wild Fox, did not.

"Nice ace," Andrew complimented, his fox ears perking up atop his head like an anime character's. "I wish my remote worked that well."

"I'm not an ace," Jim corrected him, "just a latent who knows how to read directions."

Andrew stared, his fox tail twitching behind him. "Seriously?"

"Of course," said Jim, offended. "Why would I joke about that?" Despite being in his thirties and having a five-o'-clock shadow you could grate cheese with, Jim gave an expression of childlike innocence without peer.

Lenore broke the conversational awkwardness by proclaiming, *"Acem quzghyn!"* Then again, more emphatically, *"Acem quzghyn!"*

Jim laughed, his green eyes wide with delight, then turned to Roger. "When did you teach her Kazakh?"

"That's Kazakh?" Roger looked at Lenore, then back at Jim. "What did she say?"

" 'Beautiful raven,' " Jim translated.

"When did you learn Kazakh?" Andrew asked.

"When it was in the news," Jim said, turning his attention back to his eggs. "I ordered one of those 'learn any language in ten days' courses."

Andrew stared, incredulous, then glanced to Roger.

Roger contemplated the fruit plate he was having instead of creole delicacies and explained, as he had many times before, "Like he said, Jim is just good at reading directions."

Andrew's tail twitched as he regarded Jim. Despite a plate loaded with eggs Benedict, Cajun sausage, and far more bacon than should ever be healthy, Jim maintained the physique of a male model and athlete. He also maintained a subscription to the *National Enquirer*, turned, as always, to the page with the Charles Atlas testimonials, miracle pheromone ads, and fad diets.

Roger ate his cantaloupe, wondering where Lenore had heard Kazakh. But he recalled Cottle had taken on new crew in New Orleans. A bunch of soldiers had returned from the horrors of Kazakhstan, and those who weren't hospitalized with PTSD were looking for work. Compared with what they'd seen, the boiler room would seem a vacation.

Then, out of the corner of his eye, Roger saw Andrew's ears perk up.

Roger looked where Andrew was looking, up to the calliope atop the *Natchez*. The three guys from last night were there. The curly-haired blonde with the solar tat waved his gizmo at the self-playing calliope while the Person in Black with the tribal armband talked excitedly to newsboy guy's camera. "Who are they?" he asked Andrew.

"*The Dead Report*," Andrew answered, his face becoming a mask of mischievous glee. "Don't you watch the Explore America channel?" Then he turned to Jim. "Could you make the calliope play something more ghostly?"

Jim shrugged. "Sure." He glanced at his remote and pressed a button labeled with a child's Halloween pumpkin sticker. "The Entertainer" abruptly switched to the *Casper, the Friendly Ghost* theme song.

Andrew cocked an ear. "I was thinking more *Haunted Mansion* or *Phantom of the Opera*, but I can work with this." As he said that, the steam from the calliope began to drift and coalesce, forming into a towering and terrifying ghostly figure behind the calliope's keyboard.

Roger could work with opera, too, and not just singing. He reached into his frock coat and removed his opera glasses—the real deal, heirloom Aldons, black Bakelite and Art Deco chrome with Rodenstock optics, not the gag glasses that gave you a black eye and were always a hit with children—and brought the trio from *The Dead Report* up close. Combined with lip-reading and a good memory, they gave him excellent information to fake ace mentalism or advice from nonexistent spirit familiars.

"*Keep filming!*" cried the Person in Black. "*Keep filming! This is going—*" He turned so Roger couldn't see his lips, but a moment later, turned back, "*—umentary Emmy!*"

Roger sipped his orange juice. He had grown up with Jim and knew the chaos his ace could cause. When you added in Andrew, who'd come to fame on *American Hero* as Wild Fox, master illusionist and all-around prankster, whose illusions could be seen but not recorded on film, it was a recipe for disaster. Or hilarity. Possibly both.

The ghostly figure forming from the calliope's steam condensed smaller and smaller, becoming more and more opaque as it did so. The empty hollows of its eyes shrank to doll-like pupils, the horrifying rictus of its gaping mouth contracted to a single black line, and the whole of its being became the size of a small child, a levitating cartoonish undead parody of a little boy. His mouth opened in a wide smile as his ghostly hands attempted to match the fingerwork of the possessed keyboard playing his theme song.

Roger put away his opera glasses and glanced to Jim and Andrew. They were both adults, in body at least. And the *Natchez* had hired them for entertainment, as was the case with him, so it was time for the Amazing Ravenstone to make his exit before Caitlyn, their cruise director, came by with comments and concerns about the divertissements they were providing.

"Have fun, gentlemen," Roger said, taking a last pineapple spear for himself and a strawberry for Lenore. "It looks like you already are."

◆

Roger had his magician's table set up, the drape in front embroidered with THE AMAZING RAVENSTONE in the same lettering copied from the antique trunk. The velvet mat atop was perfect for close-up magic. "Now find the lady. . . ." He fanned the three cards.

The girl in front of him was about thirteen, with red hair, freckles, a pink gingham sundress obviously new for the trip, and a face so bershon it could be used as the definition photo on Instagram, her expression equidistant between apathy and disgust with shades of bored resignation. "She's been chopped up and turned around. They're trick cards. I saw this on YouTube."

Roger took his gloved hand away. "Then show me."

The girl turned over the jack of clubs, then the jack of spades. She frowned, then turned over the last card, revealing the jack of diamonds.

Roger reached out, pulling a card from her ear. "Ah, here's the lady." He revealed the queen of hearts.

The girl looked at him squarely. "Okay, that's kind of cool, but still lame compared to Wild Fox." She glanced back over her shoulder to the woman behind her, who had the same hair and a matching sundress. "I can't believe you ever had a crush on this guy, Mom."

Her mother turned almost as pink as her dress. "How—"

"I read your diary," the girl said. "You can pick the lock with a hairpin." She then looked at the man standing with her mother, who Roger assumed to be the girl's dad. He looked like a taller, fatter, balding version of Roger, without the horns, but still sporting a Vandyke.

Roger exchanged a look of commiseration with him and his wife, then their daughter dropped the other shoe: "She still has all your albums, you know. Even listens to them sometimes." After a moment, she told Roger, " 'Jokertown Blues' was their make-out song."

Her mother went from pink to red. "Marie, that's enough!"

"Is it?" asked Marie. "You named me after the joker witch from your sex song. How fucked up is that?"

THERE'S A MIGHTY MEAN MOMMA NAME OF JUJU MARIE . . . . Roger kept from singing the line, but only just. "Jokertown Blues" was an old standard. C. C. Ryder had covered it before them, and Mr. Rainbow before her.

"Marie," her mother reasoned, "you were named after your great-aunt Marie."

"Yeah, that's what you told everyone," said Marie, "but remember, I read your diary!"

"Juju Marie!" cried Lenore. "Juju Marie!" Then, as Roger had taught her to do—though not under these circumstances—she hopped to the corner of the table, producing a card from the hidden pocket but making it look like she'd pulled it from under her wing. She presented it.

Marie took it. On the front was Sam's pen-and-ink portrait

of Juju Marie, the legendary hoodoo witch of Jokertown, throwing her cards in the air. On the back was an *admit two* pass for the Jokertown Boys show that evening in the Bayou Lounge.

Marie gazed at it, her face a study in bershon, then handed it to her father. "I can't even . . ." She pronounced her damnation on the three of them, much like her namesake, and walked away, her hand raised in abject dismissal.

Her parents gave Roger mortified looks, then Marie's mother said, "I should . . ."

She left the thought unfinished, the sentence unfulfilled, but took off after her daughter regardless.

Marie's father looked at the card, then Roger, then the card again, then finally tucked it in his breast pocket. "Very kind of you," he said with a southern drawl. "I think." He shook his head and pulled out his wallet. "This ain't the way I planned life, and I reckon it's the same for you." He handed Roger a twenty, adding, "I'd be obliged if you could point me to the bar."

Roger did.

♥

Roger ended up at the bar himself that evening, the smaller lounge that had once been the *Natchez*'s smoking room, a place for gentlemen to unwind without their ladyfolk.

Marie's father was not there, which was all to the good. Roger did not think he could deal with that conversation. He'd had an endless number of fangirls back in the day. He'd even gone to bed with some of them, a couple even long term—and Portia, at least, was still on speaking terms. But having a woman marry you because you were the closest nat boy she was going to find to her bad-boy devil joker teen idol crush? And by the way, it was likely a shotgun marriage because you were both southern Christian abstinence teens, and abortion was even more unspeakable than joker boys, even fake ones, not that you knew that.

Marie was right. It was all sorts of fucked up. Roger "couldn't even" either.

Of course, this was not the only fucked-up thing in his life. The Jokertown Boys—the famous ones—had broken up years ago, or really just splintered off piecemeal.

Sam had left first. But Sam had never really been that into it, and he'd wanted to pursue his art career. And he and Roger were still brothers, so they kept in touch, if not as much as they should. Then Paul, their lead vocalist and only tenor, had left to pursue his own music career and drug habit, not necessarily in that order, going on to celebrity followed by celebrity rehab.

Roger was scrupulously square on the drug front, not so much because of moral objections so much as knowing the number of aces and jokers who'd turned their cards while stoned, and more concerningly, the number of black queens drugs had produced.

Then again, anything could be a trigger. Losing your virginity could be a trigger. Even someone else doing that—Alec had been a full-on medieval romantic, drowning himself in King Arthur and tales of chivalry, and his card had flipped when he found out his girlfriend wasn't a virgin, turning him into a unicorn. And it took a virgin to get him to change back.

Alec was now turning into a unicorn for Renaissance Faires around the country. His wife played Maid Marian, and they had a little girl who could get Daddy to turn back into Little John. It made for spectacular if screwed-up *Robin Hood* pageants and nice family Christmas cards.

As for Dirk, aka Atlas, their drummer who could lift a piano, last Roger had heard, he'd dropped out of music completely and was working as bouncer, bodyguard, and roadie for stars famous enough to need him.

And those who weren't? Well, Roger and Jim had kept the Jokertown Boys name, for what it was worth. What it was worth, currently, was a spot on the *Natchez* so long as Jim also played the calliope and Roger wandered the boat as the Amazing Ravenstone.

He sat at the corner of the bar, wondering what magic he should perform next. The scotch and soda coin trick was a pub classic. Satan's Barman? Likewise a solid choice, but liable to piss off the actual bartender by cutting into his business, so unless Roger got him in on the act, not a great plan. And the *Natchez* had picked up a new bartender in New Orleans. He was old and weathered—at least in his late seventies was Roger's guess—but moved with the familiarity of an experienced barman. "What can I get you, young man?" he asked with a Cajun accent and a toothy grin. Despite his age, his teeth were perfect.

"Scotch and soda," Roger replied, "and a name?"

"Jack," said the barman.

Roger considered revealing his horns. "Jack and the Devil" stories were classic and always good for a laugh, but the horns were best saved for a later reveal, especially in the South, where there were a few more people who actually believed in the Devil.

Instead, Roger produced his card with a magician's flourish. "The Amazing Ravenstone, at your service." He tilted it to indicate his raven. "And this is Lenore."

"*Nevermore!*" cried Lenore, on cue, then, "*Acem quzghyn! Find the Lady! Juju Marie!*" Then she snatched the card from his hand and began tearing it into confetti, which drifted to the bar.

Jack looked askance, but the torn-and-restored card was an old trick, despite Lenore's garbled patter. Roger gathered up the scattered bits of paper and squeezed them tight. "Now say the magic words."

"*Sim sala bim!*" Lenore cried, and pecked his glove. "*Hocus-pocus! Acem quzghyn!*"

That was not the usual third magic phrase, but like Wild Fox, the Amazing Ravenstone could improvise. Roger displayed the card, rumpled but miraculously restored all but for one shred pecked out of the center. He located it on the bar and showed that it matched. Then he did another pass and swapped the calling card for the employee ID that got him discount drinks and let him run a tab. "Welcome to the *Natchez*."

"Roger, hey?" Jack asked.

"When I'm off duty," Roger said. "For now, 'Ravenstone,' if you please."

Jack handed the card back along with a scotch and soda with a generous pour.

Roger started to take a sip, but was startled by an exclamation: "It's Mr. Scratch!" The Person in Black wearing the goth store display case of silver jewelry sat down next to him abruptly, extending his hand in an aggressive handshake. "Ryan Forge, *The Dead Report*."

Roger accepted the handshake. "The Amazing Ravenstone." Ryan's grip was strong, either overenthusiastic or a power play. Roger returned it with equal firmness, allowing him to mark the back of Ryan's hand with the pre-inked invisible ink stamp he had slipped over the thumb of his glove. "And you have already met Lenore." He gestured with his off hand, providing the necessary distraction to Ryan while also blocking the angle of the camera as he slipped the thumb tip off and into a vest pocket. "My thanks for helping find her. I am in your debt. And all debts must be repaid. . . ."

"Well, we know you're not really the Devil." Ryan grinned, outing him. Roger regretted skipping the "Jack and the Devil" patter with Jack. "Sean uploaded the video, and some of our new fans are your old fans. You used to be bigger than ShockSnack, part of the Jokertown Boys!"

"Still am, but thank you, Ryan—and to you as well, Sean," Roger added with his most charming insincerity to the cameraman with the cap. "One can never have too much publicity."

"Nah, that's my brother, Kevin," Ryan corrected. "The guy with the awesome EarDrums there is my cousin, Sean Venters." He pointed one silver-beringed finger to the blonde with the solar backpiece who was wearing a pair of garish and overbranded headphones. "But for a repayment deal, we were hoping you could tell us about the ghosts here."

"I assume you don't mean the . . . friendly kind . . . like at brunch today."

"Fucking Wild Fox," Sean swore.

"Sean, you idjit." Ryan glared at him. "Now we have to bleep that out."

"Won't be the first time."

"Well," Roger said, considering, "I assume you've read the brochure and know about the ghost of Captain Leathers, how he's sometimes seen to appear in the steam. You've heard of the other ghosts who've perished on the *Natchez*, poor lost souls one and all. But there is one other spirit that may be here, or more than one. It's a tale I was told down in New Orleans, at the start of this journey. Have you heard the legend of Delphine LaLaurie?"

Jack dropped a glass, which shattered with a loud crash, causing Ryan to nearly leap out of his skin and Jack to swear in French. *"Merde!"* Roger just sipped his drink. "Don't be talkin' 'bout her," Jack admonished. "This boat's got enough haints without callin' up ol' Madame LaLaurie."

It really couldn't have gone better if Roger had planned it.

"What's the deal with Madame Lorelei?" Ryan asked. Kevin pointed his camera up at the barman.

"LaLaurie," Jack corrected, but kept his mouth shut tight otherwise, sweeping up the broken glass, until Ryan got out his wallet and laid a twenty on the bar.

Jack took it, nodding to Roger, then leaned down conspiratorially toward the camera. "Well, since he's set to tell you about her anyway, let me tell you what my ma tol' me: Madame LaLaurie was the wickedest woman in New Orleans, and that takes doin'. She was a slave master, a murderess, and what's more, a witch. She had this big house on Royal Street, and one day, the kitchen caught fire. Folk came and they found this ol' slave woman there, chained to the stove. Woman swore Madame LaLaurie said that tomorrow, she'd take her up to the attic to 'serve her.' But nobody ever came back from that damned attic, so she set the fire. Then the police asked Madame LaLaurie for the keys, so they could see if the ol' woman's story was true, but Madame LaLaurie was proud and refused. But police back then were worth more than they are now, 'cause they broke down that attic door. And there they found seven slaves chained to the wall, each tore up worse than the last. But there was ain't much they could do for them, and they all died within a week."

Ryan's eyes were wide with horror. "What happened to Madame Lorelei?"

"LaLaurie. She flew off, free as a bird. Went back to Paris they say, or maybe Hell. But nobody ever heard from her again."

"Not quite," Roger corrected, embroidering Jack's story in his mind. "The truth is, like Jack said, Delphine LaLaurie was a witch, one descended from the Merovingian kings and their ancestress, the fairy princess Melusine. But as everyone knows, the fey are fickle. Those they favor, they kiss on the hand, sweet as a courtier, and treat to every delight—but to keep their immortality, the fey also have to pay the teind to Hell, a price of seven souls. And the Devil's price is always those they favor most." Roger gave a deep Mephistophelean chuckle. "From what I heard from an antique dealer on Royal Street whose shop was in the shadow of Delphine LaLaurie's accursed house, that attic door had seven locks and her key ring had seven keys, and after she left, in the ashes of the fire the old woman had set, they found them all."

With that, Roger produced a skeleton key. "And he sold me one." The key was iron, pitted and rusted, but well-preserved for its appearance, almost two hundred years in age. "Here." He tossed it to Ryan.

The ghost hunter caught it, then immediately dropped it onto the bar as if it had burned him. "It's hot!"

"It always is," Roger lied, failing to mention the skier's chemical hand warmer he'd activated in his pocket a minute before. "The fires of Hell, and the fact that, they say, since Delphine LaLaurie wasn't able to pay the teind properly, the seven souls remained trapped in the vestibule of Hell, tied to the keys to their prison." Roger picked up the key with his left hand, then placed it on the palm of the right. "Want proof?"

The key was perfectly balanced. On the internet you could buy dozens of haunted key illusions in silver or gold, but they were all too shiny and new to seem genuine. But the trick was centuries old, and the Regency-era way to work it was to sort through assorted old keys till you found one with good balance. Steampunk jewelers now sold bags of reproductions.

Roger held his hand perfectly still, but perfectly still was never perfect. The faint imperceptible tension and flexing to hold the palm open was sufficient to unbalance the key and, by degrees, to cause it to turn as if by a ghostly hand. "The soul still tries to escape its fate, to open the lock to its prison, but the lock is no longer there." The key turned another few degrees. "But it's good that it's not, because the antique dealer said if all seven keys are returned to that attic on Royal Street, they can unlock the Gates of Hell to let Delphine LaLaurie pay her teind."

Roger waited, letting the key turn until Ryan took the bait and pointed to it in wonder.

Roger gasped sharply, the sudden intake of breath causing Ryan to freeze. "What?" the ghost hunter asked. "What is it?"

"Can you not see?" Roger asked in tones of melodramatic horror. "But no, of course not. You do not have the Devil's eye. Look, see what I see!"

With that, Roger raised his left hand to his left eye, lifting the eye patch and revealing the eye blacked out by the blackout contact, at the same time depressing the button of an antique dealer's black-light penlight secreted in his left hand and pointing such that it looked like the beam was emanating from his eye.

"The spirit of Madame LaLaurie is here!" The invisible ink on the back of Ryan's hand fluoresced, revealing the shimmering impression of a kiss, as if from a beautiful woman's lips. "She has marked you as her favorite!"

"Juju Marie!" cried Lenore. *"Find the Lady!"*

Ryan Forge screamed and ran out of the bar as if the ghost of a slave-holding serial killer fairy princess devil witch were after his soul. Kevin Forge followed with his camera.

Sean Venters remained as Roger flipped down his eye patch and put away the key. "Invisible ink and black light, right?"

Roger didn't respond, then Sean pulled out an antique dealer's penlight of his own.

"A magician never reveals his secrets." Roger tipped his hat, briefly flashing his horns. "But I must now bid you adieu. I've a show to prepare for."

Roger produced a few passes and laid them on the bar. "Until anon, gentlemen."

♣

The crowd at the Jokertown Boys show that night in the Bayou Lounge theater was the usual: most of them passengers with nothing better to do; some of them of an age to have heard the songs and liked them for nostalgia's sake, even if they'd never bought the albums; some too young to have heard them as adults, but not minding oldies from their childhood; the rest some variety of fan, but mostly there to revisit or recapture lost youth, or worse, those who'd never left it.

Shirley was parked in the front row, dressed like a Spanish dueña had raided the jewelry trays at the same goth shop as Ryan Forge. Roger wasn't certain whether he'd never learned her last name or had blotted it out of his memory or she'd had it changed legally, but it didn't matter. She was Shirley Ravenstone now, or worse, Mrs. Ravenstone, which is what she introduced herself as to everyone but Roger, causing no end of confusion to Jim, whom the wild card had left the most gullible or at least the most literal-minded man in the universe. Jim had eventually sorted it out to Shirley being married to some completely different Roger Ravenstone, hence the confusion. Shirley also claimed to be the Jokertown Boys' biggest fan, which Jim still believed.

Roger, sadly, believed it, too. Shirley had always been obese—not a joker, just a fat nat—but now she got about in a scooter. She'd had her enormous breasts tattooed with both his names, *ROGER* on the right, *RAVENSTONE* left, done in florid brushwork courtesy of Sam's tail, always proudly displayed with a low-cut top, today in black lace.

Sam had apologized for this many times since.

Shirley had been the head of the Newark chapter of their fan club, coming to all their New York shows. She'd followed them to Vegas, staying even after Paul split, taking more than half their fans with him and most of their hits, not to mention their joker street cred.

The rest of the boys were all some variety of joker-ace, with emphasis on ace, except Roger, a latent who faked it really well. They could all pass for nats with little or no costuming.

But Paul had had the wild card turn his flesh to rubber and his bones to jelly, and the only way he could stand upright was by means of an elaborate armature of braces and polio crutches. His perfect teeth were dentures glued in. And while his elasticized vocal cords and ridiculously expandable lungs gave him an increased vocal range, he'd practiced for years to turn his joker into anything approaching a deuce, let alone an ace. Calling himself "Pretty Paulie" was as much self-mockery as bragging about his mimicry.

Lenore had learned most of her obscene vocabulary from Paul.

The fact was, Paul hurt. Not just the mental anguish of being a joker and having the world view him as a monster or at best a pitiful freak, but actual physical pain. Paul hadn't been the first of the boys to turn his card, but when they'd found him at the base of the orphanage stairs, he'd screamed like every bone in his body was broken, and the screaming never stopped.

Paul's drug addiction started with the prescription painkillers he needed to keep him upright, and when the doctors' drugs began to betray him like his jellied bones, he had to turn to less legal ones. Roger couldn't blame him now, but he had then.

The trouble was, Paul was the talented one. Not that the rest of them didn't have their own talents—Roger was a good musician and a better showman, Sam had drawn their album covers, Jim was a wizard with a synthesizer, Alec with his passion for history had dug up some Childe ballads and Tin Pan Alley classics that had done well for them, and Dirk . . .

Well, Dirk had answered their ad for a drummer, was a joker-ace who fit their image, was easygoing and an awesome roadie.

But Paul had his pain and had turned it into beauty, taking teen angst and the tragedy of a crippled joker boy whom no one could ever love and distilling it into songs that a million lovelorn nat girls had taken as the answer to their own loneliness. Combined with a heartbreaking tenor, it was a recipe for success.

But the tenor was gone now, along with a bass and two baritones, leaving all the Jokertown Boys' complex five- or six-part harmonies out the window. Ditto Paul's hits.

But Roger still had his bass, opera-trained if not top operatic caliber, and used it as he strode across the stage, talking the audience up. "Anyone sad tonight?" A hubbub of voices murmured vague agreement from the *Natchez*'s ballroom. "Anyone who's feeling a bit down?" Again, agreement, slightly louder and obviously drunk. "Anyone who's got the blues?" Heads nodded like a collection of bobblehead dolls. "This song goes out to someone in the audience. . . ."

Shirley squirmed in her scooter, making her breasts bounce *ROGER* and *RAVENSTONE*. "Little lady right here in the first row . . ." Roger looked down at Shirley and smiled—always the same showman's smile—but then kept looking until his gaze and the spotlight Jim was controlling landed on a young girl, about thirteen, with red hair and a pink gingham dress. "Little lady named Marie . . ."

Marie glared defiantly. Her parents were beside her, Mom three sheets to the wind, Dad about four.

"Juju Marie!" cried Lenore. *"Juju Marie!"*

Marie had a highball glass beside her, cola brown, a cherry

marking it as a Roy Rogers children's mocktail. The lime atop her father's cola marked his as an unvirgin Cuba libre. Roger watched as Marie reached for her drink and, with a deft magician's pass, swapped the garnishes, took her father's glass now with the cherry on top, and raised her Roy libre in salute.

"Marie who knows magic . . ." Roger winked. ". . . and something about a little number we call 'Jokertown Blues.'"

The crowd roared as he launched into the old standard: "If you go down to Jokertown anyone you might see might be a little old lady name of Juju Marie. . . ."

Marie proceeded to join her parents in their drinking binge. It was probably all to the good. Dad had had too much, and it looked like Marie could use a stiff drink, even at thirteen. Especially at thirteen.

Sam had originally recorded "Jokertown Blues," his one song on their first album and an easy number for a baritone, their voices one of the few traits that set the Washburn brothers apart. The song, however, could also be done by a bass, especially with a tempo change to Cajun drop blues, a switch that Roger had found went over well with the crowds along the Mississippi.

What also went over well was anything to do with devils, at least for Roger. But when you'd gone to the trouble of getting dik-dik horns implanted into your skull, you took every safe opportunity you had to show them off.

Roger could understand Shirley's pride in her tattoos. "You'll get no release!" He sang the first line of the blues' final quatrain. "You'll get no reprieve!" The SS *Regret* had sailed long ago, and part of being an adult was owning one's teenage decisions.

Roger turned to Marie's drunk parents for the penultimate line. "And if you go down to Jokertown," he wailed, and looked to Marie for the kicker, "you might never leave!"

He raised the mike dramatically and dropped it. Halfway through its descent, it vanished in a flash of hellfire.

Marie applauded slowly, with grudging admiration. Roger had

impressed her. It wasn't forgiveness, but it was still a step toward understanding him and her parents.

Roger bowed, the actual mike up his sleeve, pulled out of the flash paper sheath with elastic. He glanced to Shirley and gave a wink. Tattoos and horns were both still less of a complication than children.

After basking in applause, he sauntered over to his bottled water, took a swig, then strapped on his electric guitar. "Anyone ever been attracted to someone who was wrong for them, but oh so right?" Roger asked after idly transforming the clear water bottle into a black microphone to more applause as he sauntered back. "That bad boy or bad girl your parents warned you to stay away from?" He glanced to Marie's parents but they were too blotto to care.

"Surely this woman knows what I'm talking about." Roger turned his gaze back to the next table, and Jim's spotlight followed. "Shirley." Roger repeated her name, punning, and she wriggled with delight, his names bouncing for all to see. "I'm talking about the 'Black Magic Woman' who helped make me the devil I am today!"

With that, Roger doffed his hat, revealed his horns, and launched into Santana's greatest hit and one of the Jokertown Boys' most requested cover tunes.

"Black Magic Woman" was a great song, and Roger enjoyed performing it, but Carlos Santana had covered it, too—the original was by Fleetwood Mac. Roger just wished he'd written it, or at least one of his friends had. But Paul's songs had left with Paul, and nothing the Jokertown Boys had originated since had broken the Top 40, let alone the Top 10.

Paul had. He'd left his boy band persona behind along with his joker-ace nickname, taking a page from Xavier Desmond, the old mayor of Jokertown, now being plain Paul O'Nealy. And when Drummer Boy, the six-armed joker-ace leader of Joker Plague, the hardcore joker rock band that had replaced them at the top of the charts, had dissed the Jokertown Boys and especially Pretty Paulie in interviews with talk about Joker Plague not being "pretty boy jokers who can pass for nats," Paul had dipped his pen into his pain and written "Fake Aces," including the lines "Fake aces with their fake faces / and their hard-edged bitter style / don't know the hard and bitter places / I hide with my own fake smile."

Paul's dentures had once fallen out onstage. Roger, thinking fast, had made it look like one of his parlor tricks, stealing his own smile next by use of toothblack, then tossing a pair of wind-up chattering teeth into the audience.

The Jokertown Boys and Joker Plague had had a long and public rivalry despite, or perhaps because of, fans shared in common. Today's audience was no exception. But where before the double agents had kept their love for Joker Plague on the down-low, today they wore it on their sleeves—quite literally, with cheap black crepe armbands silk-screened with *JOKER PLAGUE. You keep your card hidden / but it's now plain to see / the high horse you rode in on / once was ridden by me.*

The time for rock rivalries and artistic feuds, petty or otherwise, was now dead, along with more than half of Joker Plague, torn apart by a terrorist's bomb. The Voice, JP's invisible lead singer, had been made visible and silenced at the same time, permanently. The second had also happened to S'Live, Joker Plague's monstrous keyboardist, who the wild card had turned into a bald disembodied head the size of a weather balloon who floated over the synthesizer like the Great Pumpkin, depressing the keys with a thousand canary-colored tentacular tongues.

Roger thought his name had been Rick.

But the death that truly touched Roger was Ted, aka Shivers, Joker Plague's guitarist and resident devil. Except Ted's skin was bloodred and his horns were real and his fingerwork was preternaturally quick, a demon with the strings.

Fans had had endless fun comparing the two of them, and they'd both enjoyed playing up their devilish rivalry. But when Roger had finally met Ted backstage at the Grammys, all Ted had wanted to do was bond with a fellow devil joker and compare transformation stories.

Roger forgot what Ted's was. Catholic catechism? Heavy metal satanic rock rebellion? Too much D&D? It didn't matter. Roger had been too busy retelling his old lies to listen to Ted's truth.

Later, in "Fake Aces," Paul had written the lines "You cast your spell / but I always knew. / I almost tell / but I never do." Paul knew Roger's secret, but had never told, despite the distance that had come between them. "I've made mistakes / and in the end / I'm just as fake / as you, my friend." Roger had never repeated any of Paul's confidences either.

Lenore was another matter. *"Fuck Joker Plague!"* she yelled into the microphone in Paul's voice at the end of the Santana / Fleetwood Mac number. *"DB can blow me!"*

Gasps echoed across the audience, followed by an eerie silence. One guy spewed his beer.

Roger looked out at the fans, equally aghast, then turned to his pet. "Shhh, Lenore," Roger chided. "Shhh. The feud's over." He placed a finger on her beak for silence and gave the audience his most mortified look, which took no acting given the circumstances. "I think tonight we Jokertown Boys will dedicate the rest of our set to DB and Bottom, the surviving members of Joker Plague, as well as those who were lost, both fans and band members. Especially Ted, who you probably remember as Shivers, my fellow devil."

Lenore pulled her beak out from under his finger. *"The Devil made me do it!"* The raven crowed the vintage punch line, taking her cue from his final word as he'd taught her. *"The Devil made me do it!"*

No laughs were elicited, even from the older members of the audience, and the silence was palpable. Roger made a decision, unstrapping the ax and swapping it for his electric fiddle.

Usually he saved it for later in the set, but a showman did what he had to, and there was one cover song that a fiddle player could never escape requests for, especially in the South. And when he had horns?

"Speaking of devils like me and Shivers," Roger began, applying rosin to his bow while at the same time using a lighter fluid-filled thumb tip and some slips of flash paper to make flames shoot from the tips of his fingers, "I notice three gentlemen in the back there who said they saw one chasing Poe's raven. Isn't that right, Lenore?"

"*Find the Lady!*" cried Lenore, again off cue.

"Oh, I think they were trying to get away from a lady," Roger said, looking at the three members of *The Dead Report*, who'd slipped in near the theater's rear doors and had just gotten beers. Ryan Forge's hand looked red and raw, like he'd gone full Lady Macbeth on it in an attempt to wash off Madame LaLaurie's black-light kiss, "but they were also asking for ghost stories and tales of the supernatural, and while we're on the Mississippi now, I think I might recall one tale about that time 'The Devil Went Down to Georgia.'"

Roger doffed his hat and used his horns and the title to launch into the Charlie Daniels Band's masterpiece and death march for fiddlers. Jim played the rest. His ridiculously tricked-out synthesizer had originally started as one of those '70s electronic organs that promised it could reproduce the sound of any musical instrument, but by the time Jim and his ace were done with it, it did, plus everything from the voices of angelic choirs to the Devil's backup demons.

The demonic wails, however, had never sounded this authentic. While Roger knew it was just a stop on the organ, it sounded like Athanasius Kircher's legendary katzenklavier, except when the keys were depressed, instead of pinching the tails of chromatically tuned kittens and alley cats to make them scream on key, it did the same with Satan's minions, torturing the fiends of the pit till they blasphemed in musical Enochian.

The infernal invocation succeeded in lightening the mood of

the room, aided by liberal assistance from the Demon Rum and his associate John Barleycorn. Roger concluded the Devil's rock showstopper with a triumphant Mephistophelean laugh, conjuring and unfurling his best and most cherished prop, an infernal contract written in Latin in gothic Fraktur script by means of Sam's fountain pen fingernails, illuminated with square-dancing demons, hellcats playing golden fiddles, goetic sigils from the *Lemegeton*, and hex signs cribbed from an Amish wedding certificate. At the bottom, after much calligraphy coaching from Sam, was the Devil's wickedest signature in Roger's own hand, and below that a blank spot above a dotted line. But when exposed to cold air—such as, for example, the hellish fog wafting from the dry-ice machine Jim had kicked on at the beginning of the Devil's performance—a name developed in blood red in shaky, childish cursive: *Johnny*.

Audiences never failed to gasp at this reveal. Some snapped pictures. Another snap, this time of the wrist, made the contract furl up like a window shade, then once it had disappeared up his other sleeve, the flash paper sheath went up in fire. Roger then clapped his top hat back on, covering his horns, and spun around, turning his uncovered blue eye to the audience and doing a posture change so he'd look like honest, if prideful, country boy Johnny, ready to defend his soul and reputation as the world's greatest fiddler.

"*Acem quzghyn!*" Lenore cried in Kazakh, winging across the audience. "*Find the Lady!*"

Her jesses trailed behind her, trailing sparks from where they'd been burned through with flash paper. Roger then realized that his frock coat's right epaulet was on fire.

Roger could get out of a straightjacket upside down in a water tank with chains wrapped around him and his hands handcuffed behind his back, so juggling a fiddle, bow, and microphone while shrugging off a flaming frock coat and stamping it out was child's play.

"Set break!" Roger cried, leaping off the stage and onto Shirley's table, then onto the next table and the next, sprinting for the raven flying through the vent window above the doors at the end of the theater and out into the Grand Saloon itself. "Jim, follow me!"

Roger ran, dodging pillars and passersby, getting out the main doors of the Grand Saloon just in time to see his raven winging left around the corner. He chased after, seeing Lenore dive over the railing down to the main deck, winging down until flying up and darting through the curtains of a small high window directly in line with the inner door he'd heard her behind before.

"Where'd she go? Where'd she go?" asked Jim.

Roger turned. His bandmate had caught up but was jittering as if he'd just downed the daily output of an espresso machine with his hair standing on end like he'd seen one of the ghosts *The Dead Report* was looking for.

Roger had learned long ago not to question anything odd around Jim. Matters either would be explained or they wouldn't. Asking Jim what was going on was tempting fate.

"Main deck," Roger snapped. "Follow but be very quiet."

He led the way downstairs, through the inner hallway, past the boiler room, to the locked door. Roger put a finger to his lips for silence, then began to examine the locks. Six padlocks, three combination, three keyed, plus the original lock of the door. Simple enough.

From behind the door came Lenore's voice, speaking more words in Kazakh counterpointed with the beautiful singing of the crewman's caged bird.

Illicit knowledge gleaned in middle school and a little spinning of dials and tugging on bolts dealt with the combination locks. Lockpicks dealt with the padlocks. And the final lock only needed the head clerk's master key, which Roger had lifted from Mickey Lee, her assistant, and copied as a matter of habit.

The door opened inward and the songbird's trill became louder, then abruptly stopped. Roger stared. There was no poker game. Lenore sat on a reinforced epaulet as per usual, but instead of being attached to the flaming frock coat Roger had left back onstage, it was on the left shoulder of an Asiatic robe, claret velvet embroidered and trimmed with gold. A woman's coat, rich and lovely, but it looked like it had been through a war, and the same was true of the woman inside.

She wore a matching cap and she looked at Roger with wide, frightened eyes as the birdsong died in her throat, which was, Roger noted, covered with a patch of soft gray feathers. At her feet sat two children, a girl whose three hands clutched a doll dressed in a folk costume similar to the woman's, and a boy whose large oval eyes, formless hands, and translucent gelatinous flesh trailed off into tendrils of glistening ectoplasm, like Casper, the Friendly Ghost manifested in corporeal form.

Roger had grown up in Jokertown, so was used to seeing jokers, but there were more: two more women, one older, one younger, both apparent nats, but as Roger knew himself, mild jokers could be disguised; a fourth woman, young, her plain face beautified with Maori-style tribal markings that widened slightly as she gasped, revealing them to be gill slits; a short middle-aged man with one hand ending in a hook, which had speared open a tin of sardines, and the other ending in a stainless-steel spork, still with a sardine impaled upon it as he stared in terror; an older man, also frozen in terror but apparently a nat until a lizard head emerged from his neck, stole the sardine from the other man's hand-spork, and dove back into its host's flesh with its prize; a massive man with a turban fashioned not from cloth, but a single overgrown spiraled horn; and two teenagers whose embrace of affection had transmuted to one of fear, the girl with stumpy legs but overlong arms wrapped around her boyfriend and herself, the boy with arms the usual length, but four of them—still two less than Drummer Boy.

Or at least one less. Roger understood DB had lost one from

the bomb. And the donkey-headed Bottom had lost both an arm and a leg and had most of his hair burned off.

But the four-armed boy had all of Bottom's hair and then some, simply covered in it. This, mixed with eyes as big as teacups, made him resemble the dog with eyes of the same description from Andersen's *The Tinderbox*, assuming, of course, the dog also had four arms and a joker girlfriend.

One other joker sat to one side, balanced on a broad chitinous tail like an ergonomic rocking chair designed by H. R. Giger. Male, probably, Roger thought, but if he played an instrument, he would totally nail an audition for Joker Plague.

Roger winced inwardly. The thought was unworthy and unbidden. But also possibly helpful. Were DB and Bottom going to try to reform their band? Or would they continue as a duo like him and Jim, limping along? Literally in Bottom's case.

Roger winced inwardly again. He had sent flowers but had received no response except a polite thank-you card from Bottom's wife.

But Roger was a showman and a businessman. The plain fact was that, just as the Jokertown Boys were all joker-aces with passing privilege or close enough, Joker Plague's image was jokers without. And there was no way this joker could pass as a nat short of in an internet chat room, and even that was questionable: his webbed, clawed hands were built for swimming, not typing. He looked like the love child of a beaver mascot and the Creature from the Black Lagoon.

The air stank with human sweat, fear, and a fishy smell that was not just sardines. A dozen people, a dozen berths built into the walls of the room, six to a side, stacked double, the only ventilation being the tiny window covered with a heavy drape. A cord had been strung across the chamber with a makeshift privacy curtain rigged up from one of the *Natchez*'s dining service tablecloths, pushed aside now. They were all looking at him.

Sometimes passing as a nat was not a good thing. Roger

quickly removed his hat, smiling his most devilishly charming smile, and saw everyone relax as he revealed his horns. "I'm Roger," he said politely, "and I see you've already met my friend Lenore."

"*Devil*," Lenore responded on cue.

The younger and shorter of the two apparent nat women stepped forward, still cautious, but by her confident stride, Roger pegged her as an ace, and not a new or weak one either. He had been doing his best to emulate that swagger for more than twenty years. And as she stepped into the light, he could see that her skin shone with a slight golden sheen, not luminescence but iridescence, like you got from high-quality bronzer or expensive eye shadow. Ace. "Do you know Jack?" she asked. Her English, barely accented, still missed the idiom the way that usually only Jim could.

Roger knew Jack, and not just the card. Jack was the new barman. And that made a great cover for a smuggler. But smuggling refugees from Kazakhstan, especially jokers?

Roger didn't know if Jack was a Harriet Tubman or a coyote like the ones paid to smuggle folks up from Mexico, but either way, it was dangerous business. "I know Jack," Roger said, then followed that with, "Jim—get in. Shut the door."

Jim, though not precisely simpleminded, took simple orders well. "Okay," he said cheerfully as he did so. However, while he was an insanely powerful ace, part of that ace kept him from ever realizing it, leading to the body language of a nat, and a ditzy if curiously unflappable one at that. Jim glanced around at the jokers, including the beaver from the Black Lagoon and Casper the gelatinous ghost, as if they were nats having a tea party, then asked the woman with the songbird's voice and Lenore on her shoulder, "Are you going to finish the fairy tale?"

"Fairy tale?" Roger echoed in confusion.

" 'The Enchanted Garden of the Poor,' " Jim answered. "It has camels and songbirds and merchants and everything!"

The woman with the feathered throat let out a trill of surprise, and then Lenore asked, *"You speak Kazakh?"*

"Ärïne!" Jim exclaimed gleefully. Roger didn't know if this was good Kazakh or bad Kazakh, but Jim began to natter in Kazakh happily with Lenore while the woman sang with a songbird's voice, and then everyone began talking and Roger felt rather lost.

The ace spokeswoman eventually tapped Roger on the arm and asked quietly, "Your friend, he says he is not an ace?"

"It's better not to ask," Roger whispered back. "Trust me."

The spokeswoman nodded, watching Jim, as did Roger, until Jim, pausing to listen to some stories in Kazakh, took an energy bar out of his back pocket and took a bite.

Suddenly Jim began to jitter, then his hair began to float in the air with static. Sparks danced in his eyes like a Jacob's ladder, then a huge surge of electricity shot out of the top of his head, leaving him with a mad-scientist coiffure and replacing the smell of stale sweat and sardines with the clean scent of ozone.

Everyone stared at him aghast, even Lenore. "ShockSnack!" Jim explained, holding up the energy bar like he was in a commercial. "It gives you a jolt of energy!" He then examined the electric blue wrapper, which, Roger noted, was stamped with the logo and likenesses of the trio from *The Dead Report*. "I don't know how the FDA ever approved this. . . ."

"We call him Gimcrack," Roger explained to the spokeswoman. "Jim believes in advertising. . . ."

Her brown eyes went wide. "I am called the Tulpar." She fidgeted with a little bronze luckpiece. "I . . . can take the form of a winged horse." She glanced up at Roger, as if used to that sounding much more impressive.

Roger chose not to mention Alec turning into a unicorn, instead conjuring a flame and turning it into a calling card. "The Amazing Ravenstone, at your service," he said, presenting it with a flourish. She dropped the luckpiece into her pocket, but while she was reading the card, he pickpocketed her. "Parlor magic, my ace specialty." He produced the medallion from her ear, then dropped it back into her hand and gave a wink. "Or you can call me Roger."

The Tulpar eyed him, holding her luckpiece tight. "You may call me Inkar. . . ."

The others were then introduced. The teenage couple were Aiman, with the long arms, and Tazhibai, the four-armed teacup-eyed dog boy. The young woman with the gill slits was Anara, and the older woman was Aliya, the one nat in the group. But since Aliya was wife to Jyrgal, the Handsmith, who could reforge his hook and spork hands into other tools, and they were the parents of Casper, whose actual name was Nurassyl, it seemed likely Aliya was a latent like Roger. The little girl with the doll and the three arms was Sezim, a playmate of Nurassyl's, and though it was never stated outright, Roger gathered she'd been orphaned during the war.

Roger could sympathize. He and Sam had been orphaned as well.

The man with the resident lizard and the man with the turban horn were Bulat and Timur, two elders from the same village, and the giant scaled beaver was Erzhan, the elder of Aiman and Tazhibai's village.

"*And I am Bibigul,*" Lenore concluded, translating for the storyteller on whose shoulder she perched. "*My name means* nightingale, *and that's the bird whose voice the wild card gave me. I used to have Serik, my parrot, who could speak for me, but I lost him in our flight from Kazakhstan. It has been so long since I could communicate by any means except writing.*" Tears rolled down her cheeks. "*Please, I beg of you, let me keep your raven. I need her so. . . .*"

"You can't ask that," said Erzhan, the monstrous beaver man, his accent thick and weird with his Jabberwocky buckteeth. "Can't you feel her love? He's her father. . . ."

Bibigul looked at him, then Lenore, then began to twitter to her. Lenore croaked softly in response, and Bibigul began to weep anew.

"I think I may have another way," said Roger. "Jim and I have adjoining rooms, and it's not like we haven't bunked together before. Bibigul can share my room with Lenore. And when I go around the ship, she can play my assistant."

Bibigul sang a sharp trill. *"But I cannot speak!"* protested Lenore.

"Not a problem," said Roger. "Silent magician's assistants are not only traditional, they're currently in vogue."

Bibigul said nothing, only gestured in wordless protest to the gray feathers at her throat.

Roger smiled and equally silently conjured a long gray scarf for her to wrap around her neck and then a hand mirror for her to admire her new look.

♠

The only complication was that Roger had not had a magician's assistant in years, not since Portia, and the outfit she'd abandoned in Vegas he'd long since disposed of. But thankfully Roger was enough of a fop and clotheshorse himself to be able to cobble together something. Outfitting Bibigul with his gray top hat with the feathered cockade, gray morning coat, a silk cravat, a bird whistle for misdirection, and a black Battenberg lace parasol with the handle accessorized with a Bad Badtz-Maru sulky penguin key chain coin purse to imply that she was Japanese instead of Kazakh, she made a character halfway between gothic Lolita Harpo Marx and Papagena from *The Magic Flute*: the Beautiful Bibi, ready to assist the Amazing Ravenstone in his feats of legerdemain.

The first feat the next morning was getting her an employee badge. The head clerk's key and a couple minutes alone with the badge machine would usually be enough, but Ms. Potts would be in all day except for her lunch break, and while Mickey Lee, the mud clerk, always snuck out for a cigarette break somewhere during that period, timing could get dicey. Plus Ms. Potts scrutinized everything, including badge blanks. She was a middle-aged black woman who always dressed to the nines, but her lower lip stuck out in a permanent pout of disapproval, and there were few things her sharp eyes missed. So Roger made a point of avoiding them.

Instead, Roger sought out Caitlyn Beaumont, the cruise director, at her favorite place on the boiler deck, and led with an apology. "I am so sorry, Miss Beaumont," he groveled. "It won't happen again. The Jokertown Boys pride ourselves on our professionalism and—"

"Think nothing of it," she pronounced magnanimously with a southern lilt. "I remember when my Muffin got out. Almost missed a pageant finding her." Caitlyn did not mention whether Muffin was a cat or a dog, but recounted the double entendre with obvious relish. "Glad to see you found Lenore."

"Find the Lady!" Lenore replied from Bibigul's shoulder.

Caitlyn dimpled. She was young and beautiful and knew it. Today, her latest party dress, apricot chiffon set off with pearls, fit her well, almost too well, which was, Roger suspected, the point. "That said, since you boys weren't able to make it back for your second set, I had to cover. Happy to help—putting out fires is my job—and I was able to get a good karaoke night going. But people were still disappointed. So I told them that if they came to tonight's karaoke, there might be a surprise performance."

"Not a problem," Roger agreed promptly.

"Good," said Caitlyn, "because I heard it was a good show. So much that some folk were concerned Johnny might lose his soul because he skipped out on the Devil."

"You'd like me to come in on the second half of the karaoke number."

"Exactly." Caitlyn dimpled again, then looked past Roger. "And who might this be?"

"Ah, yes," Roger continued, "Miss Beaumont, may I have the

pleasure of introducing my sometime assistant, the Beautiful Bibi." Roger smiled his most devilishly charming smile. "As you can see, Lenore is quite taken with her, and that was the reason for last night's emergency. Bibi had been feeling poorly so had been resting in my room since New Orleans, and Lenore took off to find her."

"Since Naw'lins?" Caitlin stared in disbelief. "You poor thing! You feeling better now?"

Bibigul stared back, clutching the parasol in alarm, and waved in protest with one hand, covering her mouth.

"You're gonna hurl?"

"No," Roger explained quickly, "she's a mime."

"Oh!" said Caitlyn in realization. "I'd been . . ." She left the thought unfinished, but Roger didn't have to be a real mind reader to know what she'd been thinking. Their first meeting, Caitlyn's pupils had visibly dilated when he'd first revealed his horns, but she was too well-mannered and well trained to betray anything beyond that. "Your assistant, you said?"

"Yes," said Roger, "and if you check our contract, you'll see that assistants, like former members, are welcome to perform with us and stay in our accommodations."

Caitlyn unclasped her matching seed-pearl clutch and took out her phone. After a bit of review, she remarked, "Ah yes, I see it. But at no additional charge."

"For either," Roger added. "A service for a service."

"I see." The cruise director zoomed in on the fine print. "Interesting clause."

"Contracts are a specialty of mine." Roger grinned, tipping his hat and flashing his horns.

Caitlyn didn't react, displaying the admirable poise of a pageant princess. "Anything else I might do for you, Mr. Washburn?"

"Perhaps a name badge for Bibi?"

"Will she be with us long?" Caitlyn asked, glancing to her. Bibi appeared to be attempting to portray that she was trapped in an invisible box. Mummenschanz she was not.

"A while," Roger said noncommittally.

"I see," said Caitlyn. "How did she get aboard without one?"

Roger raised one eyebrow and stroked his goatee. "Truly, Miss Beaumont?"

She laughed, a practiced laugh, but a charming one all the same. Roger could respect that. "Touché. Say no more. A magician has his secrets." She gave him and Bibigul a wink. "I'm just impressed that you got her by Ms. Potts." She paused then, musing. "And I see now why you came to me. But fine, I'll get Bibi her badge. Bibi like short for Bibiana, right?"

Bibigul nodded, and Caitlyn smiled and saluted with her purse before marching downstairs in her impressively high heels, the princess off to beard the dragon in her den.

After the cruise director left, Bibigul let out a soft trill, and Lenore asked Roger, *"Can we go back to the room now?"*

"Of course." Roger realized Bibigul felt overwhelmed, so offered her a solicitous arm for the short promenade back to his stateroom, now hers.

He shut the door, and she sang a nightingale's sigh of relief, Lenore translating, *"I am sorry. I was almost as frightened as when I first saw the spirit of Captain Leathers."*

Roger paused. "You saw the ghost?"

Bibigul nodded, trilling, and Lenore said, *"Yes, but he is very kind. He welcomed us."* Another whistle. *"Would you like to meet him?"*

Roger was rarely at a loss for words, but this was one of those times. He nodded.

Bibigul smiled, then looked about the room. She picked up one of Roger's assorted magician's wands, then went to the radiator and began to tap a tempo on the valve.

Tap tap-tap tap-tap. Tap! Tap! After the first sequence, Roger thought he was mistaken, trying to parse the message as prisoners' tap code: B, F, and then something unfinished on the first line of the classic Polybius square. But after Bibigul repeated the sequence, he heard it clearly. After the third time, there was no denial: *shave and a haircut, two bits.*

Bibigul sang a nightingale's song welcoming nightfall, a beautiful but eerie melody, and Lenore cried, *"Captain Wilbur? Steam Wilbur, are you here?"*

The radiator valve suddenly sprang a leak, then, in the escaping steam, Roger saw a form taking shape, a face like the one in the ghost tour brochure: a man in his late twenties dressed like a steamboat captain from the Gilded Age.

"Welcome to the Natchez," the ghost said. *"Thank you for helping the refugees."*

"You're welcome," said Roger, tipping his hat and revealing his horns. "It was the least I could do for fellow jokers."

"Will you help me?"

When you styled yourself a devil, it became force of habit to avoid promises and open-ended bargains. "I can try," Roger allowed. "Tell me what you need."

"I'll be in contact," Steam Wilbur said. *"Boilers cooling. Can't stay much—"*

A banging sounded from the radiator, a clanking of pipes down the line, and the steam stopped, Wilbur fading from view.

Roger was left in his room, now Bibigul's room, with his raven on her shoulder. Roger also realized he hadn't had anything since dinner the night before, and Bibigul had had even less. "Would you like lunch? We can order room service."

Bibigul trilled in delight. *"Room service?"* Lenore asked. *"Yes, please. We've had very little to eat except sardines and crackers."*

Roger got the menu. Bibigul looked overwhelmed at the choices.

"Chef has a daily special. That's what I usually order."

Bibigul warbled. *"Then I shall, too,"* said Lenore.

Roger called the order in, but when he turned back, Bibigul was crying, her sobs the liquid trill of the nightingale. *"I'm sorry,"* croaked Lenore. *"You are so kind. You do not know how hard it has been. I lost my whole village, my father, everyone I knew. And once I lost Serik, I could not tell anyone. . . ."*

Roger conjured a handkerchief on reflex. "My brother, Sam, and I lost our parents when we were kids. Virus."

"You are like Sezim," Lenore declared as Bibigul sang, dabbing at her tears. *"I worry about her. She is such an innocent child."*

"Sam and I were around that age, so yeah."

"I always wanted children," Lenore confessed, *"but my card turned at my engagement feast. I loved singing and I had a beautiful voice—like a nightingale, everyone said—and then . . ."* Bibigul wiped at her tears. *"Now here I am, a joker and an old maid of thirty."*

Roger grinned. "Thirty-three here, but who's counting?"

Bibigul laughed and so did Lenore, the chuckling of a nightingale mixing with the raven's chortle.

A knock sounded at the door and Roger got it. "Chef's special t'day's shrimp creole." Jack the barman was outside. "Creole's not as good as Cajun, a' course, but still, pretty good," he said, moving the trays to the table. "An' I know you didn't order it, but Chef sent some of his special bread puddin' as lagniappe. So treat yourself." He gave a toothy smile. "Thanks for helpin' out. Gonna need t'get some better padlocks and ask folk to keep it down."

"I wouldn't have noticed if Lenore hadn't flown off. It's hot down by the boiler room."

"That it is, young man, that it is." He glanced at Bibigul's ensemble of gothic frippery and smiled. "Looks like you should be buskin' at Congo Square."

"That was the general idea," Roger admitted.

"Treat her right, y' hear?" Jack told him as he left. "This one's a lady."

"I will," Roger promised, one of his few promises. Bibigul gave him a curious look, and Roger grinned. "My reputation precedes me." He gestured to the walls, the assorted Jokertown Boys tour posters and album covers, photos of their shows with thousands of screaming fangirls. The pictures were all at least ten years old, of course, but even faded laurels could get you laid.

Bibigul trilled in wonder. *"The Jokertown Boys?"* asked Lenore, mystified.

"Our band," Roger explained. "Famous, once. Now it's just me and Jim."

Bibigul sang three querulous notes. *"Your friend . . ."* said Lenore, *"he is . . ."*

"Yeah," said Roger. "That." The fact was, he didn't exactly know what would happen to Jim without him. The boys had always looked after Jim, but everyone else had splintered off with their own lives, leaving Roger with his best friend.

Jim had been there at the orphanage when he and Sam got there. He'd been there before all the other boys, too, and even then it had been clear that Jim was an ace, but with his mind twisted with his inability to realize it. Unlike the other boys, Jim had not been orphaned, but abandoned. A child who lived in a world where breakfast cereal mascots would show up in your kitchen unless you were careful to only stock generic granola was more than most nats could deal with. To say nothing of the monster under the bed. It took Sam forging a *Monster-Be-Gone GUARANTEED!* label and sticking it on a pack of firecrackers Roger got from Chinatown before Jim or any of them could sleep sound at night.

Jim kept hoping his parents would come back, never realizing they wouldn't, or understanding why they'd left him, since so far as he knew, he was just a normal little boy. The breakfast cereal mascots agreed. "Jim's like Sezim."

Roger offered a chair to Bibigul, unsure of Kazakh customs and manners. She accepted. Then he removed the cover from her dish, revealing a beautifully plated mound of rice with a medley of shellfish and vegetables. She viewed this with familiarity and delight, then glanced at the knife and fork with somewhat less of both.

"Allow me." Roger covered them with one hand. Rare earth magnets sewn into the palm of his glove picked up the steel flatware but did not affect the cheap but prettily lacquered chopsticks he'd palmed and laid down beside them. "Better?" He moved his hand away.

Bibigul smiled with delight and picked up the chopsticks. Then, hesitantly at first, she tried the shrimp creole. She began to eat ravenously. Lenore wanted to do the same, so Roger slipped her a dead mouse, getting her to go to his glove and then to her perch.

Roger uncovered his own tray and handed Bibigul his bowl as well. "Eat," Roger insisted. "You've been starving, and I've been trying to stick to salads anyway." The side salad was coleslaw, which was not exactly dietetic but would work for his main meal. "Jim's the only one miracle diets work for."

Bibigul laughed a nightingale's joyful trill, which was echoed by Lenore's raven chortle.

Roger ate his coleslaw, but stole back one shrimp when offered. Bibigul ate both bread puddings, washing them down with sweet tea. She laughed the nightingale's laugh, crying again, but happy this time, then twittered a scrap of song. *"I don't suppose you have a* dombra?*"* Lenore translated.

"What's a *dombra?*"

Bibigul gestured to his electric guitar, whistling. *"It is like that,"* explained Lenore, *"but with a fat body like half a pear."*

Roger went to a pile of instrument cases. "Like this?" He pulled out a small Neapolitan mandolin, which Alec had bought, then realized was too small for him. Of course truth was almost everything was too small for Alec; he just wanted Roger to accompany him on medieval music.

Bibigul received the mandolin with curiosity and wonder, plucking a few notes and listening to the sound, then finally nodded and began to play a tune. It was a simple folk song, something a musician would choose to test an unfamiliar instrument, but pretty, and the notes she sang with her nightingale's voice were beyond lovely, punctuated by Lenore singing the words in Kazakh, and then again in English.

"There's an owl feather on Kamazhai's head.
I left Kamazhai so they laughed at me.
After leaving Kamazhai, wishing we were wed,
There's no way in the world I can be happy. . . ."

The song was simple, sad, and beautiful, a song of *hiraeth*, as the Welsh would put it, a deep longing for home.

"Kamazhai, my sunlight, you stayed behind. . . ."

Bibigul's fingers strummed the mandolin and touched the frets, surer now of their way, concentrating on the melody, returning to the next stanza.

"There's a golden ring on Kamazhai's finger.
She's watching the horizon from her mountain slope.
She couldn't live without me, wished that I could linger.
Oh, my Kamazhai, did you truly lose hope?"

Bibigul broke down in tears. Lenore stopped singing, croaking in alarm. Roger pulled his chair around, hugging Bibigul, supporting her so she could cry on his shoulder.

It was a long cry, but she had a lot to let out. Roger understood. Sezim and Nurassyl were children, and one had to keep up a facade of false cheer for their sake. With them no longer in the room, and with Lenore to give a human voice to her sorrow, Bibigul could finally grieve.

"Those were my last human words," Lenore said as Bibigul chirped, querulous. *"The wild card changed my voice before I could finish my song."* She reached up to Roger's head, touching his horns. *"How did—"*

"Winter concert." Roger told the old lie. "I was singing the Devil's song. It stuck."

"We are a pair"—she warbled laughter—*"marked for our love of*

music." Bibigul ran her fingers through his hair. *"I have never seen such a color except in pictures. Like a lion."*

"That's natural." Roger grinned, glad to be telling the truth for once. "Didn't get that from the wild card or out of a bottle. Always been blond."

He slipped his right glove off and reached out and touched her hair then. It was black, thick, and silky. Then, hesitantly but with her permission, he reached his fingers down, slipping them beneath the silk cravat, letting him feel the patch of feathers across her throat—soft and warm, like Lenore's down when she'd been a raven chick.

Bibigul put her hand up and snagged him behind one horn, pulling his head forward to her. Roger didn't tell her how many women had done that before, let her believe it was original and unexpected. But what was unexpected was Bibigul's kiss. Shy, hesitant. She was the first girl since Stephanie, his nat girlfriend in high school, who'd kissed him like that, wanting to kiss Roger Washburn, not the rock star Ravenstone, fake as his ace and faded as his star might be.

Steph had dumped him when he got his horns but had shown back up when he got famous. Telling her he was no longer interested had felt sweet at the time, but in retrospect, that was the last time Roger had been around a woman who'd ever wanted him for him.

Bibigul's left hand slipped down from his left horn, and, after reflexively stopping her, Roger let her flip up his eye patch. He let her gaze on his black contact until he flipped the patch back down and they went back to kissing, Bibigul twining her fingers behind both horns.

Some women had a fetish for them. Others covered their revulsion, in varying degrees of transparency, with their lust for money and fame.

This was different in all the right ways. Roger twined his fingers in her hair, kissing—

A knock sounded at the door again.

Roger paused, then the knock repeated. Then a voice: "Mr. Ravenstone?"

There were very few who called him that, and he recognized the voice: Shirley.

"A moment," Roger promised Bibigul. He stood and went to the door, donning his right glove before opening it. "Hello, Shirley."

She sat in her scooter and beamed. She wore a blue satin gown today, with a plunging neckline. Across her lap was his frock coat. "You forgot this last night at your show." She offered it to him and smiled plaintively. "Is Lenore okay?"

"She's fine. Thank you," Roger said, both for her concern and the coat.

"I know how much she means to you," Shirley said. "That's why you've always been my favorite."

"What?"

"My favorite Jokertown Boy," Shirley explained. "Alec's the romantic, Sam's the artist, Paul's the sad funny one, Dirk's easygoing, Jim's odd, and you're supposed to be the mysterious devil, but you're not. You're the boy who rescues baby birds. You took care of the rest of the boys until they could fly on their own." She smiled a sad smile. "You're still looking after Jim."

Roger didn't know quite what to say so just conjured a pass for a later show. "You know I'm supposed to have secrets, right?"

"*Solamen miseris socios habuisse doloris,*" Shirley quoted in excellent Catholic high school Latin as she tucked the pass into her bodice.

It was Mephistopheles's line from Marlowe's *Dr. Faustus*, the explanation for why the Devil wanted souls for Hell. "'It is a comfort to the wretched to have companions in misery.'"

Shirley nodded. "You've had my soul since high school, Devil. See you at the show." Shirley waved and rolled off in her scooter, calling over her shoulder, "And at karaoke tonight."

Bibigul looked at Roger questioningly as he shut the door and leaned against it. "My life," Roger explained. "Just my life." He got his top hat and put it back on over his horns. "Care to go out and help me live it?"

Bibigul smiled, and Roger grinned back.

◆

Karaoke went well and likewise the next night's concert, though this time Roger decided to swap out "The Devil Went Down to Georgia" and slip in one of Alec's old numbers, not one of their greatest hits, but a solid B side in public domain: "Greensleeves."

Bibigul joined them. In the *Natchez*'s wardrobe room she'd found a green dress that fit, more of a fanciful bridesmaid gown in chartreuse taffeta than a proper medieval garment, but combined with a henin and cointoise and Alec's wife's forgotten wimple to cover her throat, it gave the right impression. And what Bibi lacked in mime skills, she made up for with musical ability, nailing "Greensleeves" despite only practicing a day, making Caitlyn Beaumont, standing at the bar sipping her customary daiquiri, smile and nod with approval. By some greater miracle, Ms. Potts had provided Bibi with her employee badge without comment or even requesting a meeting.

The negotiating skills of a former beauty queen and debutante were mighty indeed.

The best part, however, was having Lenore sing the name "Greensleeves" at all the right places. Bibigul wore a bird whistle set into a harmonica mount, and at appropriate times, she put her lips to it, singing the nightingale's note to signal Lenore to sing the corresponding English. It was a gimmick Roger had been trying to get Lenore to do for years, but outside of a studio, wasn't anything reliable. But with Bibigul's ability and a bit of misdirection, it worked.

The crowd loved it, and Roger did even more.

For magic shows, the Beautiful Bibi's main job was to stand there and look pretty. There were more elaborate tricks, of course—disappearing cabinets and the like—but Roger hadn't brought any aboard, and part of keeping the charade going was making do with what he had. But Caitlyn was amenable to fewer hours of close-up magic on deck so long as that corresponded with more hours onstage, and since their shows were better attended now that the Jokertown Boys had added a girl to the act, it was all to the good. Drink sales were up, pleasing Ms. Potts.

She sat on the boiler deck's promenade, sipping a mint julep, dressed in her Sunday best and crowned with an impossible bit of millinery involving bows, white peacock feathers, and scads of rhinestones, sparkling like *Das Rheingold* in the morning sun as the *Natchez* pulled into Memphis. Jim was up at the calliope, as per contract, playing "Let Me Call You Sweetheart," and passengers were lined up down the stairs to the main deck to disembark, concluding their voyage or ready to spend a pleasant Sunday. Caitlyn Beaumont stood by the still cordoned-off gap in the railing, ready to thank them for their visit and remind them when to be back if continuing on, and Mickey Lee Payne bustled about, finalizing receipts and credit card statements and being dogsbody for Ms. Potts, who took Sundays off to attend church.

Roger stood with Bibigul on his arm, again in her lolligoth Harpo Marx costume, Lenore jumping between their shoulders as it amused her. *"Pretty Polly,"* Lenore cried, followed by *"Find the parrot!"* Bibigul smiled. Memphis was a large enough city to browse pet shops, and there they might find the parrot or mynah bird or maybe a cockatoo who would become Serik II.

The boat docked, the cordon set was pulled aside, and the gangplank went down, but before anyone could disembark, someone came up. She was a middle-aged black woman like Ms. Potts, but where Ms. Potts was small and round, this woman was tall and statuesque, if not precisely svelte either. Her hair was straightened as well, worn in a stylish updo with ringlets, and she wore an immaculate women's suit in houndstooth. She also held up a badge.

Roger got out his opera glasses. The badge read IMMIGRATION INSPECTOR, arranged around a US Department of Justice seal. The woman's lips read, "Evangelique Jones, ICE. My agents are going to check the credentials of your passengers as they disembark, and then we're going to do an inspection of this vessel."

Mickey Lee inspected the badge and the warrant while Caitlyn Beaumont apologetically scurried up the stairs to fetch Ms. Potts, who stormed down, her julep still in hand. "What is the meaning of this?" Roger couldn't hear a word she said over the calliope, Jim having segued to "Here Comes the Showboat," but could easily read her lips as angry as she was. "Don't you people take a day of rest like the Good Lord commanded?"

Evangelique Jones smiled sweetly, but Roger knew a fake smile when he saw one, having done enough himself. "The Good Lord may rest on Sundays, but the Devil does not. We've received intelligence that this boat may be carrying illegal aliens."

"What intelligence?" demanded Ms. Potts.

ICE Agent Jones took out her cell phone, tapped for a moment, then handed it to Ms. Potts. The screen was filled with *The Dead Report* logo, then lurid lettering spelling *Natchez Investigation: The Devil's Door. The Seven Locks of Madame Lorelei.*

LaLaurie, Roger corrected mentally, then saw the image of Ryan Forge gesturing dramatically with an EVP meter toward the locked door opposite the boiler room.

Roger put down his opera glasses. Those idiots couldn't tell Kazakh from the whisperings of the damned, but ICE certainly could.

Bibigul looked at Roger in alarm. He didn't know what to tell her. If he were a real ace, he could get the disappearing cabinet trick to work, teleporting the refugees to safety, or mesmerize the ICE agent with his pocket watch, or use smoke and mirrors to make the door disappear. But he wasn't. He was a fake.

But he was a fake with a cell phone and magician's hands. *Wild Fox,* he texted. *Disguise yourself, go down by the boiler room, and follow my cues. Joker emergency!!!*

There was no response, but there usually wasn't. Andrew's favorite pastime was to disguise himself with his illusions, for which purpose he left his phone on silent in his pocket. Roger scanned the crowd. He didn't see Andrew, but Andrew could be anyone.

Roger took Bibigul by the hand and led her round the back way to the crewmen's stairs, down to the main deck and the boiler room access passage. The door was still locked, but it wasn't long before Ms. Potts came down the hall along with Evangelique Jones, trailed by a concerned and flustered Caitlyn Beaumont.

Ms. Potts's lower lip stuck out even farther than usual. A religious woman, she had a particular dislike for the Devil, and by proxy that meant him. "Mr. Washburn," she said firmly, "I do not know what you want or what you're doing here, but it is my day off, I'm not supposed to be working right now, and I do not have time for any foolishness."

"Nor do I," Roger agreed. "Contracts are serious business, and if you will examine ours, you will see there's a clause where the Jokertown Boys not only take a portion of the concert proceeds but are owed a percentage of the bar sales if it is above a certain base level."

"I'm certain this conversation can wait till tomorrow, Mr. Washburn," Ms. Potts snapped.

"It most certainly can," agreed Evangelique Jones. "I am an agent of the federal government on an official investigation, and I have here a warrant to search these premises."

She brandished it dramatically. Roger stared, raising his right eyebrow and looking askance until she at last looked herself, realizing she was holding a copy of the *Natchez* ghost tour brochure. The warrant was safely in Roger's pocket.

Evangelique Jones turned to Ms. Potts. "Well, you saw it earlier. Now I will ask you to open that door," she said, pointing, "and if you don't, you'll be obstructing a federal investigation."

"I don't have the keys," protested Ms. Potts. "Mr. Cottle locked it after a steam leak injured some of the crew. It's a matter of safety."

"It's true," Caitlyn agreed. "We don't talk about it in front of the guests, but some of the men were terribly scalded!"

This was the first Roger had heard of this, but the safest place to hide someone was where no one else wanted to go, and such a history had obviously served to keep the crew out.

Evangelique Jones smiled and stepped over to the door, placing her palm against it flat. "Seems cool enough now. Or at least no hotter than anything else here." She opened her purse then, and with a reveal Roger both envied and hated, produced a pair of folding bolt cutters. "Now, let's see what's behind this door."

Bibigul clutched his arm, and Roger felt a stabbing pain in his left eye. He'd been wearing his contact too long, and what he needed was Wild Fox there to project an illusion. "The room is empty," Roger stated as forcefully as he could, hoping Andrew had slipped in the back. "No one's inside. There's nothing but steam and an OSHA suit waiting to happen."

"We'll see," said Evangelique Jones, snapping the first lock. It fell to the deck with a dramatic *clank*, and the pounding in Roger's head increased. Two. Three. Four. Five. It felt like an ice pick in his eye driving deeper and deeper. Six. The pounding increased, moving to his horns. For the seventh and final lock, she just beat the lock with the bolt cutters till the brass rang like an anvil in his skull, and then the door flew open.

Roger's sight was clouded by a red mist but then it cleared and he saw the room was as he described it. Empty. A tiny tendril of steam floated from the faulty radiator, but beyond that it was barren and boring.

Roger didn't know whether Andrew had cast his illusion to make it appear as he'd described, or he'd finally turned his card, gaining illusion or teleportation or some other ace to save the day. But he was afraid it was the second and he'd drawn a black queen along with it because a nightingale's cry of alarm sprang from Bibigul's throat, and Lenore cried, *"Roger, you're bleeding!"*

"Stage blood," Evangelique Jones snarled dismissively. "I recognize you now—you're Ravenstone, the parlor trick devil. I should arrest you now for that stunt with the warrant. But whatever. Found one Kazakh at least, and a joker, too!"

With that, she reached out and grabbed Bibigul's cravat, pulling it down and exposing her feathered throat.

"Unhand her!" Roger roared in his most dramatic and Mephistophelean voice. "She's my wife! We were married in New Orleans, and by law that means you cannot touch her! Here, see our marriage contract!" With that, Roger produced it, unfurling the document with a flourish.

Usually it would have dancing devils and demonic sigils, but now the only thing it held in common with the former hellish contract were a few heart-shaped Pennsylvania Dutch hex signs.

The ICE agent took the contract and examined it, finally remarking, "Damn, Naw'lins is making fancy marriage licenses these days. . . ." She handed it back. "I expect you've got her green card?"

"No," said Roger acidly, his temples still pounding, "but she does." He pointed to Bibigul's penguin coin purse.

Bibigul opened it and in wonder removed a green card.

Evangelique Jones took it and examined it, finally handing it back. "Well," she said at last, "I suppose everything is in order. Thank you for your cooperation."

She marched stiffly and proudly down the hall until rounding the corner left, like a classic villainess making her exit.

Roger's head was still pounding, and he was afraid he was hallucinating, but then he saw a fox tail emerge from the skirt of Caitlyn Beaumont's latest party dress. Then she shook her head and fox ears emerged from her perfectly highlighted hair. Then the illusion completely dissolved and Andrew Yamauchi stood there, grinning.

Then Andrew's face fell, and Roger dropped to his knees, his head swimming. He reached up, feeling blood seeping from the base of his horns, then he saw a ghost.

No, not a ghost—a translucent little boy. Nurassyl reached his chubby arms up, and the tentacles where his hands would have been touched Roger's forehead. The pain went away, fleeing before his touch, replaced with a feeling of well-being, like a mother's cool hand on a fevered brow.

Nurassyl pulled up Roger's eye patch, touching the burning lid of his eye. Roger blinked and the contact fell out. Nurassyl brushed it aside like an inconsequential bit of black jelly, then put his arms around Roger's neck and hugged him, and everything was all right.

"Lord almighty," proclaimed Ms. Potts, "saved by the Devil and Br'er Fox. You do work in strange and wondrous ways. . . ."

Nurassyl went and hugged her as well.

"And you, dear child," she said, hugging the joker boy.

Roger reached up and felt his horns. They felt longer and slightly sharper than usual.

He reached into his jacket and pulled out the silver hand mirror, checking. They *were* longer and sharper, and his left eye, despite having lost the contact, was still jet-black.

He'd drawn his card. He'd drawn his card and lived.

A nightingale's voice trilled and Lenore said, *"Oh, Roger, are you all right?"*

"Fine, I think."

Bibigul embraced him, trilling. *"Did you mean what you said?"* asked Lenore. *"Do you truly want to marry me?"*

"Yeah," Roger said, "I think so. But we're going to have to get a better marriage contract." He picked up the scroll, which was once again Sam's calligraphic masterpiece, fiddle-playing hellcats and all.

The bottom shimmered for a moment, the spot where Johnny's signature was written in disappearing reappearing ink. The name that appeared there in blood red letters, however, was *Shirley*, then just as quickly it faded away.

Roger rolled up the contract, tucking it back into his jacket, while Bibigul warbled happily.

"I know who can marry us!" cried Lenore. *"Captain Leathers! Would it not be perfect?"*

"Yeah," Roger said uncertainly. "Perfect."

♣ ♦ ♠ ♥

In the Shadow of Tall Stacks

Part 6

ROGER ASKED WILBUR IF he would marry them, but Wilbur refused. After all, what marriage bureau would be willing to accept the signature of a dead man on a really soggy marriage license? "No," he told them flatly. "I'm very flattered you'd ask, but you really need to find someone else to marry you. Why not talk to Captain Montaigne?"

Captain Montaigne informed Roger and Bibigul that, despite persistent rumors to the contrary, a boat's captain can't legally marry anyone, and that they needed to find a clergyman or a justice of the peace.

Which is what they did: when they stopped at Cape Girardeau, Roger and Bibi, accompanied by Wild Fox and Sylvia, went ashore to the local Recorder of Deeds and applied for a marriage license, with Wild Fox providing the required identification for Bibigul via illusion; later, a minister was brought on board and the marriage performed.

The reception took place in the Bayou Lounge. Wilbur stayed for a while in the lounge for the celebration, even if drinking or eating cake was no longer possible for him. He stayed mostly in the corners (remaining invisible since the *Dead Report* crew was also there), watching the people dancing and singing and Roger performing impromptu magic as Lenore fluttered around both him and Bibi.

Wilbur found himself enjoying the celebration and the memories it dredged up in him.

His own marriage to Eleanor, as well as the reception they'd had afterward, had been more traditional and elaborate, which made him, honestly, rather uncomfortable, though Eleanor had enjoyed her role as the lovely bride. The hall her parents had rented in Charleston had been decorated as a steamboat, with fluted steam stacks holding flowers as the centerpieces for the table and a cake in the shape of the *Natchez*—the hull of which had already been laid. The *Hamiltonian*'s large oak and steel wheel, newly purchased by Wilbur for the *Natchez*, stood on a frame near the head table (surrounded by the smaller cousins of the two families, who were pretending to "steer" the hall and making loud steam-whistle noises). A small orchestra played swing and classic songs on the stage, even—rather wincingly, in Wilbur's opinion—attempting some New Orleans jazz.

Wilbur sat next to Eleanor, holding on to her hand in the midst of the chaotic revelry. He knew few of the people there; the majority of those at the reception were Eleanor's relatives, as his parents were dead, he'd been an only child, and his relatives lived far from the East Coast and had declined to attend. Eleanor seemed to have sensed his unease—she had leaned over to him, placing her head on his shoulder. "Just be patient, dearest," she said. "We'll leave as soon as we can, and after that, I'll always be with you. We can start our own lives and live as we want to live."

Wilbur had squeezed her hand tightly, bending his head down to kiss her as people tapped their glasses with their silverware and laughed.

As they were doing now. Wilbur shook off the memory to see Roger and Bibi kissing, and he smiled as he had then.

But things were less joyful when he visited the remaining

refugees again early the next morning as the *Natchez* was steaming on toward St. Louis.

The refugees, after Agent Jones's blatant entry into their cabin, were increasingly nervous about being discovered and deported, and, through Jyrgal, complaining loudly to JoHanna. Wilbur popped in in the midst of one such conversation. ". . . understand your concerns, but I assure you that you're safer here than anywhere else."

A mingled, incomprehensible babble of Kazakh and Russian and poor English answered her statement (very little of it comprehensible to Wilbur despite the smattering of Kazakh he'd picked up from Jyrgal and Nurassyl). Erzhan was the loudest among the protesters, slapping his beaver's tail on the floor for emphasis, and shouting something in Kazakh that Wilbur couldn't understand and Jyrgal declined to translate.

"Miss Potts," Jyrgal said finally in his heavily accented English, his mittened hands waving to quiet the uproar of the others, "we have been nearly discovered by ICE agents twice now. That has us all worried, as you can see. Not me, you understand, but some of the others are wondering if—rather than leaving in twos and threes where you've made arrangements—if it wouldn't be better for all of us to leave the boat and take our chances on our own as a group. Maybe some of us could, perhaps, simply disappear in the joker section of your big cities. We don't wish to end up imprisoned on Rathlin Island with the others."

JoHanna was already shaking her head well before he'd finished. "The plans have been made with the JADL, and they're still the best path to follow. The authorities can't easily reach you in the sanctuary cities, and half of you are already safe. *All* of you will be safe if you just continue to follow the JADL's directions. Please, Jyrgal, you have to convince them."

Jyrgal lifted a shoulder. "I will try," he said, and again: "I will try."

"Please do your best, then," JoHanna told him, her hands on her wide hips. "It's in *all* of our interests to keep you from being caught, after all." She glared around the room, looking in the eyes of each of the refugees and pausing at Erzhan for a longing stare before heaving a sigh and leaving the room.

Wilbur remained behind. He took in enough steam to become easily visible and to make his voice audible. *"Keşiriñiz,"* he said, looking at all of them, but especially Jyrgal, Nurassyl, and Erzhan. *I'm sorry.* "I wish I'd learned enough to speak to you in your own language, but Jyrgal will tell you what I'm saying." He paused. "JoHanna—Ms. Potts—is right. You will all be safest if you stay here. Believe me, I understand wanting desperately to get off this boat—better than any of you might believe. I especially understand how frightened some of you are after what happened with that ICE woman. But I assure you that you have people watching over you here, and they . . . we . . . only have your best interests at heart. We want you *all* to find a safe place, and we'll do all we can to make that happen. I promise you that."

The words sounded like platitudes and empty promises, but there was nothing more he could say. He looked around as Jyrgal finished translating, trying to read in their faces whether they believed him or not, and not seeing anything that convinced him. Erzhan, especially, seemed unconvinced. Behind the joker's back, he could see Aiman and Tazhibai whispering to each other.

But this was all Wilbur could do to settle them; he was afraid words of hope and promises might not be enough.

For anyone. For anything.

♥

"Your shift over?" Wilbur heard Roger Ravenstone say to Jack, the bartender. Roger and Bibi were at the rail just outside the doors of the Bayou Lounge with Jack as Wilbur was passing by, unseen.

The *Natchez* had docked in St. Louis near the Arch that

afternoon; cargo destined for the city had been off-loaded—as had a quartet of the Kazakh jokers, since St. Louis was one of the sanctuary cities in which the JADL had contacts. Several of the passengers had signed on to travel only this far, leaving the boat while new passengers came aboard who were going onto the Tall Stacks festival. Many of the passengers staying with the boat took the opportunity to do some sightseeing, while curious onlookers at the riverfront paid their money to tour the boat—that last group, at just past eight thirty P.M. now, had all been escorted off the boat.

It had been a chaotic day.

"Soon," the elderly Cajun said to Roger. "Just on break right now. I'm thinking about checking out Laclede's Landing. Mebbe." Jack looked toward the sky. Dark thunderheads were rising in the west against high clouds still illuminated by the just-set sun. They could hear thunder grumbling in the distance. "Or mebbe not," Jack added. "It s'posed to rain?"

Roger pulled out his smartphone and touched the weather app. "Yep. Looks like it. There's a severe thunderstorm warning here until midnight. Check out the radar—that looks ugly to me."

Jack glanced at the phone Roger held out, but Wilbur doubted the man really understood what he was looking at. For that matter, neither did Wilbur; the red and yellow blotches looked like a bad abstract painting. At the time he'd last cared much about the weather, radar was still in its infancy and used to track airplanes and ships, not storms. With a showy wave of his free hand and a grin, Roger made it appear that his phone had simply disappeared from the hand in which he'd been holding it, displayed his empty hands dramatically, then plucked the phone from Jack's bar jacket pocket. "Well," he said to Jack, "Bibi and I got another set to do. We'd better get to it. You have a good night whatever you end up doing with it, Jack. C'mon, love."

He touched Bibigul's arm and the two went back into the lounge hand in hand. Jack stayed at the rail, looking out at St. Louis, the Arch, and the onrushing storm. Wilbur thought of staying with Jack for a bit and just watching the storm front come in, already trailing a gray sheet of rain underneath its clouds. Instead, he chose to stay invisible and just move on. The threatening weather seemed to fit his mood at the moment, with the coming storm a metaphor for his inability to come up with a solution to his and his steamboat's apparently intertwined fates or his inability to calm the fears of the remaining refugees.

Steamless and powerless. Tied down and stuck. Forever. It's coming on fast, that fate. . . . And who knows if that Agent Jones will come back. I wasn't there to help them when she showed up. . . .

Doubts and guilt whirled in an uneasy mix in his head.

Wilbur continued around the boiler deck toward the bow of the *Natchez*. The promenade area was deserted, the passengers either in the city, in their cabins, or in the lounge. He went to Jeremiah's cabin and found the old pilot with fountain pen in hand, writing another letter. His desk lamp gleamed off his balding, age-spotted scalp. Wilbur glanced over the man's shoulder: *Dear Mr. McDonough, I'm writing to you as I understand McDonough Marine Services has need of an experienced river and barge pilot . . .*

"Any luck?" Wilbur said, and Jeremiah nearly dropped the fountain pen at the sound of his voice. The old man craned his head over his shoulder, one white eyebrow lifting on his dark, wrinkled face.

"That just ain't right, sneaking up on an old man without so much as a 'hey.' You could give someone a heart attack." Jeremiah capped the fountain pen and swiveled his chair around. His head tilted appraisingly. "You look troubled, Wilbur."

"I guess . . . I guess I'm just feeling sorry for myself tonight."

Jeremiah looked back at the letter, then at Wilbur, shaking his head slowly. "I kin understand that with all that's goin' on. There's gotta be a way out for you somehow, Wilbur. I can't imagine but that your kind of existence ain't been nothing but awful."

Wilbur shook his head. "Awful? Not really. Awful was when

I lost Eleanor and our child; that's a terrible hole I can't ever fill. But past that . . . ? There have been bad times and despair since, plenty of it, but I've also had some good to leaven it. I made friends over the decades, friends like you. I have *family* here." He saw Jeremiah grin slowly at that. "I've enjoyed the trips up and down the rivers and seeing the slow changes in the landscape, even though I've wanted often enough to be able to get off at the towns and cities and explore. But awful? No. It was just . . . life. My life. It's only now, with the thoughts of my poor *Natchez* being no longer a living boat . . ." *And me stuck on it. Steamless. Powerless. Just an empty ghost with nothing but memories.*

"Sometimes what you have to do for family, what you have to do to achieve what you want, is to refuse to give up on them, to change whatever needs to be changed and make whatever sacrifices are necessary." Eleanor's words.

Am I willing to do that? Wilbur asked himself. And the answer that came back was a resounding yes. He *had* changed over the decades. He'd had thoughts and emotions and experiences he'd never imagined in his life. If he no longer had Eleanor, he still had friends, and he still had his boat.

He would find a way. He'd make whatever sacrifice he needed to make.

He was suddenly no longer sad. Just angry and determined.

Lightning flashed to the west. A rumble of deep thunder answered.

"Sorry, Jeremiah," he said. "I'm working on things. I promise. Maybe we can make it so you won't need to be writing letters like that."

♣ ◆ ♠ ♥

Under the Arch

by David D. Levine

ACK THE BARTENDER LEANED on the promenade rail, looking forward and up at the Gateway Arch as the *Natchez* steamed into St. Louis just after dawn. From river level the Arch seemed impossibly tall and impossibly clean, gleaming in the light of the rising sun as it swept up, up, up from the riverbank into a blue sky dotted with a few puffy clouds, then down again in a majestic arc. Diminishing in size as it rose, it seemed even taller than it was.

Gateway to the West, he thought; *gateway to freedom for the Kazakhs*, he hoped. It was about the midpoint of their journey to Cincinnati, and their most northerly port before Cincinnati itself. The trip so far had been much more turbulent than he'd expected, and he really hoped that this gleaming gateway was an omen of smoother sailing going forward.

Somehow, though, he doubted it.

St. Louis, important though it was in Mississippi River history, was an unfortunate detour for Jack and his remaining Kazakh charges. After this stop they would head back down the Mississippi to the confluence of the Ohio River, which they had passed in the night some days ago, then take the Ohio fork toward Cincinnati and the Tall Stacks, where the last of the jokers would depart.

He would miss them. Some more than others, to be sure, and he would not miss the hassles, the arguments, the language barrier, and the moments of near-panic. But this litter of lost puppies he'd wound up taking on, almost against his will, had turned out to be as much of a joy as a burden in many ways. Little Sezim, always clutching that filthy little doll, melted Jack's weathered heart, and Nurassyl, the "ghost boy," had such compassion for others that he made everyone want to help him. And some of the others appealed in other ways. . . .

Jack shook his head. No. Even if his interest were reciprocated—and why would anyone, even a misshapen Kazakh joker, be interested in an ugly old Cajun bartender?—he had learned enough about Kazakh culture's attitude toward gays to know that he didn't have a prayer it would lead to anything.

He sighed. He'd been single for . . . how long now? Twelve years, at least. You'd think he'd be used to the idea by now, and at seventy-nine he had few years and fewer prospects remaining. But watching Ravenstone and Bibi's budding romance, as well as Tazh and Aiman's puppy love, reminded him of what he was missing, and filled his heart with despair of ever finding someone to call his own.

Natchez's whistle blew then, a shrill blast that made the rail beneath Jack's crossed arms vibrate, and it was answered by a foghorn call from shore. The dock where they would be berthing for their three-day stay in St. Louis lay waiting, and Jack had work to do.

♣

The rest of the morning was spent shifting luggage, answering questions from their new passengers, helping to haul carts of sheets and towels to the laundry, and preparing the bar for lunch. Then came the lunch rush, which kept him busy serving drinks, snacks, and sandwiches to customers old and new. One of the former was Leo Storgman, whose tipple of choice was a boiler-maker. He had been a regular since New Orleans, and they had chatted frequently during slow moments; they actually had quite a bit in common.

"How long you been retired?" Storgman asked Jack as he sliced limes.

Jack had to think for a moment. "I took early retirement back in . . . ninety-six. Over twenty years. Jesus, where does the time go?" He shook his head. "You?"

"2011."

"You were a cop, right?"

"Detective. Forty-two years on the force." Storgman raised his glass in salute, then drained it. "Anyway . . . do you have any kind of handle on that piece-of-shit website they make us use for our pensions?"

Jack smiled sadly. "What I don't know about computers would fill a book."

"Damn." Storgman tapped his glass, and Jack refilled it. "The world just keeps moving faster and faster."

"Don't I know it."

♠

After two endless hours Jack shooed the last of the lunch customers out and shut the bar for the afternoon. For a long moment he leaned heavily on the closed door. What he really wanted to do right now was sleep for a week.

What he did instead was haul himself vertical, load and start the dishwasher, and wipe down the bar and tables. Then he picked up the basket of wrapped sandwiches he'd prepared at the start of his shift and set off down the hall to deliver them to the Kazakhs.

The scene behind the door labeled STEAM LEAK—UNSAFE was pretty much the same as it had been for the last few weeks—a little wearier maybe, a little stinkier, a little more stir-crazy. Bibigul, at least, was off with Ravenstone, rehearsing for the evening show, but the tiny space was still crowded with jokers. "Lunch," Jack said, handing the sandwiches to Timur.

"Thank you very much," the old joker replied with a courteous nod, then began distributing Jack's largesse to his flock. His English was improving every day, Jack noted; he would probably be able to get work wherever he ended up—if he could find an employer who would accept a Kazakh with a horn that curled like a turban around the top of his head. Timur was strong, warmhearted, reliable, patient, and generous. Anyone would be happy to have him.

Aiman and Tazhibai, Jack noted, had chosen to share a single sandwich—roast beef on rye with horseradish. But as Jack had not bothered cutting the Kazakhs' sandwiches in half, Aiman cut it herself with a large chef's knife, which Jack recognized as one that had gone missing from the kitchen. The kids made a big show of dividing the sandwich with ridiculously exact precision, Aiman edging the knife this way and that by tiny fractions of an inch until both were satisfied, the two of them giggling madly over the process. Then, once the sandwich was divided, they fed the halves to each other, Aiman's freakishly long arms curling around Tazhibai's four hairy ones until Jack was afraid he would need an insulin shot to overcome the sweetness of it.

Jack rolled his eyes at Timur, who smiled and shrugged. But one of the other jokers watched the kids' antics with a sour expression.

Erzhan, a tough and burly joker who resembled a cross between a giant beaver and the Creature from the Black Lagoon, was Aiman's father. He was a bad-tempered traditionalist, and Jack knew that he barely tolerated the fifteen-year-old Tazhibai's attentions to his fourteen-year-old daughter. But with quarters so close, there was no way the kids could get up to anything really inappropriate. Jack hoped that the three of them would find a way to work out their differences before their journey came to an end. There might be trouble after that, but at least then they would be out of Jack's thinning hair.

◆

After finishing up with the Kazakhs, Jack finally did get a brief disco nap before he had to go help the kitchen prep for dinner and set up the bar before it opened. The bar was lightly populated all evening—he supposed that many of his usual customers were enjoying the nightlife in nearby Laclede's Landing rather than the admittedly limited pleasures of the boat's Paddle Wheel Lounge—and after he closed up at midnight he found he still had some energy left. And the boat was docked right in the heart of a pretty big city.

He hesitated at the lounge door after locking it, heart pounding, then swallowed, nodded, and returned to his cabin, where a quick flip through a well-thumbed *Damron Men's Travel Guide* revealed that there were several gay bars within a short cab ride. Some didn't close until three in the morning.

He looked at himself in the mirror for a long while. He didn't really like what he saw, but he knew that some guys liked 'em weathered and wiry, and who was he to judge? Finally he blew out a breath, combed what was left of his hair, and put on his best pants and silk shirt. He topped this with a light jacket and an LSU trucker cap; it was a warm night, but there was rain in the forecast.

He slipped the *Travel Guide* and some condoms into his jacket pocket and shut his cabin door quietly behind himself.

♥

Jack paused at the top of the gangplank, looking up at the Arch. It was even more dramatic by night, illuminated by spotlights against a background of racing, lowering clouds. But those clouds promised rain—indeed, it was already starting to drizzle—and it looked like a pretty good hike across the wharf's parking lot to the nearest street where he might catch a cab. And besides, did he really want to subject himself to the unknown St. Louis bar scene? If he didn't manage to hook up he'd come back even more miserable.

As he dithered, trying to nerve himself up, a curse behind him caught his attention. Though he didn't speak Kazakh, the emotion behind the word was unmistakable—someone was royally pissed about something. And none of the Kazahks should be out of their cabin at this hour.

Half annoyed and half relieved at the interruption, Jack went back inside. He soon found Timur, the horn-turbaned Kazakh elder, snooping about the corridors with a little flashlight and muttering curses under his breath. This raised Jack's level of anxiety still further—the man was usually unflappable. Anything that could worry him this seriously must be pretty serious. "*Psst*," Jack whispered to draw Timur's attention without alarming him.

Timur started, then relaxed when he saw it was Jack. "I thank Allah you are here, my friend," he said.

"What's wrong?"

Timur sighed. "It is Aiman and Tazhibai. They are not in the cabin. They left . . ." He gestured up and down his body. ". . . clothing, in their beds, so we would not know."

"Oh boy." Jack blew out a breath. "If they've left the boat . . ."

Timur shook his head definitively. "They are not that stupid." He paused, then gave a sad little smile. "I think they have found a place to . . . be alone together."

"Oh boy oh boy," Jack repeated, the implications sinking in. "We have to find them."

"Before Erzhan."

"Yeah." Erzhan's reaction to discovering his little girl in Tazhibai's four arms would not be charitable.

Thinking quickly, Jack opened a cabinet on the wall and pulled out a flashlight from between the life preservers. "I'll check the engine room, you look in the kitchen."

Again Timur shook his head. "We work together. You know the boat, I know Kazakh."

Jack smiled, impressed that the man could think clearly in such a difficult situation. "All right." They set off down the stairs to the main deck.

Moving as quietly as they could, they checked first the laundry, which was closest to the stairway, and then the kitchen. Both were locked, but Jack suspected the teenagers' nimble fingers—driven by lust—might have been able to overcome that obstacle. He used his keys to enter, then he and Timur shone their flashlights around, whispering the kids' names and listening hard for any reaction.

Finding nothing in the kitchen, Jack closed and locked the door behind them. "Paddle Wheel Lounge next," he whispered to Timur, "then engine room." They crept down the corridor to the lounge, shielding their flashlights with their hands. "Have they done this before, do you think?"

Timur sighed. "I do not know. I fear yes."

Then they came to the Paddle Wheel Lounge door, which Jack had locked less than an hour ago. It stood open. "Sonofabitch!" Jack whispered, then raced through with Timur right behind him.

Jack hurried between the tables to the EMPLOYEES ONLY door at the aft end, which also stood open, revealing the grimy antechamber beyond. The left door led down a ladder to the engine room, the right one to the paddle wheel itself; both were closed. He hesitated, then heard a muffled cry through the door on the right. He hurried through.

The space between the paddle wheel and the outer bulkhead was a crazy quilt of light and shadow, the harsh mercury light from the parking lot cut into strips and triangles by the complex shapes of the paddle wheel itself and its driving hardware. Greasy connecting rods, dripping with river water or condensed steam or both, cut across the space in every direction. Despite the urgency of the situation, Jack paused, not wanting to brain himself on a protruding rod or pipe. The greasy waters of the

Mississippi slapped rhythmically against the hull below; the space smelled of filthy river water, oil, and diesel fuel.

But then another cry—this one clearly the voice of a terrified teenage girl—drove Jack forward. "Hang on!" he called. He kept his head down and held out one hand in front of himself as he moved. "Don't do anything stupid!" He wasn't sure who he was talking to, but it was good advice in general.

Behind him Timur shouted something in Kazakh, maybe translating Jack's words, maybe not.

A moment later Jack emerged into night air, freshened by the increasing rain. He found himself in a protected corner between the paddle wheel and the cabin on the boat's starboard side, with the lights of Illinois on the Mississippi's far bank providing a semiromantic backdrop. A pile of blankets and life vests cushioned the entwined and far too numerous arms of the lovestruck teenagers. And above them loomed a black, scaly, and clearly enraged figure: Erzhan.

Erzhan dismissed Jack with a glance, turning his attention to Timur. He spoke in Kazakh, something angry and disapproving and heartfelt, pointing to the frightened teenagers even as they tried to disentangle themselves from each other and get into their clothes. Timur replied in equally heartfelt tones, but placatingly, patting the air with his hands and stepping slowly forward to position himself between Erzhan and the kids. For his part, Jack held back. . . . This was someone else's family business, and he didn't feel qualified to interfere as long as no one was in immediate danger. But his heart went out to Timur, who was clearly doing the best he could in a very sticky situation.

Erzhan seemed to be listening to Timur's argument, though his face registered severe disappointment and anger. But as soon as he realized that Timur was trying to get between him and his daughter, he lashed out, slapping Timur backhand with surprising ferocity. As Timur staggered back, catching himself on the paddle wheel, Erzhan moved toward the kids with murder in his eyes.

Almost before he knew he was doing it, Jack ducked beneath

a pipe and slammed into Erzhan's side with his shoulder. Jack had played football in high school, though he'd been too skinny to be a serious player, so he thought he knew what he was doing. But this felt more like running into a concrete pillar than hitting a tackling dummy, and Jack found his own breath knocked out by the impact.

Though Erzhan barely reacted to the blow, Jack's unthinking action managed to distract him just long enough for the kids to scramble to their feet. Still only half dressed, a gangling tangle of arms, they scurried across the deck toward the door. Erzhan growled like an animal and lunged toward them in pursuit—and then there came a resounding *clang* and he dropped to the deck, stunned by his head's impact with one of the paddle wheel's drive rods.

Jack took a moment to assess the situation. The kids were nearly out the door, Timur was regaining his footing, and Erzhan, shaking his head, was quickly recovering his wits. In just a moment he would be after the kids again, and this time he would know to watch his head.

Jack leapt onto Erzhan in a flying tackle.

Erzhan was nearly twice his weight, but Jack's speed and the element of surprise sent the two of them slamming into the paddle wheel blades behind Erzhan. That must have hurt—the big joker roared like a bear and clutched Jack in a painful embrace that drove the breath from Jack's lungs.

Jack struggled ineffectually in Erzhan's grip. The scaly arms seemed strong as steel, crushing his ribs like a constricting python. Breathless, Jack started to panic, fighting for his life against the pressure.

Somewhere within Jack, rage began to rise. It was an alien presence in his breast, yet one he knew well, one he had fought many times in his seventy-nine years.

He feared it, and yet under the circumstances a part of him welcomed it.

But before Jack could give in to the anger, another factor intruded. Timur, rushing head down and horn-first from the other side of the space, slammed into Erzhan from behind, catching him right between the shoulder blades with the hard, twisting horn atop his head. Erzhan gasped from the pain and relaxed his grip, letting Jack squirm free.

For a moment Jack lay panting on the deck, recovering his breath. Then he turned painfully over and levered himself to hands and knees, shaking his head to clear it. He was too old for this shit, too old by half, but he had to do *something*.

The kids were nowhere to be seen. They had left the vicinity and would almost certainly flee the boat—a pair of frightened, underage illegal aliens, in the middle of a strange city, who barely spoke English. Jack should follow and help them. But Timur and Erzhan were struggling together like a pair of monstrous wrestlers from some Grecian urn. Jack should help Timur. Again he felt that sick rage boiling up beneath his breastbone, and again he tamped it down. That *really* wouldn't help.

Suddenly Erzhan got the upper hand in the fight, smashing Timur in the chin with a fierce uppercut. As Timur fell stunned on the deck, Erzhan straightened and rose above him with both hands clenched together, poised for a killing blow.

Jack bellowed—a savage, reptilian sound like something from the Jurassic—and leapt, slamming into the scaly joker with the full force of the anger within him. Unprepared for the impact, Erzhan fell over backwards . . . and splashed into the oily Mississippi waters below.

Jack nearly followed him overboard. But something snagged the tail of his jacket, barely preventing him from tumbling after. Instead, he landed heavily on the deck with his head and shoulders over the edge.

Lying there with the breath knocked out of him, Jack watched Erzhan flail for a moment in the dark waters, fitfully lit by the blue-white light from the parking lot. But Erzhan quickly recovered himself, and in a moment he was speeding through the water toward the shore, propelled by strong strokes of his beaver-like tail.

Jack's rage tried to drive him into the water—to follow Erzhan, to swim and fight and tear and kill—but whatever had hold of his jacket tail hauled hard on it, pulling Jack back on board. A hand grasped his shoulder, turning him over onto his back. It was Timur, of course, bruised and with blood seeping from a cut above one eye. "Are you . . . all right?" he panted.

"Unh," Jack managed, then, "Uh, yeah. You?"

Timur shrugged, then looked out over the water, seeking Erzhan.

Jack closed his eyes hard and again shook his head to clear it. It didn't help much. "He's going after the kids!" he said. "We have to stop him!"

Timur sighed heavily. *"Eyah,"* he said—that meant *yes*, one of the few Kazakh words Jack knew—but it was delivered with weary resignation. Nonetheless, he helped Jack to his feet.

They were a sorry pair of heroes, Jack reflected as he considered Timur's battered face and his own painful, exhausted, elderly body . . . feeling very frail now, as the adrenaline of the fight drained away. But there was no one else, on the boat or off, he could think of to help in such a sticky situation.

Then, to Jack's surprise, Timur enveloped him in a warm, fierce hug. He smelled of engine grease and spices and honest, manly sweat. "Thank you," he murmured into Jack's shoulder.

Jack patted Timur's back—wanting to do more, much more. "C'mon," he said. "Let's go."

They hurried up the stairs as quickly as they could. "What will he do if he catches them?" Jack panted as they went.

"Honor killing," Timur replied—a grim statement of fact, as though the question were "What happens if you step off a cliff?" and the answer "You fall."

"Well, shit."

They reached the top of the gangplank. The rain was really coming down now, but despite the distance, the dark, and the rain, Jack immediately recognized the two small figures fleeing across the parking lot. No question, it was Tazh and Aiman. "Hey!"

he called. "You kids get back here right now!" Timur, beside him, shouted something in Kazakh. But they didn't hear, didn't understand, or didn't want to obey—they neither looked back nor slowed their pace.

Then a splash from Jack's right drew his attention. It was Erzhan, crawling onto the riverbank from the water. The harsh white mercury light gleaming on his dripping black scales made him look even more like the Creature from the Black Lagoon from the old black-and-white movie. Without hesitation he took off running, following the kids with pounding strokes of his powerful legs. The beaver tail flapping behind him didn't seem to hold him back at all.

"Sonofabitch," Jack growled, and took off down the gangplank with Timur right behind him. But though Aiman's stumpy little legs slowed the teenagers, they had a lead on him—thirty feet in space and sixty years in age. By the time he reached the bottom of the gangplank they were maybe fifty feet away. Even as he ran after them, rain splatting in his face and his pounding feet splashing in the parking lot's growing puddles, he felt his wind failing and they pulled farther and farther ahead. *Shit shit shit*, he thought, but didn't have the breath to curse out loud.

Finally he had to stop, panting hard, hands on knees. The rain hammered his back, ran down his neck, and trickled past his collarbones to his chest. He looked up to see the kids reach the edge of the parking lot, look both ways, cross the street . . . and vanish into a storm drain.

Storm drain.

"Aw, Jesus," Jack said, and looked up. Low, thick clouds rushed past, their dark bellies dimly illuminated by the city's sodium lights, and a torrent of rain came pouring down into his face. "Jesus fucking *fuck*."

He was just trying to decide whether to follow them down the drain or go back to the boat for help when Timur passed him, running full tilt, charging after the kids without question or pause. Then Jack heard heavy, splashing footfalls off to his right:

Erzhan, also running for the storm drain. He was younger and fitter than Timur, but Timur had a head start and would reach the drain first. But what would happen after that?

Looking at Timur's retreating back, Jack couldn't help but notice how well-defined his shoulders were, not to mention the firm ass that strained the wet fabric of his trousers. "Jack, you are an idiot," he said, and ran after him.

♣

Timur slipped into the storm drain as neatly as a Louisiana gator sliding from the bank into a rushing river. Jack, not far behind him, had a harder time of it, but made it down into the catch basin below the drain inlet without breaking anything.

The catch basin was big enough for the two men to stand erect, and Jack found Timur peering both ways down the adjacent pipe, clearly trying to determine which way the teenagers had gone. Water cascaded from the inlet behind them to splash in the pool at their feet; it already was running nearly knee-high.

Jack wiped the water from his face, but it was immediately replaced by drops bouncing off the walls. At least it was rainwater, not sewage. "What the *fuck* were they thinking?" he shouted over the splashing and gurgling. "Storm drain's no place for civilians."

Timur shrugged. "We must find them before Erzhan does. I go this way, you go that way."

"No." Jack stopped Timur with a hand on his shoulder. "Never go alone. Too dangerous." He pointed down at the water; it was black and completely opaque in the sodium light that filtered down from the street. "There could be a drop-off under that, and you'd never see it before you stepped into it." He held out a hand. "Hold on. If one of us falls into deep water, the other pulls him out."

Timur took Jack's hand. His palm, though wet, was warm and hard as a bear's paw. "Fine. Which way?"

Jack held up a finger for silence, closed his eyes, and listened hard. His hearing wasn't quite as good as it used to be, but above the white noise of the water's flow he made out a rhythmic sloshing—with the tempo of short-legged footsteps in deep water—off to the left. He heard high-pitched vocalizations as well, but whether they were the giggles of a lovestruck teenager on an adventure or the panicked cries of one whose feet had been swept out from under her by a swift current he could not say. "This way," he said, pointing definitively.

But following the kids proved a much harder task than it had appeared at first. St. Louis, like many U.S. cities, seemed to be in the midst of a big storm sewer project, and the pipes they found themselves traversing were huge, new, only mostly finished, and not very well labeled. The watercourse forked and forked again, and the echoes multiplied; several times Jack discovered after a turn that Tazh's and Aiman's sloshing footsteps were receding, not growing closer, and they had to double back to the last intersection. Jack soon realized that he was quite thoroughly lost, and there was no telling where Erzhan might be.

Even worse, the sounds of the fleeing teenagers were beginning to be overwhelmed by a great rushing noise. Jack, to his concern, knew this sound well. The clouds above were really letting loose now, dumping buckets of rain on the city, and the sewers would soon begin to fill with water.

A deep rumble of thunder echoed down the tunnel then, as though the storm wanted to confirm Jack's fears. "Hurry!" he shouted to Timur, pulling the horn-headed joker forward.

Timur came along willingly, but the fast-running water was now up to the men's hips, slowing their progress and occasionally knocking one or the other off his feet. But their tightly held hands and Timur's determined strength made sure neither one was washed away. Jack could only hope that the shorter Tazh and Aiman were coping as well.

The only good news was that the fresh rainwater barely stank at all, by Jack's standards; even so, it smelled of compost and dead fish and old motor oil. Timur's nose wrinkled with distaste, but he said nothing.

Suddenly a loud and very clear cry of dismay sounded from around a curve in the tunnel, accompanied by panicked splashing. Jack and Timur shot worried looks at each other and sloshed forward as rapidly as they could. The increasing current was now coming from behind them; the challenge was to stay vertical.

They rounded the corner and saw two heads and six arms thrashing above the water's churning black surface; the kids' intermittent, gurgling cries could barely be heard over the water's rush and splash. Timur and Jack moved as fast as they dared, the strength of their shared grip keeping them upright as they accelerated to nearly a running pace.

They both stepped off the edge at the same time.

Jack's head went under immediately. He managed not to inhale any water, but he was forced to let go of Timur's hand, thrashing back to the surface with a ragged gasp. The current swirled him around, disorienting him.

Suddenly a rough, rusty pipe whacked his shoulder, and he grabbed it instinctively, hauling himself up until his head was above the surface. He took two shuddering breaths, shaking his head to clear his nose and ears. Thin stripes of yellow sodium light shone down through grates overhead, vaguely illuminating a large chamber where three main feeder channels joined together. The water stank of gasoline and tar.

From here he could see Tazh and Aiman, thrashing panicked and helpless as they floated downstream in the chaotic current. They clung together, which Jack wasn't sure was the best strategy for staying afloat, but with six arms between the two of them they seemed to be keeping both heads above water . . . for now. They were plainly inexperienced swimmers and tiring rapidly.

But there was Timur, heading right for them with a powerful, assured breaststroke. Jack could see his mouth move—no doubt shouting something calming and encouraging in Kazakh— but over the thundering current Jack couldn't hear a thing. The teenagers' noses were barely above water, eyes wide from terror and heads shuddering with the uncoordinated thrashing of their arms and legs. They reached out with all six arms for their rescuer . . .

. . . who was suddenly dragged below the surface in a flailing, splashing thrash.

A moment later the reason for his mysterious disappearance became clear as a black, scaly, beaver-like tail rose briefly from the roiling water.

Erzhan! He must have caught up with them by swimming beneath the surface. Jack held his breath, hoping that Timur could defeat or escape the younger joker. But though Timur's horn-topped head popped up, gasping, from the churning foam, he didn't seem to be winning. In fact, the expression in Timur's brown eyes told Jack he was losing badly.

Jack clung to the pipe, panicked and uncertain, looking for an opportunity to act—to grab a flailing arm or leg and haul Timur to safety, or to kick Erzhan in the head. But the battling jokers were too far away, the light too poor, the action too chaotic. Or was it just fear that kept him from acting? Fear that he, too—a weak, skinny, none-too-buoyant old man—would be pulled under, pointlessly raising the evening's death toll from three to four?

It was not an unreasonable fear.

But he had an alternative. It was not one he welcomed, but it was the best one he had.

He concentrated on his anger—the fierce, burning, unreasoning rage—at Erzhan, at the terrible situation, at all the obstacles and disappointments and prejudice he'd faced in his seventy-nine years. He focused it into the deep, primal force that had shaped his life ever since the wild card virus had infected his body.

And then he let the gator go.

Jack struggled to retain his human consciousness, even as his face lengthened and his tail stretched out and his hands and feet warped into scaly, webbed claws. But it was fading quickly, drowned beneath the dark, hot awareness of his giant-alligator alter ego.

Sewer Jack had come to St. Louis.

♠

The alligator thrashed in black, stinking water, struggling against imprisoning bonds. Rolling over and over in frustration and rage, he tore free of the fabric and leather that wrapped him, shreds of cloth drifting away in the churning current.

He was in an enclosed space, all hard surfaces and strange angles; the current pushed him every which way, threatening to drive him into a wall or pillar at any moment. The water was vile, rank with chemicals and gasoline, and nothing lived in it. No, wait . . . there were other living things here. Two forms struggled nearby, with two others paddling clumsily away beyond them. Food? Perhaps. Their scent was blocked by the foulness of the water.

With smooth strokes of his webbed feet he thrust himself toward the nearer pair. Food they were, indeed; the scent of fresh, hot blood was rich in the water, and growing richer as the larger of the pair tore at the smaller with fierce claws. Either one would make a satisfying meal. With unerring instinct he drove for the smaller, injured one, great jaws agape . . .

. . . and something intervened, closing his mouth and making him strike between the two with his snout, separating them and pushing them away from each other.

Angrily he thrashed his head from side to side, as though to shake off some clinging parasite. But again that alien impulse seized him, forcing him to swim beneath the smaller, bleeding one and bear it upward on his back. The bigger one—the dark one with the broad tail—tried to climb aboard as well, its claws biting painfully into his scaly hide. The alligator pitched and twisted in the swirling current, legs beating against the water, fighting to regain control of himself even as he battled his unwanted passenger.

Then the current drove him into something hard and angular, striking him right between the eyes. He saw flashing lights and bubbles escaped his nostrils. Both food things were thrown from his back into the water, but before he could turn and bite them the smaller one grabbed something above the surface and hauled itself out. Stunned by the blow, he was too slow to seize the other in his jaws before it too got away, propelling itself rapidly through the water with its broad tail.

Filled with fury, he followed, his whole great body undulating in pursuit. But the thundering, filthy water obscured all his senses, and the swimmer was swift, and the black, scaly creature soon vanished into the turbid darkness.

He surfaced, sniffing and peering all about, hoping to spot his prey by sight or scent. But it was the prey that spotted him first—a great weight struck just behind his head, thrusting him back beneath the water. His nostrils snapped shut instinctively, but the blow drove the breath from his lungs.

The alligator thrashed and rolled, trying to shake his adversary off. But though the enemy was much smaller it was frighteningly strong, its legs clamping around his neck like a vise. His own front legs, with their lethal claws, were too short to reach the creature on his back, and though his jaws snapped and his head whipped back and forth his teeth closed on nothing but water.

Down he dove, water rushing past his sides, but still his adversary clung to his back. He struck the hard, filthy bottom and pushed off with his legs, driving both of them back to the surface—and above it, splashing into the air in a rush of droplets that glimmered for a moment in the fitful light from the streetlights above. Then the combatants crashed together into the water again, waves reflecting back from the walls to batter them as they sank.

Pain! Claws dug in on either side of his lower jaw, pulling upward with unbelievable force. The alligator fought back, writhing and bucking in the water, but still found his head pulled back and back, exposing his throat and making vertebrae creak in protest. His lungs burned from effort and lack of air.

The enemy's grip shifted. Still clinging to his neck with its powerful legs, it got one arm under his jaw, pulling back with all its considerable strength while the other hand's talons clawed at the soft scales beneath his chin. The alligator's legs thrashed ineffectually.

He tasted blood, and the flow of hunger and rage that served him as a mind became tinged with fear.

Suddenly the enemy let go of his back, and two bodies fell heavily into the water beside him, struggling together in a haze of bubbles. The smaller creature had returned—still bleeding, still weak and awkward in the water, but with the element of surprise it had managed to dislodge the larger one from the alligator's back.

The alligator surfaced, drawing in a deep breath and letting it out in a great roar of pain and anger, then breathing in again and diving deep.

The two creatures still fought each other, the churning water around them now black with blood. Over and over they tumbled, a fog of bubbles obscuring the scene. He could not defeat the larger creature. It was too strong, too fast, too clever. He should swim far away, find easier prey.

But he could not let it kill the one that had helped him.

Again he drove himself between them—this time obeying his own instincts rather than the alien presence that had directed him before—battering the combatants apart with his great snout.

Once the two were separated, it became clear which was which. He snapped at the larger one, feeling flesh tear between his teeth and tasting sweet blood, but it wriggled free and vanished into the murky depths. Fearing another counterattack, the alligator caught the smaller, drifting creature with one forelimb and, with swift strokes of his legs and tail, carried it away downstream.

For a moment the alligator felt relief at his escape. But the channel was narrowing as the current dragged them along, and again he was slammed against a protruding object. Before he could recover himself, another unexpected blow stunned him, and another.

In fury and confusion he lashed out at everything, battering his tail and snout against rough unyielding concrete. But the water pushed still harder and faster as the channel grew tighter, beating him against the sides with repeated punishing blows. He snapped at the things that struck him but succeeded only in breaking a tooth on the fast-moving wall.

He was weakening—he was running out of air. He had not surfaced in too long, and this place was so hard and strange and disorienting. He struggled to the surface, to take a breath, but at the top of the tunnel he found only more hard concrete. Panicked, he flailed his legs and tail, not knowing which direction to swim. He needed air!

And then, out of nowhere, a warm hand gripped his shoulder. Another rested between his bulging eyes, gently massaging his scales.

The much smaller body moved against him, its touch calming his panic and its swimming motions guiding him around until his snout faced into the current. Reassured, reoriented, he stroked hard with his legs until the concrete that scraped against his back fell away, leaving only blessed air. He drew in a deep, comforting breath, as the other's hand continued to soothe his scaly brow.

This was something new in the alligator's experience. In a long, long life of rage, hunger, and fear he had never before felt such an emotion. It was strange, and frightening, and yet also somehow comforting.

He closed his eyes and let himself relax into it.

◆

Jack awoke with a gasp as Timur surfaced. The turban-horned joker was swimming on his back like an otter, holding Jack to his warm tummy with one arm, paddling with the other arm and his sturdy legs. "I have you, friend," he murmured in Jack's ear. "You are safe now." His voice rumbled low against Jack's shoulder blades.

Jack realized he was naked.

He didn't care.

The current seemed to be slowing. With strong, smooth strokes Timur brought them to a ledge, then helped Jack to drag himself from the water up onto it. He lay there on his stomach, retching foul water, shivering from cold and exhaustion. He was battered and bleeding and every muscle ached.

"Erzhan?" he choked out. Timur shrugged. "The kids?"

"There." He pointed, and Jack saw them clinging to a pipe on another ledge, some thirty feet distant across a roaring current. They looked like a pair of miserable drowned rats, but they were in no danger.

But then came a crashing splash and a roar of rage, and a black scaly figure burst from the water onto the other ledge.

Erzhan was bleeding from multiple gashes on his back and side, and his broad beaver-like tail dragged as he crawled across the ledge toward his daughter and her lover. But he was still moving, and as Jack contemplated the churning waters between them he realized that he lacked the strength even to swim that distance, never mind to fight the younger joker on the other side of it. Timur released Jack's shoulders, dragged himself to the water's edge . . . and collapsed there, too exhausted to move any farther, staring across the current with hopeless despair.

Erzhan reached the gasping lovers and levered himself upright, pushing Tazhibai aside to land in a heap like a discarded blanket against the wall. The water that ran from Erzhan's face, Jack saw, was more than just storm runoff . . . his expression left no doubt of the anguish he felt. But though it might be more in sorrow than in anger, still he gripped his daughter's throat and began to squeeze.

Aiman's eyes bulged, looking up aghast at her father, her

murderer . . . and with one long, flexible arm she reached around behind him and stabbed him in the back.

The knife was long and sharp—it was the same one Jack had seen before, stolen from *Natchez*'s galley, and he had sharpened it a time or two himself—and Erzhan reared back with a roar of pain and surprise. But Aiman was small and weak and exhausted, and in just a moment her father would snatch the knife from the wound and end her life with it.

But then a snarling mass of hairy arms swarmed over Erzhan from behind. It was Tazhibai, love and rage overcoming exhaustion and fear, and though Erzhan weighed nearly three times what he did, his four thrashing arms were enough to momentarily confound him. Erzhan growled and fought back, the two of them slapping and grappling with each other, but despite his numerical disadvantage in arms the larger joker soon gained the upper hand. He lifted the wriggling Tazhibai over his head, preparing to dash his brains out against the concrete ledge. . . .

And then he gasped and let the youngster go, falling heavily forward onto the concrete himself. A knife handle protruded from his back, the blade deeply embedded in his heart.

Behind him Aiman stood panting, eyes wide, long arms spread out with fingers clutching the air. But as it became clear that Erzhan would not rise again, she rushed to Tazhibai, already struggling to his feet. The two of them embraced each other with the fierce passion that only young lovers with an excess of arms could express.

Then a warm, muscular arm laid itself across Jack's shoulders. He smiled and let himself slump against Timur's strength.

♥

Once they had all recovered a bit, Jack looked around and spotted a ladder leading upward. With Timur's help, he and the kids swam over to it, then climbed the ladder and managed to shove the manhole cover at the top aside.

They emerged onto a dark street just above the rushing Mississippi. The rain was still falling but had decreased from a downpour to a gentle shower. Jack's watch was gone, damn it, but he guessed it was three or four in the morning. He peered upstream and down.

There, maybe half a mile upstream, lay *Natchez*, her smokestacks gently steaming in the lights of the adjacent parking lot. It would be a long walk, and they were wet and exhausted—and, in Jack's case, naked and barefoot—but they could do it.

Jack put an arm over Timur's shoulders and they began walking.

♣

Despite the hour, Chief Engineer Cottle was awake when Jack knocked on his door. "Yeah, what—" he said as he opened the door, then stopped dead, dark-circled eyes widening behind his thick glasses.

Jack stood there dripping and naked, with a filthy, flattened, tire-marked paper bag held before his privates. He had left the three jokers hiding beneath a table in the lounge. "I'm afraid I lost my pants," he said, in as straightforward a manner as he could manage. "Could you let me into my cabin?"

Cottle did, with an admirable lack of questions, and with a sigh of relief Jack put on his work pants—with the heavy ring of keys still attached to the belt. It was a very good thing he had taken only his cabin key with him when he'd left. "Thanks," he said to Cottle.

The chief engineer blinked twice, shook his head, and headed back to his own cabin, muttering something about "this trip just gets weirder and weirder."

♠

The next day wasn't easy, not for Jack and not for his Kazakh friends. Jack, despite his cuts, bruises, and exhaustion, had to work a full day without letting on about what had happened in the night. He pretty much got away with it, he thought, except that Wild Fox winked at him and made a suggestive comment about "rough trade." Jack just glared at him for that.

But Aiman and Tazhibai, Jack thought, had had an even rougher night—they had not only nearly died, but Aiman had been forced to kill her own father, leaving her an orphan. Fortunately, Aliya and Jyrgal had taken both kids in with open, loving arms—they were not nearly as closed-minded about young love as Erzhan had been—and Nurassyl's healing powers had gone a long way toward soothing their injured bodies and psyches.

They told no one the truth about how Erzhan had died. The story they had concocted on the walk back to the boat was that the kids had run away; Erzhan, Timur, and Jack had followed them; they had tried to hide in the sewer and got caught in the currents; and Erzhan had drowned rescuing them. Jack wasn't happy that a man who'd tried to kill his own daughter wound up being portrayed as a hero, but Timur had convinced him to go along with the fiction for the good of the community.

As for Timur himself . . . he had given Jack a very long, warm embrace before retiring to his own bed for a well-deserved rest, but Jack had barely seen him since. At least, not with his eyes. The noble, fearless joker who had saved Jack's life so many times in the last twenty-four hours was rarely far from his thoughts . . . or his imagination. But, he thought, that was probably the closest he would ever get.

So when Jack locked up the bar that night and trudged back to his cabin, he was pleased as well as surprised to find Timur waiting. "We talk?" he said.

"We talk," Jack replied.

Over a series of stiff drinks—vodka neat for Timur, top-shelf cognac for Jack—they had a long heart-to-heart, with many gestures and much drunken laughter at their difficulties of communication . . . and eventually they discovered that the language barrier was far from insurmountable.

◆

Afterward, they walked out on deck together, not willing to let go of each other just yet. The clouds had cleared away, the Arch gleamed gold in the light of the rising sun, and the full moon was just setting behind it.

In that glimmering light they shared a passionate kiss.

♥

When a very tired but happy Jack opened the bar at eleven, he found Leo Storgman waiting at the door. "I can't sleep on this boat," Storgman complained. "It's too quiet."

"Nothin' like New York," Jack agreed with weary camaraderie. "Boilermaker?"

"Yep."

Jack fixed the man's drink and set it in front of him. He looked to either side; there were no other patrons yet. "You were a cop, right? You know anything about immigration? Green cards?"

"A little . . ."

"I was just wondering." He folded his arms on the bar and leaned in close. "Can a guy gay-marry another guy—a foreigner—and bring him into the States?"

Storgman snorted. "These days? I suppose anything's possible. But it's not easy."

"I'm prepared to do whatever it takes."

Storgman's gray eyes met Jack's bleary red ones, taking his measure. Then he shook his head and grinned indulgently. "I play poker with a lawyer back home. Dr. Pretorius. You might have heard of him?"

Jack nodded. "Yeah, maybe."

"If anyone can work out an arrangement for you," Storgman continued, "it's him." He pulled a smartphone from his pocket. "I'll drop him a line right now."

"Thanks. I really appreciate it."

That afternoon, as *Natchez* pulled away from the dock, Jack came out on the promenade to watch the Arch receding into the distance behind the paddle wheel. *Gateway to the West*, he thought. *Gateway to a new life, maybe, for both of us.*

He could hardly wait.

In the Shadow of
Tall Stacks

Part 7

WILBUR NOTICED AN ENTIRELY naked Jack, Timur, and the two young refugee lovers Aiman and Tazhibai (all four of them soaking wet) coming back aboard in the early-morning rain. He watched, curious, as Jack took the Kazakh trio and hid them under a table in the lounge, then padded down—still naked but wielding a paper bag in front of his privates—to the main deck. Since neither Jack nor Timur appeared terribly concerned about their bedraggled and beaten appearance, Wilbur decided he didn't need to be concerned either.

In any case, the steam was back up in the boilers and Wilbur was feeling simultaneously excited and morose about being on the last leg of the trip, the storm battering both the boat and St. Louis fitting his mood. He stayed in the lounge to guard the jokers until Jack returned (wearing clothing now) to take the Kazakhs back to the relative safety of their cabin.

As to what he saw with Timur and Jack . . . he only shook his head. It was just another indication that the world continued to change around him. As with Captain Montaigne, he might not entirely understand or approve of those changes, but there was nothing he could do about it. Eleanor would likely have only told him, *"Love is love, dearest. Leave it alone and let them enjoy what we have, Wilbur."*

So that's what he did.

That afternoon, the *Natchez* left the St. Louis dock and headed downriver to the confluence of the Ohio River with the Mississippi just south of Cairo, Illinois, a small town surrounded by tall levees on a spit of land flanked by the Mississippi on one side and the Ohio on the other, though the town gave its back to the Mississippi and instead looked out over the Ohio to Kentucky on the opposite bank.

In the evening with the skies finally beginning to clear, the *Natchez* made the sharp left turn at Fort Defiance State Park, where a Civil War fort was once commanded by Ulysses S. Grant, to enter the Ohio River. They docked for the night in Cairo; several of the passengers strolled out to examine the town's tiny historic district, but it was a new passenger coming aboard there who garnered the most attention from Wilbur: Paul Lewis. Wilbur watched a fully dressed Jack greet the man on his arrival and escort him up to JoHanna's stateroom as Wilbur followed, curious.

Lewis was a tall, ginger-haired man with a face was so florid as to appear permanently sunburned. His hands moved constantly as he talked, as if he were unable to speak without waving them about. "The final arrangements are set," Lewis was saying as Wilbur entered the room. If Jack or JoHanna noticed the remnants of Wilbur's wet entrance on the wall, neither said anything. Wilbur noted that Jeremiah wasn't present, nor were Wild Fox and Sylvia, who—after Wild Fox's help with Evangelique Jones—were now part of the group whenever they consulted about the Kazakhs. Wilbur wondered if Jack and JoHanna simply didn't want Lewis to know about the others. "I have the transportation arranged in Cincinnati to take the group to Theodorus in Charlotte. There will be six of them still on the ship at that point, right?" Wilbur winced at that and stifled the impulse to grab steam so he could correct the man: *It's a boat, not a ship.* . . .

JoHanna did it for him. "This isn't a *ship*; it's a steamboat," she told him, her dark features stern. "They're never, ever called ships."

Lewis simply shrugged at that and continued his monologue. "Sure, fine. Whatever. Here's how I see this all playing out. You'll have a full load of paying customers for the race in Cincinnati; what I plan to do is to bring the Kazakhs out just after the last passengers have disembarked for the evening after the race, like they're just some late-leaving group. JoHanna, you can help me with that. I'll escort our refugees to a van parked close by on the Public Landing, and we'll be off to Charlotte. By the morning after the race, they should all be safely with Theodorus, which is our target goal, eh?"

"And you're with the JADL?" Jack asked. "Forgive me, but that seems . . . strange to me."

"Because I'm a nat?" Lewis asked. "Hey, both of you look normal enough, and you're working with the JADL. Even jokers sometimes have nats working for them. Look, my brother was infected by the wild card; he drew the black queen and died. After I got out of law school, I decided to work for nonprofit human rights agencies, and the JADL had an opening. Dr. Pretorius didn't seem to mind that I'd never experienced what most of them had. He just wanted a good lawyer. ICE is still looking for the Kazakhs you have, and they'd especially like to get their hands on Nurassyl and the Handsmith. The rest they'll just pack off to Rathlin with the others, but those two . . . That's why I'm coming aboard now—my expectation is that you're going to have at least one other 'visit' from ICE before we get to Cincinnati, so I'm aboard just in case that happens. Now, is it only the three of us who are aware of our secret passengers?"

Jack and JoHanna looked at each other. "That's correct," Jack said. "No one else is involved. So, Mr. Lewis, you can stop ICE from taking them?"

Wilbur snickered silently at that. So Jack and JoHanna didn't entirely trust Lewis. . . .

"I can tangle them up in bureaucratic red tape locally and fly in Dr. Pretorius from New York at need. He's been working on this from when they arrived in New Orleans and on. At the very least, we can make everything terribly uncomfortable for the Van Rennsaeler administration. They won't want the publicity we'd give them." He nodded to Jack and JoHanna with the last statement, still smiling broadly with white and perfect teeth.

Make everything terribly uncomfortable for the Van Rennsaeler administration . . . Wilbur snorted at Lewis's overblown, stiffly formal language. *I swear, the man should be speaking in one of those upper-crust British accents.* Frankly, he thought the man rather a pompous ass, but if he could deliver on his promise, then he was at least a decent pompous ass.

All that mattered was that the rest of the Kazakhs ended up safe. If it took an ass to do that, an ass would do just fine.

♠

Louisville was the last stop before Cincinnati itself: Kentucky's largest and most populous city, perched on the Kentucky side of an Ohio River bend with its attendant satellite towns of New Albany, Clarksville, and Jeffersonville slumbering across the river on the Indiana side. The *Natchez* had docked along the Riverwalk area east of the Louisville Locks, at the U.S. 31 bridge next to the *Belle of Louisville,* which would be accompanying them up-river to Cincinnati and the festival, and along with the *Delta Queen* would be taking part in the race with the *Natchez.* Wilbur had visited Louisville often in his mortal days and seen it from the deck of the *Natchez* countless times in the years since his death.

He looked out now over the small downtown area from the

hurricane deck. There was a small fair under way in the area, and the Jokertown Boys had temporarily abandoned the Bayou Lounge to entertain on a stage there. Wilbur could hear the throb of the sound system and Roger's low voice echoing from the nearby buildings, competing with the hum of traffic crossing the bridge. Visitors who purchased a five-dollar ticket were being allowed to tour the boat, and Wilbur watched a line of the curious constantly entering and leaving over the extended gangway.

He also watched a trio of the Kazakhs leave the boat under the cover of other tourists—Louisville was the final sanctuary city in which they would stop. Cincinnati was *not* a sanctuary city, but it was as far east as the *Natchez* would be going, and would offer a short drive to Charlotte and Theodorus for Nurassyl, Jyrgal, Aliya, Timur, and Tazh and Aiman.

As the Jokertown Boys launched into "Jokertown Blues," Wilbur found himself staring down at the gangway with a grimace. He recognized the African-American woman striding up toward the main deck: the ICE agent who had nearly discovered the refugees back in Memphis, Evangelique Jones, accompanied by a man in a dark suit and sunglasses whose appearance also fairly screamed "federal agent." *So Lewis was right about another ICE visit.*

As quickly as possible, Wilbur headed down to the main deck, not even caring that he was passing through people and leaving them somewhat dampened in the process, though he heard the shouts of surprise and outrage that followed him: "Hey, is there a leak somewhere? Is someone spraying water? Who the fuck just spilled their drink on me?"

As tall and striking as Jones was, she wasn't hard to spot in the crowd. Wilbur saw her ascending the bow stairs to the boiler deck, and he hurried after her in time to see her sit down in one of the plastic deck chairs near the forward rail. It was who she chose to sit beside that surprised Wilbur the most.

Paul Lewis. Their man from the JADL. Mr. Sunglasses stood directly behind the two, pretending to pay no attention to anything at all and undoubtedly watching it all.

Wilbur moved to stand directly in front of the trio, in the small space between Lewis's and Evangelique's legs and the railing. They looked out through him toward the river, the *Belle*, and the bridge, and their words were both quiet and alarming. "I take it your offer of a reward for the remaining Kazakhs still stands, since the ones you're *really* after are part of that group?" Lewis asked. His hands swept through the air as if conducting their conversation.

"Actually, we prefer that people *give* us information and help us because they understand it's their patriotic duty." Jones turned to look at Lewis directly, with a moue of unconcealed distaste on close-pressed lips. When Lewis just stared back, she continued. "But yes, our offer still stands, assuming you can deliver on it. The Kazakhs we wanted most are still . . . missing. So where are the Kazakhs? Martin"—she said the name with a quick nod of her head at Mr. Sunglasses behind her—"can have our people here in ten minutes. Less."

Lewis shook his head. His right hand waved in a gesture of dismissal. "It can't be here or now," he said.

"Why not?" The look of annoyance deepened on Jones's face.

"First, Louisville's a sanctuary city, and so there's a legal issue," Lewis answered. "Dr. Pretorius would be on you immediately for grabbing them here—and fire me for letting you. Not a complication you want, believe me. But more importantly, the Kazakhs aren't currently on the ship." Wilbur knew that for a lie, as he'd visited the refugees not an hour before; judging from Jones's expression, she had the same thought. *And it's a* boat, *not a ship, you idiot.* "I have to protect myself; I can't have the JADL knowing I gave up the refugees. I'd lose my job, be sued, or worse." Both hands waved at that. "Cincinnati's *not* a sanctuary city, so taking the refugees in Cincinnati's a much better option, and safer for everyone involved, too. I can tell you just when and how the Kazakhs will leave the boat, and let you take them without a crowd around to witness it and record everything on their smartphones. You don't want video posted two minutes later on Facebook."

He gestured at the crowds filling the two boats. "I can guarantee you'll be able to grab them easily, with no fanfare and no one plastering it all over social media. No bad publicity for the White House and the administration at all. And most especially, I can say that I was just as surprised as everyone else when you showed up, thus keeping my reputation, my salary, and your reward." Lewis's grin widened. "My creditors will be very happy, all around. What's another few days, Agent Jones? You've been looking for these people a lot longer than that. A little patience is all that's required, for both of us."

I could grab some steam, slip into the woman, and just stay there until her insides have been boiled into a soggy stew. . . . But no. He couldn't—wouldn't—kill anyone else. That wasn't the answer. But after all Nurassyl had done for him, after making friends with the Kazakhs and starting to learn their language, he wasn't going to allow Lewis to give up the joker refugees who he now considered friends.

Jones lifted her shoulders and let them fall again, her dark eyes closing once and opening again as she stared off toward the river. "All right," she said. "Cincinnati it is. You will be my eyes and ears on the *Natchez*, and I'll be calling you twice a day from now until Cincinnati, just in case anything you're going to tell me happens to . . . go awry. And you're going to tell me—right here and right now—exactly what you and the JADL have planned. I want every last little detail, and if I don't like them, maybe I change my mind."

"I'm sure you won't." Lewis grinned. Wilbur saw him reach out as if to touch Jones's hand on the armrest of her chair, but the look she gave him made the smile disintegrate and he pulled his hand back with a showy flourish worthy of Ravenstone, as if that was what he'd intended to do from the beginning. "Well then. Here's what I've arranged . . ."

As Lewis started to tell Jones what he'd outlined to Jack and JoHanna, Wilbur slid away from them. *No, this couldn't happen.* He wouldn't let it happen. There had to be a way to get the refugees safely away, as well as some way to stop the *Natchez* from being scuttled and moored. There had to be. *Didn't there?*

◆

"Everything is all fouled up," Wilbur said, the end of a tirade to Jeremiah. It had been a long monologue, starting with Kirby Jackson and just how deeply Wilbur feared being stranded steamless on a docked *Natchez*, then without so much as a segue, the new trouble with the Kazakhs. He'd laid out Lewis's betrayal; even in steam form, he'd been shaking in anger as he spoke. He'd had to take in steam twice before he finished the rant, but it felt good to be filled with heat; it matched his mood.

"I can understand the way you're feelin'," Jeremiah told Wilbur. "But it's good you caught the greedy bastard before it was too late. Now we mebbe can do somethin' 'bout it."

"What?" Wilbur husked angrily. "What can we do?"

"Dunno exactly yet. Gotta talk to the cap'n, JoHanna, Jack, and Wild Fox first, and we can all think on it. But for damn sure we gotta get 'em off the boat before ICE and this Agent Jones grabs 'em. We'll be in Cincinnati tomorrow."

"And I can't leave the ship, Jackson's refused Captain Montaigne's offer—again—and Agent Jones is waiting there to grab poor Nurassyl and the others."

Jeremiah leaned back in his ancient desk chair, the half-broken mechanism threatening to spill him over backwards. Wilbur unconsciously put his hand on the split leather there as if he could hold it up; droplets of steam condensed and soaked into the foam under the cracks. "Sure has been full'a problems, this trip," Jeremiah said.

"Any luck finding a new job?" Wilbur asked, feeling somewhat guilty that he'd been going on for so long about his own concerns and ignoring how Jeremiah had been affected.

Jeremiah snorted. "Hell no. Nothin' yet. Maybe if the cap'n turns down the comp'ny's offer and finds herself on another boat that just happens to need a good pilot . . ." He shrugged. Wilbur saw his gaze flick over to the pictures around his desk and the room: drawings of the earliest iterations of the *Natchez* and photos of the last few built by Thomas Leathers, and a large sixteen-by-twenty photo of Wilbur's current version. There were pictures of other steamboats as well: a poor print of the huge painting in the *Natchez*'s main salon depicting the race between the seventh *Natchez* and the *Robert E. Lee*, with huge clouds of black smoke pouring from their stacks into a tumultuous night sky; a dramatic drawing of the fatally overloaded *Sultana* exploding and burning on the Mississippi River in 1865, killing more than 1,600 former Union prisoners of war, the worst steamboat disaster in history; a photograph from 1922 that showed the *Island Queen*, the *Tacoma*, and the *Morning Star* all burning in the Ohio River off Cincinnati's Public Landing after a fire started by a welder on the *Morning Star* quickly spread to the other two boats; and, almost ironically, a photo of the replacement *Island Queen* burning, from 1947 when a boiler exploded and sent the boat afire on the Monongahela River in Pittsburgh, sinking her and killing twenty-four.

Wilbur stared at the pictures, a sudden realization coming to him. "You need to talk to those insurance investigators—the guy with the horns and his wife," he said, "and I need to get back into Jackson's stateroom . . ."

♥

Cincinnati. Tall Stacks.

Wilbur had to admit that the sight made him helplessly nostalgic. There were sixteen or so boats all lined up along the

Public Landing and Yeatman's Cove area of the Cincinnati riverfront, some of them just replica party boats, but a few were
actual steamboats like the *Natchez:* the *Belle of Louisville,* the
Delta Queen, the *Mississippi Queen,* the *President,* the *General
Jackson,* the *Majestic,* and (to Wilbur's mind) the obscenely
bloated *American Queen.* Even in Wilbur's earliest memories of
the river, back in the 1930s, there was rarely such an array of
steamboats gathered in one place, the prime days of the steamboats having already passed half a century earlier.

For that alone, the Tall Stacks was magnificent and splendid
and wonderful. This was a fantasy come to life, an image of a
past that had gone all too quickly. The riverfront area was packed
with the curious, with period-costumed presenters, with families and children, which filled Wilbur with a double regret. *I never
had the chance to know my child or to show him or her anything
like this, or to walk along the riverboat hand in hand with Eleanor,
our child running along in excitement in front of us. I would have
loved that. Eleanor would have loved it.*

The Ohio River itself was alive with recreational vessels of all
description. Loud music blared from the main stage just upriver—
several regional acts had been booked to play (though not the
Jokertown Boys), and a bluegrass band was set up under a tent
in front of the *American Queen,* flailing away at "Ridin' That Midnight Train" with banjo, fiddle, guitar, and upright bass. The
Natchez was parked in the blue shadow of the Roebling Suspension Bridge, designed by John A. Roebling (who would go on to
create the Brooklyn Bridge)—when that bridge had been completed in 1866, Wilbur had been told often enough in his visits
to Cincinnati, it was the longest suspension bridge in the world.
The riverfront parks on both the Ohio and Kentucky sides of the
river were lined with painted facades of period shops and booths
selling everything from Cincinnati-style chili to ice cream—and
though it would have been wonderful to have been able to stroll
the riverfront and board the other boats, or to walk into the city
just a few blocks away, that was nothing Wilbur could do.

The irregular festival had been held in Cincinnati every three to five years since the mid-1990s, and the *Natchez* had been one of its attractions several times now. Wilbur would have enjoyed the spectacle of this one as well, even if only from the boat, but he couldn't. All that had happened on the voyage, all that was threatening to happen soon, drove out any pleasure he might have felt: the thought of his steamboat docked permanently here afterward; the issue of the refugees they were smuggling and Lewis's betrayal.

Tellingly, the consortium that owned the *Natchez* had purchased airline tickets or passage back on the other boats for their passengers, since the *Natchez* would not be leaving Cincinnati after the festival. As a result, many of the boat's contingent had already disembarked, taking to hotels downtown or new staterooms on another boat to enjoy what the festival had to offer before they left.

That didn't mean that the *Natchez* was anywhere close to deserted. The festival had sold thousands of "port passes" that permitted attendees to board the various steamboats to look around them (and have their pass stamped by each as a souvenir). They also sold tickets for thrice-daily short cruises on the Ohio: morning, afternoon, and evening. That meant there was always a crowd aboard the *Natchez* that first day—and crowds had to be watched so that they didn't stumble across the remaining Kazakhs prematurely, all of them now ensconced in stateroom 3 on the texas deck. Even the traitor Lewis helped with that.

The second day featured the evening steamboat race between the *Natchez,* the *Belle,* and the *Delta Queen:* the *Natchez* would be packed with people who had purchased tickets allowing them to be aboard for the race.

It wasn't until the morning of the race that anyone heard from Leo and Wanda. In the captain's stateroom, Leo scratched his forehead under the curl of his right ram's horn, frowning. "We've checked with our contacts, did some digging, and your suspicions were right, Jeremiah," Leo said to the group gathered around him: Jeremiah, Captain Montaigne, JoHanna, Jack, Wild Fox, and Sylvia. And Wilbur, watching silently and invisibly in a corner. "I can tell you that the *Natchez* is insured to the hilt and well over. The Natchez Consortium—and Jackson as its majority shareholder—would stand to make a tidy little profit if something catastrophic would happen to the boat."

"Converting the *Natchez* to a casino or a hotel or even just an entertainment center would cost a small fortune for the necessary renovations," Wanda added. Wilbur noted that she was taller than Leo by a few inches, even in flats. He liked her voice: smoky and low and sensual without any deliberate attempt on her part—it reminded him of Eleanor's. "My bet is that it would be better all around if once they dock the *Natchez* to start that work, someone conveniently starts a fire on the boat and burns her down to the waterline. Probably at night, when no one's around to raise the alarm. No one gets hurt to complicate things, and the insurance gives the consortium a tidy last profit before they dissolve the company."

Wanda shrugged. Jeremiah looked toward the corner where Wilbur was standing.

"A welder cutting steel creates a spark, it smolders for hours on some oily rags and later ignites: voilà! A perfect insurance fire," Leo said, picking up Wanda's thread. "Happens all the time, and absent any obvious sign of arson, too often the insurance company just has to pay up."

Cottle. The certainty hit Wilbur immediately. *That's what Jackson was talking to him about back in Memphis. He'll be the one to do it. He knows the boat as well as anyone, and he'll be there to help the contractors to remove the boilers.*

"We're still having our people in New York look over Jackson and the consortium," Leo added. "We'll let you know if we find out anything else. But if I were a betting man, I'd say that's why Jackson has zero interest in any offer you've made to buy him out."

"Thanks for following up on that," Captain Montaigne told the couple. "We appreciate it."

The Storgmans both smiled. "No problem," Wanda told them. "As Leo said, if we hear anything else interesting, you'll be the first to know."

Leo and Wanda left the room. Jeremiah was already shaking his head as the door closed behind them. "So that's it," he said. "We'll get the last of the Kazakhs off the boat, then we'll all have to start looking for new jobs. And poor Wilbur . . ." He left that sentence hanging.

Poor Wilbur indeed, Wilbur thought. *I'm the one with no options at all. What happens to me if they burn the* Natchez *down around me?* He had no answer to that . . . or, rather, the answers that rattled through his head scared him more than he wanted to admit.

He plunged his hands into the wall, seeking the steam and taking it in. When he had enough, he allowed himself to become visible. "I have some thoughts about the refugees, at least," he said.

♣

Wilbur went up to the pilothouse as Jeremiah backed the *Natchez* away from its dock to lead the other two boats upriver to the race's starting point at the Manhattan Harbor Yacht Club in Dayton, Kentucky, about five miles from the finish line of the Suspension Bridge (itself packed with onlookers). Wilbur had taken in steam so he'd be somewhat visible in the dusk, though the two of them were alone in the pilothouse. Jeremiah's face was more lined than usual.

"You're still okay with everything we planned out?" Wilbur asked him.

"Yeah, I am," Jeremiah told him. "I just want it all to be over. One way or t'other."

The three steamboats moved majestically upriver, Gimcrack

loudly playing the calliope and Jeremiah dutifully sounding the steam whistle between tunes. Wilbur, looking out from the pilothouse window, saw the horned head of Leo Storgman moving toward the pilot house, pushing through the crowds permitted up on the hurricane deck to watch the race. Wilbur released enough steam to make himself invisible again as Leo hurried up the stairs and hammered on the door. Jeremiah raised eyebrows in Wilbur's direction and opened the door.

"I need to find the captain," Leo said rather breathlessly. "I looked on the boiler deck and knocked on her cabin door. Wanda and I just had a call from New York; it seems that the *Natchez* isn't the only thing your Mr. Jackson has insured. Several of the crew—Captain Montaigne, JoHanna, Cottle, and you, Jeremiah, and a few others—he took out heavy life insurance policies against each of you—a couple of months ago."

Jeremiah's head went back, startled. "Life insurance? You gotta be kiddin'."

Leo shook his head. "Nope. I don't think he's planning to torch the boat while it's empty. I need to talk to Captain Montaigne."

Jeremiah plucked a microphone from a clip on the instrument panel. "Captain Montaigne," he said, and they heard his voice reverberating from the speakers around the boat, "please report to the pilot house."

Wilbur was already slipping through the wall of the pilothouse and out before the captain could answer, a cold fear running through his head. *A policy on Cottle? I thought he and Jackson were working together. And if not, then . . .* Wilbur shuddered.

Wilbur went first to the refugees' cabin, stopping to take in steam again before he entered. Jyrgal and his family, Timur, and the two lovers, Tazh and Aiman, were the only Kazakhs remaining aboard. Their belongings were packed and ready in the room for them to leave once the race was over and the passengers started to disembark. "There's something going on," Wilbur said immediately on entering the room. "Our plans may have to change. If you hear alarms, you need to leave the room and head for the lifeboats. Look for JoHanna, Jack, or the captain; they'll know what to do."

"There is danger for the boat?" Jyrgal said.

"Maybe," Wilbur said. "I don't know."

"And you, Wilbur?" That was Nurassyl, speaking the little English he had picked up from their lessons. "You leave, too?"

"I . . ." Wilbur shook his head. "I can't."

"Cannot?" Nurassyl persisted.

"It's not possible for me. I've tried. I can't leave. The boat . . . it holds me." He hugged himself in illustration. "Look, I have to go. Just stay ready. There's something I need to check."

Nurassyl took a step in front of Wilbur as he started to leave, reaching out toward him as Wilbur stopped. Again, the mass of tentacles that served the joker for hands stroked Wilbur's form as Nurassyl hissed in pain from the touch. The tingling he'd felt when Nurassyl had given him the ability to speak returned, but stronger this time, then Nurassyl staggered backward away from him. Wilbur could see blisters rising on the tentacles even as Nurassyl cradled his arms to his body. "Nurassyl, I'm so sorry . . ." Wilbur said. *"Keşiriñiz."*

Nurassyl was shaking his head. "Not sorry," he said. "Now— you go."

"I hurt you."

"You go," Nurassyl told him.

Wilbur nodded. He left the cabin.

♠

By the time he reached the boiler room, Wilbur felt *Natchez* making the turn to head downriver again. He could sense the hull trembling and the steam rising in the pipes, ready to be released as the race began. He could see the boats roughly aligned and pointing toward the lights of Cincinnati and the bridges there:

the *Delta Queen* closest to the Ohio side, the *Belle* in the center, and *Natchez* nearest the Kentucky shore. From the entrance to the Manhattan Harbor Yacht Club, a puff of white smoke erupted from a small cannon, followed quickly by the thunder of its report echoing from the hillsides around them, signaling a fair start to the race. There were cheers from the riverbanks and from the passengers lining the decks of the boats in response. Smoke billowed from the stacks of all three boats and their paddle wheels tore at the water. Steam whistles screeched and wailed.

Despite the urgency he felt, Wilbur couldn't help but watch for a few moments, at least. Steamboat races were somewhat stately affairs, the boats generally capable of top speeds of perhaps ten miles an hour. As heavily laden with passengers as they were, Wilbur doubted they'd manage to exceed that speed, but that was also the case for the other boats. Even at full steam, with the boilers and engines pushed to capacity and the paddles lashing angrily at the river, it would take them half an hour to cover the roughly five miles of river to Cincinnati and the finish line. At the moment, Wilbur could see the *Natchez* was already ahead of the *Belle of Louisville* by half a boat length and was slowly widening the lead, with the *Queen* lagging a full boat length back of the *Belle*. The boats were close together; he could see the excited faces of the passengers on the *Belle* and hear those on the *Natchez* exchanging insults and challenges back and forth from the railings, over the clamor of the engines and the steam whistles. Crowds lined the shore on both sides, all of them cheering. Pleasure boats drew white trails on the river ahead of them as they paced the racing steamboats. The excitement from those on the boat was palpable and contagious. Wilbur wanted to shout along with them.

They were still pulling ahead, and Wilbur could feel the engines throbbing against the deck planks. As they approached the I-471 bridge, it was apparent to Wilbur that the *Natchez* was destined to win the race.

Or would be, under normal circumstances.

Wilbur slid through the wall and into the boiler room. He was immediately enveloped in steam and heat; from long experience, he knew at once something was wrong. Cottle should have been visible, opening valves, checking pressure gauges, and shouting commands to his crew over the furious din of the boat's engines. But no one at all was visible in the boiler room, though he could hear two crewmembers shouting farther sternward in the engine room. Wilbur heard the engine telegraph chime. "It's time to give me all she's got, Mr. Cottle," Jeremiah's voice thundered tinnily from the ancient speaking tube connected to the engine room.

There was no answer, but Wilbur quickly scanned the boilers: all the steam valves were cranked wide open. The boilers hissed and fumed, and the whining engines in the wheelhouse were now pounding at the frame of the *Natchez* like mad drummers beating on a hundred drum sets at once. Wilbur could see the gauges all up against or slightly past the red safety lines and still rising.

Still rising. "Cottle!" Wilbur called out, his voice lost against the furious noise. He glimpsed a pair of feet between the boilers. Gliding closer, he saw Cottle lying on the deck, his uniform shirt off to reveal a soaked wifebeater tee and blood pouring from a deep cut in his scalp.

Wilbur knew then what Jackson had planned. It had happened to steamboats often enough in the past, most famously the *Sultana*, but there were dozens of others: the *Lucy Walker*, the *Pennsylvania*, the *Eclipse*, the *Dubuque*. . . .

Every steam line, every boiler, every surface in the room was shaking from holding the increasing pressure, the banging and clanging deafening. Wilbur realized it was impossible to shut down the system now or contain it: Cottle, or whoever had struck him, had tampered with the pressure-relief valves, which by now should have kicked in. He could hear the steel shells of the boiler creaking as they expanded, the explosion imminent.

Three of the crew came rushing into the boiler room and

stopped, their faces reflecting terror at the scene in front of them. Wilbur shouted at them, "Get out! Run! Tell the captain to ground the boat and get everyone off! Move!"

They stared at him, an apparition of steam, then the boilers creaked and groaned and a rivet went flying through Wilbur and past the others, pinging loudly against the wall. The stasis broke and the crewmembers fled.

Wilbur knew what he must do, the only thing he *could* do to avert this disaster. He stepped fully into the inferno of the boilers, letting the steam fill him, letting it fill and expand his own body. He *was* the steam now, rising and expanding. He felt one of the boilers shatter and explode within him with the sensation of a hundred knives tearing into his guts, yet he contained and held that power as well, rising taller and wider in a tower of white steam, passing through the boat and the decks until his head loomed above the hurricane deck, rising above the boat itself, and he looked down at the scene as if he were a cloudy giant. The second boiler also burst, and now his body was stretched and thin, like a balloon with far too much air in it. The steam hammered at him; the explosions he contained threatening to rip him apart as a shower of condensing hot rain fell from his body.

They were passing under the Suspension Bridge, and Wilbur could see that Jeremiah had abandoned the race, nosing the boat toward the Kentucky shore at the Public Landing of the city of Covington, across from Cincinnati. None of the lifeboats had yet been deployed; the passengers still crowded the boat, staring upward at the roiling white specter of Wilbur rising, rising over the *Natchez* and above the river. He stared back at them; he took a portion of the steam within him and shaped it. "You must leave the boat!" he shouted in a god's stentorian, steam-whistle voice. "Get away! I can't hold this!"

He heard them shouting back at him, but he could no longer think, no longer hear. There was only the steam and the pressure. Memories and thoughts and fears hammered at him. *"We make whatever sacrifices are necessary,"* Eleanor said to him. Her face floated in front of him, smiling. *"This boat holds all of your dreams, and because of that, it's my dream as well."*

"I don't deserve you," he told her, and she laughed.

"Then you'd better get working to make sure you do," she told him.

"But I don't know how. I can't hold this. I can't."

Eleanor didn't answer. Still smiling, she vanished.

He heard another voice, and Nurassyl was shaking his head in front of him. *"Not sorry,"* the joker said. *"Now—you go."*

"I can't go. You know that."

"You go." Nurassyl lifted blistered tentacles toward Wilbur. *"You go,"* he repeated.

They weren't going to reach the landing in time. Wilbur looked down at the panic below him, at the crew desperately trying to launch the lifeboats and hand out life jackets, as Captain Montaigne shouted unheard orders, as panicked passengers streamed down to the main deck like a mass of writhing ants, as JoHanna and Jack herded the Kazakhs from the cabin toward the stairs.

He couldn't hold the pressure, but if he released it here, now, most of those below would die as a result.

You go . . .

"I can't. Eleanor . . ."

The steam giant roared her name as if it were a prayer, but he could not vent the pressure that way. He was as full as possible. The agony of holding in the steam and the explosion pulsed inside Wilbur, throbbing like Brobdingnagian fists hammering at him. Wilbur could see flashing lights wheeling onto the landing and hear the *whoop-whoop* of a Coast Guard fireboat. He looked over his boat and the river one last time, at the glittering of city lights on the rippling water of the Ohio.

Desperately, he took a step away from the *Natchez.* River water boiled around his foot, and he screamed with the pain of it. He took another step. Another. And yet another, and he was *away* from the boat. Impossibly outside his prison. He kept moving, deeper into the river and away. Steam bubbled and frothed around him. Wilbur turned, still a massive, gigantic form: a Colossus of Rhodes made of cloud and steam and attired in his captain's uniform and hat, standing knee-deep in the middle of the Ohio. He looked at the *Natchez* one last time: he saw Jeremiah in his wheelhouse, saw Captain Montaigne at the rail of the hurricane deck, saw the *Dead Report* trio filming him and jabbering at one another.

Closing his eyes, Wilbur finally permitted the forces he held inside to release. It was as if he'd set off a bomb: fire, steam, and river water erupted from his body, all of it showering outward but falling short of the *Natchez*. The furious, Wilbur-shaped cloud rose even higher above the river and the bridges, the wind shredding it as it blossomed until it was no longer recognizable as a human shape at all. The thunder of the explosion shattered the sky and rebounded from the tall buildings on either side of the riverbank, the reverberations slowly dying away.

A warm, quiet rain began to fall.

In the Shadow
of Tall Stacks

Part 8

H E WOULD ONLY FIND out later just how events afterward had played out. . . .

Once he'd released the boiler explosion, Wilbur had found himself in the river, his largely steamless and invisible body floating unseen. As he watched, exhausted, the *Natchez* grounded itself on the Kentucky shore, the gangways were lowered quickly, and people scurried madly away from the boat toward the police cruisers and emergency units already on the Public Landing.

The plan had been that the Kazakhs would leave the boat following the race, cloaked by Wild Fox so that neither Lewis nor Evangelique Jones would notice them. Jack would then be the one to drive them on to Charlotte and Theodorus (and, most likely, stay there with Timur). That plan still remained in place even though they landed on the "wrong" side of the river. When the boat landed suddenly on the Kentucky side and everyone poured off, Agent Jones was reduced to frantically trying to get from Cincinnati to Covington over the packed and gridlocked bridges and calling Paul Lewis on his cell, telling him to make sure the Kazakhs stayed in their cabin. But thanks to Wilbur's warning, Nurassyl and the others had already left the cabin before Lewis reached it (and found it locked); Wild Fox had disguised the Kazakhs as nat passengers while Jack escorted them from the boat, rented a van, and drove them off to Charlotte, where they were able to successfully rendezvous with Theodorus.

Agent Jones and her ICE companions stormed aboard the *Natchez* during the waning confusion; by then, the Kazakhs were already in the van and on their way. Captain Montaigne shook her head (according to JoHanna, who was also there) at Agent Jones's insistence that the door to stateroom 3 be opened or she'd have it forced. Lewis was still standing guard outside the room. "I have no idea what you're talking about," the captain said (according to JoHanna). "What Kazakhs? What jokers? I don't know this Mr. Lewis or what tale he's been telling you. Yes, we took some refugees aboard before we knew ICE was looking for them, but they were gone before your first visit." She slid the key into the lock, opened the stateroom door, and stepped aside as Agent Jones pushed through. The room beyond was empty.

As for Kirby Jackson and the Natchez Consortium, Travis Cottle, despite Wilbur's fears, hadn't been killed. When the engineer regained consciousness, he was more than happy to point to Jackson as the man who had wanted him to sabotage the boilers—which in the end Cottle had refused to do—and who struck Cottle over the head with a wrench so he could blow up the boilers himself. The local police, the FBI, and eventually the federal prosecutor were delighted with the circumstantial evidence that Leo and Wanda provided them regarding Jackson's insurance scams. The minority shareholders of the consortium couldn't plead their ignorance and disavowal of Jackson's plans fast enough—and were just as quick to accept Captain Montaigne and JoHanna's renewed offer to buy out Jackson.

The *Dead Report* trio, with their stunning video of Steam Wilbur saving the *Natchez*, had been able to parlay that into a new and lucrative contract with the Syfy channel. *The Dead Report* with *Ryan Forge* was now an hour-long show in prime time on cable—at least for the current season.

And Wilbur . . . he finally managed to flail his way ashore a few miles downstream from the *Natchez*. It took him several hours to return to the boat, and—temporarily steamless and thus invisible and powerless—he could only watch things unfold around him, and rejoice silently when he heard Captain Montaigne declare that the *Natchez* would be repaired and put back on the river.

It was three months before new boilers were installed and repairs were completed to the *Natchez*, but she finally steamed back downriver away from Cincinnati, toward the Mississippi and home with—after all the publicity—a full load of passengers once again being entertained by the Jokertown Boys as well as Wild Fox and Sylvia. They were close now to their final destination. Wilbur was in the pilot house with Jeremiah, watching as Jeremiah maneuvered the *Natchez* around the last bend before they reached their landing in the French Quarter.

Faster. Go faster. I want to be there. I need to be there. . . .

At the wheel, Jeremiah stirred, as if he had heard Wilbur's thoughts. "Mr. Cottle," Jeremiah said into the speaking tube for the boiler room, "how about a little more steam? I believe our Mr. Leathers is impatient to be home."

Cottle's voice emerged thin and tinny from the tube. "My pleasure, Mr. Smalls," he answered. Jeremiah pushed the engine lever forward a notch. The *Natchez*'s paddles tore at the Mississippi, leaving behind a shimmering white trail in the brown water. Wilbur stared ahead, watching as the lights of New Orleans moved slowly around them. *I'm coming back to you, Eleanor. I'm coming back to you at last.*

It seemed forever before the *Natchez*, with Gimcrack playing the calliope, was able to nose up alongside its familiar wharf, as the deckhands tossed out lines to be snugged around the dock cleats, before the gangway was swung over to the shore and secured. "Keep the steam up, Mr. Cottle," Jeremiah called into the speaking tube. "Mr. Leathers will be needing it."

"Yessir, Mr. Smalls," came the reply. "Understood."

From the rail of the hurricane deck, Wilbur watched the passengers disembarking and flowing outward into the early-evening lights and music of the Quarter. Captain Montaigne and Jo-Hanna stood on either side of the gangway, saying good-bye to the passengers as they left. But Wilbur's gaze lingered on a van parked to one side of the parking area off Toulouse Street. As most of the crowd cleared from the gangway, the driver—a middle-aged or perhaps slightly older man with balding gray hair—left the van and went to the rear hatch, pulling out a wheelchair. Wilbur stared at the driver, trying to see his features and wondering as the man opened the collapsed chair and wheeled it to the passenger door and opened it, extending a hand to the person inside.

Wilbur left the rail before he saw the person in the passenger seat. He hurried down to the boiler deck, going into a small private dining room just off the main dining area. He took in steam from the pipes he passed, letting it fill him so that his form was easily visible in the dimness of the room. He could see himself in the mirror on one wall: an apparition of cloud in the shape of a man, bled of any color but dressed recognizably in his old captain's uniform and hat. It would have to do. He waited, anxiously, for several minutes before someone knocked on the door, and it opened, and Captain Montaigne entered, followed by the middle-aged man pushing the wheelchair. Captain Montaigne nodded to Wilbur and stepped back into the main room, shutting the door behind her.

And in the chair . . .

Wilbur inhaled, his breath quavering in a half sob. Even with the wrinkled, liver-spotted face, the sunken eyes, the sparse white hair, the withered arms, he knew her. He saw her hands tightening on the wheelchair's arms, her clouded blue eyes staring at him. Her tongue licked dry, cracked lips. "Wilbur?" she said. "Wilbur, is that truly you? The captain told me, but I didn't know if I could believe her. . . ." Her voice was Eleanor's but not Eleanor's, ravaged by time and only a husky shadow of its former self. "I must look a fright," Eleanor said, lifting her hands to her face. "I'm so *old* . . ."

"And I'm just steam and don't dare even touch you," Wilbur told her. "To me, you look lovely."

Twin tears tracked their way down her cheeks, and Wilbur wanted to rush forward to wipe them away, wanted to kiss her, to fold her into his arms. But he couldn't. He could only glide closer to her, sinking to cloudy knees before the wheelchair, marveling. She reached toward him, but he slid back so she wouldn't be scalded by the touch. "It's me, my dear," he said in his voice of hissing steam. "My God, I missed you so much. . . . Eleanor, I never once stopped loving you. Never. You don't know . . . All the time together that we lost . . ." His voice failed him. He was weeping, water falling from his face to the carpet. "I would have left this boat a thousand times to go and find you, but it wouldn't let me."

"And I wanted to come here a thousand times to see the *Natchez* once more," she answered. "But the memories were so painful . . ." She stopped.

Wilbur could only stare at her, seeing the young Eleanor through the mask of time. "So many years gone," he whispered. "So much for us both to tell each other. I don't even know where to start."

The man behind the wheelchair put his hand on Eleanor's shoulder as she sniffed back her own tears. Wilbur glanced again at the man, wanting to ask the question in his mind but afraid that the answer wouldn't be what he hoped. "I never stopped loving you either," Eleanor told Wilbur, patting the man's hand as Wilbur remembered her doing to him so many times in their too-brief time together. "After I lost you . . . Well, that's a long tale, and I'm not sure I remember it all now. But I know where to start. Wilbur, my dear Wilbur, this is Thomas."

Thomas looked at Wilbur, taking a long breath. "Hello, Dad," he said. "It's good to finally meet you."

♣　♦　♠　♥